I0673466

SONG
OF THE
Sinner

A FIVE DIRECTIONS PRESS BOOK

SONG
OF THE
Sinner

A NOVEL

C. P. LESLEY

This is a work of fiction. All names, characters, places, and incidents are products of the author's imagination or are used fictitiously. Any resemblance to current situations or to living persons is purely coincidental.

ISBN-13: 978-1947044319

Published in the United States of America.

© 2022 C. P. Lesley. All rights reserved.
Except as permitted by the U.S. Copyright Act of 1976, no part of this publication may be reproduced, transmitted, or distributed in any form or by any means, or stored in a database or retrieval system, without the prior written permission of the author.

A Five Directions Press book

Cover images: Viktor Vasnetsov, *The Frog Tsarevna* (1918), public domain via Wikimedia Commons; "Spring Meadow" © Larisa Koshkina via Pixabay

Book and cover design by Five Directions Press

Five Directions Press logo designed by Colleen Kelley

FIVE DIRECTIONS PRESS

Whether the charmer sinner it or saint it,
If folly grow romantic, I must paint it.
—Alexander Pope

BOOKS BY C. P. LESLEY

The Not Exactly Scarlet Pimpernel

Songs of Steppe & Forest
Song of the Siren
Song of the Shaman
Song of the Sisters
Song of the Sinner

Legends of the Five Directions
The Golden Lynx (1: West)
The Winged Horse (2: East)
The Swan Princess (3: North)
The Vermilion Bird (4: South)
The Shattered Drum (5: Center)

Tarkei Chronicles
Desert Flower
Kingdom of the Shades

Contents

PRAISE FOR SONGS OF STEPPE & FOREST

"In *Song of the Sisters*, against the tense political backdrop of 1540s Moscow, C. P. Lesley brings us into the domestic world of the women's quarters and enchants with a quiet novel about two sisters who wield their limited power to determine their own destinies."

—Finola Austin, author of *Bronte's Mistress*

"A vividly told tale full of magic and mysticism, passion and betrayal. The story of Grusha will grab you by the heart and throat as you travel through the medieval world of Russia and the steppe."

—Terry Gamble, author of *The Eulogist* and other novels

"From Tatar shenanigans on the steppe to the machinations of Moscow's elite, trained historian C. P. Lesley weaves historical facts with a prodigious imagination and a passion for sixteenth-century Russia."

—G. P. Gottlieb, host of New Books in Literature

"Across half a millennium comes this tale of a complex and fascinating heroine with threads that will rouse and resonate with women even today. Juliana is a woman at turns privileged, abused, coveted, and marginalized for her beauty and existentially threatened when misfortune robs her of it. Faced with a no-alternative 1,500-mile journey across a frozen Polish-Russian landscape that throws her into the jaws of her past in order to save her future, she summons a steel courage born of desperation. The current of smart dialogue throughout the book weaves together a cast of characters—of whom we're never quite sure who to trust—through betrayal, hope, fear, conflicting loyalties, determination, and love. Juliana ultimately emerges as a champion for all who think they are broken but instead find undiscovered, unimagined strength."

—Ellen Notbohm, award-winning author of *The River by Starlight*

If you enjoyed this book, please consider leaving a review at your favorite online bookseller and/or on GoodReads.

Cast of Characters

(in alphabetical order by first name)

Alexei Bulatovich: Maria's husband; a high-ranking Tatar, descended from Genghis Khan, in service to the Russian grand prince; Nikita's patron. As the son of a khan, he bears the title *tsarevich.*

Alya: Darya's maid.

Anatoly Anfimov: Anfim's son, known as Tolya.

Anfim Fadeyev: Clerk involved in foreign affairs, later promoted to state secretary of the Treasury; father of Lara and Tolya; hero of *Song of the Sinner.*

Anna Semyonovna Kolycheva: Solomonida's daughter by her first marriage.

Darya Petrovna Sheremeteva: Younger daughter of the deceased nobleman Pyotr Alexandrovich Sheremetev; Nikita's wife and Andrusha's mother.

Demid Timofeevich Vorontsov: Uncle of Ekaterina, Dmitry, and Yuri; brother of Gavriil.

Dmitry Ivanovich Vorontsov: Katya's younger brother; Nikita's friend and comrade-in-arms; Yuri's cousin.

Ekaterina Ivanovna Vorontsova: Known as Katya; neighbor of Darya and Solomonida; Igor's wife, Dmitry's sister, and Yuri's cousin.

Eva: Solomonida's maid.

Father Faddei: Anfim's elderly father, a retired Orthodox priest.

Fyodor Mikhailovich Koshkin: Father of Maria and Lyuba; a high-ranking but incurably ambitious Russian nobleman.

Gavriil Timofeevich Vorontsov: Katya's uncle, Yuri's father, and, briefly, a suitor for Solomonida's hand; his sister-in-law *Elizaveta Vadimovna* also appears in the novel.

Igor Grigorevich Bezzubtsev: Second cousin of Darya and Solomonida; Katya's husband.

Kirill Fadeyev: Anfim's middle brother, who lives in Smolensk with his wife, Oksana, and their sons.

Laika: Igor's dog, left with Darya and Nikita after Igor's marriage.

Larisa Anfimova: Anfim's daughter, nicknamed Lara.

Lyubov Fyodorovna Koshkina: Maria's sister and Fyodor Koshkin's youngest child, known as Lyuba; Anna's best friend.

Makar: The servant in charge of Igor's wardrobe, the equivalent of a valet in modern usage.

Maria Fyodorovna Koshkina: Wife to Alexei Bulatovich, eldest daughter of Fyodor Koshkin, and a friend of Solomonida and Darya. Her marriage to Alexei gives her the title of *tsarevna* (khan's daughter or, in this case, daughter-in-law).

Masha: A kitchen maid in the Sheremetev household.

Mishka: Steward of the Sheremetev household.

Nikita Andreevich Monastyrev: Son of Pyotr Sheremetev's closest friend; Darya's husband and Andrusha's father.

Pavel Ilich Shuisky: Scion of a powerful princely clan and potential suitor for Anna's hand in marriage.

Petka: A servant in the Sheremetev household, next in line to Mishka as steward.

Postnik Fadeyev: Anfim's eldest brother, who trades with his two sons, mostly in the east.

Pyotr Alexandrovich Sheremetev: Solomonida's and Darya's father, who died less than a year before the story begins, after a long battle with dementia. His third wife, *Xenia*, is also mentioned.

Semyon Pavlovich Kolychev: Solomonida's deceased first husband; Anna's father.

Solomonida Petrovna Sheremeteva: Older daughter of Pyotr; ex-wife of Semyon Kolychev; Anna's mother; heroine of *Song of the Sinner*. Various characters in the novel use her nicknames, Shura or Shurenka.

Yuri Gavriilovich Vorontsov: Youngest son of Gavriil Timofeevich.

Chapter One

I'D NEVER REALIZED HOW LONELY ONE COULD FEEL IN THE midst of a crowd. Indeed, I had never *felt* lonely in the midst of a crowd. I loved parties and people, chatter and song, the glitter of gemstones in flickering candlelight, the swish of silk and velvet, the twang of zithers in the background—and yes, the social and political games that masqueraded as idle conversation, rumors, and gossip but in fact determined the ins and outs of everything from war to governance to marital happiness.

Yet as I gazed at this special gathering, aware that I should be in my element, I instead experienced a haunting sense of isolation. The guests at the party—limited to the family and close associates of my next-door neighbors—mingled, for the most part, in pairs.

Perhaps that was what bothered me—the lack of a partner. After seven years of widowhood, I would have sworn I'd grown accustomed to my single state. Indeed, I had no desire to remarry. But tonight, watching husbands and wives whispering as they passed me, I knew I missed what I had never had: a man who loved me. A man who would catch my eye as he laughed with his friends, wink at me across the crowded room, mutter in my ear as he moved from one group to the next.

"Solomonida!" Katya Vorontsova, my hostess, bustled over. Vivacious and, at twenty-seven, a few years younger than I, she looked, as always, very fine. Although we both had blue eyes, her dark hair allowed her to wear bright shades that would drain my pale complexion to ashen. I complimented her on her choice of a cobalt silk robe cuffed in cloth-of-gold and a jeweled headdress suitable for a bride—which Katya was not, having returned to her father's home after losing her elderly husband eighteen months ago. It was something we had in common: unsatisfactory spouses, fortunately deceased.

She blushed and gripped my sleeve between finger and thumb. "I wish I could wear that color. Bittersweet suits you perfectly. I'd love to be blonde."

While I searched for a reply, she pointed to loaded tables at the far side of the room. "Supper is served." I let her tug me toward the food, because I had eaten next to nothing since late morning. And because listening to her chatter gave me something better to do than bemoan my own lack of company.

The Vorontsovs had done themselves proud, I saw as we came close. Salmon and sturgeon, cheese straws and caviar, roast beef and capon and noodles floating in butter, baskets of bread and rolls—these celebratory dishes clustered thick as soldiers on parade. I topped a pancake with salmon and another with sour cream and caviar, then accepted a porcelain dish to hold them and the mushroom turnover Katya insisted I try. Plate in hand, I moved away to let the next hungry diner approach and surveyed the room, waiting to see if

Katya would rejoin me or depart to usher more guests to the tables. Taking care not to drip butter or sour cream onto my red-orange robe, I bit into one of the pancakes. It was as delicious as I'd hoped, and for a moment I forgot my distress in the pleasure of satisfying my appetite.

In response to the zithers I'd noticed earlier, as well as flutes and tambourines, a few of the bolder guests had already begun to dance. From where I stood, I saw a nobleman strip off his outer robe to leap and squat with the freedom conferred by trousers and leather boots. Others clapped in time with the instruments and would no doubt join him as the liquor continued to flow. Off to my left, concealed from the sight of those in the main hall but visible from where I stood, several women—girls barely old enough to wed but also their mamas and grandmas—traced sinuous circles with their arms, waving silk scarves. My feet tapped the rhythm, my skirts swirled in response to the sway of my hips, and I yearned to join them. I'd fit right in, more self-assured than the maidens but not yet old and creaky. And to dance, I didn't need a partner. I'd blend into the group, one woman among many.

A clay stove covered in patterned tiles kept the rooms warm enough to discourage much activity, but although it would be unpleasant to end up sweaty and disheveled, I struggled to resist temptation. I hadn't danced in years.

Temptation won. I set my empty plate aside and edged toward them, only to stop when someone caught my arm. I turned to find Katya holding out a goblet, which I took. The rich crimson of the liquid led me to expect cherry juice, but my first sip convinced me otherwise. "Fine Italian wine," I said to Katya. "Thank you. Your father has spared no expense tonight."

"It's a special evening," she said. "If being halfway through the Christmas season isn't reason enough to celebrate, I don't know what is. Walk with me while I check on the other guests. It may be our only chance to talk."

No dancing yet, alas. But I could hardly refuse my hostess, and conversation would keep my nagging sense of loneliness at bay. I strolled at her side, taking the occasional sip of wine. Katya had a keen eye and a sharp tongue, and she loved to share her acid comments on all and sundry. More often than not, her gimlet gaze led to revelations as accurate as they were entertaining.

A small, dapper boyar in his early forties with dark hair turning to gray crossed my line of sight. "Fyodor Koshkin," I said, unable to conceal a flash of anger. Not long ago he had involved himself in my family's affairs in ways that still made my blood boil.

"Did you *have* to invite him?" I asked Katya, directing her away from Koshkin. "I haven't forgiven him for trying to steal our estate six months ago. If I have to talk to him, I may empty this goblet over his head."

Katya laughed, but she didn't resist the tug of my hand. "Your cousin Igor brought him. So Koshkin can make his peace with my family now we're back in favor at court, I assume. You did hear about the scandal at the Kremlin two days ago?"

I nodded. "Everyone here is buzzing with the news like so many bees. Your uncles took their revenge for the Shuisky princes' attack on them last September. And Grand Prince Ivan stood by and watched while his boyars ordered the head of the Shuisky clan executed."

"Not just executed," Katya said. "They stripped him naked in public and gave him to the dogs—or at least their keepers. A nobleman, the head of the most powerful clan in these lands!"

The shock I heard in her voice mirrored my own every time I thought about it. "Worse than the beating he administered to your family," I agreed. "Although he would have killed your uncle Demid if not stopped, so I suppose your relatives wanted to even the score. I do wonder why the grand prince, young as he is, let things get that far."

"Ivan lost patience," Katya said with an airy wave that shocked me with its casual dismissal of judicial murder. "The Shuiskys dishonored him, too, by attacking his favorite. And Ivan blames the Shuisky princes for his own mother's death."

I shivered despite the heat, tormented by memories of Grand Princess Elena's blue face and tragic eyes as she died, poisoned by a concoction of yew delivered as a tisane. I'd served as her lady-in-waiting, and I witnessed the agony of her final hours. More than five years later, the horrors of that day—our desperate and ultimately unsuccessful attempt to save her—still gave me nightmares.

"He's right to do so, from what I've heard." It was another Shuisky prince's wife who had unwittingly delivered the poison at her husband's behest. I didn't mention that detail, which was not known to those outside the small circle of ladies-in-waiting, but I couldn't disguise the tremor in my voice.

Eager to deflect my hostess onto a different conversational path, I tipped my chin toward a rotund middle-aged man, his once red hair fading to gray. It was one of her aforementioned uncles—not Demid, beaten by the Shuiskys, but his brother Gavriil. He stared at us with a fixed expression on his face, like a man struck by lightning. Or perhaps someone behind us had attracted his attention.

"Gavriil Timofeevich seems to relish his return to favor," I said. "Has he settled on another bride now that my sister is taken?"

"Not he." For some reason I couldn't detect, that brought a flush to her cheeks. "Although I suspect he will after he settles into his new position at court. He got back to Moscow less than a week ago."

I narrowed my eyes at her. "Why does that question make you blush like a girl in love?"

She giggled in a way I'd expect from my daughter Anna, not a mature woman. "You'll find out soon enough. It's a surprise!"

"A surprise? What kind of surprise?"

She shook her head, still laughing. "Soon, I said. Look, there's Aunt Liza. I need to get her some food before she makes a scene. Talk to you later!"

I watched her as she dashed off, leaving me alone once more. I could dance now, if I wished, but the music had stopped during my conversation with Katya. The massed groups of men and women had split into quartets and trios and pairs, husbands and wives together, as if anticipating an announcement of some kind. My stomach knotted at the sight. I might as well be a ghost, gazing on a human realm forever barred to me. At this darkest time of the year, people said, the boundary between the heavenly sphere and our own thinned, and those on the other side could pass through it.

A superstition worthy of slaves and peasants! My dead father's voice sounded in my head, and I chided myself. I had no cause for complaint. In a few months I would turn thirty-two. I had a daughter I adored, home and family, rank and wealth, neighbors and friends. What possessed me to yearn for a partnership I might not want if I found it? I could have remarried anytime these seven years, if that had been my goal.

Gavriil Vorontsov continued to stare, as if he couldn't take his eyes off someone behind me. Glancing around, I saw only a quartet of elderly ladies, deep in discussion of their various ailments. Turning back, I raised my eyebrows at him, asking a silent question. He looked away, but when I moved, I realized that he followed me with his gaze.

So he *was* watching me. How odd!

And how disturbing. Not only was I alone at the party, but the one man showing an interest in me had grandchildren older than my daughter. Having passed thirty, it seemed, I'd lost whatever charms I once possessed.

Determined to rid myself of melancholy, I decided to seek out my sister, Darya, last seen gazing with adoration into the eyes of her new husband while he muttered secrets into her ear. In their pleasant and undemanding company, I could reimpose order on my rebellious heart before moving back into the party to look for my friends.

Or were Darya and her Nikita the true source of my misery? My jaw dropped open at the thought, and I hastily shut it again before I attracted more unwanted attention.

The truth struck me hard, like a blow between the eyes. I was jealous. Darya, once my closest companion, had found a state of wedded bliss that I had not enjoyed as a wife. Not that I begrudged them their happiness, but in that moment I realized that witnessing it so often over the last two months had sent my thoughts reeling toward a destination abandoned so long ago that I'd forgotten ever wishing I could reach it.

No wonder I pine for a man of my own.

"Solomonida!" As if conjured from the midst of the crowd, Darya pushed past a pair of large Vorontsov aunts and grabbed my arm. "Look who's here," she said in excited tones. "Anfim Fadeyev! I haven't seen him since before he went back to the Treasury! Let's go and greet him, shall we? He looks very elegant, I must say."

"He certainly does." I followed the line of her pointing finger. At the far side of the room stood a man a hand's breadth above medium height with a mobile, clever face; a body strong and solid but not given to fat; and, as I knew from experience, a pair of dancing light blue eyes and a smile that seldom failed to coax an answering smile from me.

"I've missed him!" The words burst out of me without conscious thought, and I instantly regretted them. I liked Anfim, who had proven a good listener, but I had no business missing him. The difference in our ranks meant that we must always remain at arms' length.

We were too far away, with too many people between us, for Anfim to hear me. Nevertheless, he raised a hand, as if he spotted us across the room.

"Me too," Darya said. "Who are those men he's with?"

"Nobles who direct government offices," I told her. "I recognize some of them. That's Ivan Tretiakov—the treasurer and keeper of the seal—talking to Anfim, for example. And that tall, distinguished-looking, dark-haired man with them is Prince Alexander Gorbaty. I'm surprised, though. Until now I thought everyone here was friends or family."

"The nobles could be family," Darya pointed out. "In-laws and other relatives. And the lower officials are connected to *them*. Let's go and greet him." She pulled on my elbow, which she had not released, and started toward Anfim.

"Should we?" I asked, but she had already set off across the floor. I moved with her rather than lose her again in the mob.

But we had underestimated the many obstacles in our path. We did move forward, but not enough to get close to Anfim and his companions. Dozens of people blocked our way, imperiling our progress with careless gestures and outflung hands, many of them holding goblets. The noise level rose steadily, to the point where I struggled to hear Darya, walking right next to me.

"Do you think one of those men got Anfim his job back?" my sister shouted as she dodged yet another stout noblewoman, narrowly escaping a deluge of red wine that would have stained her apple-green robe. Her hair was darker than mine, matching her hazel eyes, but we were about the same height—a little taller than normal—and had the same slender build. Anyone would recognize at a glance that we must be related.

"No idea." I sidestepped the puddle left by the wine, holding my robe above my ankles. "One day he was at our house, and the next he packed up his papers and left." She'd been away then, helping her new husband move his things from the subordinate principality of Staritsa, where Nikita had served for a year before Tsarevich Alexei took him on as a resident artist and occasional warrior. "I asked him who put in a good word for him, but he said he didn't know. Like you, I haven't seen him since."

"When did you ask him? I didn't think you spent much time with him."

We pushed our way to a relatively secluded corner, which made it possible for me to lower my voice. A good thing, because my cheeks warmed in response to her astonished question. I had no desire to yell the answer to all and sundry, however small the likelihood they could hear it.

"I saw him often in that month. I had no one else to talk to with you gone," I said, making light of it, although the memory of those hours in Anfim's office sent delighted shivers down my spine. "No one except servants. Even Father Job was busy with his family and stopped by just long enough to perform services and hear confessions."

"Why not tell me, then? I've known for a while that he appeals to you." She looked at me, her eyes keen, and I wondered what she made of my attraction to a man I hadn't considered a suitable match for either of us. But that was an avenue I had no wish to explore.

"I forgot," I said. "He'd left by the time you came back, and it didn't seem important."

Darya accepted my somewhat deceptive explanation with a nod. "Oh look," she said, gazing at Anfim once more. "He's laughing. I haven't seen him laugh like that since the day we told him about pelting our cousin with acorns. Even then, he tried to hide it."

"He's very proper. He would say it's not appropriate to laugh at one's employer." I sighed, recalling the occasion she had in mind. "Although he does, and often, whether he tries to hide it or not."

"I'm glad to see him laugh outright," Darya said. "Maybe he'll share the jokes with us now that he's back in the government and his own man again."

"I hope so." From halfway across the room, I studied Anfim. His eyes crinkled at the corners, and he raised his goblet in a toast. I didn't recognize the official who'd amused him, but I liked this new view of him.

Was *he* the man missing from my life?

I was dreaming. I didn't want another husband, and however much I liked Anfim, I couldn't risk falling in love with him. I was a boyar's daughter with a child approaching marriageable age. I had to put her interests first. An alliance with a man from a line of merchants would undermine everything I'd worked for over the last decade.

Not that Anfim and I had ever expressed an interest in each other. Darya had told me last summer that he was in love with someone. Over the course of months, our conversations in his office had evolved from lady of the house and resident clerk to something approaching friendship, but there they stopped—and rightly so.

Watching him from a distance, though, I couldn't help feeling drawn to him. His light brown hair gleamed in the light cast by the torches placed at intervals along walls painted in patterns of scarlet and sky-blue; and he was, as always, discreetly but luxuriously dressed—tonight in rich brown velvet with clasps formed from gold braid. Next to the brilliantly clad noblemen and noblewomen he looked like a wren amid a flock of peafowl, but at the sight of him my heart gave a skip.

Stop, I told myself. I had never known a noblewoman who took up with a merchant. In the occasional tales I'd heard while I was growing up, the women came to bad ends—like the girl who ran off with a bandit chief, only to be murdered out of jealousy. I could do my best for my beloved daughter or imperil both our futures by giving way to a foolish whim. Not much of a choice, put like that.

Determined to be sensible, I tugged at Darya's arm. "I don't think we can get much closer," I told her. Indeed, the crowd had become ever more tightly packed as we progressed—and more masculine. Soon we would be lucky to catch even a glimpse of Anfim.

"Very well." With a shrug, she turned back to face me. I thought she sensed my reluctance, even if she didn't grasp the reason for it, until she spoke again. "I'm sure he'll seek us out. And if he doesn't, I'll ask Niki to fetch him later."

Searching for a way to dissuade her, I surveyed the room, only to realize that the time for objections had already passed. As I watched, Nikita and his patron, Tsarevich Alexei, approached the group of officials. The two of them detached Anfim from his companions with the aplomb of skilled horsemen separating a stallion from the herd and ushered him in our direction.

"I don't think you'll have to," I said. "They're heading this way."

A flash of joy suffused my body, scattering every one of my good intentions. It was all I could do not to groan. I was hard-hit, indeed.

To reestablish control of my unruly emotions, I studied the three men as they came toward us. Alexei—tall, dark, and blessed with extraordinary good looks—stood out among the party guests for his kingly bearing, the result of a lifetime as one of Genghis Khan's descendants. Nikita's coloring resembled Anfim's, although his eyes were warm brown instead of blue. Niki was taller and more slender, with the long fingers of an artist and an air of confident serenity that concealed a sharp mind and a wicked sense of humor. But what struck me most was Anfim's comfort with them, now that he'd returned to his own sphere—as well as the gleam that lit his eyes when he bowed to me in greeting.

"Look who we found." Niki gripped Anfim's shoulder, although he showed no signs of wanting to escape. I returned Anfim's bow, then stood on tiptoe to kiss Alexei's cheek.

"Welcome," I said. "Darya and I tried to cross the room to say hello, but we had to stop. Between the aunties and the boyars, we feared for our skirts and our toes."

"Especially our toes." Darya kissed Anfim as well as Alexei, making me wish I'd done the same. "I barely avoided an auntie with a goblet and an unsteady hand. I dodged the wine, but it's the nearness of having my feet crushed that will give me nightmares."

My upper arm brushed Anfim's sleeve, sending a trickle of warmth flowing from shoulder to elbow. *Anna*, I thought, trying to sound as stern with myself as I would with her under similar circumstances. *I can't afford to yearn for an unsuitable man. Anna's future depends on me.*

Alas, my self-chiding had no effect on my heart whatsoever.

"How are you?" I asked him. Surely even the strictest moral arbiter must approve of so simple a question. "You look as though your return to government work pleases you."

"Very much." He gazed at me, an expression I couldn't read in his eyes. "Except for not seeing enough of my friends. And what of you?"

"Life has become very quiet since you left." I didn't want to complain about not having heard from him in more than a month, so I searched for a friendly but not intrusive way to find out what occupied his time these days. Before I could settle on one, another voice intruded.

"Family, friends, honored guests," my cousin Igor Grigorevich Bezzubtsev called in ringing tones. "I have an announcement to make."

At first, his words had little effect. The chatter continued, intermingled with songs and toasts, the twanging instruments, the hum of flirtation, giggles and guffaws. Still at Anfim's side, I turned toward my cousin's voice, wondering what kind of announcement he might have kept for an audience such as this.

Gradually the din faded. Igor strutted toward a long table at the back of the room, the place where the family would sit at meals. As usual, our cousin had dressed in a style designed to cast every other guest into the shade. Today he'd outdone himself in a cloth-of-gold robe tied with an embroidered cobalt sash, its hue repeated in his leather boots and silken cap trimmed with white fox fur. A gem-studded collar that would not have looked amiss on the grand prince himself adorned Igor's thick neck. Glancing at Anfim, I saw amazed delight in his wide eyes and twitching lips and knew that he shared my reaction. I hastily looked away, lest I send both of us into floods of laughter that could only cause offense.

That was when I realized that Igor's extravagant robes were designed to complement Katya's. She strolled at his side, her hand on his arm, and the glee on her face gave me pause. Katya had been chasing Igor, most often in vain, since the day she first met him at our house six months ago. From her proud stance and those matching outfits, I concluded she had caught him at last. No wonder she'd blushed when I raised the subject of marriage.

I flicked my head toward my sister, and her quick nod told me she'd had the same thought. At that moment, Igor raised his goblet and announced in ringing tones, "Congratulations are in order, my friends. Katya Ivanovna's father has given her to me in marriage, and our wedding will take place on Sunday, six weeks from now, before the onset of the Great Fast." He stared straight at us as he added, "We will be managing this estate until her younger brother, Dmitry, returns from his military assignment in Kolomna, because their father has decided to enter a monastery after the ceremony." The assembled company roared its acclamation.

I repressed the unwomanly curse that sprang to my lips, although I heard it echoed in Niki's muttered expletive. Igor had aided and abetted Fyodor Koshkin's attempt to wrest our home from us, and now he would be living right next door. A lesser evil, admittedly, than tearing our own house from our hands, but still infuriating.

I glanced at Darya once more and found her shaking her head in disbelief. "We'll never get rid of him now," she said with a sigh. "And here I was hoping he'd get posted to the Far North."

Igor raised Katya's hand to his lips and pressed a kiss on her knuckles, then gazed deeply and yearningly into her eyes. "I am honored by your trust in me, my darling. I will take good care of you."

Knowing him, I didn't believe it for one moment. The crowd disagreed, yelling congratulations. As I applauded with the rest, I had to admit that it was a lovely sentiment. And for some reason even the expression on *his* face brought me to the brink of tears.

The evening went downhill from there. My sister strolled off with her husband and the tsarevich to greet Alexei's wife, Maria—the older sister of Lyuba, Anna's best friend. I'd already thanked Maria for inviting my daughter to stay overnight, a favor that she brushed off on the grounds that it kept both girls out of trouble. So despite my better judgment, I chose to stay and chat with Anfim.

Still looking for that safe topic, I settled on asking him about his children, who had visited us often in the days when he worked for us. "I miss Lara and Tolya. How are they coping with your new assignment? Does it mean longer hours away from home?"

"It does." Anfim took the goblet from my hand and, when he saw it was empty, beckoned to a servant, who refilled it and handed it back to me. "They miss you, too—and Laika as well."

The shouts and celebratory toasts increased in volume, making it harder to hear. I leaned forward. "Laika's still with us, although I suppose Igor will want his dog back once he settles in here. Bring the children to our house whenever you like. Anna loves teaching Lara embroidery, and there's a horde of kitchen boys eager to help Tolya slay his dragons. It would be good for them, too, to have the company of other boys and girls."

"You're very kind. I'll think about it." His face, which had been open and accepting—less guarded than usual, in fact— closed down. "But you're right, it would be good for them. The atmosphere at my house is pretty grim. My father's dying. Between caring for him and completing my work, I haven't been paying the children enough attention."

So that explained his withdrawal. "I'm sorry to hear of your troubles," I told him. I'd never met his father, although my sister had, but I knew too well the pain of losing a parent. My own father had died less than a year ago. "You must definitely send Lara and Tolya to us, then. And let us know how we can help."

He asked me about Father Job and the servants, about how I was spending my days, whether I enjoyed having Darya and Nikita back in the household. After a while, my head started to throb. The smells of liquor and rich food lost their appeal. The toasts flowed nonstop, and although as a woman I could get by with a few sips each time, the sheer number meant that over the course of the evening I had downed several goblets of wine. It escaped me how the men, expected to drain their cups with every salutation, managed to stay upright.

"Are you unwell?" Anfim asked when I pressed my hand to my forehead. "Shall I see you home?"

The concern I heard in his voice heightened my distress. Darya had achieved happiness, and even Katya had wrung a commitment out of my cousin by sheer force of will. Yet here I stood, alone and unloved, in conversation with an attractive man my age whom I could not have and should not want.

I opened my mouth to turn down his offer, but the words would not form on my tongue. Although we lived right next door, an announcement that I planned to return to the house at this hour of the night would unleash a furor of activity. Niki would insist on escorting me, and Darya on fussing over me, and they would both miss the rest of an event that gave them pleasure. I'd tell them, of course, rather than disappear without a word. But a quick statement that I didn't plan to brave the wintry streets alone would release them to enjoy the rest of the evening and worry about me, if they must, tomorrow morning.

"You wouldn't mind?" I asked Anfim. "I would appreciate your escort. I won't keep you from the party long."

He tipped his head and treated me to that delightful smile of his, the one that lit his eyes from within and heightened his resemblance to his uninhibited son. "If you leave," he said, "the party will lose its luster. I've already spoken with the officials I came to meet, so it's no inconvenience to walk you home. Or should I call for a sleigh?"

If you leave, the party will lose its luster? That unexpectedly flirtatious comment lit a glow about my heart. Or perhaps it was the wine talking. My headache lessened, and I returned his smile. "Let's walk," I said. "It's cold, but I have ample furs. Give me a moment while I tell Darya and Niki I'm leaving, and I'll meet you at the front door."

"It will be my pleasure," he said with another small bow. I thanked him and went, with a noticeable spring in my step, to explain the new plan to my sister.

Chapter Two

DESPITE THE DISTINCT CHILL IN THE AIR, I TINGLED WITH warmth, inside and out, as I strolled along the planked sidewalk, one hand snug inside my fur-lined cloak and the other tucked between Anfim's sleeve and his ankle-length coat. The sky above glistened with stars, their brilliance unmuted by the occasional lantern marking this noble estate or the next. Flakes of snow sparkled against their midnight backdrop—so soft and fresh they gave the whole scene an unworldly glow, as if we walked in a glittering dream world.

People surrounded us—laughing and drinking, dancing and singing to the accompaniment of horns and drums. Many wore costumes, masquerading as beasts to celebrate light's cautious return to our darkened world. A tall Grandfather Frost—his long hair braided into wild curlicues and his beard flowing to his waist—stood in one corner, waving his arms as if conducting the musicians rather than handing out small gifts to passersby, his usual practice. The free swing of the sack slung over his shoulder suggested he'd emptied it before the children went to bed.

Jesters in bright-colored suits and belled hats searched for candle-lit windows marking houses that welcomed their services. Girls eager to learn whether and whom they might marry in the coming year called down past open shutters to the bent old women who earned their bread telling fortunes, tempting them with promises of coin and hot drinks. Floating on a sea of magic, I happily lost myself in *this* cheerful crowd.

A man in a bear suit, blinded by his mask, stumbled into me. Knocked out of my illusion, I clung to Anfim, who put a steadying arm around my waist and said, "Watch where you step, fool." He shoved the other man in the shoulder, but his tone was more friendly than harsh, and the "bear" responded with abject apologies. I laughed and waved him on his way. Anfim pulled me closer at the sight of another would-be animal, antlered like an elk, staggering toward us. I blinked, experiencing a flash of recognition. Then the elk veered off, avoiding a collision, and I forgot about him.

Wandering along the wooden sidewalk, I savored the lingering taste of wine, the smooth and comforting sensation of Anfim's arm around my waist, the musky scent that clung to him. I asked for more details about his new position and listened as he told me how it pleased him to handle international documents again. In truth, he could have said anything: I welcomed the sound of his rich tenor voice.

A slight flush suffused his face, visible as we passed under the lantern near the gate of the estate where I lived. The result of all those toasts, perhaps. "And your father?" I asked. "When did he fall ill?"

"He's not ill," he said. "Not in the usual sense. He's been failing for years. And he's in his sixties. He clings to life even as it slips away from him, but each day he weakens a bit more. He will join the angels soon." He tightened his hold on my waist, and I leaned closer, not wanting to miss a single word. I'd waited months for him to confide in me. "I will miss him, but in a sense he's already left us. He doesn't know where he is, most of the time. That's my greatest fear: to linger endlessly, incapable of caring for myself or even aware of what goes on around me."

"I understand. Papa's death was the same—not painful or upsetting, once he stopped realizing how much he'd forgotten, but so drawn-out we didn't know whether to grieve or rejoice when he at last left this earth. Your father is a good man, from what you've told me. He will go to Heaven, I'm sure." In this phantasmagorical space, I could talk with Anfim as an equal, and I relished the opportunity. "But it's hard on you and the children, especially when they lost their mother a year and a half ago. Who looks after them?"

"A nanny." He stared straight ahead, but the tightening of his lips showed me how much the situation troubled him. "But she watches my father as well."

He didn't admit that he couldn't afford a second nurse, but I knew that government salaries often weren't paid in full or on time. "Bring the children to our house," I said again. "We'll look after them, and that will free your caretaker to concentrate on your father's needs."

"I will." The tension I'd sensed in him dissolved as he looked down at me and smiled, sending a shiver of delight down my spine. "Enough about my family troubles. I'd like to say that I'm glad you agreed to walk with me this evening. I've long wanted to see you outside the confines of that office."

Ahead of us, the main entrance of the estate stood open—an unusual sight so late at night, but not during the Christmas season. I heard the servants celebrating in the courtyard and kitchens beyond. I don't know what possessed me—the wine, perhaps, or the closeness created by walking arm in arm—but I lost control of my tongue and blurted out the question that had plagued me since my sister revealed the truth last summer. "Have you? Darya told me you're in love with someone else."

The voice in my head clanged in warning, like a bell. *Why did I say that?* In response, I pulled away from him. "Forgive me. I have no right to ask you such a question."

His smile turned to laughter, and he clasped my hand in both of his, the warmth of his gloves defeating the icy pull of the air around us. Another "bear" lumbered in our direction, and Anfim caught me around the waist and turned us so that my back pressed against the fence that ringed our estate. He waited until the pretend bear had passed before speaking again. "That was my father talking. Did Darya Petrovna believe him?"

"It's not true?" A bud of hope bloomed in my chest, so close to his. "Why did your father say it, in that case?"

Anfim sighed, and his face became serious once more. "It's not completely false, but as I told your sister at the time, the whole thing ended sixteen months ago. If I can even call it a 'thing.' It started when I was captured by the Tatars—you know about that?"

I nodded. "Darya told me. The people in charge of foreign affairs sent you on a mission to Crimea, and two renegade princes ambushed your group. Tsarevich Alexei's half-brother rescued you, but your companion died during the escape and his men couldn't find the other envoys. So when you got back to Moscow months later, your supervisors questioned your loyalty, wondering how you escaped when no one else did."

"Exactly," Anfim said. "They didn't want me around for a while. If it hadn't been for Igor Grigorevich …"

He let the sentence trail off, but I knew that part as well. His government salary might be unreliable, but its loss had left him struggling to support his family. "We'd never have met," I said instead, keeping my tone light to comfort him. "I don't often feel grateful to Igor, but I do thank him for that."

"So do I." He rubbed my cheek with his thumb. My skin warmed at his touch, as I pushed my doubts away and leaned into his hand.

"And the woman your father thought you loved?" If I didn't ask for the full story now, when he seemed willing to talk about it, I might never hear it.

"It's no secret," he said. "I met a woman in the horde. The only Russian woman there. Grusha, they call her—"

"Grusha? I remember Grusha!" I spoke without thinking, as one does when a name leaps out of the past. "It must be the same one, if she's in Ogodai Khan's horde."

"You do?" He couldn't have looked more astonished if he'd tried. "How do you know her?"

"She used to work next door, in the house we just left. My husband manipulated her into joining his criminal scheme, and she fled to avoid arrest. It gets more complicated from there, but I did hear that she went south with Ogodai after her man died. Maria and Alexei are in constant contact with his half-brother, so they give me news of the horde. Grusha has a son, Maria told me, and she became the camp shaman."

"Yes, that's right. I saw her as a good mother, someone who would help Lara and Tolya. She's not above my station, as you are." He said that last with a certain bitterness, and I winced.

For a moment, his tone pulled me out of my wine-warmed, light-filled idyll. I didn't belong here, with this man I couldn't have. I should flee through the gates and leave him here on the street. But I stayed, because I wanted to hear the rest.

When I didn't answer, he gazed over my head. His voice, too, sounded faraway, as if he traveled back in time. "Grusha's

22

son is Lara's age. He needs a father. It seemed we would make a good couple, each providing something the other lacked. Not a grand passion, you understand, but I thought we could become comfortable together after a while."

"But she didn't agree? Why not?" I strove to keep my voice level, to conceal my distress. My *illogical* distress. Such arrangements were standard, and this one had been proposed and come to naught before we met. Yet I couldn't help wondering whether he still cared for this woman who was not denied to him by virtue of their birth.

This time, his laughter had a rueful edge. "I behaved like an ass." A blast from a horn greeted his words, and I glanced to my left and laughed at the sight of someone in a horse costume twirling and hooting, as if he took Anfim's comment as an instruction.

I shook my head at Anfim, who seemed perplexed by my response. I explained about the horse, then added, "You behaved like an ass? I don't believe it. You're the soul of discretion, the most courteous man I know."

"Not that summer." He too shook his head, as if disgusted by his own boorishness. "Everything about the camp unsettled me. Being stuck there. Having no idea what would happen, whom I was dealing with, when I'd see Lara and Tolya again, whether my father still lived. At first I couldn't even communicate in Tatar, although I've studied the language for years. I'd lost my wife three months before, and I was grieving more than I understood at the time."

The sorrow in his voice gripped my heart. "And Grusha?" I asked tentatively after a while. None of what he'd said so far constituted behaving like an ass, so far as I could tell.

He met my eyes then. "Yes, Grusha. She both drew me and repelled me. I'd never met a woman so certain of her own worth—because of her service to the horde as a guide to the spirit world. How could I, a priest's son, pursue a woman who saw her pagan visions as equal to the love of Christ? Yet the more I learned about her, the more interesting she became. And she *is* a good mother. I tried to persuade her to reject her calling—the very thing that attracted me to her in the first place. I didn't grasp until too late what she kept telling me: that she valued her gift more than marriage. I didn't want to hear it, but in the end she left me no choice."

His description didn't sound like the Grusha I'd known. I'd considered her weak-willed and gullible, especially around men. My husband exploited her without effort, according to his own boasts. Either becoming a shaman had changed her, or Anfim saw a strength in her that others didn't.

I chose not to deflect him by again bringing up the past. Instead, I gazed at him in silence. Anfim seldom spoke so personally or for so long; I'd found him to be a master of the noncommittal phrase. Yet I heard both regret and remorse in his words. *Did* he still care for Grusha, whatever he said about it being over?

Even if the answer was yes, it should make no difference to me. Yet somehow it did.

He clasped my hand once more and raised it to his mouth. A rush of heat suffused my body as his lips brushed across my fingers. "It's not Grusha I love," he said, his husky voice setting off new ripples in my insides, drowning the scolding voice in my head. "I admire her, it's true, just as I admire your sister. I miss my wife, who was a steady, undemanding companion. But only one woman has my heart, and I must have drunk too much at that party, because I'm tempted to throw caution to the winds and confess how passionately I want you."

"Me?" I'd never expected such a declaration from him. He was so concerned about propriety, so aware of the difference in our ranks—more even than I. But again my heart warred with my head, and I didn't know how to respond.

Snow drifted past my face, strengthening my conviction that this night existed in another realm, a mystical sphere that only resembled my home. The tightening of his grip on my waist—combined with the warm glow of wine, the brilliance of the night, and the caress of his lips across my fingers—chased the last of my reservations into a cave.

"Oh, Anfim, I want you too." I pulled my hand free and wrapped my arms around his neck. Greatly daring, I touched my mouth to his.

He responded by kissing me with an intensity I hadn't experienced during six years of marriage. I fell into bliss, oblivious of my surroundings. At last, to my great regret, he pulled back and regarded me with troubled eyes. "We shouldn't do this," he said. "*I* shouldn't do this. I have no right to tempt you to sin."

The sparkling snow formed a nimbus around his head. My lips tingled from his kiss. My heart beat fast beneath my cloak, matching the thump of the drums, the stamping rhythm of the dancers' feet. Bears and wolves and horses surrounded me, blowing flutes and sounding horns. Roughly costumed bison and birds pranced among them. Figures in horned masks clapped their hands and sang. The flickering flames of bonfires cast elongated, distorted shadows against the buildings. Lost in this fantastical realm, what sense did it make to resist the lure of wine and the promise of a man's touch? Tomorrow would arrive soon enough, and with it the pull of duty and loneliness.

I twisted free of the spot where Anfim had pinned me against the fence, caught his left hand in mine, and tugged. "Come home with me," I said, "if only for tonight. I've lived without love for too long."

Having spent most of my life on the estate, I knew every entrance, every room, every seldom-used passageway between the front gate and my bedchamber on the third floor. I led Anfim without hesitation to the women's quarters, capturing a tray holding another jug of wine and two glazed clay cups on the way.

He didn't resist or protest, although I sensed a certain hesitation in the sidelong glances he sent my way from time to time. Only when we reached the sewing room on the third floor did he take the tray from me, depositing the cups on a table before claiming the jug, pouring wine into both, and handing one of them to me.

"Stop," he said. "Believe me, I want this as much as you do, but what of your daughter? Your sister, if she comes upon us? What of you, tomorrow morning? Will you regret what we do tonight?"

I sipped wine, considering his questions. He had a point—several points—but my sense of existing inside a fantastical dream blinded me to thoughts of tomorrow. I yearned to discover what lay beyond that kiss. "Anna isn't here," I said. "She begged to stay the night at Alexei and Maria's, and I agreed. Darya and Niki won't return for hours. You can be home long before then."

"Leaving you to rue a hasty decision?"

"Why must I rue it?" I gripped my cup in frustration. Although I appreciated his reluctance to take advantage of a woman who, in truth, had drunk more than she should, I didn't *want* to stop and think. I wanted, for once, to feel. "You say you love me. And I love you. Who knows when circumstances will favor us again? What I'd regret in the morning would be letting this chance pass me by."

"And what happens if I get you with child?" He, too, grasped his cup so tightly his knuckles showed white.

"You won't. Anna's birth did something to me. I didn't quicken again after I bore her. Not in three years." I took another gulp of wine, this time for courage. "I'm tired of doing what's expected of me. I've lived like a nun for almost a decade. Just once, I'd like to break the rules. I know you desire me." I'd felt him pressing against me when we kissed, and the thought of what I'd experienced in that moment heightened my yearning to throw caution to the winds. "Will you refuse to give me sweet memories, show me what love can be like if you care about someone?"

He'd watched me without speaking, as I'd gazed at him while he spoke of Grusha. As I finished, he drained his cup and reached for me. I noticed the grace with which he moved, the sense of discretion that clung to him even as he pulled me into his arms and bent his head to embrace me with the ardor I craved. His hands roamed over my body, brushing my most private places, leaving a trail of burning ecstasy in their wake. I responded in kind—stunned by my boldness, as if watching myself from a corner of the ceiling.

After a while, he pulled back enough to say, in the same unsteady voice I'd heard eons ago in the street, "If we're going to continue, I think we need a more private place."

"Yes," I said. The flames of passion filled me, driving out every sober thought. I stepped back and took his hand, then led him toward my bedchamber. "Let me show you."

At that point, I lost track of time and couldn't have cared less. What use have magical worlds for time? I heard nothing to suggest the return of my sister and brother-in-law, but the servants were still carousing in the courtyard as I sat on my bed and watched Anfim gather his clothes. Only when he finished dressing did I rise, still naked, and kiss him farewell.

He stopped then, shaking his head and wrapping his arms around me. "I can't bear to leave."

"You must," I told him. "But thank you for indulging me. I didn't know it was possible to enjoy the act of love so much."

He blushed like a schoolboy caught with his hand in the sweets. "Indulging you? Myself, rather. I've dreamed of this night. I only hope my selfishness won't cause you distress."

"Not in the least," I said to reassure him. "I would say you've brought me back to life, but it's more than that. I realize now that I never truly lived before. You have released me *into* life, just as Prince Ivan and the Firebird freed the maidens held in thrall by Koshchei the Immortal."

That made him laugh, as I'd expected it would, although I meant exactly what I'd said. I hadn't known I could feel so fulfilled, so beloved. "Steal the golden apples whenever you wish, my Firebird," he said. "I'll be waiting in the shadows for a sight of you."

I freed myself long enough to pick up the chemise he'd pulled off me earlier in the evening and tossed to the floor, then dropped it over my head and went to unlock the bedroom door. He followed me, then left after one last, lingering kiss. I watched him until he passed through the door leading out of the sewing room.

When he pulled it shut behind him, I ran to the window like any foolish girl eager to catch a last glimpse of her lover and stared into the courtyard, searching for him amid the still-noisy crowd. A flash of gold in the dark next to the wall caught my eye, and I saw one of the small side gates open. At the very last minute, as if he knew I stood there—how was that possible?—he stepped into the light from the lantern and raised a hand. Then he was gone.

I resisted the insane urge to run after him. The barriers between us had not lessened. Society would frown on our union. I had no desire to remarry even if that obstacle did not exist. And as Anna's mother, I did not have the right to put my own selfish desires ahead of hers.

Yet no matter how hard I tried to be sensible, I longed passionately for what I could not have and until tonight would have insisted I did not need. I'd failed to predict how Anfim's gentleness would thaw my iced-over heart or how hard it would be, having spread my wings for the first time, to stand meekly by and let them be clipped once more.

With a sigh, I left the sewing room for my bedchamber. I had just enough time to gather and put away the clothes I'd worn to the Vorontsovs' party when I heard the swish of sleigh runners against the snow—Darya and Niki on their way home.

Thank every saint in creation they hadn't come sooner. The risk of discovery had been greater than I'd thought.

Although saints would not exert themselves to protect me from the results of my misdeeds, would they? If they did, they wouldn't be saints.

At the sound of footsteps in the passageway, I blew out the candle and dove into bed. When the door opened with a creak, I kept my eyes closed.

"Are you awake, Solomonida?" my sister whispered. "Do you feel better?"

I didn't answer, and the door closed again. My secret sin was safe, for a while.

I woke at first light and stretched, peaceful and luxurious as a cat. I reached a hand across the mattress, but of course Anfim was not there. Fragments of last night's spell clung to me like wisps in the woods, and for a moment I almost believed I could summon him to me through sheer force of will. How would it feel to wake up each morning with such a man at my side? Rivulets of sensation rippled through me as I imagined what we might do together. My breasts and belly tingled, and other places as well.

I pushed those sinful thoughts away and stared at the ceiling, going over the events of last night. What possessed me to seduce a man, however kind and responsible and caring? Because I couldn't fool myself that Anfim would have urged me to make love. He had revealed an unexpected depth of feeling but also the capacity for restraint. The responsibility for our night of passion lay squarely on my shoulders.

I could blame my behavior on the wine or the carnival atmosphere that turned reality on its head—that sense of otherworldliness that consumed me from the time I left the party with Anfim until the moment he waved goodbye. I knew the Church would see our congress as evidence of the devil's work—coupled with women's notorious frailty and lack of self-control. Even dear Father Job would look askance if I confessed this sin. Yet try as I might, I could not feel remorse. For once, I had given myself over to desire, and I didn't regret what Anfim and I had done together. Perhaps the priests were right to castigate me as morally weak.

Other questions pushed thoughts of repentance from my brain. Why did I have to wait until the age of thirty-one to discover the pleasure of the right man's touch, only to find it in the arms of a man barred to me because of the difference in our ranks? Could life be more unfair?

And when will I see Anfim again?

I pushed that last question out of my head. I'd escaped once without attracting attention that would harm both my daughter and myself—and Anfim, too, if the gossip mongers learned that he'd forgotten his place and entered into an affair with a noblewoman. I must get my passions under control, be grateful that I'd not already doomed Anna's chances, forget my one stolen night of bliss.

Well, forgetfulness might be beyond my powers. But I must not *act* on my yearning to be alone with Anfim, to lie with him again, to feel the rapid beat of his heart close to mine.

A treacherous thought intruded. Suppose social convention did not exist, and Papa had wed me to a merchant like Anfim instead of Semyon Kolychev, a nobleman who thought of women as fortresses to be conquered with as little expenditure of effort as possible? Sixteen and wholly innocent, I'd had no warning of the brutality that lay behind my new husband's striking façade. When Semyon ripped my virginity from me as he might tear an apple from a tree, I wept, but I didn't complain. No wonder I had vowed never to remarry.

In the years since, I'd felt no impulse to break that vow. But today, fresh from the arms of a lover who understood tenderness, I sensed the leaves of change unfurling. Perhaps there was still time to find happiness in love.

Or would be, had I not fallen for a man I could not wed.

Chapter Three

Despite my determination to put that night out of my mind, I obsessed over Anfim for the rest of the Christmas season. I did not seek him out, and neither did he visit me. When Epiphany arrived without sight or sound of him, I tried to take heart from the notion that I'd fallen for a man with so much common sense.

Instead, I stewed in an unholy broth of chagrin and betrayal. Our night together meant nothing to him. My loose morals had undermined his respect for me. Or worse, I'd been just a passing fancy, and he'd lied when he said he loved me.

Yet try as I might, I could not put that evening behind me. As I stood near the frozen Moscow River—watching the priests raise their crucifixes in the ceremony that symbolized the Baptism of Our Lord, then leaping back to avoid the surge of residents racing to dip themselves and their children in the sanctified water through holes cut in the ice—I intermittently gave into temptation and searched for him amid the throng.

"Where's Anfim?" I asked Darya when my efforts proved fruitless. "Do you see Lara or Tolya?"

She stood on tiptoe, peering in every direction. "Not a sign. But the crowd is huge, Solomonida. The entire city must be here. Look at those people over there, bringing their horses to drink from the river!"

"You're right," I said. "One man and two children—they could be anywhere in this mob." I shrugged in an attempt to appear calm. "Let's go home, shall we? The priests have driven out the devil, and the ceremony's over. My toes will turn into icicles if I stand here much longer." She agreed, and we left.

Despite my disappointment, I was glad we had attended the Blessing of the Waters. Although I didn't yet feel strong enough to confess my sins, I worried about the state of my soul. Taking part in the rituals of the Church might convince God to forgive me for my misplaced passion.

The days continued to roll by without word from Anfim, and I'd more or less given up on him by the time Nikita walked into the second-floor sitting room waving a piece of paper in his right hand. It was the fifteenth of January, exactly two weeks since my unwise but cherished evening of love.

"A note from Anfim Fadeyev," he said without preamble. Darya and I exclaimed, and Anna, perched on the window seat stitching, said, "At last! I've been waiting ages for Lara. Is she coming soon?"

Niki dropped onto a chair. "I don't know, sweetheart," he said. "Her grandfather died the night before last. They can't bury him with the ground frozen solid, but her papa is arranging a memorial service. After that, probably." He glanced at Darya, then at me. "Anfim apologizes for the delay. Apparently he promised to visit you ten days ago. He says life has been unbelievably hectic, what with his father's illness and the children's needs. And once Christmas ended, he had to work as well."

"When did he promise?" Darya asked me. "The night he walked you home?"

At least I knew, at last, what had kept him away. Yet I struggled to reply, not because I had no answer—"yes" would do—but because a sea of emotion threatened to engulf me and I feared what my simple response would reveal.

When my silence lengthened, Darya raised her eyebrows, as if repeating her question without words. I felt heat in my cheeks and hoped I wasn't blushing too obviously. "Yes. He said his father needed a lot of attention, so I invited him to bring the children here. I knew you wouldn't object. He agreed, but when he didn't follow through, I thought he'd changed his mind." About me, not the children—I didn't add that part.

"Hmm." She fixed me with that keen gaze of hers. "You've been very quiet about that evening. What else are you hiding, I wonder?"

"Nothing important," I said, which was probably the worst lie I'd ever told. "We talked about his work at the Treasury and the celebration in the streets. We only came from next door, after all. There wasn't time for much else."

Except his confession of love and my seduction of him …

A devil caught hold of my tongue, and I blurted out the next phrases before my better self could censure them. "I'll visit them tomorrow and express our condolences, shall I? Laika can come with me. And I'll bring Eva, of course, for propriety's sake."

"You're welcome to use the sleigh," Darya said. "The weather's colder than a sinner's heart." I winced at that expression, but my sister appeared not to notice. "Anna and I could go with you, then," she added, "although not the dog."

I should have grasped at the offer and been thankful for it, but instead I yielded once more to temptation. "Next time," I said lightly. "Igor's getting married in less than a month, and pestiferous man that he is, I expect he'll demand that we give Laika back once he settles in with Katya. It's a short walk, even in winter, and I promised the children a chance to play with her. From what Anfim writes, it could be a while before he can bring them here."

Again my sister treated me to that assessing gaze, but she said only, "Very well. Ask him what they need most, and Anna and I will deliver it in a day or two."

I agreed, and our conversation turned to other topics. Niki left, claiming a prior appointment. But as I worked on an embroidered cuff for Anna's new robe, the second half of a pair, and chatted amicably about what Darya had overheard about the plans for Katya and Igor's wedding feast, I noticed her eyes never left my face. I thought of asking her what she saw there, but I feared I might not like the answer.

The next morning, I trudged through the Moscow streets on my way to Anfim's house, Laika's leash in my hand and my maid Eva trailing me as promised. The moment I left the confines of our own courtyard, I regretted my foolish impulse. The gale howled with a force strong enough to cut through my winter cloak and chill my bones. Snow, melting under my feet, seeped into my boots. Even so, I pushed on through the fierce wind and flying chips of ice.

Laika dashed this way and that in pursuit of errant flakes and sent powdery fountains into the air as she slid through one drift after another. Like a good servant, Eva kept her thoughts to herself, although I heard her muttering prayers under her breath as we reached the end of our street and turned onto the next.

But indeed, it was not a long walk. I knew from Darya's directions that Anfim, like us, lived within the small trading quarter called the Kitaigorod. The district covered not much more than three long avenues with a labyrinth of cross-streets, mostly narrow lanes. These days, nobles, wealthy merchants, and officials occupied most of the homes. Rising prices had driven artisans and petty traders beyond the massive wall that protected this part of the city from invaders.

At the next intersection I saw a modest house with carved wooden cornices above the shuttered windows, exactly where my sister had told me to look for it. My hands tingled at the sight, and excitement quickened my breath as well as my steps. *So close!* What would Anfim say when he saw me? What would he do? How should I greet him?

I forced myself to stop and beckoned to Eva, so intent on her prayers that she almost stepped on my heels. "We're here," I told her, pointing to the house. "Go and announce our arrival, but quietly, respectfully. God claimed the father of this family not long ago."

Her face turned ashen; she shuddered and crossed herself. "A recent death? Is the corpse still here?"

"I doubt it," I said. "Some days have passed. The Church will have taken charge of him by now. And his spirit won't bother you. He was a priest who reached the end of his life and was taken to the Lord in peace. Only those who perish from violence roam the earth unsatisfied." A superstition I did not believe but Eva, like most of the servants, did.

A modicum of color returned to her cheeks, and she dipped her head in acquiescence. Once I'd seen her enter the servants' entrance on the ground floor, I led Laika up the stairs in search of the main entry. I hoped the walls would provide some protection from the gale.

I needed it. My hands and feet were chilled, and my ears burned, despite my fur hood. I wasn't sure, right then, where I would find the strength to undertake the short walk home. No Anfim would await me at the end of *that* journey.

"Lady Solomonida!" Anfim's voice, high with surprise, cut across this dismal thought. "Come inside and warm yourself. What brings you here?"

He ushered me into a tiny entryway lined with benches, untied my cloak, and hung it on a peg. Then he caressed my face with his thumbs, a gesture not unlike the one with which Nikita rubbed charcoal against paper to produce his drawings.

I threw caution to the winds and kissed his cheek. He hugged me and brushed his lips across mine, then drew back.

I repressed a sigh. Of course, his children must be nearby. I tried to take comfort in the thought that their presence would keep us from doing anything foolish.

"You're frozen," Anfim said. "Did you walk here by yourself?" He pulled off my fur-lined mittens. I shivered and shook my head.

Laika pushed past us and headed for the room beyond as if she had entered the house many times. When I exclaimed and called her name, she pressed against the door, which swung open. I called again. She turned and took three long steps toward me, then shook her soft chestnut coat free of snow, showering us. Anfim laughed, although in the greater light visible through the open door I saw lines of strain around his eyes.

So he too had doubts about what we'd done together. Or did he wonder what to make of my visit? I hastened to reassure him. "We received your note yesterday. May your father's memory be eternal. I came to find out what you need. Darya Petrovna and Nikita Andreevich send their condolences, and she and Anna will visit you soon. And yes, I did walk here, but not alone. Eva accompanied me."

"Then, please, come and warm yourself by the stove." He extended his hand toward the room beyond. "Lara and Tolya are with their nanny, but I will send for them soon." The hint of a smile creased his mouth. "They would hate to miss a visit from Laika. But first let me find out where Eva went. I'll fetch you some hot cider at the same time. I have something to say to you."

Again I heard restraint in his voice. More concerned than before, I followed him into the room, an unexpectedly cheerful place for a house in mourning. The children were not in fact present, but they would arrive before long. Whatever we needed to discuss, we should do it now.

But I didn't know what to make of his subdued manner, and I feared what he might say. Had I been right to construct a sinister explanation for his silence? And if I had, how should I respond? I didn't regret our night of passion, only the damage it might do to my reputation if discovered—and then mostly because it would undermine my daughter's chances. And I'd made it clear that I neither expected nor wanted an offer of marriage. All that made me a thoroughly disreputable woman—in the eyes of the world but possibly in Anfim's eyes, too. He was a man who played by the rules.

A tendril of dread uncurled in my stomach and spread throughout my body as I sat in the only chair and held out my hands to the beehive-shaped clay stove. Without so much as a hint of what he wanted to tell me, Anfim ducked through a smaller door at the far side.

To distract myself, I surveyed my surroundings. Bright red and blue cushions on the benches echoed the rainbow colors of the woolen rug. An embroidery frame holding a project I recognized as Lara's lay on a table—probably the place where the family ate, given its size—but none of Tolya's toys scattered the floor. A smaller table that might double as a desk, a pair of lively carved wooden bears, a shelf holding pottery cups and bowls: that was the extent of the furnishings.

Laika plopped herself next to the stove and lay still, her eyes closed in bliss and a doggy snore emanating from her nostrils. The odor of damp fur pervaded the room. Exhausted from exercise and emotion, I rested my head against the chair and let the warmth permeate my limbs. But anxiety over Anfim's greeting tugged at me.

What does he want to say to me?

Before I could fret myself into a frenzy, Anfim returned, alone, carrying a wicker basket and a clay jug that he placed on the large table. Wisps of apple-scented steam rose from the jug, displacing the odor of damp fur and mingling with the mouthwatering aroma of gingerbread. He poured cider into a cup plucked from the shelf and handed it to me, then held out the basket. I accepted the cup and drank from it, savoring the sweetness and spice, then balanced a piece of gingerbread across the rim and placed both on the arm of the chair where I sat.

While I studied him, he avoided my gaze. I noticed that he did not help himself but instead took a place on the bench closest to me, leaning forward with his elbows on his knees.

"You had something to say to me," I prompted, repressing a childish impulse to sit in silence until Lara and Tolya raced in, looking for the dog.

His cheeks reddened, and he still did not meet my eyes. "I do," he mumbled after a while. "I owe you an apology. I behaved like a lout. You're a beautiful woman, and I took advantage of you after drinking too much wine. There are no excuses I can make. As a man, I bear responsibility for our sin. I imperiled your immortal soul as well as my own. That's what I wanted you to hear—that I have confessed my fault and will not repeat it. I have nothing but respect for you, although I didn't show it then. Please believe that I am truly contrite."

It was worse than I'd feared. Every drop of moisture drained from my throat, and I couldn't think straight. Anfim *regretted* making love to me. His passion embarrassed him. He didn't share my wicked delight in our shared sin; instead, it repelled him.

His rejection crushed me. The whirlpool inside spun off into an ache that masqueraded as a single pounding thought. *Anfim does not want me.* Despite everything he'd said to me that night, Anfim did not want me. I'd plowed through ice and snow to offer my support, and he did not want me.

It took every scrap of self-control I possessed not to throw the cup at his head, followed by the gingerbread, then dash from the room without even my cloak. For far longer than I liked, I stared at him, unable to harness even one of the furious, heartbroken words that roiled my brain.

But I was a former lady-in-waiting to the grand princess of all Russia, a survivor of Europe's most savage court, and I would not—*not!*—show my wounds to this pitiful man who had stolen my heart and did not even have the sense to appreciate the gift that had fallen into his arms. I stood, chin high, and returned the cup and cake to the table with trembling fingers. I walked to the entryway and put on my cloak, mittens, and hood before whistling to Laika. The dog opened one eye and glared before shuffling to her feet and joining me. The brief wait gave me time to master my voice.

"I see," I said in a tone frostier than the wind outside. "I ask your forgiveness, both for my behavior after the party and for visiting you uninvited today. I will not make that mistake again. Please tell Eva to meet me in the street. And I wish the best for you and your children as you adjust to the loss of your father. May his soul rest in peace." A peace I did not feel and had not earned.

"Solomonida, you don't understand—"

"I understand perfectly," I said, biting off each word. "You could not have been clearer."

I turned away, unable to bear another word. Tears pricked my eyes, and I refused to cry in front of him. I grabbed Laika's leash and left the room.

There was no sign of Eva when I reached the bottom stair. Without looking back, I swept through the courtyard, then directed Laika to the side of the street, just beyond the entrance to Anfim's house. There she would be safe from traffic—although there was little danger, since few people chose to brave the outdoors in this weather. The gale-force winds had abated during my short time inside, raising the temperature from frigid to chilly. But looking up, I saw the flat, slate-gray sky and realized more snow would fall soon.

A flurry of footsteps signaled Eva's arrival. The maid skidded to a stop beside me, panting as hard as the dog. "Lady, I'm sorry. I just found out you'd left."

"And a good thing I did, Eva." I pointed at the sky. "We must run, or we'll get caught in a blizzard."

"Yes, Lady." She took Laika's leash from me. "C'mon, dog. Let's race." And race they did, as snowflakes swirled slowly, then ever faster around them.

Not wanting to risk a stumble on the icy, muddy lane, I followed at a more measured pace until we turned the corner onto Varvarka Street, where wooden planks lined the sides of the road and I could make better time. The need to watch my feet distracted me from my grief, but inside I was keening, and when we at last entered our own gates to find my sister leaning out the sitting-room window, I struggled to hold back my tears. She disappeared from view, slamming the shutter closed, and reappeared at the top of the stairs as I put my foot on the last step.

"Shurenka," she exclaimed, using my childhood nickname. I realized then how worried she'd been. "You can't have set off for Anfim's house in this weather. Where did you go?"

When I didn't respond, she touched my cheek as Anfim had done. I closed my eyes against the agony that filled me then and felt her hand on my elbow, pulling me inside.

"Take Laika to the stables," I heard her tell Eva. "Order the grooms to rub her down well and keep her warm. We don't want her getting sick. I'll take care of Lady Solomonida." I opened my mouth to protest, but again I couldn't find the words. A life bereft of even the promise of love stretched out before me, with no hope in sight.

After a brief greeting to my daughter, I slumped onto the window seat in the sewing room on the third floor and listened to Darya shoo Anna out with a combination of assurances and promises. "Your mama's fine," she said.

"She needs rest and hot food because she went out in this horrible weather. I'll send for you soon, but for the moment I want you to practice reading. Do you have the book Niki gave you?"

I heard Anna's murmured assent, followed by a closing door, as I tried to marshal my scattered thoughts. Only then did I realize that the secret Anfim and I shared would remain hidden from the world, keeping Anna safe. I need no longer feel pulled in multiple directions, my desires at war with my deepest goals. Strangely, that thought did not comfort me one bit.

Memories of the embarrassment on my lover's face rekindled my grief. The heat from the tiled stove, a stark contrast to the air outside, caused my cheeks to burn, and I pulled off my mittens so I could pat my face without further chilling it with snow. Even my hands were cold, though, so after a moment I picked up a square of linen to use instead.

I hadn't yet decided how much to tell my sister when the aroma of steaming cider overwhelmed the last of my composure. The scent thrust me back into the anguish of that moment when Anfim denied the love I cherished, holding up a mirror to my own doubts, then going beyond them into a realm I had no desire to enter. Overwhelmed with emotion, I burst into tears.

Darya must have set the jug aside, because in no time she was beside me, hugging me the same way that I hugged Anna when her world collapsed around her. I wept for what seemed like ages, sobbing out not only the tension that had been building in me since the Vorontsovs' party but the long agony of the years before, when I'd hidden my pain even from those I loved most because to open the floodgates would drown both me and them.

At last I pulled away and accepted the fresh linen cloth she handed me. "I must look like a mess," I said shakily. "You have the patience of a saint."

She didn't answer directly. Instead she said, "Tell me what's going on, Solomonida. It's not like you to keep secrets."

But what could I tell her? My night of passion, hidden at the time because it was so precious, had become evidence of colossal misjudgment.

I could share some of it, though. "That night when I let Anfim walk me home," I began, "I asked him about the woman he loved. The one you told me about the first time you went to his house. It was Grusha. Do you remember her, the Kolychev maid who ran away?"

"Grusha?" She looked as astonished as I'd felt when I heard the news. "Seriously? Anfim fell in love with that silly girl who let your husband bully her?"

"The very one," I said. "He met her in the Tatar horde. Offered her marriage, but she refused." My breath caught in my throat as I thought about what he'd said next.

"Why not tell us, then?" Darya frowned. "I don't think much of his taste."

"Either she's changed, or he saw something in her we never did. He called her strong and sure of her own worth." When Darya scoffed at that, I inhaled, a long, sobbing sound. "But there's more. He told me his father got it wrong: he admired Grusha, but he loved me. We kissed. It was so special, Darya, not like anything I'd experienced before. I realized I love him, too."

The tears threatened to choke me again, but I pushed them aside. Through a blur, I saw her watching me, her face taut with unexpressed feelings, her eyes wide with questions. She liked Anfim, I knew, but the rules of society were as plain to her as they were to me. "You don't have to say it. We can't marry; it would wreck Anna's chances of making a good match. I don't even want another husband, after Semyon. But to have a good man declare his love for me, to kiss him and feel joy instead of dread—it was like a door opening onto a world I hadn't dared imagine. And I was sure he meant it, until this morning."

I couldn't go on. I blinked furiously as she patted my hand and made encouraging noises that made me feel about six years old.

"What happened this morning?" she asked gently when the silence lengthened.

With a great effort, I pulled myself together, determined to act like a grown woman. Even so, my voice shook as I answered her. "He apologized," I whispered. "Blamed his behavior on too much wine and human frailty. He rejected me, Darya. I hope I never set eyes on him again."

Chapter Four

Darya waited a few days for the blizzard to clear. When Anfim still didn't appear, she summoned her sleigh and her best aristocratic manner and visited his home, just as I had done. When she returned, I pretended disinterest. I cringed inside whenever I thought of that last visit with the man for whose touch I still yearned, sinner that I was.

"The children will arrive a week from Monday," she announced. "I talked Anfim into letting them stay here for a while so he can get his affairs in order. Masha can take care of them."

"But she's a kitchen maid," I said, my head reeling with this turn of events. Lara and Tolya were welcome, of course, but how had Darya talked their father into permitting them to stay at our house for more than a few hours?

My sister's new air of authority impressed me. She had ordered the servants for years, but with her family and her peers she tended toward the shy and retiring. Marriage had changed her. Under other circumstances, I'd have rejoiced to see her coming into her own, but in those dark days my spirits hovered near the ground, like fog.

"Yes." Darya waved a dismissive hand. "But she has half a dozen younger brothers and sisters. She will do well. I think she'd enjoy being more than a kitchen maid."

"I'm sure you're right." Masha was an intelligent woman, but ... "Her looks won't scare the children?"

"The scars on her cheek are much less visible since I gave her cosmetics." Darya sounded thoughtful, as if she were imagining the effect of Masha's burns on a child. "I think we can explain to Lara and Tolya that someone hurt her by accident."

"Let's make the effort, at least," I agreed. "She deserves a chance to look after something besides pots and pans. She'll make a reliable nanny." I paused before adding, almost as an afterthought, "Did Anfim say anything else?"

Darya laughed. "You're not fooling me, Solomonida, so don't even try. Yes, he asked after your health. He says you misunderstood him, whatever that means, and apologizes for expressing himself badly. And from the wistful expression in his eyes, I'd guess he cares a lot more for you than you think."

"Let him show it then," I said, still acting as if the news meant nothing to me. But inside, a seedling of hope sprouted in my heart. Perhaps I *had* misunderstood Anfim, as he claimed. Although I couldn't see how ...

As I hovered once more on the edge of an emotional whirlpool, Nikita arrived. The grin on his face caught my attention right away—and Darya's. "What is it?" she asked. "You look like you just heard the best joke in the world."

"Oh, I did." He turned the wicked smile on me. "Gavriil Vorontsov has asked me for your sister's hand. Says he was smitten by her beauty at the Christmas party and has thought of nothing else since that night."

"Smitten by my beauty?" I repeated, incredulous. I would have sworn that Gavriil Vorontsov saw women as one step above the animals, tolerable only because of our ability to bear and rear sons, something I had failed to do at sixteen and certainly could not promise now.

Although "smitten" did explain his staring at the party. "He must have lost his mind. If nothing else, he proposed to Darya six months ago, and she turned him down. Has he no pride?"

"A man in love has no pride," Niki said, winking at Darya, who reddened and dipped her head in a way that made me want to shake them both. Lovely for them that they had each other, but the man *I* desired had broken my heart, and Gavriil Vorontsov was no substitute.

No, that was my misplaced passion talking. I should regard Vorontsov as the answer to my prayers. He equaled—even exceeded—me in rank; he had ample resources; and he had spent decades cultivating the connections that would help me find the right husband for my daughter. So what if he didn't stir my blood? Nothing in life is perfect.

"Would you consider him, Solomonida?" Darya asked, echoing my unspoken thoughts with uncanny precision. "With the power he wields at court, he could assure your future—and Anna's."

"You didn't take him," I reminded her before turning to Nikita, who regarded me with those shrewd eyes of his. "What did you tell him?"

Niki shrugged. "What do you think? That you're a grown woman, and he'll have to persuade you himself. He's waiting for you in my study."

Without another word, I swept out of the room, stopping in my chambers to change my outer robe and forcing aside memories of Anfim's touch. *Anna comes first*, I reminded myself.

I hoped she would appreciate my sacrifice.

When I entered the study, I found Vorontsov pacing the room like the ponderous beast my daughter's friend Lyuba had pointed out in one of Alexei's books—an elephant, she called it. Vorontsov lacked the ivory tusks on either side of his mouth, of course, although his luxuriant whiskers produced some of the same effect. And this elderly elephant thought I should marry him.

An image of Anfim laughing, the remembered sensation of his hand caressing my bare skin, flashed through my mind. I shoved it aside, but with it went my certainty that my future didn't matter, so long as I secured my daughter's.

My lumbering suitor produced a creaky bow as I shut the door. "Solomonida Petrovna," he said with his usual solemnity. "Your brother-in-law has told you of my offer?"

"He did." Impatient with my own waffling, I crossed the room and took one of the chairs, gesturing toward the other. "Gavriil Timofeevich, please sit." When he did, I got straight to the point. "Your proposal does me great honor, but have you considered that I may not be a suitable wife? I have a daughter by another man, and my age means that I can no longer bear you sons." If he harbored delusions as to what he could expect from me, best that I rid him of them as soon as possible.

He winced at my candor, then leaned forward, resting his elbows on the arms of the chair. After a while, he said haltingly, "That doesn't matter. I have four adult sons already. I approach you because, when I saw you at the party, I noticed how lovely you are—and how lonely. I offer comfort, admiration, a home of your own. And I can help you find a suitable match for your daughter. She is twelve, Nikita Andreevich told me."

Hearing him list the reasons that had brought me to this room, my volatile emotions lurched in his direction once more. I leaned forward as well, then drew back as I realized I was mirroring him. "She turns thirteen in February," I clarified. "I don't seek a husband for her yet, but in a few years …" I left the phrase unfinished; he knew the rules of our world as well as I did. Many families married their daughters as young as fourteen. I wouldn't do that to Anna. But leave her unwed beyond sixteen or seventeen and people would wonder what was wrong with her.

"Perfect," he said.

I watched him, wondering at the note of self-satisfaction I heard in his voice. The evidence of discomfort I'd noted earlier had vanished.

"Perfect for what?" I narrowed my eyes at him as I asked the question.

"The bride show. The boyars will hold one in the next two or three years." He pronounced these cryptic phrases with the air of a traveling magician pulling an object from thin air. "It's only a matter of when. King Sigismund of Poland turned down our offer for one of his daughters. The Habsburgs won't send us a princess; they never do. In the end, Grand Prince Ivan will take a Russian noble bride as his father did. And your Anna is an ideal candidate: highborn, healthy, about six months younger than the bridegroom, and with no pack of hungry male relatives at her heels. I need only bring her to Ivan's attention."

My mind reeled. I'd spent too much time away from court the last five years to judge his assessment of international diplomacy, but I had no reason to question it. I got the important point, and it went far beyond my wildest dreams. If I accepted Vorontsov's proposal, he would do his best to ensure that my daughter became the next grand princess of all Russia. A promise he could keep, if he chose, because he had the grand prince's ear.

But did I want him to? I could think of few fates I desired less for my daughter than marriage to Grand Prince Ivan. Becoming a ruler's wife sounds wonderful on the surface, but few grand princesses manage to wield real power. They live under constant pressure to produce male heirs within a court characterized by intense scrutiny and competition. To thrive, they require a strength of character my Anna did not possess. And this particular ruler was already revealing capricious tendencies and an alarming capacity for unbridled rage.

Vorontsov took my hand, and I fought the childish temptation to tug it free. "Marry me, Solomonida Petrovna," he said, staring deep into my eyes. "I will take care of you both. You will not regret your choice."

His obvious sincerity and the kindness on his face touched me. I realized he was more than the lumbering beast I'd considered him. I doubted he would mistreat me as Semyon had done. Katya had described her uncle as a good man when he offered for my sister.

Suppose I did accept him? I wouldn't experience passion, of course, but I might find companionship. And companionship lasted, while passion fled the scene with notorious haste. A union with Vorontsov would make it easier to fulfill my goals for Anna, too. If nothing else, once I wed him, he—not my cousin Igor—would have the final say in choosing her husband. I felt certain I could sway Vorontsov more easily than Igor, whose behavior at the Christmas party had shown he still bore a grudge against me and my sister.

I shouldn't rush to decide. If Vorontsov's influence could work to Anna's and my advantage, it could also hurt us. If I turned him down, I must phrase my refusal carefully to avoid giving offense.

I freed my hand from his clasp and rose. "I need to think about what you've said," I told him. "I will give you my answer soon."

Without acknowledging the amazed delight that lit his face, giving him briefly the appearance of a much younger man, I left the room.

Back on the third floor, I discovered that Darya was entertaining our friend Maria. Her sister Lyuba rose to greet me. After I returned their hugs and kisses with words of welcome, Lyuba dropped back onto the window seat beside Anna and resumed her chatter without, so far as I could tell, stopping to take a breath. "Ah, what it is to be young," I said to Maria. "How lovely that you came to see us. Darya, did you already order refreshments for the girls?"

"And for us." Darya pointed at the empty space between her and Maria. "Sit and tell us the whole. Did you give Gavriil Timofeevich reason to hope?"

I took the seat she indicated, unsure how to explain why I'd acted as I had. "Yes," I said slowly. I repeated what he'd told me—that he expected the boyar council to hold a bride show and select a highborn Russian girl to marry the grand prince—and about the promises he'd made to care for me and for Anna.

"If he's right"—I looked at Maria as I finished—"Lyuba will be summoned as well."

"Without a doubt," she said. "Papa would never let the opportunity slide to make himself the father-in-law of the grand prince." She sighed. Her father—the same Fyodor Koshkin who'd tried to steal our estate for his protegé Cousin Igor—had a long history of political scheming, often unsuccessful. "I wouldn't put it past him to start the rumors of a bride show himself."

"I'm glad you took Vorontsov's proposal seriously. He could be of real help to you." Darya patted my hand. "Still, there are other well-connected men out there. Are you sure he's the one you want? You're lucky, being a widow. You actually have the right to choose whom you wed. Is it worth being stuck with an elderly husband—even an influential one—solely to see Anna selected as grand princess?"

I gazed at her, hearing my own uncertainty reflected in her questions. "I don't know," I said after a moment. "I'm not set on Anna wedding Grand Prince Ivan. He's difficult, from what I hear—autocratic, stubborn, volatile, mistrustful. And making one's mark at court requires a steely strength that Anna lacks. That's not the point."

"What is the point, then?" Maria sounded genuinely curious, and I struggled to explain the disconnected thoughts that kept pushing me one way, then the other, in response to Vorontsov's proposal.

"I want Anna to marry well." I pleated the soft wool of my dress between my fingers, examining the folds as I searched for the right words. "By well, I mean a young man who has rank and wealth but also the capacity to love her. Having Gavriil Vorontsov as her stepfather would aid me in finding such a husband, and his opposition would make it more difficult. It seems like tempting fate to declare a goal, then resist the first good opportunity to achieve it."

"But what about …?" Darya's voice rose in pitch, and I stretched out my hand to quiet her. She hesitated, then added, "those things you told me a few days ago?"

"That wasn't real," I said, fighting back tears. The gap between myself and Anfim remained as vast as ever—

widened, even, by our last encounter. "I can't risk my daughter's future on a dream."

"You don't have to wed Vorontsov," Darya said with a confidence I envied. "If you like him, that's one thing, but if not, Niki and I can find a good husband for Anna when the time comes. I'm sure Alexei and Maria will help."

"Darya's right," Maria put in. "You have friends and family. You don't need to pledge yourself to an old man you barely know to make a good match for your daughter or even to keep loneliness at bay." She paused before adding with a mischievous smile that revealed a startling resemblance to her younger sister, "You never know. That unreality that's brought the gleam of tears to your eyes might be worth waiting for."

"I like Vorontsov well enough," I said, "but I promised only to consider his proposal, which I will."

The conversation turned to other topics then, and I let it flow over me, setting my quandary aside for later resolution. And I didn't contact Gavriil Vorontsov with my decision. Not then.

Despite his promise to Darya, Anfim did not bring the children the next Monday or even the Friday of that week. He sent messages explaining the delay, but each excuse further confirmed my belief that he wanted nothing more to do with me, despite Darya's assurances to the contrary. She didn't know the whole, so how could she tell? I tried to take comfort from my close escape and focus on my responsibilities toward my family, especially my daughter. But, stubborn as ever, my heart refused to comply with the demands of my head.

For ten miserable days I turned the advantages and disadvantages of accepting Gavriil Vorontsov's proposal over in my head without reaching a decision. So far, he seemed content to wait, so he too might be having second thoughts. I welcomed every moment in which he didn't force my hand, although I knew I must respond soon.

Then, on Monday, the twenty-eighth of January, not long after the noonday church service, I heard Laika barking in the courtyard, followed by high-pitched children's voices. Darya emerged from the washhouse, where she had gone to supervise the laundering of the family's linens, as I ran from the kitchen. The cook, abandoned in the middle of my instructions for the day's meals, called after me.

I stopped and turned. "Someone's in the yard," I told her. "Get the maids started on chopping onions and carrots, and I'll be back as soon as I find out who it is."

"No need," Anfim said from behind me. "It's us. Laika rushing to welcome Tolya and him running and shouting to greet her, mostly. I hope he didn't bother you."

I whirled to face him. He was smiling and holding out his arms, and although I managed not to throw myself into his embrace in full view of the household, I knew he must see his expression reflected on my face. For that moment, I didn't even try to suppress my joy.

Memories of our last meeting soon wiped the smile from my face. I took a step back as he clasped my hands and looked deep into my eyes. "We must talk," he said.

More talk? Didn't you do enough damage the last time?

Yet I couldn't bring myself to pull away. I'd yearned for his touch for too long. "If you like," I told him, wondering if I'd lost my mind.

"Please." He stepped closer and kissed my cheek. "I won't hurt you again," he said into my right ear.

While I searched for a reply, Darya joined us. Lara and Tolya followed—Laika strolling between them, her head held high. Both brother and sister had a hand on her fur, and the sight of them made me laugh. The dog looked like nothing so much as a proud landowner showing off her property.

"Welcome, Lara," I said as they approached. "You too, Tolya. I'm sorry I missed you that day Laika and I came to your house." To my credit, I succeeded in getting the last phrase out without a quiver, although grief constricted my throat. "We had to run straight home because of the snow."

"You're here to stay with us for a bit," Darya told them. "And we're happy to have you. Come with me, and I'll show you your rooms. You can meet Masha, who'll be looking after you."

The children hesitated. Even brave Tolya gazed at his father as if he feared Anfim might vanish into thin air, while Lara bit her lip and blinked back tears. I recalled then that Anfim had left them once before, on the mission to the Tatars that lasted months. Such young children wouldn't understand that this time was different.

"Papa won't leave before you say goodbye," I told them. To Anfim I added, "Would you like to see the nursery as well?"

"No need," Darya said. "We won't be long, so go upstairs with Solomonida, please. We'll meet you in the main sitting room."

Suspicious, I stared at her. Had Anfim told her he wanted to talk with me alone, and if so, why was she encouraging him? She was the one who'd urged me to give Vorontsov a fair chance, even if she turned around later and announced I didn't need to wed him!

But if she supported Anfim's cause, whatever it was, I might as well find out what he'd come to say. "Follow me." I gestured at the main staircase. "Darya, will you let the cook know I'll rejoin her later? I left in the midst of telling her what to prepare for supper."

"Of course," my sister said. "Don't worry. I'll take care of it as soon as I finish with Masha. Come, children, wouldn't you like to see your rooms? Laika will show us the way."

The three of them left, Lara and Tolya casting the occasional glance over their shoulders. I accompanied Anfim up the stairs, wondering what I'd let myself in for this time.

Settled in facing chairs, we spread our hands toward the stove. Despite that effusive moment in the yard, neither of us reached for the other after we entered the room. I felt off-balance, still smarting from my last encounter as well as torn by conflicting loyalties. Anfim gazed at me without speaking, his expression, as usual, hard to read.

"Are Lara and Tolya afraid that you'll be away for a long time?" I asked to fill the silence. "As you were when you went on the mission to Crimea?"

"I *will* be away for a long time," he said. I heard a note of puzzlement in his voice. "Your sister and brother-in-law didn't tell you?"

I frowned, trying to remember what Darya had said about the children. "Just that Lara and Tolya would be staying with us while you set your affairs in order. I thought she meant for a week or two. Where are you going?"

He planned to leave again, and for a long time. The glimmer of hope rekindled by his smile flickered and died. I should stop talking to this man altogether. He depressed me more with each conversation.

"East, and south. To Kazan, Astrakhan, maybe Bukhara and Persia. I don't know how long it will take. A year, perhaps more."

"How is that possible? You just got your government job back." I felt bewildered and betrayed. "I thought that mattered to you." I thought *I* mattered to you. I didn't say that, though.

He sighed, then reached for my hand. "It's a journey with my brothers. You know they're merchants, but you have no reason to care that they trade along the Volga. Rather, Postnik does. He's the eldest. But Kirill wants to join us this time. He loves an adventure, and he has partners who will watch over his business in Lithuania."

"And the government?" I blinked, trying without much success to make sense of what he was saying. I must look like a tipsy owl.

"I'll be working for them, too," he said. "I can't tell you those details, but it's an important part of the plan."

I heard excitement in his voice, but I didn't share it. A lead weight settled on my heart, and I struggled to breathe. "Why?" I asked.

"Because that's the only way I can improve my fortunes enough to propose marriage to a boyar's daughter. Money alone won't advance me much, but money and connections … If I fulfill the tasks assigned to me, Ivan Tretiakov, the royal treasurer, has promised to promote me to state secretary. I still won't be your equal, but at least you could wed me, if you choose, without raising too many eyebrows."

"Wed you?" This I hadn't expected. "You want to marry me?" My fears and hopes collided, leaving me teetering at the edge of an emotional chasm.

He drew back, loosening his clasp. "Is the idea so ridiculous? It seemed natural to me, after what happened between us that night. I hoped …" He rose from the chair. "In that case, I will remove myself from your sight. My apologies for presuming too much."

I grabbed his hand in both of mine. "Anfim, don't. When you apologized for making love to me, I thought you regretted what we did together. It never occurred to me that you might offer marriage. You took me by surprise, that's all."

A shudder went through me as I said the word "marriage," as if hearing an echo of Semyon's cruel laughter. I didn't know if I could bind myself to another man, even Anfim. And if I did, what of Anna? Gavriil Vorontsov, at least, could secure her future, whatever the cost to me.

I kept those thoughts to myself. Anfim would go soon— and might never return. Time enough to discuss the future if he did.

He didn't remark on the shudder. Perhaps he didn't notice. More likely, he couldn't imagine the reason for it. We still had a lot to learn about each other.

But he did resume his seat. "Solomonida, I'm sorry you misunderstood me that day. I meant only to assure you that I took responsibility for my actions. How could you think I regretted my night with you? It was the most precious of my life. I told you I love you. I would marry you tomorrow if you'd have me. But I know the constraints on noblewomen. Give me a chance to prove myself worthy of you."

It was my turn to stare. He understood and accepted the barriers we faced. His declaration of love and the grip of his hand, warm and strong, made my heart sing. For a moment, I let myself believe that, with him, I might find a way out of my dilemma. But …

"When do you leave?" I asked.

"As soon as I say goodbye to Lara and Tolya. My brothers reached Moscow yesterday. Will you help Darya look after my children? Will you wait for me, or is that too much to ask?"

"And if you don't return?" I could barely form the words. "Suppose I lose you forever?"

"I will return." He brushed my cheek with his free hand. "And when I do, I swear I will be close to you in rank."

"Then I will do as you ask," I told him, although my doubts remained. He pulled me into his arms, and we kissed until the clatter of feet in the hallway caused us to pull apart.

Still floating on a sea of passion, I sent my polite rejection to Gavriil Vorontsov that very afternoon.

Chapter Five

January 14, 1546

"I SEE SLEIGHS!" TOLYA, BY THEN SIX AND A HALF, LEANED SO far over the balustrade that I grabbed his shirt from behind and hauled him back before he could dive headfirst into the courtyard. "Lots of sleighs—big ones and small ones and pack horses. Look, Auntie Shura!"

By "Auntie Shura," he meant me. Darya and I had realized within hours of Anfim's departure that our full names were too much of a mouthful to pour from a child's lips hundreds of times a day, so he and Lara called us Auntie Shura and Auntie Darya.

I rose on tiptoe to get a clear sense of the frozen river beyond the estate walls. I saw the usual market stalls and carcasses of flayed cows, pigs, and sheep, standing upright and rigid with ice, arrayed near the shore. The center, kept clear to allow sled traffic to move swiftly throughout these months of intense winter, did seem unusually busy today.

"You're right, Tolya," I said. "A big party is coming in. Merchants, probably. Look at the size of those sleighs. They must have traveled far to collect so many goods."

"Papa!" he shouted, as he did whenever we saw a group of traders, or even soldiers. I wondered—not for the first time—how well he remembered his father, whom he hadn't seen for two years.

And might never see again. Anfim had already stayed away twice as long as he'd predicted. I shivered as a spectral hand squeezed my heart. I'd loved both Tolya and his sister even before I agreed to take primary responsibility for their care, and my affection for them had only grown since they came to live on our estate. I'd gladly oversee the rest of their upbringing, if fate demanded that of me. Yet I couldn't help wondering whether their father had forgotten them—and me—or, more likely, lay buried in some distant land.

During his absence, though, I had brought Anna to the brink of adulthood. Her fifteenth birthday lay three weeks ahead of us, and once she passed that milestone, we could start looking for a husband for her. Then the main obstacle to a future with Anfim would be my own reluctance to remarry—especially if he achieved his promotion, thus narrowing the social gap between us.

But we would have no future together unless he returned. If he'd fallen ill, been captured once more, or drowned on the Volga, would I ever find out? However great my love for his children, I hated to think that their presence in this house might be the only vestige of my brief but passionate affair.

Belatedly, I realized I hadn't responded to Tolya's shout. "I don't think it's your papa, sweetheart. He'll write us a letter when he gets close enough, the way he did when he first left."

Letters I had not then learned how to read, as Anfim well knew, but Darya shared each one with me. "Give Solomonida my love," he wrote at the end of each missive.

I'd taken lessons since then, starting with the alphabet, then poring over his notes until I mastered every stroke of his handwriting. I kept the messages still, in a chest in my room, and pulled them out from time to time to remind myself that he was out there, somewhere. But as the months dragged on, then turned into years, it became ever harder to open the letters, knowing that the man who wrote those words might have passed into the world beyond, leaving only shadowed memories of his love—and the two children who brightened my life.

These days, I could read Anfim's missives for myself, if he would only send one.

Darya appeared at the doorway to call us to the midday meal. "What keeps you hanging around at the top of the staircase? Tolya, you'll catch your death! Solomonida, how could you let him stand out here in the cold?"

"Papa is coming," Tolya said. He ran past Darya, and I heard him shouting, "Lara, Lara, where are you? Papa is coming. I saw the sleighs!"

"There's your answer," I told my sister. "A party of merchants drove past. You know how he is: whenever he glimpses a big group, he's convinced Anfim has returned. I thought if I waited with him, I'd have a chance of helping him understand that his father isn't with them—or at least console him when the truth dawns."

She nodded her comprehension. "It's hard for him and Lara, but I have faith in Anfim. One of these days, he'll be back. Surely we'd have heard if he fell sick or worse."

"One would think so," I said, following her into the house. "But I can't get it out of my head that it didn't work that way when the Crimean Tatars captured him. The government knew nothing until after Ogodai Khan rescued him. And then they found out only because Ogodai and Alexei worked together to get Anfim back to Moscow. There are so many hazards along the Volga. Pirates and nomads and boat accidents, plague and other illnesses, theft. For all I know, the whole pack of them got lost and is wandering around in circles far from home!"

"May the Virgin Mother protect them." Darya's eyes twinkled, and I heard laughter in her voice. "I see you've put a lot of time into imagining disasters."

"And what would you do in my place?" I demanded.

She raised a shoulder. "The same thing."

My irritation at her gentle mockery dissipated. Squabbling with my sister wouldn't bring Anfim back. "Perhaps we could make inquiries," I said in a pacific tone.

"Good idea. I'll ask Niki to find out what he can from the foreign affairs people." She glanced at me as she shut the door. "Do you ever regret turning down Gavriil Vorontsov—or not marrying someone else?"

"What?" I made no effort to conceal my surprise. I rarely thought of my rejected suitor, and never with regret. As for marrying another, no one else had asked me, and with my thirty-third birthday behind me, I doubted anyone would.

"No," I told her. "I have everything I need here. I like Gavriil, but at this point in my life, I wouldn't consider marriage other than for love—and then only if it doesn't imperil Anna's prospects. Why do you ask?"

Darya laughed, openly this time. "Just reminding you that you chose this path." She took my arm. "Come and have dinner, then we'll go to the nursery and coo over Andrusha. We haven't visited him today. He'll be wondering where we are. And it will take Tolya's mind off the sleighs."

"Oh, Darya, you're as transparent as water. Of course, your son is not wondering where we are. He's barely a year old!" But I laughed with her because, really, she was too absurd.

Arm in arm, we walked to the dining hall, where the servants awaited our arrival. When we got there, we found Tolya standing on the window seat, explaining to Laika that the many sleighs on the river meant that his papa would arrive soon. The dog regarded him steadily with her wide-eyed gaze, as if she understood every word. The pair of them looked for all the world as if they were in the midst of a conversation. Although I'd expected Igor to reclaim her after his wedding, he hadn't, because Katya refused to share her house with a dog. Tolya's affection for the Polish scent hound, already strong, had quadrupled in the years since. They were now inseparable.

Lara leaped to her feet as we entered and ran forward. "Look, Auntie Shura." She thrust a piece of paper into my hand. "I finished the sums Father Job left for me."

I studied the scribbled sheet, filled with columns that made far less sense to me than I assumed they did to Lara, who seemed to have been born with a gift for mathematics. In addition to learning to read and write, I attended the children's lessons so that I could help them with their homework. Even so, I found Tolya's love of stories far easier to share than Lara's affinity for numbers. "How clever you are," I told her. "You'll make an exemplary merchant's wife someday."

She beamed with pride, and I handed the paper back to her. "Father Job will be proud of you, and so am I. Now put the sums in a safe place, and you can show them to him after dinner."

Instead of obeying, she gripped the paper in both hands and said, "Is Tolya right? Has Papa arrived in Moscow?"

In response to the mixture of anxiety and hope I saw on her face, I reached out and stroked a stray wisp of hair away from her forehead. "I don't think so, darling. Merchants come and go all the time, and Papa hasn't written to tell us that he's nearby." Her lip trembled, and she nodded. "Put your work in a safe place," I repeated, "and let's have dinner."

While she did as I asked, Darya pointed at the laden high table. "Let's eat. I'm starving. I'm beginning to wonder if Andrusha will have a brother or sister before the year is out."

"So soon? Then we must take good care of you." I slid into my usual place and gestured to Father Job, sitting with the men on the other side of the room, to say the blessing.

But as I bowed my head to pray, then helped myself to various dishes that I consumed without tasting them, just as I heard without absorbing the babble of conversation rising from the long tables where the maidservants sat, I wondered anew about the path I had chosen. Not whether I should have accepted Vorontsov's proposal, nor even whether I had done the right thing by taking on the role of mother to Lara and Tolya, but whether I should have promised to wait for Anfim's return, no matter how long that took.

Suppose I waited the rest of my life, and he never came back?

The moment the midday meal ended, the servants, eager to escape a wintry wind and clouds that threatened to drop their burden before nightfall, fled for the kitchen and storerooms. Those who lived outside our compound left for their own homes. Lara showed Father Job her page of sums and clapped her hands in delight when he complimented her on her neat writing and correct answers. "I'll bring a new set for you tomorrow," he promised.

I glanced at Tolya, who sometimes became jealous when his sister received attention from the grownups, but he had retreated to one corner of the room, where two lines of opposing chessmen were engaged in all-out warfare under his command. His simulation of battle cries and Laika's encouraging barks drowned out the priest's words.

When Father Job, too, departed for his home and the Great Battle of the Chessmen ended, Darya and I withdrew with the children to the third-floor nursery. I was wishing I had Niki's skill with charcoal and could capture the scene—chattering children, laughing baby, indulgent adults—on paper when the sound of runners against snow, the neighing of horses, and the jingle of harness broke the near-silence of the courtyard.

When it came to identifying visitors, our location put us at a disadvantage. The nursery overlooked the gardens and orchards that lay behind the house. Anna reacted first, looking up from where she'd been shaking a painted wooden rattle to entertain Andrusha and saying, "Niki? Isn't it too early for him?"

"Unless he finished the illustration he was working on for Alexei," Darya agreed. "But we aren't expecting anyone else. Perhaps Katya decided to stop by."

"So late in the day?" Although less than three hours had passed since our midday meal, the sun already hung low in the sky, and few visitors would leave the warmth of their hearths on a winter evening. "More likely, it *is* Niki, trying to reach home before the snow starts." I stood and stretched out a kink in my spine. I loved Andrusha as any devoted aunt would, but he had plenty of playmates at the moment. He didn't need my undivided attention as well. "I'll go and see, then send a message if it's a guest."

She thanked me. Already halfway to the door, I waved a hand in response, then passed into the hallway and went down the stairs.

I found no one in the sewing room, also on the third floor, or in the main sitting room beneath it. I checked the dining hall and Nikita's study in the room beyond, in case Niki had gone straight there. Puzzled at finding both empty, I looked around, then headed back toward the hallway that led to the outside stairs. Niki couldn't have reached the nursery without passing me, so where was he? In the office below?

No, he wouldn't go there without letting Darya know he'd returned. Perhaps my sister was right, and the recent arrival was Katya after all. I must have missed her as she headed up the stairs.

I reached the hallway and saw a line of light under the door of the main sitting room, the same chamber I'd checked not long ago without results. Odd.

Still, it was a natural place for a visitor to go. I approached the sitting room and opened the door.

A man with light brown hair and a proud stance, richly dressed in velvet the color of autumn leaves, stood gazing out the window at the courtyard below. Beyond him, snowflakes drifted against the mica panes. A large leather bag, like a saddle bag, lay near his feet.

No. It can't be. Anfim, after so long without a word?

But the man was the right height, had the right coloring. I recognized his profile. He seemed a bit taller—no, straighter, more self-assured—but otherwise he looked the same as I remembered him.

I gasped as the reality of his return sank in, and at the sound Anfim turned. "It's you," he said with a smile. "I hoped you would be the one I saw first." He held out his arms.

Tempted to run to him, I stopped as a torrent of fury ripped through me without warning. "Why didn't you send word?" I demanded. "I learned to read for you. I looked after your children for you. I stayed awake at night imagining everything that could go wrong. And here you walk into my sitting room after two years and smile at me without so much as sending a note to say you're alive and well and on your way?"

My reaction took him aback. Literally—he jerked and stepped away from me, closer to the window. But he recovered quickly. "I'm sorry, love," he said. "By the time I got close enough to send a message, we'd reached the river road. It was clear our sleighs would outpace any courier we might send. So we decided to press on. We haven't stopped since Kazan except to change horses. I came here right after making my report to Tretiakov. I was desperate to see you."

I burst into tears, overcome by the rush of emotion. A whirlpool of surprise, delight, disbelief, relief—and yes, the remnants of anger—shocked me into silence. I felt his arms close around me. As incapable of rational thought as a child, I gave into instinct, pressing against his body. His lips brushed my hair, and he murmured apologies, mingled with expressions of love and statements about how much he'd missed me. After a while, the stream of words and the power of touch calmed my unruly heart. I wiped my cheeks with one hand and pulled away enough to look at him. "What kept you so long?" I asked, my voice still unsteady. "I feared you'd been captured by pirates, lost in the river, robbed by Tatars, dead of the plague. And worse!"

He stroked my cheek. His right arm still clasped my waist. "We traveled all the way to Persia. And since I, at least, will never go so far again, it made little sense to argue with my brothers to save a week here or there. What I failed to understand was that it would take us twice as long to get back. The current of the river works against those going upstream, and men must haul the boats along by brute strength. I'd hoped to find people going north while we went south who could carry messages, but that never happened. I'll tell you the whole, I promise, over the days and weeks to come. But first I want to hear about you. How are you? How are Lara and Tolya?"

By the time he reached the end, I had control over my voice once more. I couldn't quite grasp the extent of his journey, but the sincerity of his apology allayed my anger. I clasped my hands behind his neck. "They are well. We're all well. Let's go and see them. You won't believe how much they've grown. Tolya, especially. He's missed you so much, and now he'll feel vindicated. He's been insisting since midday that his papa has come home, and I told him it couldn't be true. I swear, I thought you would never return."

"And desert the most beautiful woman in the world?" He shook his head, but I sensed a new confidence in him, a comfort with his feelings for me that hadn't been there before, and I liked it. "What cad would do such a thing? I look forward to greeting the children, of course—and your sister and brother-in-law and daughter. I have gifts for everyone."

"Then come with me. Everyone but Niki is in the nursery, and he'll no doubt be home soon." I pulled back and, indicating the door with one outstretched hand, clasped his with the other.

"Nursery?" he asked. "Aren't they too old for that? Lara must be almost ten by now, and Tolya more than six. I'm wondering if they'll even recognize me."

Tempted to say that it served him right if they did not, I refrained. "Darya has a baby," I explained. "They named him Andrei, after Niki's father, and we call him Andrusha. He had his first birthday at the end of November."

"That's wonderful news. I must congratulate her." Anfim turned me to face him once more. "But before we go, can the two of us spend some time alone together this evening? I earned my promotion, and we can marry whenever you wish."

I flashed back in my mind to the day he left, my conviction that I could delay my decision on his proposal until he came back, if he ever did. That moment had arrived, and I still had no answer. Marriage itself threatened me as much as ever—the permanence of it, the vulnerability it imposed on women. Anna's future remained murky. But I knew better than to start such a discussion so soon after his unexpected return, and I wanted very much to be alone with him. "Yes," I told him. "I would like that. We have a lot to catch up on."

"Good." He stroked a finger down my cheek, and a lump caught in my throat. How I had yearned for his touch! "Thank you for taking care of my children for so long," he went on. "That's a debt I can never repay."

I released my tangled emotions in a deep sigh. "Seeing you safe and well is payment enough. As for your son and daughter, I enjoy looking after them. Let's go upstairs. We can continue our conversation later."

The clamor in the nursery when we entered defied belief. "Tolya," I said as I walked through the door. "You were right. Your papa was in one of the sleighs that arrived this morning."

Tolya, racing from one corner to the next, skidded to a stop midway. "Papa? You said it wasn't him."

"I was wrong. Here he is." I stepped aside to let Anfim enter the room.

Tolya continued to stare, but Lara dropped the stuffed bear she'd been dangling in front of the baby and ran toward us, calling, "Papa, Papa, you're here. What took you so long? We missed you!"

He caught her up in a hug. "My goodness, look at you. I left a little girl and returned to a young lady. A beautiful young lady, at that!"

"I can read and write and do sums," she said as he released her. "Father Job says I'm especially good at sums. And my embroidery is much better than when you went away."

"I'm sure it is." Anfim's voice sounded choked. He looked over her head at Tolya, still staring as if his mind couldn't accept what his eyes saw. Again I wondered whether he recognized his father.

Then Anfim said, "And here's my favorite bogatyr." He held out his arms. "You didn't forget me, did you? I'm sorry I was gone for so long."

Tolya tore across the room. Anfim grabbed him midleap, laughing, and submitted without complaint to what looked like a death grip around his neck. Only after his son let go did Anfim return Tolya to the floor and come forward, kissing Darya on the cheek and admiring Andrusha.

"Won't you stay and eat supper with us?" Darya asked. "You can tell us about your journey. I know I have questions galore, and so must your children!"

"I would love to join you." Anfim stroked his daughter's gleaming hair. "Will you sit next to me, *dochka*, and tell me your news?" Lara, beaming at being called his dear daughter, took his hand and nodded.

By then, the sound of boots on the stairs signaled Nikita's arrival, and we headed downstairs for supper. At Darya's suggestion, I ran ahead to catch the steward before he could leave the dining hall and asked him to bring food for six to the sitting room. By the time I rejoined the others, Tolya was digging through the saddle bag as if it were Grandfather Frost's magic sack of toys while his father watched with an indulgent smile.

Lara stood next to Anfim, showing him her paper filled with completed sums. When he said, "Excellent, *dochka*," she traded the paper for her latest embroidery project: a long strip of cross-stitched flowers in shades of blue from indigo to the hue of a summer sky. "It's for this blouse." She ran a finger around the neckline of her shirt, showing him where the band would go when she finished it.

"It's beautiful," he told her. "Your stitching has improved tremendously since I last saw it."

"You won't go away again, will you, Papa?" She sounded wistful. "We missed you a lot, Tolya and me, even though Auntie Darya and Auntie Shura and Anna were lovely to us. Anna even gave me her dolls, because she's too big for them now that she's almost fifteen."

"Not soon, sweetheart," Anfim said. "At least, I hope not. And never for so long. Your uncles and cousins and I saw many marvelous places and things, but I plan to stay with you from now on."

"Will you tell us about them, the marvelous places and things?" She stood, her eyes wide and her hands twisting the fabric strip as if she couldn't quite accept that Anfim was real.

"Of course," he said. "So will your uncles. We'll visit them tomorrow. But first, come and see what nice presents I found. Tolya, show us what you have there."

It was an embroidered cloth, unlike anything I'd ever seen, covered with stitches forming long overlapping branches laden with red apples, a brown trunk, and huge bright-green leaves against a cream background, the whole bordered in multicolored, interlocking diamonds. "Ah," Anfim said, "the cloth is for Darya Petrovna. It represents the Tree of Life, the merchant told me."

Tolya placed it on Darya's lap, and she fingered it appreciatively. "How lovely. Thank you. It's so soft. Look at the sheen on that silk, and the embroidery is gorgeous."

"I'm glad you like it. The style is called suzani, a bit different from your exquisite altar cloth, but it reminded me of you. What have you there, Tolya?" Anfim took the stack of three books his son was holding out and opened the top one, then the second. "Those two are for Nikita Andreevich," he said, "because of the miniatures." Tolya passed them to Niki, who exclaimed at the beauty of the pictures, and returned to collect the third.

"For Solomonida Petrovna." Anfim looked at me over his son's head. "I didn't know you'd learned to read until you mentioned it a while ago, but it won't help with this book; it's written in Arabic script. But the tale is a love story, and you can tell that from the drawings." He smiled then, his eyes warm, and I felt my cheeks burn in response, especially when Darya sent me a mischievous glance.

"Here, Auntie Shura." Tolya held out the book, and I took it with thanks, rubbing the burgundy cover in my fingers as Darya had done with her silk. Someone had found a way to inset intricate patterns in the leather, and I traced them with my finger. Most of the books I'd seen had only sanded wood covers, but this was a work of art from start to finish. I turned the pages, admiring the exquisite detail and bright colors of the paintings, the veiled, moon-faced women and turbaned men. I hadn't reached the fifth page before Tolya returned with a folded length of brocade. I set the book aside to admire the exquisite design of the silk.

"It's gorgeous," I said. "I've never seen anything so fine. It will make the most wonderful gown."

"I can't wait to see you in it," Anfim replied.

Servants arrived with food as Anfim reached into the saddle bag and pulled out a small, jeweled headdress, pointed in the center and adorned with gold wire twisted into arcs that resembled the etchings on my book cover. He placed it on Lara's head and, when she turned around in response to his command, tied its ribbons in the back.

"I have fabrics for you too," he told her. "But I left them at the house. I'll find someone to make dresses from them later."

He reached into the bag and pulled out a brass oval, then held it up before her face so she could see her reflection in the polished surface. She oohed with delight, and he handed her a broad collar, stitched with long curlicues of sky blue and rose against a dark green background, saying, "For Anna Semyonovna."

"Thank you!" Anna said as she took the collar. "I didn't expect anything, never mind anything so fine." With help from her aunt, she clasped it around her neck, where it stood out against her blush-pink robe.

Tolya stood next to his father, shuffling his feet and looking downcast. A year ago, he would have blurted out a demand for his gift, but Darya and I had worked hard with him the last few months, and he managed not to put his disappointment into words.

"That leaves just one more present." Anfim reached out and rumpled his son's already tousled hair.

"Me, me, me!" Tolya shouted.

Anfim broke into laughter. "You, you, you," he said in a teasing tone. "I put it at the bottom because it's the heaviest, so dig down until you find it."

Tolya dove for the bag. After a while, he pulled out a child-sized helmet, gleaming steel with a pointed tip and a long strip to protect the wearer's nose. As the boy balanced it over his head, Anfim took it away from him. "The other part goes first," he said.

Tolya dug into the bag a second time and, after some rummaging, extracted a mail shirt and a leather belt. Whooping with joy, he pulled on the shirt, which fell past his knees even after his father adjusted the belt. Anfim deposited the helmet on the boy's head and said, "A bit large, but you'll grow into them. I wasn't sure how much bigger you would get during my time away." He pulled off the helmet once more and set it aside, saying, "Eat first, son, and you can test out your armor later."

Tolya responded with a fierce hug and incoherent thanks, then joined his father, who was pointing to the cushion on his right. Lara nestled on Anfim's other side, as if her closeness might prevent him from disappearing once more. The three of them occupied one long bench, leaving the individual chairs for the rest of us.

Darya handed each of us a bowl of braised beef, fragrant with carrots and herbs, and a piece of bread before taking a seat opposite Anna and me. Niki positioned himself at her left, and I was next to Lara, so as a group we formed a rough circle. Small tables between the chairs provided handy resting places for the dishes when needed.

"We want to hear about your journey," Darya said once we were settled. "Where did you go that kept you on the road for two years?"

"A long way." Anfim dipped the bread in his stew but didn't eat it. "I've traveled east before, as far as Kazan. But never south, and the river goes on for what seems like forever, widening the whole way. We sailed from one town to another—each with its own governors, its own customs duties, its own requirements for bribes and gifts and papers. I had no idea, even after that fateful journey to Crimea. But oh, the experiences! We rode down the Volga on a dragon-prowed ship, like something out of legend. We crossed a huge, choppy sea, dodging live sturgeon almost as large as our tiny boat, and made our way to the city of Tabriz—where the Persian emperors live. It has an astonishing covered bazaar, unlike anything I've ever seen, and it's surrounded by huge mountains that put our Urals to shame. From there, we traveled to Tehran, then to Bukhara. My brothers wanted to push on to Samarkand, at the edge—so the merchants in Bukhara said—of mountains even higher than those of Tabriz, so tall they must reach Heaven itself. But that would have delayed us another year, so I argued that we should go home before our families forgot us altogether. In Bukhara we saw live peacocks—like the ones you, Darya Petrovna, embroidered on your altar cloth—and the elephants in the book I just gave Solomonida Petrovna. I wish I could have brought you a live bird, but I doubt it would have survived the journey, even if we'd discovered how to feed it."

They peppered him with questions, the children especially, and between bites of delicious beef and chewy, crusty bread I listened, my head turned toward him. Although I paid close attention to his answers, at first I asked no questions of my own. Instead, I studied him as he talked, listening for nuances and emotions, clues to how his long absence had changed him. Again I noticed that he seemed more sure of himself, more comfortable in his own skin. I didn't know if that was the result of his journey or just a reflection of his status now that he'd earned his promotion. I recalled that night at the Christmas party, when I'd first noticed the change, even before he left for his years of travel. Watching him, listening to him, I sensed the yearnings of desire reawakening, my heart softening with each word that left his mouth, each longing gaze sent my way.

The meal had almost ended when Niki asked, "Did you get your promotion?"

I already knew the answer, so it didn't surprise me when Anfim said, "Yes. I am now State Secretary Anfim Fadeyev, in the upper tier of the Treasury." Darya and Niki showered him with congratulations while he gazed at me, an expression I couldn't read in his eyes.

"As a senior official," he said after a while, "I also have a new house, just around the corner from this one—even closer than before."

"A new house?" the five of us said in concert.

"Can we live with you again, Papa?" Lara added.

"Without question," he said. "I need a few days to get everything in order, but then I look forward to having both of you with me." He dipped his head to me, then to Darya and Nikita. "But you've done enough for me, the three of you. I can take them to the old house, and my brothers can look after them. We needn't impinge further on your hospitality."

"No, please let them stay." Darya clasped her husband's hand and leaned forward. "A few more days until you get settled is nothing. It will make the transition easier for them, and it will give us time to get used to their living somewhere else. We've loved having them with us, and it will be a wrench to see them go." She looked at me. "Don't you agree?"

"Of course. I'd hate to say goodbye so suddenly." A flash of sadness ran through me at the thought of losing them. Then I remembered that our parting would not last long if Anfim and I married.

My stomach seized up at the thought. How well did I know him, despite our brief affair? Yes, we'd been friends for six months before his journey. My one night of love had revealed him to be capable of tenderness as well as passion. Yet I had no real assurance that the permanency of marriage would not turn him into a version of Semyon. And since the great clans would always look down on him because of an accident of birth, even though he had, through his own merits, come close to us in standing— enough that he and I could wed—I could not justify my choice by claiming that this match served Anna's interests as well as my own. Marriage to Anfim might still imperil my daughter's chances of attracting a highborn husband.

"That's very kind of you," Anfim said. "In that case, I accept."

Lara and Tolya looked downcast at the news, although they didn't protest. "If you've finished your meal, it's time for bed," Darya told them. "Say goodnight to Papa. Masha will be waiting for you in your rooms. You can tell her the whole story before you go to sleep." Dutifully, the two children turned to Anfim, whom they hugged and kissed.

He wiped a tear from Lara's cheek. "Don't worry, sweet girl. I was gone a long time, I know, but I'm here now, and in a few days we'll be together again." She nodded, not meeting his eyes, and he watched her leave, a small frown creasing his brow. Tolya, still in his armor, trailed after her, the picture of dejection.

It didn't last, though. He'd no sooner passed through the door than I heard him calling for the dog. Skidding paws and a welcoming bark announced her arrival.

"He'll do fine," I told Anfim. "I'm more worried about Lara. How much work does the house need?"

He turned to face me. "Why not come with me and see for yourself?" He gazed at me meaningfully as he spoke, and the pace of my heart quickened.

"What about the snow?" I asked.

He settled his bowl on the table next to him and indicated the window with his hand. "It's mostly powder. I have a sleigh, and I'll bring you back right away if the storm strengthens."

Passion urged me to agree, yet I still hesitated. So much riding on a simple decision, for good and for ill. My heart thudded as if its beats could push me in one direction or the other.

Then Anfim leaned sideways and murmured in my ear, "There are things I need to say that others shouldn't hear. I'll do nothing you dislike. Won't you come with me, if only for an hour or so?"

I didn't *have* to lie with him. I could listen to what he wanted to tell me, then come home. I wouldn't learn more about him if I refused to speak with him alone.

"Yes," I said.

The conversation turned to other topics—what had happened in Moscow and in each of our lives during Anfim's time away. He reclaimed his food and, while others talked, finished his meal.

When he left, I went with him. The snow was as light as he'd said, and well wrapped in furs, I slipped into the sleigh before the stable boys strapped the horse into its harness. Anfim took his place on the driver's seat and snapped the leather reins against the horse's back. It moved toward the gate at a rapid pace, and we were off.

Chapter Six

SOMETIME LATER, I RECLINED ON ANFIM'S MATTRESS, wrapped in a length of bronze silk, fine to the point of translucent, bordered in a wide band—gold shading to pale yellow—and decorated with embroidered roses the size of my thumbnail. A soft, citrusy perfume brushed my nostrils whenever I moved, as if someone had steeped the fabric in it. I turned my head this way and that, enjoying the brush of pearl earrings against my shoulders. My determination to keep Anfim at arm's length had lasted less than a quarter of an hour. I cringed inside at this reminder of my own sinful nature, but delight in his caresses drowned out any feeble stabs of conscience.

I sighed. More fodder for that long-delayed confession.

Anfim didn't appear to notice the sigh. Instead, he laughed. "Do you like your real presents?"

"More than I can say." I rubbed the silk between thumb and fingers, touched the earrings once more. "The gifts you gave me in front of the others are beautiful, but they pale by comparison to these."

He cut short my gratitude with a kiss. When I could talk again, I added, "Your new house is lovely, too. In good repair, and bigger than the old one." I thought of the rooms we'd walked through on our brief survey: whitewashed walls, tiled stoves warming the rooms, a spacious kitchen. "You'll need servants; I can help with that. Something to hang on the walls, to break up that solid background. But not much more, once you move your belongings. What happens to the house you have?"

"My brothers will stay there when they visit Moscow. I'll hire a caretaker the rest of the time, and I can check on the property often enough to ensure it's well maintained. We'll divide the furnishings. We also have my father's belongings in the storeroom and the items that were in my wife's dowry. They belong to Lara, but she will have the use of them here. We will all live in comfort." He smiled and caressed my cheek. "I bought goods for our use, too—carpets from Tabriz, for example. You'll have to come back and see; I'm sure you'll have good suggestions. Once I have the furniture moved and the children settled, we can talk about our future."

"Of course," I said, deciding to conceal my reservations about marriage for a while longer. I wanted to celebrate his return, not introduce complications. Besides, I needed time to decide how to answer his proposal. "Tell me more about your journey. What was your favorite part?"

"Besides seeing you again? Reaching Bukhara." He lay facing me, his head propped on his arm. His other hand rested on my waist. Despite my doubts, his touch felt like a miracle after so long an absence. "Bukhara was astonishing— so many people, such wonderful art. We saw complexes of buildings decorated in multicolored tiles that told stories— dragons Tolya would love, flowers, intricate patterns they call arabesques. The houses look the way you've described Tsarevich Alexei's home, with running water and heat pumped throughout the buildings. Then there's the market, filled with stalls carrying goods I'd never imagined and people haggling over them. The whole city smells of spices—not just ginger and cinnamon and nutmeg but things I'd never heard of, like coriander. A dozen different kinds of pepper alone."

He stroked my silk-covered hip, sparking a new flame inside me. "The market in Bukhara is where I found this. Fit for a khan's chief wife, they told me. It's called a sari. It came over the mountains from Hindustan, the tradesman said."

I fingered the embroidered flowers. "It's exquisite. How do people wear it, though? It seems wrong to cut and stitch it."

"I met a silk weaver who told me the women wind it around themselves, as you're doing now. There's a trick to tying it, but I don't know what it is." He ran his fingers along the line of my thigh, igniting flickers of passion that I tried without success to resist. "Perhaps you can leave it here, for when you visit me. But do take the pearls and the perfume."

I liked the idea of a precious gift shared only with Anfim. "Very well. And the cloth you brought for Darya? Did that come from Bukhara too?"

"Yes. It was produced there, not like this. Tolya's armor and the books came from there, too. I found the headdress for Lara and Anna's neckpiece in Kazan."

"I think Tolya will sleep in that armor." I laughed at the memory. "With Laika at his side as his knightly steed. But what of you? Are you glad you went?"

"On the whole, yes. I missed you and the children, but the memories and the friendships will last me a lifetime. I earned my promotion, so the trip fulfilled its purpose. And despite the delays, it went well: we brought back enough textiles and gemstones and spices of the east to keep my brothers in business for a good many years." Again he caressed my hip, and I responded by tracing the line of his collarbone with my thumb.

"Best of all, the woman I love waited for me." He bent to kiss me. "I suppose I'd better get you home before your sister and brother-in-law begin asking questions. Can we meet again tomorrow? I want to hear everything you've been doing for the last two years. But first …"

I relaxed into his embrace, and a considerable time passed before we spoke again.

The lazy drifts of early evening had given way to serious snow by the time Anfim escorted me back to my family's estate in his sleigh. With one last kiss, he stopped at the base of the staircase that led to our second floor. "Up you go," he said. "I'll be back tomorrow to see the children, as soon as I work out how to handle the move."

With reluctant feet, I mounted, turning every few steps to find him still watching me. As he stood there, flakes swirling around him in a madman's dance lit by the lanterns placed at regular intervals about the yard, I imagined him as a young Grandfather Frost.

"You'll turn into an ice statue," I told him as I reached the halfway point. "You don't need to wait there in the midst of a blizzard."

"I do," he said. "I want to see you safely inside. Climb faster if you'd like to spare my ears—and the horse!"

I laughed, picked up my skirts, and ran up the covered staircase as fast as I could. When I reached the top, I turned once more and waved. He moved toward the sleigh, and I stood at the door until I saw him climb in. The horse wasted no time in heading for its stable. I was still laughing and shaking my head as I entered the house, but his caring, like the memory of his passion, warmed me.

Why did I doubt him? He was different from Semyon in every way. We'd spoken of marriage only in passing tonight, but he'd made it clear that he hadn't changed his mind.

So I had to decide. When the promised conversation came, should I say yes, despite my fears, even if it interfered with my desire to see Anna settled in a household of her own?

Then again, could I bear to say no?

I found Darya in the dining hall sorting—or, rather, supervising the sorting of—linen when I got downstairs the next morning. "How did things go with Anfim?" she asked.

"Well." I strove to appear casual. "The new house is bigger than the old one. It needs decorating, and he has no idea where to start. So we walked through every room, considering the possibilities. He plans to move the family's belongings today. He'll stop by to see Lara and Tolya once he has everything in place. I promised to help him with the final touches."

She accepted this true if incomplete explanation with a nod. "He must have bought things that you can use, judging from those gorgeous gifts." She picked up a folded cloth and shook it out, and I recognized the suzani embroidery. Held at shoulder height by her extended fingers, the cloth fell past her hips. "Do you like your book and that fabulous length of brocade? The orangey pink is the perfect color for you."

"Peach." I thought of the bronze sari—even more beautiful, if that were possible—but refrained from mentioning it. "It's named after a Persian fruit, apparently. Like eating honey, Anfim said, when they're ripe. I can't wait to make a dress from it. And yes, the pictures in the book are beautiful. I wish I could read the words. I'd love to tell the story to Lara and Tolya—even to Anna."

"You could make something up, based on the drawings." She turned away to lay the suzani cloth across a side table, then returned her gaze to my face, as if studying me.

"I could. I'll look through the book and see what I can come up with. And I'll ask Lyuba, next time she visits Anna. She can probably read it." I tipped my head, showing her the pearl earrings. "Anfim brought me these, too."

"He's still interested, then. Will you accept when he offers for you? It sounded last night as if he still plans to." She seemed more curious than concerned.

"He does," I said. "He has, in fact, but I'm not sure. My experience with Semyon rather soured me on marriage."

"He's nothing like Semyon," she pointed out, echoing my own thoughts of a few hours ago.

"My head knows that," I admitted. "My heart still needs convincing. Would you and Niki object? He's not of noble birth." I'd never asked them outright. Given Anfim's prolonged absence and my own uncertainty, I'd seen no reason to worry about family opposition until then.

She shook her head slowly. "No. You're older than we are; it's not for us to tell you what to do. His rank is close enough to ours to avoid a scandal—for you, at least. But what happens to Anna if you wed? Will she stay with us?"

"Stay with you?" The question stopped me cold. I'd known for years that my own needs contradicted my daughter's, but until I heard Darya lay it out, I hadn't considered this particular dilemma. I could embrace happiness for myself, assuming I could conquer my fears, at the cost of separation from my daughter. Or I could stay to support Anna at the risk of losing Anfim's love. I couldn't do both. "Why must she stay with you?" I asked, grasping at straws.

"So we can arrange her marriage," Darya explained with the kind of patience usually reserved for dim-witted children. I gritted my teeth at her tone but chose not to interrupt. "The noble matrons will drop her from their lists if they learn that meeting her requires them to visit an official's house, even if he *is* a state secretary. As a widow, you can flout the rules, but Anna doesn't have that luxury. For the sake of a few months to a year, it seems like an unnecessary risk to move her."

I opened my mouth to protest, then shut it again, at a loss for words. "Do you disagree?" Darya added when I remained silent.

"No," I said reluctantly. "I accept your reasoning. It's just that ..."

I stopped, weighing my options, then continued after a long pause, during which Darya regarded me sympathetically but didn't speak. "There's no real alternative. I won't walk out and leave my daughter behind, even with you to guide her. Our choice of a husband will determine the whole course of her life. I want to give her every advantage I can. I've made no promises to Anfim; I'll tell him I can't give him an answer until Anna is wed."

And I could avoid facing my demons for a few more months.

The early afternoon brought an unexpected and unwanted visitor: our cousin Igor Bezzubtsev, demanding to speak with me. Katya accompanied him; in fact, she delivered her husband's "request," which didn't sound like one, on his behalf.

On the brink of refusing, as much to put my cousin in his place as from genuine dislike, I abruptly changed my mind. Courtesy required that someone in the family greet Cousin Igor. Normally, that someone would be Nikita, as master of the house, but he had gone to Alexei's as soon as the snow stopped. Darya could take over for him, but Igor had asked for me, which left little justification for leaving the unpleasant duty to my sister. Besides, I was curious to discover why our cousin had come here after more than two years without a visit.

So, grumbling to myself, I left Darya to entertain Katya in the sewing room while I went to Niki's study. The destination, too, gave rise to unpleasant memories, since it was the place where Igor first attempted to steal our estate by producing what later turned out to be a bogus will. Already in a bad mood, I ordered the steward to bring beer and smoked sturgeon with black bread, but not much. Igor didn't take hints readily, but surely even someone as thick as he would understand that I wanted to cut short our time together.

"Cousin," I said as I entered, "welcome. Please be seated."

In fact, he was seated already, but he leaped to his feet at that tart reminder. He moved as if to kiss my cheeks, but when I fended him off with a raised hand, he returned my bow before again collapsing onto the chair. "You look well, Solomonida." He gestured in a sweep that roughly matched the distance from my head to my feet. "I apologize for the long delay in visiting you."

Mishka arrived with a tray containing the requested refreshments. He poured beer into a fired-clay mug for Igor, placed the food on a small table where we could both reach it, and handed me a cup of mulled white wine, aromatic with the cinnamon that had been another of Anfim's gifts. When I took the cup, Mishka withdrew.

I sipped wine, letting the sweet, spicy taste roll around my tongue and inhaling the heady fragrance. "What brings you here?"

Igor stretched out his legs, occupying the space, then pulled them back when I kicked his ankle. "Sorry," I said. "An accident. Didn't expect your foot to be there."

He scowled before apparently deciding to accept my statement at face value, although I felt certain we both recognized it as false. "I have news," he announced. "Gavriil Vorontsov, whom you refused—I'm sure you had your reasons, although I don't pretend to understand them—has arranged for my appointment as an associate boyar. I am now on the grand prince's council."

This was news indeed. I ignored the derision in his voice in the interests of acquiring more information. Igor had married Vorontsov's niece, but was that sufficient motive for Vorontsov to take an interest in Igor's career? Maybe so, if the promotion expanded Vorontsov's sphere of influence on the council. "Congratulations, cousin. You must be proud."

"And you too have a chance to be proud, cousin, if you decide to help me." He tucked his feet under his chair and leaned forward, a pose that reminded me of Vorontsov in the midst of his proposal—a younger, slimmer, less kindly Vorontsov. Another event that had taken place in this room.

"Decide to help you?" I couldn't conceal my confusion. "You don't need my help if you're on the royal council."

"Ah, but I do." Igor raised his cup to his mouth and took a long swallow. Perhaps he drained it, because he set it aside. Instead of offering more, I waited for him to explain himself.

"An associate boyar needs a suitable estate," he said after a pause. "Katya's brother, Dmitry, will return from Kolomna in a few months. Meanwhile, Gavriil Timofeevich tells me he informed you when he proposed that the young grand prince would marry a Russian girl. I came to confirm that there will be a bride show, probably by the end of the year. Anna will be summoned, as a virgin daughter of the Sheremetev and Kolychev clans. As I recall, she will soon turn fifteen—the perfect age."

"You're becoming more obscure by the moment," I said. "You can live at the Vorontsov estate after Dmitry returns. He's unlikely to stay long before he gets another military assignment and needs you and Katya to administer the property again. It's quite suitable for a member of the royal council, too, because the previous owner was a senior boyar and tutor to the grand prince, several rungs above where you now stand. And in any case, your housing arrangements have nothing to do with Anna's entry into a bride show for the grand prince that may not take place."

"Tut, tut." Igor shook his head like a teacher distressed by a disappointing pupil. "And I thought you were the smart sister. Why else would I have asked you to join me here? Can't you see the connection between my needing an estate and Anna becoming the next grand princess?"

"No." My temper was fraying, and I wanted to deny him the satisfaction of coaxing me into playing his game, although in fact I did have a glimmer of what he had in mind. He was proposing some kind of trade. "You presume too much, as does Gavriil Timofeevich. I do not yearn to see Anna become the next grand princess of Russia."

He leaned back and stretched out his feet again, although I noticed he avoided any contact with mine. His air of relaxation seemed like an insult given that he sought to manipulate me, even if I did not yet know into what. Something to do with an estate, I assumed.

"But you have no say," he announced in measured tones that sounded false to my ears. "Nor does Anna. The boyars send out a summons on behalf of the grand prince. As the head of her clan, I have a responsibility to deliver her for examination, and I have no intention of risking disgrace for noncompliance. The members of the inner council select the final group of candidates to present to the ruler. Even if they reject her, what they say about her will affect her chances of making any other match. If, for example, rumors were to circulate that her mother consorts with a man not of noble rank who has in the past been accused of conspiring with the Tatars, then Anna would be fortunate to find even a provincial captain willing to take her on, don't you think?"

"How dare you? That is a complete fabrication!" I jumped to my feet, gripping my full skirt with both hands to keep from going for his throat. Yet his accusation froze the blood in my veins. Where had he heard that I was "consorting" with Anfim? That description was too specific for him to have anyone else in mind.

Igor stood, raising his shoulders and clenching his fists so that he appeared to tower over me. "Sit down, cousin," he ordered.

As if he had the right to issue commands in this house. "*You* sit down," I retorted. "I live here."

He dropped onto the chair, lolling with an insolence that made my palms twitch with the urge to slap him. I resumed my seat, pushing my hands under my robe to maintain a vestige of control.

"Let's bargain," he said. "Here's what I propose. You assist me in persuading Darya and Nikita to give up this estate, which they stole from me. In return, I inform Gavriil Vorontsov that Anna is a lovely girl, pure as new-fallen snow, and that as the head of her clan I would welcome nothing more than to see her selected for personal presentation to the ruler, who may then honor her with the silk scarf and ring signifying his acceptance. Or you refuse your aid, and I ensure that your daughter does not marry the grand prince— or anyone more prestigious than a peasant. Unlike the bride show, that *is* your choice."

While I gaped at him—stunned not just by his audacity and his pomposity but by the realization that, at least in pursuit of his own self-interest, he was not the utter dolt I'd considered him to be—he rose once more and bowed. "You have one month to decide." He produced an ironic tip of his head that I interpreted as expressing his complete lack of respect for me, then added, "You should have accepted Gavriil Timofeevich's proposal, you know. You or your sister—you can hardly expect a man of his standing to tolerate rejection twice from the women of one no-longer-very-exalted family. If either of you had cooperated, he would have no reason to seek revenge. Farewell, dear cousin. Send a message when you come to your senses."

He dipped his chin in my direction and left. I waited for the sound of the closing door, then took a long drink from my cup. The warmth of the liquid alleviated my shock. To steady my nerves, I walked to the small table and poured more wine, then sipped slowly as I considered what Igor had said. Freed from the drumbeat of my cousin's threats, I could think again.

He still insisted he had a right to our estate. He had the support of Gavriil Timofeevich Vorontsov, whose proposal I had spurned. And the two of them would not hesitate to destroy Anna's future if doing so would get Igor the property he craved.

This property, which once belonged to my father, who had bequeathed it to the son of his best friend. To Nikita, in short, not to Cousin Igor. And Igor believed he could frighten me into helping him steal it a second time.

My fingers gripped the cup so hard my hands hurt. If I had a weapon, I would kill him. Since I did not, I went in search of my sister.

In my anger, I forgot that Igor had not come alone until I reached the third floor and found Darya with Anna and Katya—the last person I wanted to see right then. They sat side by side on the bench near the stove, Laika stretched at their feet.

I needed to calm down before I could act as a hostess, never mind a friend. So I made a hasty excuse, ducked out of the room, and ran back to the study, hoping to avoid Igor along the way. My luck held, and I grabbed the tray of bread and sturgeon: small as it was, it remained untouched. I set aside the beer, picked up the jug of spiced wine, and carried it and the food to the women's quarters at a pace sedate enough to keep my robe safe from sloshing and spatters. By the time I got there, my heart rate had slowed and I felt capable of handling whatever came next.

"It would be a shame to waste this lovely fish," I said as I entered. "And Mishka mulled wine for us, too."

"Where's Igor?" Katya asked. "What did he want with you?"

"Didn't he tell you?" That surprised me. Katya wasn't the sort to traipse behind her husband without demanding an explanation of his purpose. When she shook her head, I set the tray on a sideboard and answered her questions. "I don't know where he went. He left the room before I did. As for why he asked for me, I believe he wanted to tell us about his promotion, but I'm sure you already shared that news with Darya."

"I did," Katya confirmed. "In fact, I told him I would. But you know Igor. He loves admiration. Perhaps he wanted to hear you congratulate him. Did you?"

"Of course," I said, wondering if she stood behind my cousin's sudden display of intelligence. I'd always regarded her as the smarter of the two. Yet here she was, acting the innocent.

About to push harder, I noticed Anna, sitting right next to Katya and staring at me with wide, worried eyes. Before I had a chance to send my daughter from the room, Katya rose from the bench and picked up her fur cloak. "I must go," she said. "If my husband has finished the business he came for, I shouldn't keep him waiting." She kissed Darya on both cheeks, then did the same to Anna and me. "Next time I'll stay longer."

"Please do," I said, not sure if I meant it. She nodded and headed for the door.

As soon as her footsteps faded from earshot, Darya turned to me. "What did Igor really want?"

My sister shared my suspicions. I found that heartening. "A moment." I held up a hand. "Anna, this isn't for your ears. Leave us for now." She obeyed, sending curious glances over her shoulder on her way out. I couldn't blame her for wondering what we were keeping from her. I would have done the same in her place.

I caught Darya's elbow and led her to the window seat. Then I told her about Igor's attempt at extortion, because there was no other word for it.

"But that's outrageous," she said when I got to the part about his proposed bargain. "How dare he threaten Anna? How can he imagine that Niki and I would meekly stand by and let that happen—or surrender our home without a fight, for that matter?"

"It's terrible, I agree. Yet we can't stand back while he spreads his poison throughout the town. I won't let him wreck Anna's chances." Unable to sit still, I rose and paced to the window and back.

"Niki will smash his teeth in if he tries," Darya said. Her voice held a note of vicious satisfaction that was quite unlike her.

Already on my way back, I stopped to stare at her. She was stabbing a needle into her sewing as if she could pierce our cousin with its bone point.

"I'm sure Niki will," I told her when she at last looked in my direction. "But it won't serve. We need to find a way to silence Igor even when Niki's not there to overhear him—and without giving in to our cousin's demands. You know what people are like: if Niki defends our honor, they'll assume Igor has cause to declare it sullied."

"Niki could threaten him privately," she pointed out.

"We'll keep that in mind," I promised—to humor her, not because I thought it would work. "Tell him, by all means. I don't want you keeping secrets from your husband. But the fact that Igor came after me suggests he's already discounted what Niki might do. Igor's a snake, and now he has access to the grand prince's council, where he can do a lot of damage without us finding out until it's too late. He also claims to have the backing of Vorontsov, who outranks everyone we know except Alexei and Maria. We need a plan that will force Igor to abandon his ultimatum altogether."

"Alexei," Darya said, her gaze thoughtful. "Is Koshkin involved in this scheme of Igor's, do you think? It sounds like something Koshkin would do."

"It does." Koshkin, a slippery character if I'd ever met one, loved plots and intrigue as other men loved their firstborn sons. He was an even more likely mastermind than Katya, and less scrupulous. He'd supported our cousin against us with the forged will, as well. "Igor didn't mention him, though, only Gavriil Vorontsov. Why do you ask?"

"Because Alexei doesn't hesitate to rein in his father-in-law, and he's very effective when he does. I'm less certain he would intervene with Vorontsov, although in a pinch we could turn Alexei loose against Igor. Niki is Alexei's adjutant, after all. Any attack on him undercuts Alexei's influence as well."

"True," I said. "Although sending Alexei after Igor is not so different from involving Niki. Igor can still cause trouble through backbiting and rumors. And Anna's not the only potential victim. Igor revived that old lie about Anfim spying for the Tatars. He accused me of consorting with a traitor. I don't know where he got the consorting part—servants' gossip, I suppose. That might hurt Anna by undermining my reputation, but the treason accusation is far more dangerous."

"We have to move fast, then." She tucked her needle into the linen and set it aside. "And I think you should choose: either marry Anfim or keep your distance. No one can accuse you of consorting if you're legally wed, and Igor's gossip loses its bite if you are no longer together."

"We already agreed that I won't marry Anfim until we settle Anna's future," I reminded her. A pang of sadness assailed me at the thought of not even seeing him, but I shoved it down. I'd deal with that later. "Although you're right: he's more vulnerable than she is. If anyone takes the charge of treason seriously, it might cost him his life. And even if they don't, he worked hard for his promotion. I don't want him undermined with a scandal right when he's getting started in his new job."

"Will you tell him what Igor said?" Darya's eyes widened.

"I'll have to, won't I? Otherwise I'm keeping secrets from *him*." It felt strange, worrying about the effects of my behavior on someone outside my immediate family. After years of widowhood, I'd lost the habit of coordinating with other adults, except for my sister. Even during my marriage, I hadn't regarded Semyon as a partner but as an adversary who issued orders that I had to obey or circumvent. Anfim deserved better. "Besides, he needs to know about Igor's threats so he can defend himself against them."

I bit my thumbnail. I wasn't sure I wanted to say the next part, but I saw no alternative. "We may have to find Anna a husband as soon as possible. Igor has nothing to gain from questioning her chastity if she's already wed."

She nodded. "I'll speak with Niki. In fact, we should go together."

To cover my distress, I walked to the sideboard and poured two small cups of the still warm wine. I handed one to Darya and raised the other in a toast. "To Igor's destruction!"

I saw the troubled expression in my sister's eyes, but she gamely touched her cup to mine. "To Igor's destruction and a good husband for Anna," she said.

Chapter Seven

NIKI WAS FURIOUS WHEN HE LEARNED OF IGOR'S LATEST attempt to grab our estate. He paced the main sitting room, smacking his hand against his legs, the table, the chairs— anything inanimate that came his way. "I swear I can shut his mouth," he said on one of his passages past Darya and me, sitting together on a settle near the stove. "I'll make him rue the day he was born."

"We all rue the day he was born." I summoned my most soothing tone. "And truly, Niki, the thought of you punching him silly warms my heart. But you can't silence Gavriil Vorontsov, who's the grand prince's favorite at the moment. You'd end up back in exile, and what would happen to us then? Your presence here is the only reason Igor hasn't moved in waving more of his forged documents and daring us to stop him."

He continued to stalk around the room, but the set of his shoulders told me he accepted that I spoke the truth, whether any of us liked that truth or not. After a while, he slumped into the room's one armchair. "Very well," he said. "I'll hold off on administering the beating Igor deserves and think about potential husbands for Anna. A kind man— well connected, old enough to protect her, young enough to appeal to her, healthy and reasonably good-looking with adequate resources. From a boyar family, of course. Did I miss anything?"

"Not that I can think of." I picked up a cushion from the settle and toyed with the fringe, considering the characteristics he'd listed. "Do you have any friends with younger brothers who might suit? Ideally, we'd find someone who'd fall in love with her."

"But also someone who could defend her against our cousin," Darya finished for me. "A man who knows his own mind, so he'll pay no heed to Igor's scandalous tales."

"Such a man would be several years older than Anna," Niki said. "Nineteen or twenty, at least. But that might serve us better anyway: an inexperienced boy won't do her much good."

I winced, unable to conceal my distaste. Niki raised an eyebrow at me. He'd noticed my reaction, obviously. "It sounds so businesslike," I said with an apologetic shrug. "I know, I started it. But I can imagine Papa having this conversation with his friends about me, and the group of them deciding that Semyon Kolychev was ideal."

Darya patted my hand in sympathy, and we exchanged glances. I'd never told her the whole story of my marriage, but she knew me well enough to hear the sounds of distress whenever I said my dead husband's name.

An image of Anfim filled my head then, his gentleness and respect, his unselfish passion. Wasn't *that* what I wanted my daughter to experience someday? So why was I so afraid of pledging myself to him in marriage?

"Maybe beating Igor up *is* the right choice," I said lightly. Warmth flooded my cheeks, and I saw them watching me, their faces intent. Wondering what caused my blush, I assumed.

"Don't tempt me," Niki said. "Alas, you're right that it wouldn't solve anything in the long run. I'll make inquiries—discreetly, or Igor will start spreading rumors right away. Meanwhile, let's consider other ideas."

Try as we might, though, finding the right husband for Anna seemed like our best choice.

Because of Igor's threats, I thought it unwise to get in a sleigh and drive over to Anfim's new house, in case our cousin was watching for evidence of "consorting," as he put it. At times, I studied our servants, wondering who had tattled to my cousin and why.

More likely, Katya had told her husband about us. She'd known of my interest in Anfim months before the party, and she must have seen us talking that night. She was sharp enough to witness the glances the two of us exchanged and draw the right conclusions from them. In fact, she'd seen us leave her house together. It wasn't proof, but it seemed like a more credible explanation than a servant risking his or her livelihood by gossiping to the master of another household.

But wherever Igor had gotten his information, I didn't want to risk Anna's and Anfim's futures by confirming my cousin's suspicions. Anfim had promised to visit that day, but to ensure that he did, I sent him a message. He arrived on our doorstep late that afternoon, to effusive greetings from Lara and Tolya.

"Are you here to fetch us, Papa?" Lara asked as the volume of noise faded to a level approaching normal. She cast an apologetic glance my way, as if she feared that her eagerness to leave would offend me.

"Don't worry," I told her with a smile. "We love you both, but we know you belong with your papa." I looked at Darya and Nikita, then at Anfim. "What do you think about letting Masha accompany them when they move to your house? She's part of my inheritance from my father, and I'd be happy to release her for as long as needed to live with you. It will make the transition easier for all concerned."

"A great idea," Darya said. "She's wonderful with the children. I hope you'll allow them to continue their lessons with Father Job as well. If you agree, we can ask him for you."

Anfim accepted the offer with enthusiasm. "I would like both of those things. We transferred the furniture and household goods this morning, so if Lady Solomonida follows through on her promise to advise me on ornaments and such, Lara and Tolya can join me tomorrow." The light in his eyes underlined that decorating was not the only reason he wanted me to visit, and the thought of what else we might do sent tremors from my chest to my toes.

I pushed such thoughts to the back of my mind. "Of course," I said, wondering how to convince him that our "consorting" must end for a while.

Well, best get it over with. I stood and extended a hand. "There is, however, a complication. Please come with me while I explain. And do join us for supper. Your children still have a thousand stories to tell, and you can share more about your journey."

As soon as we left the main sitting room and entered the empty dining hall, Anfim took my outstretched hand. The strength of his grip reassured me. Here was a partner I could rely on. I led him to Nikita's study, where no one would interrupt us.

Or spy on us? I wasn't so sure about that. But once the door closed, I nevertheless let Anfim take me in his arms and kiss me. Indeed, I kissed him with equal fervor.

"Come home with me tonight," he said as he released me. "Every time I think about you in that bronze sari, I regret not having you at my side. When can we marry?"

A tremor ran through me as another vision of my long-dead husband assailed me, and for a moment I couldn't answer. I'd expected the question, prepared to discuss it in rational terms, as a set of pros and cons. But the terror that gripped me as I recalled the years with Semyon defied logic. The words I'd intended to say congealed on my tongue.

Anfim frowned—a troubled expression rather than an angry one. "Have you changed your mind?" he asked. "I thought we agreed that so long as I got my promotion, I would be close enough to you in status that we could wed. You seemed amenable to the idea yesterday."

Too late I recalled that I had met Igor in this room. In my state of near-panic, I couldn't bear to take one of the armchairs or even ask Anfim to do so; I had enough unpleasant memories to defeat without adding the residue of prior conversations. I took his hand once more and led him to the settle on the far side of the study, near the window.

"I did leave you with that impression," I admitted, forcing the words past the constriction in my throat. "I was so happy to see you again; I didn't want to spoil our reunion with my doubts. But I do have them. Not because of anything you've done, but because we have still spent little time together. And because my previous husband made me very unhappy."

He surged to his feet, his hands clenched into fists, and I recoiled, seeing my fears brought to life. "Your husband beat you?" he asked, his voice close to a growl. I'd never seen this side of him before. "A woman like you?"

I shook my head, striving for calm. His anger was not directed at me, as Semyon's had been, but at my first husband in defense of me. "He never beat me," I said in an unsteady voice. "He didn't dare. Papa would have torn him limb from limb if he tried it. He slapped me a few times when I annoyed him, but no more than that."

I stopped. How to explain Semyon's perversions? "He mocked me at every turn, called me names, threatened to sell me as a slave to the Turks because they like blondes, rejected Anna because in his mind only sons counted; a daughter was worthless." My cheeks felt as if they were on fire with remembered humiliation, but I forced myself to continue. Anfim was my lover. He deserved to know the whole, even the things I'd told no one else. "And he liked to 'overcome resistance,' as he put it. I learned to submit to his demands, no matter what. Opposing him could only make matters worse, and if I complained—even to the Church—what could they do? He was my husband. But every time he approached me, I hated him more. The day Grand Princess Elena ordered my divorce I danced for joy. It felt like she'd lifted a huge weight from my shoulders."

For a moment, Anfim remained standing, clenching and releasing his hands as if throttling the long-dead Semyon. Then he dropped back onto the settle and wrapped his arms around me, murmuring endearments and reassurances into my hair. "Don't worry, my dove, you're safe now. I'll never let anyone hurt you again."

I pressed my face against his chest. I didn't weep; the injury had occurred too long ago, and I had no tears left. But after a while, a strange thing happened. The tension I'd carried inside for years dissipated like fog on a sunny morning. I had shared the dreadful past with Anfim, and he hadn't spurned me. Instead, he was comforting me.

When I at last raised my head, I saw the glimmer of unshed tears in his eyes. I kissed him, then said, "I didn't mean to upset you. I'm sorry."

"No, I'm glad you told me. What happened to him after the divorce?"

"He'd committed a terrible crime. He faced execution, but his uncle pleaded for mercy. The only reason Elena granted the request was because Semyon's cousins were the ones who put a stop to his wickedness. She ordered Semyon knouted, then forced him to take monastic vows and sent him to a place in the Far North. That's why she ordered the divorce, so that he could become a monk. I never saw him again." I flinched, thinking of the nights I'd stayed awake in this house, listening for Semyon's heavy tread, only to recall that I no longer had a reason to fear his return.

Anfim tightened his arm around my waist. "He's lucky he's dead. If he weren't, I'd be tempted to kill him myself. Bastard."

"Thank you." I took a long breath. "Alas, Semyon is not the only bastard we have to worry about." I told him about Igor and his threat to harm Anna's reputation—and Anfim's own—if I didn't help my cousin obtain the estate he craved. "He gave me a month, but of course I won't agree. I won't even respond," I finished. "The question is how best to thwart him." Then I explained the plan to find a husband for Anna and how it must delay any marriage between us, if only for a few months.

He listened without interrupting, but when I reached the end, he frowned once more. "Is it so important for Anna to marry into a boyar family? Suppose you and I were to wed, and she came to live with us? Among merchants and officials, it's not uncommon to have some acquaintance with a spouse before the wedding day. That would be better for her than marrying a complete stranger, one who wants her only for her bloodline and her womb. She could wait until she's ready, and Igor Grigorevich would have no power over you or your sister and brother-in-law."

I stared at him, speechless. *Not* marry into a boyar family? Despite my own association with Anfim, the thought had never occurred to me. Aristocratic girls married to serve their families, not themselves, although I hoped those two goals could be reconciled for Anna. I didn't know what to say.

"What an interesting idea," I managed after a while.

He watched me, his head tipped to one side, as if assessing my state of mind. "You seem shocked. Surely Anna's happiness is more important than her rank in society. You just told me how marriage to the scion of a boyar clan affected you."

I shivered again at the memory of Semyon's cruel face. "It's not always that way. I've known happy couples, too, and I'm sure you know unhappy ones."

"Of course," he said. "I meant only to urge you to consider other possibilities."

Again I found myself at a loss for words, but this time because a surge of regret stopped them as they reached my throat. If my father had wed me to Anfim instead of Semyon, how different my life would have been!

When I didn't respond, he leaned forward again and brushed his lips across my forehead. "I would never treat you as your husband did, Solomonida. You needn't fear marriage to me."

"Thank you," I said, touched by his understanding. "I'll think about what you've said. Maybe you're right, and I'm the one who can't see beyond the rules I grew up with. But you would still be at risk from Igor's malice."

He raised an indifferent shoulder. "Perhaps, but why should he come after me? I can't give him Nikita Andreevich's estate."

"He wants to manipulate us," I said. "He's determined to retake this property, by fair means or foul, and he's threatening to slander you if we don't hand it over. He's counting on the rest of us caring enough about you to make a deal with him to preserve your reputation—and your life."

"Yes," he admitted. "And I'm delighted to have such friends. But I worked for Igor Grigorevich, remember? All I have to do is remind him that I know about his forged will and can swear he has no claim to your family's property, and he'll realize I can damage him as much as he can me."

Could it be that simple? I remained unconvinced. I remembered Igor sprawling in the armchair, his arrogant ease, his conceit as he celebrated his own cleverness. I knew my cousin well enough to guess that he might have overlooked something that we could use to undermine his scheme, but I doubted the answer was as simple as either Anfim or Niki imagined.

"I hope you're right," I said, because I could be wrong, even though I didn't see how, and I knew Anfim had both a longer and a better acquaintance with my cousin than I did. His father had ministered to Igor's family once upon a time, and the two boys had grown up together. Exactly *how* Anfim managed to stay on good terms with my obnoxious cousin remained a mystery to me, but after three decades he must have a slew of arrows in his tactical quiver.

"So do I." He gave me the smile I loved. "Now, how are we going to get you to my house to fulfill that promise of yours about decorating the children's rooms without Igor Grigorevich finding out?"

When Anfim left that evening, I went with him, dressed in Masha's cloak—its hood concealing my face. I wore my simplest robe, left my headdress behind, and for the first time since my betrothal seventeen years before redid my hair in the single braid typical of never-married girls. Masha had retired for the night, so with a bit of luck anyone who saw us would believe that she, not I, climbed into the covered sleigh behind Anfim.

Once we reached our destination, we sauntered through the rooms, adorned with gorgeous carpets and draperies purchased in Tabriz. The bright rugs I'd admired at their old house lay in the children's bedchambers to remind them of the home they'd left two years ago, and although the walls still shone off-white with new paint, exotic ornaments of various kinds decorated the areas designed for entertaining guests.

"A good idea." I pointed to a red-and-blue rug, then to a shelf where the wooden bears frolicked in what would soon be Tolya's line of sight. I'd already applauded the creamy tints and lace-trimmed bed coverings of Lara's room, the chest where she could arrange the dolls Anna had passed down to her. "These familiar things will help the children feel at home."

I pulled out a package I'd brought with me, unwrapped it, and handed him a colored drawing of Laika seated beside a standing Tolya. "This is Niki's gift to you. He thinks it may help Tolya get used to not having the dog to play with every day. Why don't you hang it on that wall?" I pointed to a bare stretch near the carved bears. "It will be the first thing he sees when he awakes."

Anfim took the drawing from me and gazed at it with something approaching awe. "He has a gift, Nikita

Andreevich. It looks just like Tolya, right down to the mischievous smile. Clever of him to stick the paper to this wooden backing, too." He placed it atop a small chest of a type I'd never seen before, brightly painted in gleaming black lacquer, with horses romping across the door against a background of fantastic mountains. "I'll have one of the workmen hang it later. I think Tolya will want to hold it in his hands first so he can admire it."

I agreed, suggested another improvement or two, then turned toward him, laughing. "You didn't need my help. You've done a wonderful job on your own."

He sidestepped me, wrapping his arms around my waist from behind and nuzzling my neck. "Shall we get to the business that *does* require your help, then? I can hardly wait to see you in that bronze sari once more."

How could I resist an invitation like that? Dawn flushed the skies with pink by the time "Masha" found her way back home.

As planned, Lara and Tolya moved to their father's home the next day. Calling promises to stop by soon, Darya and I watched them go with a mixture of sadness and knowledge that this was the right step for them. "They'll be back," I reminded my sister, speaking to reassure myself as much as her—although a few hours a week meant little when measured against the time we had spent together since Anfim left on his journey south.

"It won't be the same," she said, stating the obvious. She pointed to Laika, straining at the leash held by a burly stablehand. "Even the dog will miss them."

"I'm sure she will," I agreed. "And Tolya will miss her. He probably can't remember a time before she became his best friend."

Darya sighed, acknowledging this reality. Anfim and his family had passed from sight by then, so we left the courtyard for the kitchen, where the cooks awaited instruction on what to prepare for the evening meal.

The day after the children left, Nikita initiated discreet inquiries as to which boyars might be looking for a daughter-in-law and about the character and abilities of any potential bridegroom. Anfim and I continued to meet, although with the children in residence at his house, our encounters were neither frequent nor intimate. We talked about marriage once or twice, but I reiterated the need to wait until I had Anna settled. Anfim didn't argue, although I could tell from his stiff shoulders that he would have preferred a different answer. In fact, I sensed he was losing patience with me: unlike many men in similar circumstances, he wanted to "make an honest woman of me," as people say, only to see his efforts to do the right thing foiled by me dragging my feet.

At the same time, his willingness to let me approach matrimony at my own pace gradually eroded the last of the fears left over from my experience with Semyon. I became more accepting of the *idea* of living as Anfim's wife even as I insisted on placing my daughter's needs above my own. I tried to reassure myself that everything would be resolved soon, but the only result was that lost love haunted my dreams.

Igor's deadline came and went without my sending him a reply. A week later, his valet delivered a letter—written by a clerk, since our cousin held to the old view that noblemen had no need to read and write for themselves—expressing disappointment that I favored the material interests of my sister and brother-in-law over the deeper emotional bonds between mother and daughter. Whatever happened next, the letter implied, I had only myself to blame.

I tore the offending document into shreds and fed it to the furnace, then sought comfort in the fact that my painful separation from Anfim appeared to have borne fruit. My cousin hadn't repeated the accusation of consorting in this latest missive, at least.

But as February passed its zenith and cleared the way for March, the whole situation made me queasy. While I refused to dignify Igor's attempts at manipulation with a response, I half-expected another visit, if only to twist the knife. Yet nothing of the sort occurred.

"Was it a meaningless threat, then?" I asked Darya and Niki on the second day of March. The three of us had again settled in the main sitting room on the second floor. "A vain hope that he could intimidate us into giving him what he wanted?"

"No, I don't think so." Niki frowned at the blazing furnace. "I'd guess he's behind the occasional rumor I've heard about Anfim's ties to the Tatars—speculations that his journey east served purposes other than trade, for example. That he's a spy passing information to Kazan, in short."

My spirits dove into a deep cave at the news. So much for my dream that Anfim, at least, would be spared, given how seldom we saw each other. "How dastardly! Doesn't Igor care that his spite could get his childhood friend arrested?"

"Igor cares only for Igor. You know that as well as I do." Niki patted my hand in a reassuring fashion. "We'll find a way to defeat him. Didn't you tell me Anfim traveled on government orders?"

What could we do against rumors whispered in the dark? Fear tied my tongue, but I nodded, and he went on. "State

Treasurer Tretiakov's no fool. He knows that a government clerk would collect information *about* Kazan, not hand it over to the enemy. It can't be a coincidence that, right around the time Anfim returned, we received news that Khan Safa-Girei had fled the Kazan fortress."

"That would fit with what Anfim told me before he left," I said. "But it doesn't change the lies the gossip mongers are spreading."

"True," Niki admitted. "It expands the circle of people Igor can offend with his antics, though. If the government had a stake in Anfim's expedition, even a small one, he will have submitted a report as soon as he returned. So there is proof somewhere of what he said and did. And he must have operated with the approval of someone in the inner circle at court—most likely, a boyar or prince interested in gathering intelligence about Kazan's defenses. Igor's rumors endanger that person as well."

My drooping spirits revived at this news. Surely a boyar or prince could restrain Igor—although Gavriil Vorontsov, a more powerful opponent, might yet prevail. "Anfim did submit a report," I said. "He told me the day he returned that he'd just come from Tretiakov's office. But why do you think a member of the inner circle is involved? Isn't the treasurer's approval enough?"

"Not for something like this." Niki tapped his fingers against the arm of his chair, as if directing a dance only he could see. "Foreign affairs are under Tretiakov's jurisdiction, so he must have authorized the mission and the expenses. The leader would be a military man, though. Prince Alexander Gorbaty, perhaps. You remember how he and Tretiakov talked with Anfim at the Vorontsovs' Christmas party, just a week or two before Anfim set out on his journey. Gorbaty oversees most of the Kazan campaigns, and he outranks Igor.

He even outranks Gavriil Vorontsov, although the grand prince's favor is one of the few things more important than birth. Frankly, I hope Gorbaty *is* the leader. He's a single-minded soldier who has no use for ambitious courtiers like your cousin, and he doesn't permit anyone to interfere with his pet project. If he's involved, he'll squash these rumors as if they were so many cockroaches. Which they are, in a sense."

"But what is the project?" I asked, struggling to follow the ins and outs of Niki's argument.

"The conquest of Kazan," he said. "It's only a matter of time."

"Kazan?" Darya sounded as bewildered as I felt. "We attack Kazan every other year. We never win."

"We haven't won *yet*." Niki mimicked an archer pulling back a bowstring and releasing his arrow. "But one day we will. What we need is the right information. If Anfim brought that home, any attempt to discredit him will blow up in Igor's face."

"I hope that's true, but even if it is, it's not enough. Igor can still harm Anfim with his lies," I pointed out. My spirits sank once more at the thought. "Gossip like that takes on a life of its own, and in this case, there are already people who believe he betrayed Russia during his mission to the Tatars a few summers ago."

Niki acknowledged my point with a rueful half-smile. "I suppose so. Can you ask him what's going on, Solomonida, the next time you see him? Sound him out, at least, as to whether he's worked with Gorbaty? Then we'll know which rumors we need to combat and what kind of support we can call on."

How casually he said it, as if he took it for granted that Anfim and I belonged together. Yet I hadn't seen Anfim in two weeks. "I can ask," I said. "I doubt he'll admit it if it's true. But I should tell him what you've heard. Learning that someone's trying to undermine him may persuade him to reveal the truth."

"Speaking of truth, are you going to confess to what's ailing you?" Darya glanced at her husband, as if deliberating how much to say in front of him, then went on. "You looked quite pallid this morning."

"A slight indigestion." I wriggled on my bench, hoping she didn't notice how much her question discomfited me. This was the fifth morning in a row that I'd experienced that particular form of nausea, and after four pregnancies I had little doubt as to the cause. And I'd felt so certain I told the truth when I assured Anfim that there could be no consequences from our lovemaking! "I drank some water, and now I'm fine."

The intensity of her gaze told me she wasn't fooled. Even Nikita raised his eyebrows, although he didn't challenge me. He retreated to a seat near the window and draped his arm across the sill, staring at the courtyard below. From that I deduced that he was no more comfortable discussing "women's matters" than most men of my acquaintance.

"Have you and Anfim decided when to hold the wedding?" Darya asked. The connection she'd made between my illness and Anfim's proposal revealed that she shared my suspicion that morning sickness, not indigestion, accounted for my weak stomach. I searched for signs of condemnation, but neither her face nor Niki's revealed what they thought of my no longer secret sin.

I gave up my efforts to conceal the obvious. "We've discussed it several times, but as I told you I would, I convinced him to wait until Anna was settled. That was before this bout of sickness, though. I should let him know that I may have a baby on the way."

My own words triggered a memory, and in a burst of light, I saw a potential solution. Before I could worry it to death with caveats, I shared it with them. "But he also asked me why Anna needs to marry a nobleman at all." They exclaimed at that, as shocked by the suggestion as I had been. "If we gave up on that idea, Anfim and I could wed right away. Anna could live with us, and Igor couldn't touch her. Even as head of the clan, he'd have a hard time arranging a contract for her behind our backs if she were living in a state secretary's home, and you and your estate would be safe from him. He'd have no reason to slander Anfim then."

Niki turned his head. "You're considering this plan, aren't you?"

"I am," I said. "Should I not?"

"If you take that step, there's no going back," he pointed out. "And she's too young to understand what's at stake. Will she resent you for stripping her of her birthright?"

"I don't know. I hate to think so, but maybe she will." I watched my proposed solution evaporate before my eyes, casting an even harsher light on the dilemma I faced. Because I didn't need to hear Anfim announce that no son or daughter of his would be born out of wedlock to guess how he would react to my news. I could no longer argue for a delay, because the disgrace of my unwed motherhood would fail both Anna and the infant I bore. Yet satisfying my needs and those of the unborn child would mean deserting the daughter I'd already raised. Would Anna ever forgive me for that?

The wages of sin, indeed.

Chapter Eight

THE CONVERSATION WITH NIKITA TOOK PLACE ON A Tuesday. By the time Friday rolled around, I could no longer deny—to my sister or myself—that the unsettled stomach I suffered each morning, which faded by noon, indicated that, God willing, Anna would have a new brother or sister by the end of the year. Knowing Darya suffered from similar symptoms only made it harder to ignore my own.

"You won't try to get rid of it, will you?" my sister asked me that afternoon. Anna had gone to spend the day with her friend Lyuba, and the two of us were in the sewing room—Darya decorating the cuffs of a loose shirt for Andrusha, who seemed to grow as we watched, and I hemming the recently stitched-together peach brocade robe.

"How can you think that?" I said, amazed. "After I watched Grand Princess Elena die trying to abort hers?" The Shuisky princes had poisoned her by doctoring the potion given to her to end an unwanted pregnancy. "I may have conceived this child sooner than I should have, but I won't compound my sin by hoping for its death."

"And if Anfim insists on a wedding?" She looked me in the eye, as if challenging me to choose between my daughter's needs and my own. "What happens to Anna then?"

"He will insist," I said. "He's not the kind of man to abandon a lover or deny responsibility for a child. And I must accept, without delay. Bearing a bastard would cause a scandal guaranteed to hurt Anna more than me making an almost suitable match. The question is whether Anna should stay here or live with us, as Anfim proposed. I can't answer that until I talk with him, although I'm inclined to leave her here until we find a husband for her." I tried to sound strong, convincing, although the thought of choosing between Anfim and Anna, Anna and the new baby, made me squirm inside.

That was when I grasped—as I had not before—the agonizing conflict that had driven Grand Princess Elena to take the potion that killed her. She hadn't known, of course, that the dose of yew leaves would prove fatal. She'd sought only to rid herself of a child whose very existence more than four years after her husband's death threatened to unseat her, whose father she loved but could not marry because doing so would undermine her ability to protect the sons she already had—sons whose legitimacy her long affair, although never confirmed, had already cast into question. I'd heard the rumors, like everyone else at court and even foreign diplomats, that Elena's two boys were the sons of her lover, conceived before her husband's death. Her fear of confirming that slander drove her to a reckless disregard for her own safety.

For a wild moment, I fought the urge to procrastinate. With the stakes so high, why say anything to Anfim, when I didn't yet know how the pregnancy would end? I'd miscarried in the past and might do so again. The Church taught that any pregnancy that ended prematurely indicated a mother's sinful state, and in that sense I was more vulnerable now than ever before. I hadn't wanted to rid myself even of

Semyon's children; still less did I desire to lose Anfim's. Yet past experience suggested it might happen. If it did, I would still marry him, but I wouldn't have to desert my daughter to do so. We could wait until we saw her settled.

I crushed that line of thought the moment it formed. Secrets were for unwed girls and brides too young to manage a household. A woman my age should practice courage and honesty, whether she preferred to wait a few months or not. What kind of marriage would Anfim and I have if I concealed so important a truth from him before we even said our vows?

"I'll invite him to visit us tomorrow," I told Darya. "Perhaps I can persuade him to tell me what information he collected for the government at the same time."

She nodded. "I think that would be best—both to let Anna stay with us and to talk with Anfim. Write him a message, and I'll have one of the stable boys deliver it."

I set my hemming aside and called for pen and ink. After two years' practice, I could craft a simple note without difficulty, but deciding what to put in it required more effort. In the end, I wrote the simplest text I could contrive.

I need to talk to you. Please visit me here, at the house—tomorrow, if possible. Your reply would be appreciated. SP

I feared that after my two weeks of not visiting him, he might ignore my request altogether, but his answer arrived before supper.

I will call on you during the third hour after sunrise. AF

Even the demands of early pregnancy couldn't ease me into slumber that night.

This time I remembered not to meet Anfim in the second-floor study, steeped with memories of unwanted encounters. Instead I commandeered the office where he used to work, empty on a Saturday as well as relatively private. Other than Father Job's domain, also unoccupied that day, most of the chambers on the ground floor stored household goods in need of repair or discarded by family members who had outgrown them. Even curious servants would have trouble eavesdropping on us here.

With considerable reluctance, I freed myself from Anfim's embrace and took a seat on the bench that ran behind what had once been his desk. I'd spent many happy afternoons and evenings in this room, and I drew on those recollections for courage. "I have news," I said in the quietest voice I could manage that would still reach his ears. "It was a surprise to me, and I fear it will be a greater shock to you. Perhaps an unpleasant one, but I hope not."

I drew a deep breath, unnerved by the silent expectation I saw on his face. Although I didn't doubt that I'd made the right choice, telling him was harder than I'd anticipated.

In the end, I blurted out the truth. "I told you I couldn't get with child," I said. "It seems I was wrong."

His face lit up with joy, and he clasped my hands. My fear of rejection dissolved at the sight. "But that's wonderful! When did it happen? How long have you known?"

"As to the last, only a few days," I said. "I'm not certain even now, in fact. But a week of morning sickness seems like too much of a coincidence. Regarding when it happened"—I counted back from Anna's birth to when I'd first guessed at her presence, although the span of intervening years made that calculation rather unreliable—"I'd say I'm about six weeks along, so either the night you came back or the next time. We probably have until June before I show, and I don't expect the child before October."

"We should wed right away, though," he said, as I'd guessed he would. "I want no stain of sin to cling to the child or to you." He squeezed my hands. "I'm so happy, Solomonida. I'd like nothing better than to care for you and our baby."

I gripped his hands in turn, searching for words that could express my complex feelings. "You're wonderful," I said after a while. "I don't deserve you. And I will marry you, Anfim, for our sake as well as the child's. But there's something we must discuss."

As soon as I reached the "but," I saw his expression change, no doubt in response to my own hesitation. When I got to the "discuss," he dropped my hands and stood, his back against the wooden wall to the outside. "We can't delay. What of the child? Do you expect me to stand by while you risk its legacy and your reputation?"

"I don't ask that," I told him. "It's Anna. I haven't forgotten that you promised to take her in. In the long run, that may indeed be the best solution. But this is a crucial time for her. Niki is looking around for a potential husband, there is talk of a bride show, and she has reached the age when many people regard her as an adult. By marrying you, I take on your rank in society. I'm a widow in my thirties; people don't care much what I do. But Anna is at a different stage in her life. The choices we make for her this year will determine her future, and the mamas and grandmas may decide she's ineligible if she comes to live with us—despite your promotion."

He winced at that, and I held out my hand to him, inviting him back to my side. "It's unfair," I said, acknowledging his distress, "but that's how aristocratic marriages work. I don't want to deprive my daughter of the opportunity to become a boyar's wife. Yet if I leave her here, it feels as if I'm abandoning her when she needs me most."

He resumed his seat next to me and clasped my outstretched fingers. "I live three streets away. She can visit you whenever she likes, and you can come here. How is that abandoning her?"

When I stared unseeing at the desk, unable to find comfort in these words, he tightened his grip. "At the same time, I know her a little. Are you sure she would regret leaving the burdens of aristocracy behind, in favor of a life with ..." He paused for an instant, then finished, "less exalted expectations?"

I hesitated, because he had a point. Anna loved her home and her family, her small circle of friends, the comfort of the familiar. She might someday become accustomed to parties and court life, but I found it harder to imagine her coping with the stress of a boyar marriage—its constant political maneuvering, the pressure to produce male heirs, and the demands of a large household—never mind a bride show and the need to manage the expectations of an entire realm. The warm simplicity of Anfim's house, his quiet demeanor, his guidance and gentle humor seemed much more likely to appeal to her. "I'll ask her, but she doesn't have enough experience of life to know what she'd be giving up. And I fear she will worry more about hurting my feelings than what she wants for herself. Ideally, I'd leave her here for a year, so that she can grow accustomed to the idea of marriage and we have a chance to see if a suitable bridegroom exists."

His brow creased in thought. "I understand. She is a young woman and very dear to you." With his free hand, he touched my belly, where the unborn child would not quicken for months. "But this little one needs you, too, and he—or she—has even less ability to choose than Anna does. You can't deny our baby a chance to grow up in its father's house."

I knew he was right. I had already decided to bear the child, if God so willed. And to marry him. Which meant …

"I agree," I said after one more pause to wrestle with my conscience. "I will confess my sins to Father Job and ask him to wed us as soon as possible. We're on the brink of Lent. If we don't marry now, I'll be almost four months gone before the Church will authorize our union. It's unfair to ask Father Job to break the rules by wedding us during the Great Fast."

"Let's approach him together," he offered. "He'll be here tomorrow, will he not?"

"Very well." The sooner, the better. "We were both married before, so it will be a simple service, without a formal crowning. We can hold the ceremony at our estate. Only Darya and Niki and the children need attend—although I will ask Alexei and Maria, because they're such close friends. And your brothers, if you wish to invite them."

"I do. You'll like them, I think. Postnik and Kirill, both older than I."

"I'd love to meet them. Do they have wives and children?" With a shiver of dread, I realized how many basic details I had yet to learn about him, despite our shared sin. It seemed odd to feel so close and so distant at the same time.

"Children, yes," he said. "But grown now. The girls have married, and the boys trade, like their fathers. Kirill's two sons came with us on the journey east; he left them in Ryazan to conduct business. His wife stayed in Smolensk, which is where he spends most of his time; he'll be leaving soon to reassure her that he came back in one piece. Postnik's wife died not long after mine, and his sons live in Nizhny Novgorod. They handle lots of different goods, but they make their best money buying horses from the Tatars and selling them to noble cavalrymen. Just wait until August, when the Tatars drive their herds up from the south. You'll see my nephews then, if not before. I plan to take Tolya this year to watch; he'll love it." He grinned again—at the expression on my face, I assumed. I could only imagine how befuddled I must look.

"It's like experiencing another world," I said. "I've always known merchants buy and sell things, of course, but I never thought about the amount of planning that must go into it. So much travel, so many goods!"

"And so many relationships to maintain," he added. "Like a grand game."

I listened to him talk, enjoying the animation on his face. What else might I learn from my marriage to this man of a different heritage from my own? From his family?

I wondered, too, what his family would make of me. But if they attended the wedding, I would soon find out.

When I gazed at him without replying, Anfim tipped his head to one side, assessing my silence. "And Anna?" he prompted after a while.

"I'll talk with her this afternoon, but the simplest thing is to leave her with Niki and Darya for now." I winced, remembering the other matter I'd promised to discuss with him. "That's not our only problem, though. Someone is spreading rumors about you. Cousin Igor, I assume, since he threatened to do just that as part of his scheme to grab this estate."

Anfim scowled at the desk as if it, not Igor, had offended him. "Devil take Igor Grigorevich. How dare he attack us for so petty a cause?"

I placed my free hand over his. "It's petty to us, not to him. And he's not acting alone. He has the backing of Gavriil Vorontsov. Did I forget to mention that?"

He shook his head. "I don't believe it. Vorontsov doesn't care who lives here. If he wants Igor to have an estate, he'll provide one. What makes you think your cousin's telling the truth?"

I frowned at my clasped hands. Igor had sounded so certain, tossed off the name so casually, that I hadn't considered the possibility that he might be lying. But it was true that Gavriil Vorontsov had not struck me as vengeful or vindictive, whereas Igor had shown himself to be both. He'd demonstrated cunning as well.

"Igor swears Vorontsov wants revenge for Darya and me turning him down. That does seem unlikely." I thought about whether it would change things if Vorontsov played no part in my cousin's scheme. Not much, I decided. "But Igor still threatens you. It can't be an accident that gossip is circulating about your split loyalties right after Igor announced his intention of spreading exactly that kind of tale. And the world contains too many people who believe whatever they hear."

"It does," he agreed. "It's time for me to pay a call on Igor Grigorevich. This has gone far enough. I can't stand by while he endangers my wife and her family."

I stared at him, shocked anew into a sense of my own limitations. I had thought of him as a loyal worker, a supportive friend, an affectionate but authoritative father, my handsome and passionate lover. But even when he told me about his tasks for the government or some of the tales associated with his expedition, I had failed to grasp that Anfim was a high-ranking *civil servant*, an international merchant, a man with skills and competence that he exercised on behalf of the rulers of the Russian lands.

Shame filled me as I realized the extent to which pride limited my understanding of how the world worked. I'd been raised in the belief that birth and blood equaled virtue. I hadn't questioned that belief—not when I fell in love with a clerk, not when he left me for two years to pursue his dreams, not when he asked me why I believed so strongly that my daughter must wed an aristocrat. But there was much more to Anfim than met the eye.

And he had given me the opening I needed. I shared Niki's deductions about the information gathering in Kazan and the expedition used to collect it. "Is it true?" I finished. "Do you have a protector, one powerful enough to defend us from Igor—or even Vorontsov, close as he is to the grand prince?"

He released my hand and leaned back against the wall, surveying me with a shrewd look in his eyes that indicated he guessed what lay behind my questions. "Nikita Andreevich has a powerful intelligence," he said after a long pause. "I'm sure you know that I can neither confirm nor deny such speculation."

I raised both eyebrows. "You can't tell the truth to your wife?"

Only when his face crinkled into a smile did I realize I'd walked right into the trap he'd laid for me. "Maybe to her," he said, laughing. "Once I have her installed in my house."

I groaned and led him upstairs. Perhaps Niki would succeed in winkling the truth out of him.

Leaving Anfim with Nikita, I ordered Eva to bring me some bread and cheese. Since I couldn't eat in the mornings (and I suspected Eva had figured out why), I was hungry by midday—especially after today's intense if informative exchange with my soon-to-be husband. Only after I'd finished the food and the cup of apple juice she brought to wash it down did I seek out Anna.

I found her in the sewing room, alone. "Where's your aunt?" I asked, surprised.

"In the nursery." She set aside the ceremonial napkin she'd been embroidering—one of many we would distribute at her wedding—and folded her hands in her lap. "Andrusha is cutting another tooth, and he's fretful. She asked me to wait here for you."

"It's good that she did," I said. "I have something to tell you." I pulled the half-open shutter closed against the frigid air outside and sat next to her, uncertain where to begin, still less how much I could share with a fifteen-year-old.

She looked expectant, innocent but engaged. I decided to start with the one point I could not conceal for more than twenty-four hours. "Anfim has asked me to marry him."

"And will you?" She sounded almost breathless.

"Yes," I said. "Quite soon, in fact. Before Lent, if Father Job agrees."

That shocked her. Her eyes widened, and her lips parted. Then she asked the one question I'd hoped she would not. "Why so soon?"

"Don't you like Anfim?" I asked in an attempt to distract her.

She blushed and looked away. "Yes, but he's not one of us, is he?"

Hearing this echo of my own prejudices, I winced, hoping that her averted gaze kept her from noticing my reaction. "You may stay here if you like," I told her. "With Auntie Darya and Uncle Niki. We've started looking for a husband for you." I didn't want to burden her with knowledge of Cousin Igor and his threats.

"And where will you be?" Anna looked straight at me, her head high and her eyes blazing. "You plan to leave me here on my own while you go and live with a *clerk*? Why are you marrying him, Mama, and in such haste? Or would you like me to guess? Eva says you throw up every morning, just like Auntie Darya. Only Auntie Darya is married, and you're a fallen woman."

I stared at my shy, gentle, acquiescent daughter, shocked beyond belief. I'd expected pleading, sadness, fear of loss—anything but rage. Not since she turned three had Anna so much as given way to a tantrum. She was the sweetest, most biddable girl I'd ever known. I would have sworn she didn't have a rebellious bone in her body, never mind a prideful one.

Her unexpected strength of character impressed me, but I couldn't let her challenge pass uncontested. I rose to my feet and gazed down at her. "Anfim is more than a clerk," I told her. "I am marrying him because I love him, and I expect you to respect my decision. Shame on you for listening to servants' tales. I had intended to talk over with you the advantages and disadvantages of moving, since you're an adult now, but I see you already know what you want. Rest assured that I will help you in any way I can. I won't be far away, and we can visit whenever we like."

Her mouth trembled, and I saw on her face a shadow of the timid, eager-to-please Anna I'd known for so long. Then she pressed her lips together and turned away without answering. Saddened, I left the room, wondering how much more damage my surely not *so* unforgivable yearning to experience passion would cause.

Chapter Nine

ANNA HAD SUBSTITUTED PUNCTILIOUS COURTESY FOR HER anger by the time Anfim appeared the next morning for the service marking the sixth hour after sunrise. She didn't fool me, of course, but I chose not to challenge her so long as she avoided obvious rudeness. My greatest fear—that I could meet my own needs or my daughter's but not both— had come to pass, and adjusting to that unwelcome reality consumed much of my energy.

The atmosphere outside did not reflect my mood, which veered from hope to despondency and back with the speed and regularity of a fairground swing. It was the final day of *Maslenitsa*, Butter Week, and from the shrieks of celebration outside our walls I deduced that the townspeople of Moscow were getting in their last round of storming snow forts, sledding, indulging in rich foods, and visiting friends and relatives before Lent began. The noonday sun stood high in the sky, and although it was already the seventh day of March, the nip of frost chapped Anfim's cheeks. He came alone, dressed in his best, and I saw no sign of a horse or carriage. A circle of white against his shoulder indicated an encounter with a stray snowball on the way.

"You left the children at home," I said. "Probably a good idea, under the circumstances. It's surprisingly chilly. Are you ready to tackle Father Job?"

"As ready as I can be. And I left the children behind because they shouldn't see their father getting scolded, even if he deserves it." He laughed as he bent to kiss my cheek, so I knew not to take his comment too seriously. "How did your talk with Anna go?"

"Ugh." I told him everything except her opposition to me marrying beneath my station. I didn't want to hurt him again with reminders that, however close he came to aristocratic status, in some people's minds there would always be a line he could not cross. "I suppose I shouldn't complain. It's heartening to discover that she's not as meek as I thought. But she's raised a barrier between us that I don't know how to breach."

"She'll get over it," he said with the casual air men use to dismiss women's fusses. "She has only one mother, after all."

Tempted to snap at him, I refrained. I needed his support with Father Job; everything else could wait. I tucked my hand in the crook of his arm. "The bell's ringing. Let's go in."

I stayed close to him throughout the service that followed. We stood near the back, a small army of servants between us and the rest of the family. I wasn't sure whether our position kept us from attracting attention in truth or only lessened my sense of being in the public eye, but it certainly prevented us from drawing the notice of Father Job, intent on one element of the ritual after another. Most of the light came from the candles near the royal doors, which hid the altar from the congregation, so we stood surrounded by a gentle perfumed darkness, in stark contrast to the brilliance outside. As my eyes adjusted to the shadows, I picked out various servants—in particular Eva, the maid who had enlightened Anna about the reason for my morning sickness. I briefly weighed my responsibility as the mistress of the house: should I chide Eva for chattering about matters that were not her concern?

I decided to leave her be for the moment. I had too many other things on my mind right then to worry about that one. But when the time came, I'd make sure to give her a piece of my mind.

Anfim and I stayed in the background until the service ended and the worshippers departed for home or for the dining hall in search of their midday meal. Then, with considerable trepidation, I accompanied him as he strode forward and asked Father Job, in the most respectful tone, to spare us a few moments of his time.

Job looked from him to me and back again, studying our faces. What did he see, or think he saw? "Of course," he said. "Please come to my study."

We followed him across the courtyard and entered the main house. With every step, the spasms in my stomach grew more painful. For a while, I feared the child would expel itself midway, but the cramps eased as we entered Father Job's study, before I had to call for assistance. Soon I sat beside Anfim on a bench, uncertain where to start. After the usual greetings and blessings, he said, "I have proposed marriage to Solomonida Petrovna, and she has accepted."

"*Gospodi*," the priest exclaimed. O, Lord. I pondered the implications of that, but Job didn't enlighten us. Instead, he waved a hand, indicating "continue."

In the light that shone through the window, I saw Anfim's color rise. "It seems best that we wed as soon as possible, Father. I fear I have committed the sins of impatience and lust. And with Lent so close, I would like to ensure that the results of my misdeeds do not damage Solomonida Petrovna's reputation."

If he'd slashed Father Job across the face with a whip, I doubt our chaplain could have been more shocked. "I see," he said after a long pause. "That was a grave error, my son." He turned his gaze my way, and my stomach clenched once more. "Hardly one you could have committed alone, however. I am disappointed in you, my daughter. I expected greater virtue and self-restraint from a woman of your age."

I lowered my gaze. Tears pricked at my eyes. I couldn't remember the last time I'd felt so ... shamed. "You're right, Father." I strove to raise my voice above a whisper. "I am as much to blame as Anfim, if not more."

"You are both to blame," the priest said firmly. "What kind of example do you set for your children?"

I couldn't have answered that question if I'd tried. The tears I'd held back so far spilled out, and I couldn't speak. Anfim put his arm around me, then pulled a square of linen from somewhere about his person and pressed it into my hands.

Will he refuse to marry us? Have I alienated my daughter without saving the child I bear? Were my nights of passion worth the cost? I cried harder as fears and doubts assailed me.

"Very well," Job said after a few more rounds of ecclesiastical admonition, his exact words inaudible past my weeping. "Neither of you may take communion for one year. That is the usual penalty for such misbehavior. And although I am loath to reward your sin, if there are indeed consequences, we must not punish an innocent child. Since, as Anfim Fadeyev notes, Lent begins at sunset, I will perform the wedding at the ninth hour. Meet me at the chapel then."

"Yes, Father," I said between sobs. Anfim echoed my words and added, "Thank you."

A cold silence stretched to an uncomfortable length. I kept my head bent, unable to recall another time when I had displeased our household chaplain to this extent.

Then I heard a heartfelt sigh. I looked up, patting my cheeks with Anfim's handkerchief, and saw Father Job shaking his head. "I'm glad you feel remorse, my daughter. Your tears are pleasing to God. Are we not all sinners? And today is Forgiveness Sunday. Go now, with my blessing, and return at the ninth hour."

Anfim helped me to my feet, and we left the priest's study for the room across the hall. No more than a day had passed since we sat there and I told him my news, yet the events of those twenty-four hours had overturned my life.

Once inside, he took me in his arms, and I pressed my face against his coat while he murmured, "Hush, love, the worst is over," and similar words of comfort. The sound of footsteps in the hall told me that Father Job was leaving, probably to seek his dinner before returning for the mid-afternoon service and our wedding. I waited until I heard the outer door close before I dared raise my head.

"That was awful." I held up my right hand, the tips of thumb and finger no farther apart than the top joint of my pinkie. "I feel about this tall."

He stroked my still-wet cheek. "Me too. The worst part was knowing that I'd earned every stern word. But cheer up, dearest. He agreed to perform the ceremony, and that's the important thing. In three hours, we will be husband and wife."

"But will he ever forgive me? I didn't realize how much I counted on his good opinion. And that question he asked about setting a good example for our children ..." I stopped, incapable of finishing the sentence.

"He relented at the end, I thought, with that reference to your tears and Forgiveness Sunday. Priests develop a great understanding of human weakness, even as they try to keep us on the straight and narrow path. It's a tough job, and he does it well." Anfim spoke from experience, I knew, having grown up as a priest's son. He kissed my forehead. "Anna will forgive you too, I'm sure, when she comes to her senses."

"I hope so," I said, but in fact I had no such hope. I wasn't sure I could forgive myself.

Anfim announced he needed to go home and check on his children—promising to return with them and his brothers, if he could persuade them—in plenty of time for the wedding. Back in my chamber, I turned over the peach brocade robe to the maidservants, asking them to baste the rest of the hem and complete the work later. They returned the garment in an impressively short time. I thanked them and dropped it over my head, thrusting the last few clasps into their loops and rubbing the as-yet-unembroidered sleeves for luck. Although my sinful state required sincere concentration on the penitential elements of the remarriage ceremony, my pangs of guilt could not obliterate glimmers of delight at the thought that Anfim and I would soon be united for the rest of our lives. If only the price of happiness were not so high.

Reaching the chapel, I surveyed the company. Anfim and his relatives had not yet arrived. As I expected, I saw only a few servants; most of our people focused their devotions on the midday communion service, as did the family. Recognizing curiosity in the stares of those present, I winced. Eva had probably shared her knowledge of what lay behind my sudden wedding with the entire household. Add public shaming to my list of penances.

"Nervous?" Darya said from behind me. I turned to find her and Niki, the first of our few guests to arrive—not surprising, since they had only to cross the courtyard. Anna followed them in but stopped some distance away, refusing to meet my eyes. Although I hadn't expected immediate forgiveness, I would have appreciated a less obvious display of hostility.

"A little," I told Darya. "Semyon still scares me, even from the grave, but I don't really believe Anfim would treat me that way. I do worry about how his family will react, though." I tipped my head toward my daughter, still staring at the chapel walls as if they contained the clue to some mysterious secret that only she could discern. "Not to mention ours. I see Anna's still snubbing me. Has she said anything to you?"

"Not a word," Darya admitted. "Except that she would like to stay with us. I'm sure she'll relent once she gets used to the idea."

"Yes." But my sister's assurance gave me an idea. I was Anna's mother; she had no right to judge me. And Forgiveness Sunday gave me the perfect opportunity to make amends.

"One moment," I told my sister, then walked forward and bowed before my daughter. "Forgive me," I said, "for disappointing you yesterday, as well as for any harm I have caused you, wittingly or unwittingly, throughout the year."

I waited, eyebrows raised, until she returned my bow with chilly courtesy. "I accept your apology, Mama," she said in a flat voice and without the hint of a smile. She paused, then added, just as I was on the point of reprimanding her, "Please forgive me, too, for my misdeeds past and present."

She had calculated the minimum effort with a kind of perfection. If we were not in church, I would have attempted to break through her reserve, but given the setting, I nodded and moved on, repeating the ritual greeting with Darya and Niki. They responded with greater warmth. Anna must have noticed, but she gave no sign that she cared. Irritated, I studied her, mulling over next steps.

I had yet to settle on a plan when Anfim appeared. Two men who bore a sufficiently strong resemblance to him and to each other that they must be his brothers followed him in. One clasped Lara's hand and the other Tolya's. I held out my arms to the children, who released their uncles long enough to run to me for a hug, then returned to their places at a word from their father. Anfim kissed my forehead before leading me forward. "Permit me to present Postnik," he said, gesturing toward the man with Tolya. "And this is Kirill." He nodded at the other man, and both brothers bent forward from the waist.

I returned the bow, ensuring I matched the depth of their salutations so they would understand that I didn't place myself above them, despite my noble rank. The pair of them regarded me with a certain wary curiosity as Anfim said, "Solomonida Petrovna Sheremeteva, my wife-to-be."

Postnik, as befit the eldest, took the lead. A large man with medium-brown hair and eyes of the same hue, taller than Anfim by half a head and considerably rounder, he had a smile every bit as charming. "Solomonida Petrovna," he said. "I am delighted to make your acquaintance."

He slapped Anfim on the shoulder, hard enough to cause a stagger, and added, "Are you sure you wish to demean yourself with this scamp?"

A chuckle escaped me. Anfim groaned, but the resigned look on his face told me this was an old game between them.

"You know," I said when he didn't respond, "I cannot think of a single word less appropriate to describe Anfim than 'scamp.' But I'm pleased to meet you, too."

"*Bozhe moi*," Postnik said. "Look, Kirill, she takes him seriously. It must be true love."

Kirill—the shortest of the three and, at least at this moment, the most solemn, with striking blue eyes and hair almost black, in stark contrast to his brothers—bowed once more. "My apologies, Lady, that my wife could not reach Moscow in time to attend your ceremony. If you had given us a little more notice …"

I winced at the unspoken rebuke. What right had Anfim's brother to censure us? I raised my chin, intending to put him in his place. Then I noticed Lara, clinging to her uncle's hand and regarding me with wide, questioning eyes. Tolya tipped his head to one side, as if waiting to hear what I would say.

Whatever I did, I must not upset the children. None of this was their fault.

I lowered my chin once more. "That would, of course, have been better," I said with a pretense of serenity. "I appreciate your taking the time to join us on this special day, and I regret that our haste inconvenienced you. I hope to welcome your wife to Moscow soon."

Kirill's mouth tightened at the corners. He definitely disapproved of me. Because Anfim and I had married in haste, or because of the difference in our stations? Either way, it would take some work to win him over, and I experienced a certain resentment at the thought. He was about to become my brother-in-law, though, and any antagonism between us could only upset Anfim. Whether I liked the situation or not, I must try to fix it.

Postnik released Tolya and gave him a little push. "Look, nephew, that pretty blonde girl is signaling to you. Lara, both of you go and join her. And keep an eye on your brother."

I glanced at Anna and realized, to my astonishment, that he told the truth: Anna *was* gesturing "come here." She was getting into the spirit of the ceremony then, no longer holding herself aloof. Perhaps my apology had touched her after all.

The children ran off, and Postnik turned back to me, his eyes crinkling at the corners as my love's so often did. "That's your daughter, I'm guessing," he said to me. "She resembles you. Anna Semyonovna, Anfim said."

"Yes." I gestured to both brothers. "Please, let me introduce you to our friends and family. Father Job will begin the service soon, so we don't have much time. And, look, here are Maria and Alexei! I hoped they would come, but I feared that they, like you, might find it difficult to join us on such short notice."

Indeed, Maria and Alexei, with Lyuba between them, stood at the threshold of the chapel. Relief flowed through me at the sight. The arrival of these dear friends, like the support of Darya and Niki, lessened my sense of isolation.

They approached and kissed my cheeks, then bowed to welcome Anfim and his brothers. "Tsarevich Alexei," I said, "you'll remember Anfim Fadeyev, I'm sure, from the Vorontsovs' Christmas party a couple of years ago. Permit me to present his brothers, Postnik and Kirill Fadeyev." I indicated Maria and Lyuba with an upturned palm, then took a step back, giving the men space. "Alexei's wife, Tsarevna Maria, and her sister, Lyubov Fyodorovna Koshkina."

"A pleasure to make your acquaintance," Alexei said with his usual calm courtesy. "Or to renew it, in Anfim's case.

You've made a great journey since I saw you last. You must tell me about it later."

"All three of us did," Anfim said. "We'll be happy to share the details with you."

Postnik bowed and murmured a greeting. I noticed his flinch when he pronounced the word "tsarevich," and although he hid his reaction quickly, I got the impression he felt daunted by such exalted company. Kirill as well— watching him blush as he echoed his brother's phrase, my indignation with him faded. Maybe he sought my acceptance as I did his. I would keep an eye out for trouble, but in its absence I could hope for the best. We had no choice but to work things out, because our love for Anfim would bind us, no matter what.

"I'm delighted to meet you," Maria said. "I can't wait to hear about your adventures." The men responded to her obvious interest (and, no doubt, her beauty) by preening like chicks greeting their mother. It was a funny image, and I tried not to laugh out loud. I saw Alexei's lips twitch at the sight, but he, too, said nothing. Lyuba bowed to Anfim's brothers before walking to Anna's side, but Postnik and Kirill, basking in the sunshine of Maria's approval, seemed not to notice either the bow or the departure.

"Come," I said, "We'll have time to talk to Maria and Alexei later. There are others I'd like you to meet." I led the three brothers to Darya and Niki, who greeted Anfim with enthusiasm and expressed a heartfelt welcome when I repeated the introductions. With this second presentation, Postnik and Kirill relaxed a bit more, and I understood that it must be hard for them to have their youngest brother elevated above them. How much more difficult to cope with being thrust without warning into a world of people who, in truth, were not much different from themselves but whom they had been taught their whole lives to honor and respect.

But when I brought the three men over to Anna, she greeted them with the same cool reserve she'd chosen to inflict on me.

I caught her arm and pulled her aside. "Behave yourself," I said, quietly but in my firmest tone. "Postnik and Kirill are our guests. We want them to feel comfortable. Whether you're upset with me or not, I expect you to treat them with courtesy."

She scowled, but I stared her down. And it worked. When I released her, she turned and greeted Anfim with a smile. He responded by telling her how pretty she looked. In a friendlier tone, she asked Postnik and Kirill about their journey. Nearby, Lara and Tolya fidgeted until Lyuba bent and muttered something to them that caused them to turn into model children, although Tolya couldn't quite keep from shuffling his feet.

I went over to the three of them. "A long wait, I know," I said to the children. "But you're doing beautifully, and I'm so glad you came to see your papa and me wed. We'll be a real family now, and I want you both to know how much I'm looking forward to that. You're like a son and daughter to me."

"Must we call you Mama?" Lara asked. A fleeting sadness darkened her eyes, and I brushed my hand across her cheek.

"That's up to you," I said. "I am your second mama, not your first. If you'd rather keep calling me Auntie Shura, I won't mind."

"We could call you Mama Shura," Tolya suggested. "I would like that." Lara nodded her agreement.

"I think that would be lovely," I told them. "Why don't you do that?"

Tolya cheered, and I touched a finger to my lips, reminding him we were in church. A relieved smile creased Lara's pretty face. I thanked Lyuba for watching them and rejoined my sister.

I had barely reached her side when the clomp of boot heels against the floor and the swish of fabrics drew my attention to the chapel entrance. There stood Katya with, to my surprise and dismay, a glowering Igor at her side. They strolled toward us—although in Igor's case it looked more like a stomp. His bootheels clicked against the stone flags that lined the floor, while Katya glided along on her high-heeled leather shoes.

The small sense of comfort I'd managed to establish vanished at the sight. "Why did you invite *him?*" I whispered to my sister.

"Niki did it," she murmured. "He wants to undermine any attempts by Igor to deny the legitimacy of your marriage. He's drawn up a document and promised to force our cousin to put his mark on it, swearing he witnessed the ceremony." She meant that Igor would make an X and Nikita would write out the name—probably with Father Job to witness it. "Igor doesn't know about that part yet, but he will soon," she finished.

"He'll have a fit," I said. "But you don't think that will stop his campaign against us, do you?"

Darya shrugged. "Probably not, but he'll have less ammunition." I was still weighing the benefits and flaws of that approach (and wondering why they hadn't shared their plans with me) when Katya reached me. I embraced her, then bowed stiffly to Igor. I didn't have time to do more than mutter greetings before the swing of Father Job's censer announced the beginning of the service. I clasped Katya's hand and said, "We'll talk later. Thank you for coming."

Igor continued to glower, but I ignored him and moved to Anfim's side.

After a while, Father Job called us forward. Having chastised us in private, dear Job expressed no hint of censure as he pronounced us husband and wife. Anfim had captured the priest's state of mind accurately, I concluded. Standing in the underpopulated chapel, the candle in my hands casting distorting shadows in this windowless space, I bowed my head and listened to Job recite the names of previous sinners redeemed by divine mercy and prayers for love and forgiveness, as the remarriage rite required. But my attempts at penitence could not shut out visions of the night to come, forcing me to conclude that I was still a sinner at heart.

Giving up repentance as an exercise in frustration, I concentrated on the service. I maintained my calm well enough until the deacon read the passage about the husband being the head of the household, and wives therefore subject in everything. At those words, a nightmare vision of Semyon floated before my eyes, and I shuddered. Anfim, holding my right hand in his, tightened his grip, and I twisted my head to look at him. Lit by his candle, his clean profile, without the scar that had marked my first husband's, offered the reassurance I needed. I released a long, relieved breath.

Father Job uttered the benediction, and the service drew to its close. Darya, Maria, and Katya surrounded Anfim and me, hugging us and issuing congratulations. Postnik weighed in with sincere good wishes; Kirill repeated the words with less enthusiasm. Nikita dropped a kiss on my cheek and shook Anfim's hand before hauling a grumbling Igor off to the sacristy—to sign the promised document, I assumed. Father Job had already headed in that direction after issuing austere felicitations.

At first, Anna hung back. I watched Lyuba huddle with my daughter, saying phrases I couldn't hear accompanied by gestures that indicated she might be remonstrating with Anna. She must not have liked the answers she received, because she shrugged, then came forward and embraced me, leaving Anna in her corner. But when Lara and Tolya tugged at Anna's sleeves, my daughter relented and brought them to join us. While Anfim dropped to one knee and caught a child in each arm, I hugged Anna and accepted her muted congratulations. Then I released her and leaned over far enough to kiss the tops of the children's heads. When Darya called to them, I grabbed the chance to chat with Katya, as promised.

"Well, haven't you been a wicked girl?" she said in a teasing tone. "And here I always thought of you as the lonely but virtuous widow. Except for that party at my house, the night Igor and I announced our betrothal. Have you been seeing Anfim all that time?"

"Yes and no." I laughed when she raised her brows. "You remind me of my stepmother when you do that—determined to winkle a confession out of me. I didn't see much of Anfim after the party, and he left Moscow barely a month later. He was gone for longer than either of us expected, and we had no contact during that time. Since he came back, though …" I left the sentence unfinished, trusting her to fill in the missing phrase. And despite my suspicions of her, I saw no reason to conceal what must be obvious. I patted my belly. "This was a bit of a surprise. I thought myself too old. But he's a dear man, and I look forward to being his wife."

"He is a dear man." She looked past me, toward the space where Anfim stood with his brothers, then turned her head toward me once more. "I wish you well. Igor's somewhere between furious and baffled, but I think you made a good

choice. Life is not only about rank and advancement."
I stared, amazed. I'd never expected to hear such words
from her. Not for the first time, I wondered whether Katya
regretted joining her life with my cousin's.

Before I had an opportunity to probe, Niki returned
with Igor, whose bad temper had, if anything, intensified.
"Congratulations, Cousin Solomonida," he said in a voice
that sent chills down my spine. "I see you've decided to
throw in your lot with the jumped-up clerk. But don't think
a silly bitch like you will get the better of me. You and your
kin stole what was rightfully mine, and I'll bring the lot of
you down, whatever it takes. It's not just about the estate
anymore. This is war."

His insult pierced my defenses like a knife between the
ribs. *Silly bitch* was one of Semyon's favorite epithets, and
Igor sounded eerily like my first husband as he said those
words. I froze in place, transfixed by the glow of triumph on
his face and incapable of summoning my usual biting retort.

Anfim spun on his heel and broke the spell. "Do *not*
threaten my wife," he told Igor. "Do I make myself clear?"

Igor whirled, his robes flaring like the tail of an outraged
peacock. "You dare challenge a member of the grand prince's
council? A petty servitor like you?"

I dragged my eyes away from them and looked around
for the children. They clung to Darya, but when I held out
my arms, they ran to me. I pulled them close, murmuring
words of comfort.

"I don't care about your rank," Anfim said. "Or how
long we've known each other. Treat Solomonida Petrovna
and Anna Semyonovna with respect, or you'll regret it.
Remember how much I know about you and your intrigues.
And if I hear so much as a *hint* of scandal associated with
their names, you'll answer to me."

He took two steps forward. Igor's face blanched, and he stumbled back as Anfim's brothers moved in, their stance combative. There was no mistaking the message conveyed by the scowls they directed at Igor—we Fadeyevs stand together.

Niki walked forward and turned, shoulder to shoulder with Anfim, to face Igor. "You'll answer to me as well," he said. "I won't hesitate to punch that sneer off your face, Igrushka, and you know it."

Igor rallied, his hands clenched. I thought he might be the one to land a blow, and in church. Someone should intervene. I searched for Father Job, but he hadn't returned from the sacristy.

Katya gripped her husband's elbow and murmured soothing phrases that became stronger and less accommodating when he shook her off. She cast an apologetic glance in my direction, and I smiled—a rather fixed expression, no doubt—to show her I appreciated her efforts.

I reminded myself that behind the bravado stood Igor, the boy I'd once pelted with acorns. "Stop it, cousin," I said in the firm tone I used with misbehaving children. "You started this fight. You can end it."

He turned his minotaur glare on me. "And why should I listen to you?"

Anfim and his brothers emitted a concerted growl. I searched for an answer that might silence him and didn't find one. But as I braced myself for a brawl, Alexei lost patience. "Enough," he roared at a level guaranteed to subdue an entire horde of raging nomads.

I blinked at him, impressed. *So much for calm courtesy.*

"This is a wedding, not a battlefield. Control yourselves," he ordered. Having shocked the company into silence, he moderated his aggressive stance, although I still heard the snap in his voice. From the stunned expression on every face but Maria's (she regarded her husband with satisfaction), I concluded that I wasn't the only one who'd forgotten that he commanded armies. This incident must not even qualify as a skirmish in his book.

"Thank you," I told him. "You are absolutely right." When he nodded, I turned to my husband. "And thank *you*, dear heart, for speaking up on my behalf." I glanced at Darya, then addressed our family and friends. "We have supper prepared. Won't you join us?" I extended a hand in the direction of the sacristy. "Where's Father Job? He's welcome to eat with us."

"He said he had to get home, but he sends his good wishes." Niki didn't step away from Anfim, but he did relax his warlike pose. "Let's move to the dining room, as Solomonida suggests."

"Let's not." The edge in Igor's voice underlined his annoyance. "You got what you wanted. You can celebrate the rest of this farce without us. Katya, come."

As if she were a dog. A flash of annoyance crossed her face, but she said, "As you wish, husband."

Head of the household, indeed. Stunned by this new evidence that Igor's amiable if foolish surface hid a roiling cauldron of resentment, I watched my cousin stalk from the chapel. Katya trailed him like a servant, discomfort evident in the set of her shoulders and her tightly gripped hands. Glancing at Anfim, I saw him shaking his head and knew he'd marked the exchange as well. I whispered in his ear, "How glad I am to have you for a spouse instead of Igor."

The door slammed behind our cousin and his wife as I reached the last word. "You remember that the next time you're upset with me," he murmured in a teasing tone. "*Gospodi*, I'm glad they left. What an uncomfortable meal that would be. I have a stone in my stomach just thinking about it."

"Agreed." I took a deep breath and released it. I would deal with Igor's malice tomorrow. Tonight, I intended to relax and enjoy my wedding after a long and eventful day.

Although I hadn't yet resolved my dilemma, I could take pride in the progress I'd made since this morning. By marrying the man I loved, I had chosen to fulfill my own needs while saving the child I bore from the stigma of illegitimacy. Repairing my relationship with my daughter and seeing her safely settled must come next, but that quest, too, could wait for another day.

I turned to the others and added in a louder voice, "Will you not eat with us?"

A chorus of acceptances enveloped us, although Anna's voice was not among them. Suppressing a groan, I took Anfim's hand in mine, and we led the way out of the church.

Chapter Ten

I SURVEYED THE MAIN DINING ROOM AND NODDED IN satisfaction at the sight of the oblong table, surrounded by chairs, off to one side. Before leaving for their homes, the servants had pushed the usual furniture against the far wall. The present arrangement would work much better for a small group.

"You can remove six of the chairs," I told Mishka. "Igor Grigorevich left with his wife, Masha has already taken the children home, and I have given Lady Anna permission to eat with Lady Lyuba in the sewing room."

As I spoke the last phrase, Mishka sent me a sympathetic glance, from which I deduced that my daughter's opposition to my marriage was no secret from the household. But like the good steward he was, he refrained from comment. Instead, he bowed and passed the order along to Petka, who summoned another man to help him remove the chairs.

When they were done, Anfim led me to the far side of the table. As a newlywed couple, we would normally sit at the center of a long board, surrounded on both sides by the members of the wedding party. With eight people spread out around one table, there was no center. No real wedding party, either, given the hasty preparations. So I sat nearest the window, with Anfim to my right and an empty chair beyond him. Darya took over as hostess, directing everyone else where she wanted them.

"I'll sit next to the new bridegroom," Postnik announced with a grin. "Someone has to raise a few toasts and embarrass him." Without giving Kirill a chance to protest (although I doubted Kirill had any such intention), Postnik plomped onto his selected chair. As the last guest settled into place, the servants entered, bearing the first course.

The men sat together and so did the women, in true Muscovite fashion. Darya had argued for such an arrangement because it eased conversation—although I soon discovered she wasn't quite right about that.

"Will you tell us more about your business?" I heard Nikita ask Postnik. "You're based in Nizhny Novgorod, your brother says. What do you trade?"

"Whatever comes my way." He launched into a long and oddly compelling tale of exchanging furs with forest dwellers, bargaining with the nomads for horses, and cutting deals on everything from pottery to leather boots with the merchants of Kazan. Some of his encounters sounded too fantastic for words, but he held the entire table spellbound.

As he talked, servants circled us, placing baskets of bread at each end, flanked by platters of sliced cheese and small bowls of fragrant roasted nuts. So close to Lent, meat and fish were already on the list of forbidden foods, but we had a few more hours to use up our dairy products and eggs. "I think this is the quietest wedding supper I've ever attended," I said to Maria as Postnik's extended yarn gave way to more general conversation among the men.

"Does it bother you?" Maria asked. "No roomful of guests, shouting toasts and congratulations?"

Did it? I loved parties, but … "No," I said after a short pause. "There's so much pressure on a bride. And this wedding will cause talk, for several reasons. I'd much rather celebrate with selected friends and family than deal with perfect strangers pounding their cups on the table and roaring demands that we kiss when they're not slipping back-stabbing comments into the toasts."

"Even in the immediate family, not everyone seems welcoming," she said, too quietly for Anfim's brothers to hear. "And I don't mean Anna or your cousin Igor, although they certainly put on a show." She tipped her chin in the direction of Kirill, indicating whom she had in mind.

"True," I admitted. "He'll take some persuading, although Postnik seems friendly enough. Kirill has a wife I must win over as well, although she lives in Smolensk, so who knows when we will meet?"

The servants distributed one more round of *zakuski*—small appetizers easily eaten with the fingers—and left the room. I watched Maria transfer a cheese straw from the closest plate to the wooden trencher in front of her, then did the same. Only when its buttery, salty taste filled my mouth did I realize the extent of my hunger. Mornings still made me queasy, and the tension of confessing to Father Job followed by our hasty preparations for the wedding ceremony had kept thoughts of food at bay ever since. With those stresses behind me, I felt ravenous. Even so, I ate slowly, sampling a mushroom turnover here, a handful of nuts there. Darya had arranged a feast, so I could anticipate many more dishes to come.

The servants returned with brass cups and jugs of red wine, traditional at weddings. Alexei raised the first toast, and I took a sip in response. The rich taste reminded me of the Christmas party that had started me on the road that led to this night. How long ago it seemed!

I drank a bit more, then set the cup aside. After a while, Maria asked, "Are you well?"

Hearing concern in her voice, I made no attempt to dissemble. "Very well, except in the mornings. The last few days have been difficult, though."

"I see," she said. "I wondered. It's as well you found out this week rather than next, in that case. Having to wait two months would be nerve-racking. Good that the priest agreed to wed you on such short notice, too. But Father Job has always responded well in a crisis." I listened for hints of surprise or condemnation, but instead she finished with, "Anna's behavior can't help."

"No," I admitted. "I do regret leaving her here." I explained the arrangement I'd worked out with Darya and the reasons for it. "If she won't talk to me, though, how can I reassure her? Her first reaction was anger—amazing because it's so unlike her, but rather reassuring. It shows she can defend herself if she cares enough. But now she's just shutting me out."

"She won't tell you what's upsetting her?" Maria asked.

"That I'm throwing myself away on a clerk," I said, again speaking in a near-whisper out of concern for Anfim's feelings. "I don't think that's her real objection, though. She likes Anfim. You saw that in the church. She loves his children, and he's a state secretary, not a clerk. Is she angry because she believes I put someone else's interests ahead of hers, because she feels abandoned, because I gave her too little warning, or for some other reason altogether?"

The servants returned, cutting off our conversation. They removed the *zakuski*, replacing them with pancakes glistening with butter and dabs of sour cream, accompanied by bowls of roasted carrots and thinly sliced sour cabbage. I had almost forgotten my own question by the time they left and we could talk again.

Maria, however, had not. "Anna's young still," she said. "You've been her unwavering protector for her entire life. I doubt she has any memory of her father—certainly no good ones—so you are her main source of support and guidance. How many of us like to think of our parents as people in their own right, capable of falling in love and acting on their desires? I remember how shocked I was—disgusted, even—when my father remarried in midlife and mooned over his wife like a man half his age. And I was twenty then, not fifteen. That you and Anfim anticipated your vows only heightens Anna's realization that you're imperfect, like everyone else. If so, she's not likely to admit what's troubling her, no matter how hard you press her. She may not know herself."

I thought about Anna and what she'd said to me. "You could be right. The comment about Anfim threw me off, because I'd begun to realize how much we"—I indicated the table with my hand, meaning the boyars as a group—"take it for granted that birth means more than intelligence or effort. Maybe it does bother her that I married an official, just as it bothers her that I'll allow her to stay here if she chooses. But it was the news that I intended to marry *quickly* that upset her most. Eva had explained to her what that meant."

"Don't worry," Maria assured me. "She'll get over it in time."

Darya had stayed out of the discussion about Anna, but now she rejoined the conversation, regaling Maria with the story of Igor and his renewed attempt to grab the estate and finishing with, "And that's why the men nearly came to blows in the church." She grinned at me. "I'm proud of Anfim, standing up for you like that."

"Did you think I wouldn't?" Anfim asked. I wondered how much else he'd overheard.

"Of course not," Darya told him. Alexei stood and toasted us again, and Niki followed his lead. Postnik joined in, raising a goblet "To my youngest brother and the beauty who has held his heart for the last three years. May they always enjoy the happiness they experience today!"

No sooner had the men downed their toasts than he continued, punching Anfim on the shoulder once more but addressing me, "Did he tell you about the Tatar maiden he spurned for you?"

"What? No, he did not!" Openmouthed, I stared at my new husband, who flushed scarlet, although a smile played around his mouth.

"Tell us now," Darya said. "You can't throw out a line like that and not explain."

"Yes, what happened?" Maria asked. "We want every detail."

"It was nothing," Anfim muttered. "My brother exaggerates."

"I do not," Postnik announced in ringing tones. "Very well, if he's shy, I'll do the deed. Kirill can remind me if I leave anything out. But you should have shared the story yourself, brother. You're too modest for your own good." He ruffled Anfim's hair as though my husband were no older than Tolya, and I couldn't help laughing at the pained expression on Anfim's face.

Then Postnik began, and I concentrated my attention on him. "We were halfway between Kazan and Astrakhan, more or less, right where the Samara River joins the Volga. Pirates lie in wait there to attack travelers as they pass, because the Great Mother shifts her course to flow south, and you can't see ships lurking in the bend."

He stopped to take a swig of wine, and Kirill, who had so far said next to nothing, picked up the tale. "Two of the ships ahead of us were captured and robbed, but we managed to slip past. We made it a good way down the river, to a place called Perevolok. There we fell foul of Sheikh-Mamai Bey and his nomadic Tatars. They dragged us to his camp and confiscated our goods. Anfim here—"

He nodded at my husband, and Postnik grabbed the chance to interrupt. "Anfim talked to them for a long time in Tatar. I've been trading in the east for two decades, but I can't speak the language like that. He insists it's because of his months in captivity, being surrounded by a foreign tongue waking and sleeping, and maybe there's something to that. In any case, he convinced them to release our boat and half of our cargo, keeping the other half as a 'gift' to show our respect for their leader. In return for being allowed to steal our goods, Sheikh-Mamai gave us a girl he'd raided from some other horde the week before, to go with the ship and our half."

"Not us," Kirill put in. "The girl went to Anfim, as a token of Sheikh-Mamai's regard."

I couldn't stop staring at this man I loved and had just married. "And you refused to accept her?" I said, struggling to make sense of what I was hearing.

"No." Anfim took over, probably because it made little sense to hold back by then. "Sheikh-Mamai would have considered that a great dishonor. He might have killed the lot of us on the spot. Besides, I recognized her from my captivity in Ogodai Khan's camp. Her mother was one of the cooks. They're enemies, Ogodai and Sheikh-Mamai. I didn't know much then about how the bey captured Kiraz, but I wanted to free her if possible. So I thanked him profusely for his generosity, and off we went."

"Pretty little thing," Postnik said, waving his goblet. "Fourteen, fifteen—she didn't seem too sure. Timid, seldom spoke even when spoken to, but if she'd been captured in a raid, that's not surprising. Being handed over to three Russians, whether or not she recognized Anfim, must have terrified her. We treated her well, though, and my brother made sure he was never alone with her. That's when I realized how much he must love his Moscow beauty." He grinned at me as he lifted the cup in a silent toast, and I felt my cheeks warm in response to his obvious admiration.

"We left with her," Anfim added. "I'd have liked to return her to her home, but that would have delayed us twice as long. Fall had set in by then, and Kiraz told us she was captured while the horde was moving to its winter grazing lands. You've never seen the steppe; it's vast. The chances of finding them in motion were almost nil, and once we reached their destination, we'd have had to make the river journey down the Volga again. We might not be so lucky the second time. We traveled with Kiraz as far as Astrakhan; then I apprenticed her to a silk weaver."

He touched the sleeve of my peach robe. "The woman gave me this in exchange."

"It's beautiful." I stared at the silk as if I'd never seen it before, wondering at the secrets it concealed.

Anfim addressed Alexei. "That was six months or so into our journey. I'm sorry: I forgot about her until Postnik brought her up. I should have told you as soon as I came back. You can let your brother know where she is, so her family won't continue to grieve. Maybe they can go after her."

"I'll do that." Alexei frowned in concentration. "And the girl was untouched when you left her? Her mother will ask, I'm sure. I may as well reassure them when I write."

"So she said." Anfim picked up his goblet and took a sip before continuing. "I have no reason to doubt her. Sheikh-Mamai has many women, and he showed little interest in Kiraz as he handed her over to us. Eighteen months have passed since then, so I can't swear she still is. But *I* didn't touch her. I wouldn't take advantage of a child." He, too, saluted me with his cup. "I prefer women old enough to know their own minds."

Alexei nodded his understanding, and Postnik started another round of toasts. I pretended to take part in every one, but I couldn't get the story out of my mind. It wasn't that I disbelieved Anfim, exactly. It seemed quite unlike him to pursue a reluctant and frightened girl—no older than Anna, from the sound of it. His brothers vouched for him, and by telling Alexei where to find Kiraz and insisting on her purity when he left her, Anfim had made statements that could be checked. But even if he *had* slept with the girl he'd received as a gift, I'd lived long enough to know that men far from home often permitted themselves such encounters without attributing much significance to them.

It was the suggestion of his own heroism that embarrassed him rather than some wrongdoing, I concluded. But the tale reminded me yet again that, despite the passion we shared and my certainty that he was different from my dead and unlamented first husband, I still had a great deal to learn about Anfim. And that, I had to admit, was both an exciting and a troubling thought.

Postnik didn't stop after revealing one secret. He continued to dig up tales of Anfim's boyhood and the long journey east while Kirill, lowering his barriers as the wine continued to flow, interjected the occasional joking reminiscence. Anfim retaliated, and soon the three of them were doing their best to top one another. I found out more about them in those hours of nonstop toasts and anecdotes than I'd learned from Anfim since we met. And the whole time, even as I laughed along with the rest, I couldn't help wondering where this journey would lead me next.

It led me first to Anfim's house, long after dark. His brothers accompanied us the first part of the way, their arms slung around his shoulders while I walked ahead. When we reached Ilinka Street, they continued on, heading for the estate where I'd visited Anfim on that dreadful day, more than two years ago, when he'd broken my heart. We turned right toward the new house. Their shouted good wishes drew the attention of passersby, who stopped and stared.

"It's good that Masha took your children home right after the ceremony," I said as I waved goodbye. "The party lasted longer than I expected."

"Yes," Anfim said. "And imagine them hearing those raucous stories. My authority as a father would be destroyed. May the devil fly away with Postnik and Kirill!" He laughed at the memory.

"Postnik is charming," I told him. "Alas, Kirill dislikes me, although I hope to win him over someday."

"He's the most conventional of the three of us, so having a highborn sister-in-law bothers him." Anfim took my elbow as we approached a cross-street. "He's not quite sure how to act around you. I expect he'll warm up once he realizes you won't snub him because he's a merchant."

I decided not to argue. Anfim might be right, and if not, there was little either of us could do about it tonight. Also, he distracted me by gripping my arm and saying, "Watch out."

"For what?" I searched the streets for signs of danger. Dusk had fallen during our wedding ceremony, and hours had passed since then. The scarcity of lanterns made passage hazardous, and no doubt cutpurses roamed at will along the crowded streets.

"I don't want you to trip." He pointed ahead to where a small snow fort, already abandoned and crumbling, blocked our path.

Flickering flames lit the sky, marking the bonfires where residents burned straw effigies of Lady Maslenitsa to mark the ending of the eight-day celebration in her name. Plumes of smoke rose above the wooden walls of the urban estates that characterized this part of town, and soot tickled the inside of my nostrils. Through one set of open gates I heard a sizzling sound and saw people in the simple clothes of servants tossing leftover pancakes into the flames. The greasy, smoky smell of burning butter turned my stomach, and I quickened my pace, hoping to escape the stink before my gorge rose. Anfim lengthened his stride to match mine. I appreciated his not demanding an explanation. Perhaps the odor got to him, too.

Despite the snow piled wherever we looked, the many bonfires had forced the lingering frost to loosen its grip, if only for a night. We crossed the street and walked hand in hand toward Anfim's new house—the home we now shared—no more than a few doors away. I asked him what the men were discussing among themselves while I chatted with Maria and Darya.

"Politics," he said. "And what to make of Igor Grigorevich's behavior at the wedding."

When I opened my mouth to ask for more details, Anfim touched a finger to my lips, then bent to kiss me. "Can't it wait till tomorrow? We've been married four hours

157

at the most, and I want to savor the magic of knowing that, no matter what happens from here on, we are one in the eyes of the Church and society. To welcome you into my home as my wife. The house is right over there." He pointed to an entrance no more than a pebble's throw from where we stood, and I realized that while we walked and talked, we'd covered more distance than I'd imagined.

I tucked my hand in his arm and laughed, comfortable for the first time with the reality that whatever I'd believed about my own fertility, I would bear Anfim's child. "How splendid it will be to share a room and have it not be a sin!"

"Indeed," he said as we reached the gate. "I can hardly wait. Let me introduce you to our house spirit." He yowled like a cat—the only animal able, according to legend, to communicate with the *domovoi*, or house spirit. From somewhere in the night, a real cat wailed in response.

"You must have been practicing," I said, still laughing. "The local felines think you're one of them."

In answer, he pulled me close and kissed me hard in full view of those passing by. They cheered, no doubt alerted by the yowl to our newly married state. Then he stepped across the threshold, proving that he would be master in his own home, and held out his hand. "Solomonida Petrovna, dear wife of my heart, meet my *domovoi*. *Domovoi*, this is your new mistress. Treat her well."

Another round of cheers sounded, and I looked around. Every Russian loves a wedding, and another small crowd of passersby had stopped tossing snowballs and lighting flames long enough to wish us well. Tears of joy pricked my eyes as I accepted my husband's outstretched hand and took the crucial step across the threshold into my new life.

Chapter Eleven

April 6, 1546

FOR THE NEXT MONTH, I IMMERSED MYSELF IN THE DETAILS of consolidating my new family and household. Although I knew that I needed to confront my cousin and heal the breach with Anna, my good intentions foundered in an apparently endless stream of domestic obstacles: acquiring staff, reestablishing the routines my sister and I had set up for the children, obtaining supplies, and hosting a party for Lara and Darya, whose name days came a week apart, among others. I hoped the party would at least advance my reconciliation with my daughter, but that was not to be. Lara's delight in turning ten and becoming the center of her newly expanded family's attention for an afternoon lightened every heart but Anna's. My daughter stayed at her aunt's house, blaming her absence on monthly cramps. Darya insisted Anna was telling the truth, but I took small consolation from that. I was not there to care for her, and until I met the needs of all my children, I could not relax.

My second marriage, in contrast, suited me well—so well that I wondered why I'd resisted taking another husband for so long. But just as I became convinced that I had made enough progress to redirect my goals toward foiling Igor and addressing my daughter's fears, life tossed a new complication my way. On Friday, April 6, Anfim returned home late and announced that he had orders to leave for Kazan the next day.

I couldn't repress a moan of dismay. "So soon? You promised to stay with me until the baby arrives!"

He kissed me in welcome before dropping onto the chair facing me. "I promised to stay with you forever, my love. And I intend to do that to the best of my ability. But I have my orders. I can't refuse to go, although I'll come back as fast as I can."

I knew, of course, that he couldn't turn down an assignment from the grand prince. He'd wind up in jail, if not worse. Those rumors about his split loyalties would grow tendrils like vines and ensnare him. "I understand." I tried not to sound as grudging as I felt. "But why you? I thought becoming state secretary meant fewer long journeys."

"It's a great honor," he said mildly. "The grand prince appointed me to accompany Prince Dmitry Belsky, who handles most foreign affairs; Prince Dmitry Paletsky, who's back in favor for the moment; and another state secretary. I told you three weeks ago that the last envoy had returned from Kazan with good news: the populace has agreed to accept the grand prince's choice as khan. We're to see Shah-Ali installed before they change their minds. The moment that's done, we'll leave for home."

"Poor Lara and Tolya—they're just starting to believe that they won't turn around and find that you've vanished once more." That was a low blow, and I knew it. I regretted the words the moment they left my mouth. "Sorry. I shouldn't have said that. Still, you'll be gone for months."

"It will be hard on them, I know," he admitted. "And on you. But it's not like the last time. We're riding on government business, so we'll change horses frequently rather than stop and rest them every few days. Three weeks to Kazan, I'd guess—perhaps less. Then the ceremony, and I can leave for home as soon as the princes decide there's no chance of an uprising. God willing, I'll be gone two months at the most."

"Don't worry. I'll explain it to the children." A lifetime's training that a wife should support her husband when service assignments called him away was resurfacing, and I abandoned my earlier objections.

An ugly thought pushed its way into my brain. Cousin Igor had gone quiet in the last month. Even Niki hadn't overheard new rumors about Anfim—just wilder versions of the originals, propagating like the weeds they were. I hadn't forgotten his threats at our wedding, though. Arranging this unexpected assignment—less than three months had passed since Anfim received assurances that his new position would keep him in Moscow for a while—struck me as exactly the kind of underhanded scheme Igor would embrace. As a member of the grand prince's council, he did have a say in diplomatic appointments.

"You're sure Igor doesn't want to put you in harm's way?" I asked. "I can imagine him distorting the details of your journey to show you in a bad light, or even taking advantage of a dangerous situation to attack you more directly. He swore he would destroy us, whatever it took—remember?"

"It's possible." Anfim frowned, then leaned forward to clasp my hands. "Although the orders came from Tretiakov. But you're right: Igor Grigorevich did declare war. I'll keep my eyes open, I promise."

At least he hadn't denied the possibility. "Maybe he seeks to separate us so he can cause trouble while you're gone."

"Maybe," he affirmed. "Let's take steps to prevent that. Nikita Andreevich will watch over you during my absence. Why not ask him to let Laika stay here while I'm away? Since Kirill already left and Postnik intends to head back to Kazan with us, I'd feel better about your safety if you had the dog in the house."

I sighed. I rather doubted Laika would offer much protection against Igor, her former master, but since Anfim had to leave, no matter what, the dog's presence would reassure him. And she would no doubt aid us against any intruder *other* than my cousin.

"That's a good idea. I'll ask." I gripped his hands in return. "And forgive me for being so crotchety. I know you have to go where you're sent. It took me by surprise, that's all. I'll miss you."

"And I'll miss you," he said. "I'd hoped to spend the whole spring and summer with you and the children."

Having no more to say on that subject, I shifted to another. "You didn't tell me why Tretiakov picked you for this mission to Kazan."

He reached forward and pulled me onto his lap. "I didn't, did I? The Treasury mostly wants me to ensure the royal gifts are delivered on time and undamaged. They always assign state secretaries to the government part of these missions, you know, even though it's the princes and boyars who will represent the grand prince at the installation ceremony. And since I visited the area recently, I seemed like the logical choice. I speak Tatar better than most of my colleagues and have more acquaintance with the local customs, so Tretiakov thinks I'm less likely to raise the hackles of the very people we want to keep on our side."

"It's a good story," I said. "Well thought out and quite plausible. But I remember the last time you traveled east. You can't expect me to believe that delivering gifts is your whole assignment. I bet you're gathering information again. Why? Moscow doesn't need to conquer Kazan if it can put a puppet khan on the throne."

Anfim laughed and tapped the tip of my nose. "How did I win the heart of such a clever woman? Alas, the nobles in Kazan change their minds about who they want to lead them as often as they change their coats. Today it's Shah-Ali, but tomorrow Safa-Girei may convince them to back him once more. So we need to be ready when that happens."

Which sounded like a confirmation to me. I sighed and put my arms around his neck. "Well, if I have to say goodbye to you in the morning, my love, let's get you packed so we can make the most of this evening."

"An excellent idea," he said.

The next day, I watched Anfim mount his horse and set off for the Kremlin, where his brother Postnik intended to join him. Government missions traveled with an escort of soldiers, and as Anfim had told me the evening before, his brother didn't want to miss the opportunity for official protection when heading out along often dangerous roads. As soon as my husband passed through the gate, I ran for the top floor in the hope of catching sight of him in the narrow streets, but I reached the window just in time to watch him turn a corner. From there, other houses and their walls blocked him from view.

I collected a melancholy Lara and Tolya from their nanny, Masha. "Let's go visit Auntie Darya and Uncle Niki," I said. "Your papa wants us to ask if Laika can stay with us while he's gone, and I expect they'll let her. But we should go and fetch her in person."

They shouted their approval, so I gathered they liked the idea of having Laika live with us until their father returned. Masha, in contrast, looked glum, although she didn't protest.

"You needn't come with us," I told her. "I remember you saying you wanted to oversee the washing." I rumpled Tolya's hair. "This bogatyr goes through shirts and trousers so fast I think his dragons must use them to rub their sweaty brows." He giggled at that, as I'd known he would. "We'll walk to the house, ask to borrow the dog, and bring her back straightaway if my sister agrees. I don't expect to be gone more than an hour, so if the maids have any questions—about dinner, for example—ask them to wait until I return."

"Yes, Lady." Masha dipped her head in acknowledgment of the orders and, I suspected, appreciation for the reprieve of not being required to give up an hour to accompany us. Tolya required constant supervision, so carving out time to perform the rest of her duties wasn't easy.

I turned to the children. "Get your jackets, and we'll go. It's a lovely day, but not quite warm enough for shirt sleeves." They ran to obey, and in what seemed like no time we were out on the street.

It was indeed a lovely day, mild and sunny. The noise from the nearby market stalls was more subdued than usual because Lent limited what foods could be eaten and therefore made purchases of many items unnecessary. The restrictions also meant that the strong odors of hanging meat and poultry were absent for once. The butchers would not reappear for two and a half weeks, and the cheesemakers and dairymen, even the purveyors of oil and fish, were banned as well. Only the bread bakers and vegetable purveyors called their wares. Anfim's new estate had ovens and a kitchen garden, though, so we hastened past the stalls, stopping only to savor the aromas of herbs and fresh-baked bread. Laika, if we brought her back, would need meat, but I had checked the stores the day after moving in, so I had no fear that we would run out before Easter arrived to fill the marketplace once more.

When I reached my sister's estate, I found her in the courtyard talking with Mishka. Laika romped near the stables, and Tolya gave Darya a perfunctory hug before dashing across the wooden planks to throw his arms around the dog. Lara gazed at me, her eyes pleading.

"Yes," I told her. "You may find Anna and tell her about Papa leaving." To Darya I added, "Is she upstairs?"

"She is," Darya said. "Off you go, Lara. You know the way." Lara ran up the stairs, and my sister turned to me. "Anfim left again?"

"This morning." I explained about the unexpected mission. "He asked if Laika could stay with us, as protection, until he returns. It will be a couple of months."

"Absolutely," she said. "How sad that he's been sent away. The two of you must just be growing comfortable with each other. Although I can hardly believe that a month has gone by since your wedding. It seems like yesterday." She put a hand on my arm. "Go inside. I've almost finished with Mishka. I'll meet you in the main sitting room, and you can tell me what you've been doing. I want to hear about the baby, too."

"I can't stay long," I said. "I promised Masha we'd be back within the hour. I haven't told the servants what to prepare for the midday meal yet." Although with only me and the children to please—and during Lent!—that hardly mattered. A diet of bread and vegetable soup didn't change much from day to day.

"We'll feed you here." Darya had obviously reached the same conclusion. "They can manage cabbage soup and buckwheat groats for themselves without your supervision. Mishka, send one of the stable boys to alert Masha that Lady Solomonida won't need a midday meal, only supper."

"Yes, tsaritsa," I said, teasing her. "How authoritative you've become! But I'll accept your dinner with pleasure. I want to hear about Andrusha and the new one on the way as well."

With that settled, I climbed the stairs to the second floor.

Nikita arrived not long after we'd finished our meal of bread, steamed slivered beets and carrots, and stuffed cabbage rolls. Although Lenten, it was not really austere: the bread dark and chewy, the vegetables brilliant in the April sunshine, and the cabbage rolls surprisingly rich and flavorful, with a meaty texture that derived from the mixture of mushrooms and barley that filled the tightly wrapped green cylinders. Niki took the seat next to me and helped himself to a cabbage roll before pouring kvass from the jug at his right. I took the opportunity to share my suspicion that Igor had taken steps to send my husband away and my fears of what might happen as a result. Niki frowned and expressed his sympathy, promised to investigate, and agreed that Laika should stay at our house until Anfim returned.

"I'm glad you're here," he said once we reached the end of that topic. "I thought I'd have to send someone to fetch you. I think I've found a potential husband for Anna." Darya and I both exclaimed at that news.

"Seriously?" I asked before my sister had rallied enough to pose what I felt certain would be the same question.

"Who?" In truth, thanks to the drama leading up to my hasty marriage, I'd almost forgotten the plan to find Anna a husband and thereby undercut any attempts by Igor to ruin her reputation.

"Yuri Vorontsov," Niki said. "Gavriil's son. That should not only tie Igrushka's hands but mollify Gavriil, if he is indeed holding a grudge against our family. Maria has invited the four of us—including Anna—to visit this afternoon. Yuri will be there, and we can talk with him."

"Talk with him?" Darya asked. "He's back from his posting in Kolomna, then?"

"He and his cousin Dmitry. They rode in together yesterday afternoon. Anna's name must have come up in conversation the first evening, because Dmitry marched Yuri over here this morning to let me know that Yuri needs a bride."

"I wonder who mentioned her. Cousin Igor would only have slandered her." I shivered at the memory of my cousin's malice.

"Well, from what I know of Dmitry, that might have been enough to send him hotfooting it over here," Niki said dryly. "He would recognize the slander for the lie it is, and he might push the match just to spite Igor. But be that as it may, Yuri's a good choice for Anna in lots of ways. Most important, his father has the grand prince's ear. Yuri's standing isn't high yet because of his youth, but he'll outrank your nasty cousin one day, and his branch of the family is more prosperous."

"His youth? How old is he?" I perked my ears at this promising development. I'd heard Yuri's name before today, but I knew little about him except that he was Gavriil's youngest son. I'd assumed the friendship between Yuri and his cousin Dmitry meant they must also be close in age. And that worried me, because Dmitry was twenty-six or twenty-seven. Twelve years' difference was a wide gap for a bride of fifteen, however appealing a potential candidate might be in other ways.

"He turned eighteen last month, so not much older than Anna. He's a good lad, a bit rough around the edges like a lot of military men but honest and plain-spoken and kind." Niki placed another cabbage roll in his bowl and tore off a chunk of bread to mop up the sauce. "As soon as we're done here, we'll visit Maria, and you can see for yourselves."

I stood. "I should take the children and the dog back to my place first. I let Masha stay behind so she could instruct the other maids on how to get the stains out of Tolya's clothes, so she's not here to supervise them."

"Oh, I remember those stains," Darya said. "How does he manage to attract so many different kinds of dirt? And his trousers! I swear when he left here every single pair had ripped knees."

"They still do," I said. "Even though I had the whole lot of them replaced when I moved in four weeks ago, they're back to looking as if they belong in the rag bag. I told Masha to get the maids sewing new ones, but how long will they last? Not to mention that it doesn't take him more than a month and a half to outgrow the few clothes he doesn't destroy. As for the dirt, you wait. Andrusha will be every bit as bad. The moment he leaves the nursery, he'll become a little mud pile with legs."

I left them laughing at that and went to reclaim Tolya and Laika.

"We'll meet you with the carriage at your house," Niki called as I reached the door. I waved a hand in acknowledgment.

I found Eva, whom I'd left to watch over Anna, in the next room. Had she been listening at the door? "What are you doing here?" I demanded. "You have no business in this room. You weren't eavesdropping, I hope."

She blushed and didn't speak. I remembered my vow to chastise her when I next saw the opportunity. "Off you go. Anna Semyonovna and Lara Anfimova are in the sewing room. Tell Lara to join us downstairs, and let my daughter know we will be visiting Tsarevna Maria in an hour or so. Then help her change her dress, if need be. But no gossiping about things that don't concern you, or I'll ensure you work in the kitchen from now on."

She blushed again. "Yes, Lady Solomonida. I'm sorry if I've offended you."

"And so you should be." I gave her a curt nod, and she hurried off. The moment I saw her go, I went to collect Tolya. Before long, Lara arrived, and the three of us headed home with Laika.

An hour or so later, dressed in a leaf green robe embroidered in a darker shade around neck and cuffs, I ducked my head and joined Darya and Anna in the carriage. Niki rode alongside. My daughter's delight at this outing won me a smile and a "Good afternoon, Mama." Progress!

I didn't comment on the change but instead returned her salutation in kind, adding, "Did Auntie Darya explain why we're visiting Maria?" Although she nodded in return, I noticed the tension on her face. "We're going to see, no more," I assured her. "No big decisions today."

Another nod. "I understand," she said. From the way she twisted her hands together and bit her lip as she stared out the window, I assumed her anxiety remained high. Even so, I saw reason to hope that the situation between us would continue to improve.

When we reached Maria's house a short time later, her housekeeper ushered us into a sitting room that already contained five people. Alexei, Maria, and Lyuba were there, naturally, since they lived in the house. I recognized Dmitry Vorontsov, the brother of our neighbor and fair-weather friend Katya: a good-looking man of medium height and a soldier's build, with gray eyes and chestnut hair. He might have left the house not long after his arrival, as Niki had said, but he had waited long enough for a servant to trim his hair and beard. His dark blue robe looked opulent enough for court.

With wavy hair of a rich auburn, obviously inherited from his father, and dark brown eyes, a clean-shaven chin, and a winning smile, the younger man sitting next to Dmitry was handsome enough to attract Anna's interest. He rose when we walked in, as did Dmitry, and the two of them bowed. I saw then that Yuri was half a head taller than his cousin, which pleased me, since my daughter, slender and willowy, already matched me in height. His eager welcome pleased me more, since it spoke of a friendly, outgoing personality. I could imagine Anna blossoming in the sunshine of Yuri's warmth.

Maria and Alexei came to greet us, Lyuba at their heels. Nikita then performed the introductions. I assessed the blush on my daughter's face as she pressed her palms together and bowed to Dmitry, then Yuri. Her voice trembled when she expressed her pleasure at making their acquaintance, but she kept it loud enough to hear. When she straightened and retreated to stand next to Lyuba, I saw Yuri's eyes fixed on her flushed face. She looked beautiful despite her discomfort— her blonde braid, entwined with ribbons and pearls, falling over her shoulder to her waist; her blue eyes sparkling; her coloring enhanced by the pure white of her tunic and the delicate rose pink of her overdress and pointed headdress. Best of all, I noticed she couldn't take her eyes off him, either.

Lyuba broke the spell that held Anna and Yuri enchanted. "We're to go upstairs." She tugged on Anna's sleeve. "The grownups want to talk."

Anna blinked and gave a tiny shake of her head, as if waking up. "Excuse me, then." She looked at me, and her face lit up in a way I hadn't seen in a month. My heart warmed at the sight.

"We'll talk for a while," I said, returning the smile. "Then maybe you and Lyuba can join us again before we go home."

She nodded agreement. Lyuba tugged on her sleeve once more, and the two of them left the room—Lyuba with a rapid stride, Anna more slowly. Yuri Vorontsov's eyes followed my daughter's every step.

With our party reduced to four on our hosts' side and three on ours, we settled on the padded benches that ringed the room and accepted delicate porcelain cups that held, as I knew from long experience, Maria's preferred beverage, a yellowish green liquid called tea. I'd drunk it so often at her house that I'd acquired a taste for it, but it didn't surprise me when Alexei offered the men beer instead. The tea reminded me of nothing so much as fragrant grass, in its own strange way refreshing but a stretch for palates accustomed to ale or kvass.

At first I allowed Alexei and Nikita to take the lead in questioning Dmitry and Yuri about their recent assignment. Kolomna, a town southeast of Moscow that often served as a staging ground for campaigns against the Tatars, was a common military posting, and both Alexei and Niki had spent time in the town. I listened for clues to Yuri's way of thinking, his approach to life, but the discussion of military strategy revealed little beyond what Nikita had already told me: that Yuri was straightforward and conscientious, with few airs and graces.

Would that be enough to satisfy Anna? I thought it might. She had no grand education, no political ambitions, no artistic inclinations beyond her embroidery. Nikita had insisted she learn to read and write, so she had access to religious works, but I hadn't detected signs of the bookishness that characterized her friend Lyuba—who not only delighted in secular stories written in at least three languages but penned her own when she thought no one was looking. Anna didn't even, so far as I could tell, share Darya's inclination toward the spiritual, which had caused my sister to toy with the idea of entering a women's monastery before Nikita captured her heart. Until Anna snapped at me about my hasty marriage, I'd have said she'd be challenged by the demands of running her own household, but her behavior since had convinced me that she had hidden strengths. Strengths she needed to learn to make more appropriate use of, but ones that would serve her well in the long run.

After a while, Yuri turned to me. "The beautiful blonde girl is your daughter? The one you seek to marry? I would be honored if you would consider me as her husband. Dmitry says she is already fifteen."

His matter-of-fact statement provoked a shudder, but I managed to conceal my reaction. I had so wanted to keep Anna at home until she turned sixteen, but Igor's threats made that decision unwise. "Her birthday fell on February 5. I'm willing to see her contracted now, if your family agrees, but if we could delay the wedding itself into the fall, we will have time to prepare her for marriage."

"I'm not in a hurry," Yuri said. "If we do sign a contract, perhaps we can break convention a little. Since Nikita's house is right next to Dmitry's, I expect we could find a way to give Anna Semyonovna and me a chance to learn more about each other before the ceremony. Her honor could not be compromised by talking with her intended bridegroom in her mother's company."

His consideration for my daughter's feelings as well as her reputation appealed to me. Listening to him strengthened my conviction that this was the kind of man I wanted for Anna, someone who would think about what would serve her, not only himself. But …

"I should warn you that my cousin Igor Bezzubtsev, who is the head of our clan, insists that your father has not forgiven my sister and me for refusing his marriage proposals. I hope Gavriil Timofeevich won't oppose the match." I tightened the grip on my clasped hands. The possibility that Igor had powerful backing for his schemes still unnerved me at times.

Yuri obviously didn't share my concerns. He burst out laughing, a sound of such genuine amusement that I readily understood how he might captivate my daughter. "I can convince my father," he said when he got himself under control. "He wants grandchildren to carry on his line. If I tell him no one but your Anna will do for me, how can he object? Besides, I don't think he *will* object. He has more on his mind than nursing grudges, including how to convince my uncle Demid that chiding the grand prince isn't good for anyone's health—especially Demid's. As for your cousin Igor, Papa hasn't much use for him, and I don't either. I can't imagine why Katya agreed to wed such a pompous ass." He clapped a hand over his mouth then, but his eyes danced. "Sorry. That was rude."

But the rest of us were laughing, too. "Alas," I said, "you'll find no disagreement here."

If only Igor's self-absorption didn't make him so dangerous.

"None at all," Darya put in. "I'm glad you've taken a liking to my niece, and that you believe your father won't object. What comes next?"

"I suppose I should approach Gavriil Timofeevich," Niki said. "In the meantime, shall we let the girls rejoin us?"

"We may as well," Maria said. "If they're not listening from some corner or bolthole I know nothing about, I will be amazed."

Which, I had to admit, sounded more than likely.

Chapter Twelve

ON THE WAY HOME, I LISTENED TO DARYA QUESTION ANNA about what she thought of Yuri Vorontsov and, in particular, whether she'd like to know him better. By interposing the occasional comment or query, I soon learned that Anna was, as I'd suspected, quite taken with Yuri. "He's good-looking," she said. "And he seems nice. Not too much older than me. Does he like me, do you think?"

"Very much," I assured her. "He called you beautiful and charming. He's willing to wait until the autumn to wed you, so you can get acquainted before the ceremony. Of course, once the contract's signed, it will be hard to end things if you don't like him, but at least the wedding won't be as scary as if you were meeting your husband at the betrothal ceremony, as many girls do. He seems like a pleasant young man, and he has the sense not to listen to Cousin Igor."

That made Anna giggle. "I've hopes the negotiations will work out well," I finished.

"I might be married before Lyuba is," Anna said, sounding both excited and wistful. "That will be strange. We've been friends for so long."

"You'll still be friends," Darya said. "Marriage won't change that. And I'm sure it won't be long before Lyuba weds. She had her fifteenth birthday six months ago."

"She says her papa is keeping her for the bride show. For the grand prince, you know." Anna wrinkled her nose. "I think I'd rather marry Yuri Gavriilovich than the grand prince."

"I would, too, if I were you. What shall we do to mark your betrothal?" I hoped that acknowledging her new status as a bride-to-be would convince her that I supported her moves toward adulthood.

She blushed and hesitated, then said, "Maybe we could have a party if Yuri Gavriilovich offers for me."

"Yes," I said. "Let's see what Niki finds out about the Vorontsovs' intentions."

The next day passed quietly, or as quietly as any day could in the presence of Tolya reunited with Laika—despite the fact that it was a Sunday during Lent, and we spent a good part of the morning in church. The evening before, Darya had sent one of the grooms from her stables to walk and feed the dog, a kindness I welcomed. He would stay with us as long as we needed him to care for the hound, but no adult could keep up with Laika's loping stride for an entire day. Even at four, the dog—bred for hunting—could run Tolya into exhaustion within the space of a few hours. The rest of us had no hope of outlasting her.

We could, however, enjoy the post-supper silence that came from Tolya and Laika both sleeping well at night.

On the Monday, I received a message from my sister, inviting me to visit her as soon as possible. Her rather cryptic note provoked a ripple of concern. Suppose Igor *had* intervened to separate me from Anfim with the intention of causing trouble of some kind—or was already conspiring to botch any contract between Anna and Yuri Vorontsov? I wasted no time before summoning a maid, sending a message alerting Masha to my absence, and heading for the estate where I had lived until last month.

One of the kitchen maids accompanied me for propriety's sake. She chattered nonstop as we traversed the short distance, but I paid little heed, my thoughts focused on what I would find when we reached our destination.

I arrived as the bells of the nearby cathedral struck two. A quick conversation with the steward led me to the main sitting room, where I found Darya working on another shirt for her son. "What's happened?" I asked as I closed the door. "Is it Igor?"

"Sit here." She indicated the bench next to the unlit stove, right next to her. I settled myself, watching her fold the shirt. "I don't want the servants to overhear us. They'll find out soon enough."

"What?!" I was even more alarmed. That the servants eavesdropped on us was not news, but for my sister to worry about them indicated that something big was at stake.

"It is Igor, in a way, but not in connection with Anfim being sent to Kazan. We still have no word on that. Niki met with Gavriil Vorontsov this morning," she said once she had the shirt stowed away in her sewing bag. "It's good news, but also troubling."

"Explain." I pushed the word past constricted throat muscles.

Darya inhaled, then released the breath in a sigh. "Yuri had already talked to his father, saying how much he admired Anna and wanted to wed her. Niki told me Gavriil agreed in principle to the match—that's the good news. But then Gavriil announced that he didn't entirely trust his son's judgment, because he'd heard rumors that Anna wasn't as pure as she appeared. From our cousin, I assume, because who else would spread such vicious lies about a girl who rarely leaves the estate?"

"No!" I forced myself to lower my voice, which had come perilously close to a shout. "That beast Igor. I'd like to throttle him. How dare he impugn my daughter?" As soon as the words left my mouth, I knew the answer. Igor had threatened to do exactly that.

Darya pointed that out. When I nodded gloomily to show I understood, she went on. "I suspect he's also the source of Gavriil's other concern: that your marriage to an official weakens Anna's network of connections and therefore lessens her value as a bride." She didn't finish with "I told you so," which was nice of her. I heard the hint of censure anyway.

"As you warned me might happen," I said, acknowledging that unspoken reproof. "But Igor's aspersions against me don't change the fact that Anna is a Kolychev, and her father died a nobleman, however undeserving of that rank. You and Nikita and Igor are nobles as well."

"Unfortunately, the entire Kolychev clan has been disgraced since then," Darya reminded me. "Although they may return to favor one day. A marriage between Anna and Yuri would help their cause, for that matter. In any case, Gavriil Timofeevich has agreed to entertain the proposal—given that Yuri refuses to consider anyone else—so long as his sister-in-law confirms Anna's virginity. That would be Elizaveta Vadimovna, the same sister-in-law he sent to confirm mine, when Igor tried to shove me down Gavriil's throat."

"Devil take him—and Igor." I groaned, finally understanding the source of Darya's discomfort. Neither of us wanted to explain the Vorontsovs' suspicions to Anna, never mind their proposed remedy. And Elizaveta Vadimovna, although at heart a decent soul, appeared fierce at first glance and was tactless in the extreme—hardly the person I would recommend for such a delicate task.

"I suppose we have no alternative," I said after an awkward pause in which I reviewed and discarded alternatives. "The Vorontsovs are well within their rights, and if they vouch for her purity, that will undercut Igor's attempts to discredit her in ways nothing else can." I sighed, anticipating a battle to come. "I can't say I'm looking forward to this, but I'll stay with her every step of the way, even if she hates me for it. Is she upstairs?"

"Yes, in the nursery with Andrusha. Courage, sister."

"I'll need it," I agreed. "Well, I'd better get started. At the rate these negotiations are moving, Yuri's aunt will be on the doorstep before we know it. The last thing we need is Anna finding out at the last moment exactly what she came to check."

Darya pulled the child's shirt from her bag once more and rethreaded the needle. "Maybe you can imagine throttling Igor throughout the examination. It will give you a glare fierce enough to cow even Elizaveta Vadimovna."

"Believe me," I said as I went to the door. "The thought of throttling Igor will be my one consolation for what I'm about to do."

"But why would they even *think* that?" Anna wailed.

"I told you." With difficulty, I kept my tone level. I'd already explained the situation three times, and I knew it wasn't only the invasion of her body by another woman that bothered Anna—although that was bad enough. "I know it sounds nasty and quite unfair, but it's not uncommon.

It doesn't mean Yuri's relatives suspect you of any specific misdeed. All the girls summoned for the grand prince's bride show will suffer the same indignity. I did myself before marrying your father. And when Gavriil Vorontsov wanted to marry your aunt Darya, she went through it with this very same Elizaveta Vadimovna."

"But why?" Anna covered her face with both hands. "I know hardly any boys. Andrusha and Tolya, who are *little*; Yuri and his cousin for a tiny part of one afternoon. How could I be impure? I don't want to lie on my back and show my private parts to an old lady I've never met."

"I also wish you needn't do that." I sat next to her and put my arm around her shaking shoulders. She turned and sobbed against my chest. Hugging her, I again wanted to throttle Igor with my bare hands. Whatever I said to Anna to calm her fears, I didn't believe that Gavriil Vorontsov would have suspected my shy fifteen-year-old daughter of impropriety without Igor stirring the pot.

Even so, I kept my anger under control. Anna needed me. I rocked her in my arms as if she were no more than five and murmured consoling phrases over her bowed head.

By the time Darya arrived to announce that Yuri's Aunt Elizaveta—Liza for short—had in fact arrived with indecent speed and was heading up the stairs as we spoke, I was so eager to finish the business that I greeted our visitor with relief, if not warmth. Aunt Liza hadn't changed since I last saw her at the Christmas party. If anything, she appeared larger and more stolid than before, with a dour look on her face that reminded me of the snarling lion depicted in the book Anfim had brought back from his journey. I hoped her grim expression reflected her dislike of the task ahead of her rather than her reaction to the possibility of Anna joining her family.

"She's very upset," I said in response to a perfunctory query as to my daughter's state of mind. "She can't imagine why anyone would doubt her when she's never left the confines of this estate except to visit female friends and family or to attend church. And if you'll forgive my candor, I can't imagine why either. Does Gavriil Timofeevich really believe that we would endanger her chances of happiness by failing to fulfill our responsibility to watch over her?"

I hoped the blunt question might discourage our visitor—or that she would repeat it to the men, underlining the absurdity of Igor's claims. Instead she harrumphed and stalked past me to take Anna by the chin and tip her head back. "A pretty thing," Liza said. "When not blubbering, I assume."

Anna mastered her courage and her manners enough to stand in welcome—lowering her eyes to indicate deference, since Liza's grip on her chin made it impossible to dip her head. I handed my daughter a square of linen, which she used to pat her cheeks dry before sneezing into the cloth. Liza hurriedly released Anna's chin, muttering a curse and crossing herself to ward off evil spirits, and from behind the older woman's back I smiled. Served her right.

Anna saw my reaction. I knew because she bit her lip for a moment.

"Well, you have manners, I see," Liza said gruffly. "How's your embroidery?"

Anna reached into her sewing bag and pulled out the exquisite hand towel, its pale lilacs and darker violets strewn across a background the color of fresh cream. She held it out to Liza, who harrumphed once more. I could see from her rapt expression, though, that my daughter's work impressed her—as well it should.

"Very nice," Liza admitted. "You have a gift. How about managing the household? Any experience with that?"

"Some," Anna said, her voice several notes higher than normal. I didn't blame her for being nervous: even without the stress of knowing what was to come, she probably felt intimidated by Liza's barking voice and imposing figure. "Mama and Auntie Darya take me with them when they order meals and assign tasks, and I direct the servants as needed, but I don't have charge of the house myself."

"Of course," Liza said as if the last went without saying. "Well, that seems to cover the essentials, except for the purity examination. My nephew Yuri seems set on having you, and it's the price of my brother-in-law's acceptance, so let's get it out of the way. Your mother told you what to expect?"

Anna couldn't conceal a grimace, but she tipped her head forward in acquiescence and moved toward the door. When I set off after them, she turned and said with surprising dignity, "I will go with Elizaveta Vadimovna, Mama. Please stay here."

About to protest, I stopped. Yuri's aunt was gazing at Anna with approval, a reaction I had no desire to undermine. This examination was a farce, and at some level Aunt Liza must realize that. "Very well, darling," I said. "If that's what you prefer, I'll wait here."

I had yet to rethread my needle before they returned, Anna blushing but relieved, Liza no longer harrumphing. "Honor is satisfied?" I asked, my tone tarter than was wise. I continued to hope that my disbelief coupled with our willingness to satisfy their demands would convince the Vorontsovs that they'd come close to making fools of themselves. In a perfect world, they would openly praise Anna's virtue, thus undoing any future damage Igor might attempt as well as his past efforts to cast us in the shade.

"Entirely," Liza said. "I expected nothing else, but the men …" She left the sentence dangling and gave me an apologetic shrug. "I'll tell my brother-in-law that the girl is everything she should be, and he will contact Nikita Andreevich to discuss the terms of the contract."

The sudden release of tension made me feel quite kindly toward her, especially when I saw my daughter relax for the first time since I'd alerted her to Liza's visit and the reason for it.

"That's splendid," I said. "Anna darling, find Mishka and tell him to bring some nice appetizers and a jug of that mulled wine he prepares. And ask Auntie Darya to join us; we have something to celebrate!"

She treated me to a broad grin and ran from the room.

Yuri's Aunt Liza must have been as good as her word, because within the week I received a message from Niki inviting me to join him and Gavriil Vorontsov at our family estate for the formal signing of the marriage contract. I was overjoyed, especially when I discovered, written on a separate enclosed sheet, a short message from my daughter telling me how happy she was at the news.

But my pleasure at seeing my breach with Anna gradually heal soon suffered a setback. I read farther into Niki's letter, and my heart sank. *Alas*, the message warned, *Cousin Igor will be present as the head of the Bezzubtsev and Sheremetev clans.* I had known, of course, that Igor must be consulted, but I'd hoped his adulation of Vorontsov would lead to instant agreement, allowing him to skip the signing ceremony. Instead, I had to worry about what mischief my cousin might cause during the meeting. Would he wait until the last minute, then raise some ridiculous objection guaranteed to scuttle the negotiations—or even refuse outright to make his mark on the document? And what would happen to my relationship with Anna if she could blame the dashing of her hopes on my inability to get along with Igor?

Then I perused the second to last paragraph, and my fears expanded to include the fate of my marriage. *You should know, too*, Niki wrote, *that Dmitry Vorontsov questioned his uncle, and Gavriil confirms that it was Igor who recommended your husband be assigned to the mission in Kazan. He claimed he wanted to honor a capable official whose unswerving loyalty to the crown has sometimes been doubted.*

I groaned. Talk about damning with faint praise: not only had Igor neatly separated my husband and me, but he'd managed to drag in the old scandal as he did so, all the while pretending that he believed none of it. He was still after us, and by separating us, he had increased his chances of a successful attack.

But, Niki wrote, *I have it on the best authority that the Vorontsovs will not permit any interference with their plans.*

I tried with little success to take comfort from that assurance. The Vorontsovs' support would help Anna, but I doubted it would extend to defending my husband and me.

The whole situation unsettled me. I yearned for Anfim's counsel, his common sense, and his physical presence. And I felt guilty about keeping secrets from him. By the time he returned, the match with Yuri would be finalized—unless Igor intervened—without my husband even having a say.

I decided to write to him as soon as I returned from the signing. A letter would not make up for leaving him out of an important decision, but it was better than nothing. And if some evil scheme did lie beneath Igor's attempt to get my husband out of Moscow, Anfim should hear about that as well.

Dressed in my best peach brocade robe, I set off for Nikita and Darya's house with Masha, the children, and Laika late the next morning. The choice to include my companions was based on more than a desire not to walk the streets alone. Although Laika had too much affection for humans large and small to make a good guard dog, in the days she'd spent with us, I'd discovered an exception to her "people are good" rule. One move toward Tolya by anyone outside the immediate family, and she bristled and bared her teeth, as if he were her pup. I still wasn't sure she would defend the children against Igor, but she would protect us from pickpockets and other miscreants, and for that reason I'd decided to bring both boy and dog along. And where Tolya went, Lara insisted on going. We made a joyful party as we wended our way through the streets. Sunlight caressed our faces, and a gentle breeze carried the mingled scents of wildflowers. I inhaled, treasuring each sign of spring.

"Let's go to the country while we wait for your papa," I said to Lara. "After Anna's betrothal party, of course. I'll ask her if she'd like to come with us."

"The country?" Lara stopped mid-step to stare at me. "What's in the country?"

"Have you never left the city?" I asked, shocked. When she shook her head, I again realized how much I took for granted. Her father traveled as an official and a merchant, but a non-noble family would not own rural estates.

Yet I could hardly bear to imagine growing up without ever walking in the majestic beauty of an ancient forest, sipping water from untouched streams, perching on a fence to watch lazy bees drunk on nectar, falling asleep to the caroling of nightingales, and breathing untainted air while racing heedlessly across flower-strewn meadows.

A life bounded by city streets—what kind of childhood is that?

"Then we must give you the chance," I told her. "We'll bring Laika with us; she can run the whole day if she wants. Tolya will catch frogs and climb trees and slay his dragons with sticks. He'll tear his clothes to shreds, but he'll love every moment."

She made a face. "I don't want to catch frogs or climb trees or tear my clothes."

"No," I said. "I don't suppose you do. But you'll enjoy the flowers—they're everywhere in this season. And there are songbirds and shady spots under the branches to sit when the sun gets high. We'll bake cookies and sweet breads, and we can embroider together. You can read and write and do sums if you want, but you won't have to. It will be a holiday."

Lara giggled at this news. "I hope Anna does come with us. That would be fun."

"I'll ask her today." The more I thought of the idea, the more I liked it. Although we might defeat Cousin Igor this time, only a fool would suppose that interfering with our plans for Anna's marriage would satisfy him for long. And although we wouldn't stay abreast of his rumor mongering if we left the capital city, there was little we could do to counteract that anyway. With luck, removing ourselves from his line of sight would create an opportunity for someone else to draw his ire.

I decided to tell Anfim about the plan in tonight's letter, inviting him to join us on his way back from Kazan. He'd reach us sooner than if he had to travel to Moscow, since the villages I owned lay southeast of the city, not far from the Ryazan road. Anfim might have passed our estate on his journey east: Bronnitsy, famous for its horses, hosted one of the courier stations where government officials stopped to rest and replace their mounts. If he stopped at the same town again on his way home, anyone in the area could direct him to our house. Yes, as soon as we got through Easter and Anna's party, we would leave Moscow for the country.

After a few weeks, even Cousin Igor might forget about us for a while.

Chapter Thirteen

BUT FIRST I HAD TO GET THROUGH THE CONTRACT SIGNING, fending off any disruption from my recalcitrant relative. Darya welcomed me on my arrival and ushered Lara upstairs, dispatching Tolya and Laika to the courtyard. "Join me afterward and tell me everything," my sister whispered to me when the three of them had gone.

"Of course," I said. "Wish me luck. Niki said Igor will be there. What's his mood?"

"Sulking, from the looks of him." She pulled a face that bore a remarkable resemblance to a toddler in full tantrum.

"Wonderful." I resisted the temptation to groan. "He's enough of a pest under normal circumstances. Why is he sulking, anyway? After making so much fuss about winning Gavriil Vorontsov's support, you'd think he would love the thought of an even closer connection."

Darya laughed. "Because it wasn't his idea? That's my impression, for what it's worth. Although he may have hoped to wed Anna to some candidate of his own. If so, no wonder he's miffed."

"I suppose. I'd better go find out." I touched her arm in leaving. "I'll fill you in as soon as I can, I promise."

"I can't wait," she said, and I wended my way to Nikita's study on the second floor.

When I reached my destination, though, Igor didn't look sulky. Instead, he displayed a deference he'd never previously extended to me. I attributed his uncharacteristic behavior to the presence of the Vorontsovs and made an effort to respond politely, then bowed to Gavriil and his son before kissing Niki on both cheeks. Father Job sat at the desk, papers spread in front of him, when I walked in. He rose and blessed my bent head when I stood before him. It was the first time I'd seen him since my wedding day, and the pleasure in his voice as he said my name warmed my heart.

The presence in the room of five men far outnumbered the available chairs. I sat on the bench next to Father Job, since my presence at the ceremony was a concession at best. If Anna's father had lived, he, not I, would have overseen the negotiations and the signing on Anna's behalf. (The thought of whom *he* might have picked for our daughter's hand sent shivers of revulsion down my spine.) I felt certain that my cousin would have barred the door against me if anyone had asked him, so the Vorontsovs' willingness to include me spoke well of them.

Father Job resumed his seat behind the desk. Nikita and Gavriil, as the people who had negotiated the contract, occupied the two chairs. Yuri settled himself on the window seat, and Igor sank onto a bench attached to the wall farthest from me. Since I couldn't ban him from the room, the arrangement suited me: I could keep an eye on him.

Within a short time, I noticed a pattern. Whenever Gavriil's attention turned elsewhere, Igor lounged, and a sullen expression came over his face, giving him the look of a petulant brat. But every glance from his patron caused my cousin to straighten his back and feign polite interest. From this behavior I concluded that Igor disliked the idea of the marriage contract, as Darya had noted, but feared the effects of opposing Gavriil Vorontsov directly.

I listened without comment as Father Job read the document aloud. Niki had consulted me on the provisions made for Anna's dowry, and he had followed my recommendations to the letter, except for adding certain household goods and a village of his own. The Vorontsovs accepted the terms without question, as I'd expected: the men would have worked out any disagreements before this formal meeting. Igor also raised no objections, despite his growing resemblance to a thundercloud, strengthening my hopes that however much he might object to the arrangement in private, he would not take the risk of refusing to sign.

That meant we had won, at least in this arena. Because once Igor's name went on the contract, his chances of terminating the match between Yuri and Anna fell close to zero. My heart pounded with the prospect of success, and I gripped my hands tightly to keep my emotions under control, rather than risk celebrating too soon. If I could see my daughter settled *and* my husband safely returned from Kazan without further damage to his reputation, my happiness would be complete.

Father Job held out a quill pen, and the other men stood. From where I sat, I could see what they were doing. Gavriil Vorontsov made an X, but his son wrote out his father's full three-part name with a flourish, then added his own beneath it. Igor and Nikita repeated this performance. Father Job signed as witness, then turned to me and held out the pen. "Will you act as the second witness, Solomonida Petrovna?"

"What? You'd let *that* woman witness the document?" Igor clenched his fists. "She's not worthy!"

"Not worthy?" Gavriil Vorontsov echoed. "Of course, she's worthy. She's the girl's mother." He nodded at me, and I felt a flush of real warmth for him. I was glad he would become my daughter's father-in-law. "Can you write?" he added, as if the answer hardly mattered.

"I can," I told him, proud of the effort I'd put into learning. Behind Gavriil's back, Igor scowled like the mythical basilisk. I stared at my cousin, challenging him with my steady gaze until he looked away.

Seeing Igor cowed, if only for the moment, I returned my attention to Vorontsov and the priest, released my anger with a long exhalation, and accepted the quill. "It would be my honor," I said. Then I dipped the pen in the ink pot and, with considerable care, wrote my full name at the place Father Job pointed out to me. He thanked me as he sanded the paper and set it to one side.

Something else to put in my letter to Anfim. How proud my husband would be of me when he heard I had witnessed a contract!

I hadn't even had time to celebrate internally, though, before the situation took a sudden turn for the worse. The trouble began with the most innocuous question imaginable.

"You'll have copies made?" Gavriil asked in his gruff voice.

"Of course," Father Job said. "A set for you, one for Igor Grigorevich, and"—he dipped head and shoulders in my direction—"one for Solomonida Petrovna and her husband."

Igor's shaky self-control snapped. "Her treacherous husband," he snarled. "As if he has anything to say about a boyar wedding. Why, she's not even noble herself, at this point!"

"Calm down, young man," Gavriil said in magisterial tones. "Are you saying you oppose a match that *I* approve?"

Igor's mouth opened and closed, like a fish out of water, and his Adam's apple moved as he swallowed hard. I could almost see the thoughts colliding in his head. "Of course not," he managed in grudging tones after a while. "Your approval means a great deal to me. I had plans of my own for Anna, but I set them aside to please you."

Why do you think we pushed the contract negotiations forward, if not to thwart your uncaring plans?

I released another slow breath, hoping his meeting would end before Igor lost all control.

But although Gavriil's reproof *should* have stopped Igor in his tracks, it didn't. "It galls me, however," he went on, "that her mother has complicated our situation by willfully abandoning her nobility—for a love match, of all things. Just like a woman to be so heedless."

The scowl on Gavriil's face didn't bode well for his alliance with my cousin, if such a thing existed. "You disappoint me, Igor Grigorevich," he said sternly. "How can you imagine another husband would do better for Anna than my Yuri? As for Solomonida Petrovna, she is quite noble enough for *me*. Or have you forgotten that I sought her hand?" He dipped his head at me in that elephantine way of his. Grateful for his intervention, I returned his smile.

Igor's jaw tightened like a vise, but after a brief pause he pulled himself together enough to respond. "I do, of course, appreciate your condescension, Gavriil Timofeevich." He bowed stiffly—first to the elder Vorontsov, then the younger. "My apologies if I implied otherwise. I hope you can understand my anger at not being consulted during the negotiations. Please forgive my boorish behavior."

"You are forgiven," Gavriil Vorontsov said with a lofty air. While Igor slumped back onto his bench and rubbed his brow, Vorontsov turned and shook Nikita's hand. "Your niece is a lovely girl, my son and sister-in-law tell me—as pretty as her mother." He winked at me, and I smiled again at this new reminder of his charm. "I'm proud to welcome her into the family. Will you deign to present her to us, now that the match is official?"

"Of course," I said. "Give me a few moments, and I will bring her here."

Igor stood once more. "Excuse me, if you please. I am well acquainted with Anna, and I have other demands on my time." He sounded wooden, as if rage boiled below the surface, but he succeeded in keeping whatever resentment he felt under control.

Gavriil Vorontsov waved a careless hand. "Go, Igor Grigorevich. Your part is done." He grinned at his son, whose beaming face spoke of both delight and relief. "Yuri and I can handle the matter from here."

"Farewell, then," Igor said with the obligatory bow. As he passed me, though, he bent and, while pretending to kiss my cheek, growled into my ear, "I'm not done with you, Shura. You may have won this round, but the real battle's still ahead. I'll bring you and that treacherous husband of yours down, whatever it takes."

Before I'd recovered from my shock, he stalked out the door and was gone.

In a thoughtful mood, I left the men to seal the contract by drinking goblets of claret and went in search of my daughter. Darya had almost certainly anticipated the presentation, so I expected to find Anna dressed in her best and looking forward to what would surely be a brief but cordial meeting.

Climbing the stairs to the third floor, I wondered how best to convince my daughter to leave her new husband-to-be in the city and enjoy the last summer of her maidenhood among the many attractions of the natural world. Could we invite Yuri Vorontsov to accompany us? There could be no impropriety given that I would be present the whole time. Niki and Darya might choose to come along as well, turning it into a gathering for the whole family. But even if one or both of them decided to stay in Moscow, I could think of no better way for Anna and Yuri to become acquainted. Life in the country moved at a slow, unpressured pace, one that the city attained only when snowbound.

As I reached the last flight of stairs, I encountered my sister on her way down. I grabbed the opportunity to fill her in on the contract signing and Igor's fury, then moved straight into my summer plans. "I would love to get Anna away from our cousin and his toadies," I said. "To give Yuri a chance to court her without constant surveillance. Is it possible, do you think?"

"Possible?" she cried. "It's inspired! I'll talk to Niki as soon as Gavriil Vorontsov leaves. Yuri asked to stay and chat with Anna for a while after they're done, so we can approach him then. Unless he has a military assignment, I'm sure he'll agree. He's quite smitten with her, which is lovely to see. And it would be so good for us and for the children to get out of the city's heat for the summer." She looked pointedly at my belly, then her own, already rounding. "The ones yet to come, as well as those we already have in our care."

"Agreed." I laughed at her eagerness. "It's far too long since we went there. Goodness, I don't think we've left Moscow since Papa fell ill. We haven't stayed the whole summer at Malinino since the year Semyon died." The name of the estate derived from the word for raspberry, *malina*, and just hearing it made me nostalgic. I had a vivid childhood memory of wandering amid patches of raspberry bushes, dodging spiny stems to grab the ripe fruit before returning home with crimson staining my hands, face, and pinafore. How our nurse, Matryona, used to scold! It never did the slightest good, though. The next day we were back in the berry patches, juice-stained as ever.

"So long? Ten years?" Darya said. "Is that possible? Yes, it can't be less."

Anna must have heard us, because she came down the stairs then, looking every bit as beautiful as I'd expected in sky blue silk and the embroidered collar Anfim had brought back from his voyage. I congratulated her on her forthcoming marriage, then mentioned that Yuri and his father were waiting downstairs for her. Before I ushered her back to the study, though, I told her about our plan to leave the city. I emphasized my hope that Yuri would accompany us.

"You will join us?" I asked as I reached the end. "You can't stay behind if Auntie Darya travels with us, and if Yuri Vorontsov does visit, you will have much more time with him there, even chaperoned, than you can ever have here."

That made her blush, which was rather sweet. "May I ask Lyuba to come, too?"

"Good idea," I said. "Let's invite her. I know Lara loves to spend time with you, but you'll have more fun if someone your own age is there as well. And although Yuri is welcome to stay as long as he likes, he may have military or family duties that call him away. Then Lyuba's company will be even more important. Let's go downstairs and find out if he's willing to accompany us, shall we? This meeting is mostly for Gavriil Timofeevich's sake, but I know Yuri is eager to see his contracted bride."

"I'm eager to see him, too," she said. And hand in hand, we went downstairs.

As I'd hoped, Yuri and Niki greeted our suggestion to spend part of the summer at Malinino with enthusiasm, and so the plan was made.

I sent my letter to Anfim that evening, with one of the stable boys acting as courier. Whatever nefarious schemes Igor had in mind, at least my husband would know to watch out for them. Because happy as I felt to see Anna's future close to being settled, I could see that Igor's grudge against us had not lessened and, indeed, appeared to have grown as a result of today's events.

Easter Sunday rolled around at last. For the all-night vigil leading into the celebration of the Resurrection I went with Darya and Nikita, Maria and Alexei, and Anna and Lyuba to the Dormition Cathedral in the Kremlin, where Metropolitan Macarius, the head of the Russian Orthodox Church, presided over a large congregation of nobles, including the young grand prince and his brother. Surrounded by candlelight, incense, and the sound of deep, rich voices, I wondered whether Anfim had reached Kazan by now. I cast my mind back to the day of our wedding, the small chapel with its sparse attendance. Although nothing like this magnificent crowded setting, it nonetheless felt so dear to me. With so much having happened in the interim, it seemed as if Anfim had left ages ago, but in fact not more than three weeks had passed since I kissed him goodbye.

By the time the service ended at sunrise, my back ached from so many hours on my feet, and I was more than ready to return to the house. We greeted those standing nearby, then walked the still-gray streets, admiring the flush of dawn as it turned the river pink. Complete strangers stopped us as we went by, calling, "Christ is risen!"

"He is risen, indeed," we called back. With the next group, it was our turn: "Christ is risen!"

"He is risen indeed!"

When we got to my house, a sleepy Lara and Tolya scrambled out of bed to meet us. Lara greeted us quietly, then waited with admirable patience while Tolya licked his lips and reached for the fruit-studded bread known as kulich. Masha slapped his hand away before balancing the tall cylinder on a plate, its round glazed top giving it the appearance of a large mushroom. He pouted, and she ignored him as she turned the loaf on its side and cut it into thick slices. Next to the bread sat a molded cheese, decorated with the Cyrillic letters X and B, an abbreviation for *Khristos voskrese*—Christ is risen. After weeks of fasting and hours on my feet, I yearned to grab a slice and slather it with cheese, but manners won out, and I let my guests serve themselves first. When at last my turn came, I relished every morsel. No food ever tastes so good as the first bite of sweets and dairy after seven weeks of nothing but vegetables and grains.

When the others left, I retired to my chamber and slept. Even Anfim's continued absence couldn't keep me awake that morning. The child growing in my belly must be more than three months along. I could tell because the fatigue that had plagued me in February and March was abating, together with the sickness that had made each morning miserable. But much as I rejoiced in the return of my usual boundless energy, the effects of the all-night vigil would not be denied.

Later in the day, I took the children with me, Masha and Laika in attendance, to Darya and Niki's home for Anna's party. The chance to combine our celebrations of Easter and the new beginning represented by her marriage contract was too good to pass up. The main celebration would involve female friends and relatives, but Nikita would naturally serve as host at his own dinner, and Yuri had promised to stop by if his family made no objection. Katya, Maria, Lyuba of course, a handful of Anna's other friends, all fifteen years old or soon to reach that marker—I expected a small but enthusiastic celebration.

Alas, I hadn't counted on Igor ...

Our cousin arrived halfway through the meal, when we were laughing and toasting and reveling in the return to the table of baked ham and roast capon, even a round of beef. Sour cream and butter glistened on the vegetables; the crust on the bread shone crisp brown from its egg wash. Niki had tapped the storehouse that held wine and beer, and the men raised toasts to everything from Anna's betrothal to the return of spring. I thought of the last time I'd attended such a celebration, on the evening of my wedding. By now, my brother-in-law Kirill must have reached his wife in Smolensk. What would he tell her of me? And Postnik, so welcoming, now traveling with Anfim, sharing my husband's everyday experiences in the way I longed to do. I wished the three of them were here today, trading stories of their journey, teasing and goading each other while the rest of us reveled in their tall tales.

The crash of a door caused my head to jerk toward the sound, and there stood Igor, with a young man at his side. Of medium height and slim, with light brown hair and hazel eyes, beardless and rather flamboyantly dressed, the young man looked pleasant enough, although I found his expression rather smug. I concluded that he was accustomed to both recognition and admiration. On the whole, I placed his age in the late teens, which made him an odd companion for Igor, now thirty. Whoever the boy was, he must have been Lara's age or younger when I served as Grand Princess Elena's lady-in-waiting. No wonder I didn't recognize him.

It was the smugness, more than any specific resemblance, that sparked a flash of recognition in my brain. But I still hadn't put a name to him when Nikita rose and said, "Welcome, Prince Pavel. Igor, your wife indicated you had other commitments. How pleasant that you found the time to join us." His tone, unusually chilly for such a festive occasion, undercut his words. Igor dipped his head but otherwise did not respond.

I rose as well—flanked by Darya and Maria on my left, Katya, Anna, and Lyuba on my right. Lara, clad in a particularly flattering rose-pink dress stitched from one of her Bukharan silks, stood next to Lyuba. I heard them whispering and snickering at the new arrivals and sent them an admonishing glance, although sorely tempted to snicker myself. In contrast to my wedding feast, the entire group of hosts and guests sat at one end of the banquet hall, looking out at a sea of servants facing each other along the series of tables. The arrangement inhibited conversation, but it did have advantages in terms of greeting late arrivals.

"Permit me to introduce my family and friends," Niki said to the newcomer before naming us one by one. He ended with, "Prince Pavel Ilich Shuisky, ladies."

I sighed—softly, so as not to call attention to myself. Pavel Ilich, indeed. So that explained my flash of recognition. I'd never met Prince Pavel—although I knew his mother—but I had vivid (and unpleasant) memories of his father, Prince Ilya Shuisky, a notorious conspirator and womanizer who bore primary responsibility for the death of Grand Princess Elena. Like his son, Prince Ilya had exuded confidence that he need only enter a room to become the center of every woman's attention. I had avoided him when I could, kicked him when he took liberties, and ensured that I never, ever, went anywhere with him alone. I dipped my head the absolute minimum to welcome Ilya's son. He did not reciprocate or even—so far as I could tell—notice, because he was staring at Anna in a way that I didn't like one bit.

Thanks be to the Mother of God that we signed that contract.

Of course, I had no reason to assume that Prince Pavel took after his deceased father in every way. He might resemble his mother, who was quite charming. But watching the expression on his face, I didn't believe it. Prince Ilya had died only the year before, and boys spent far more time with their fathers than with their mothers. It seemed likely that Ilya's influence would outweigh his wife's, and that disturbed me a good deal. I knew of at least one captive Ilya had raped, and his wife had indicated that was not the first incident of its kind. Erring on the side of caution, I preferred to keep as much distance between Prince Pavel and my daughter as possible. The contract with Yuri should protect her, but it might not protect her enough.

Cousin Igor's smile, even more complacent than Pavel's, did nothing to reassure me. I recalled him saying at the contract signing that he had intended to offer Anna to someone else. I could only guess at his motives for bringing Pavel here, but it didn't take a genius to guess that he might see the young prince as a suitable husband for my beautiful fifteen-year-old daughter. With my cousin's threats ringing in my ears, I was on high alert. Whatever he had in mind, I intended to put a stop to it.

I let my sister, as the hostess, greet them first. "Would you care to join us? I'm sure Mishka can set two more places." She gestured at the extreme end of the men's section, past Niki and Alexei. "You go to Yuri Gavriilovich's left, please, Igor. We will move him down to make room for Prince Pavel next to Tsarevich Alexei."

Maria, standing next to me, cleared her throat. I relaxed my combative stance enough to send her a mischievous glance, and she responded in kind. We could both guess how much Alexei would dislike being forced to converse with a self-satisfied lad of Pavel's age. But Darya was right to make the change: however influential Yuri's father might be at court, the demands of precedence placed a prince above a boyar's son.

Besides, the experience might prove beneficial for Pavel. Alexei could depress pretension with little more than a raised eyebrow, and his setdowns, when he chose to deliver them, must freeze the blood in the recipients' veins. Even Igor quailed under the lash of Alexei's tongue.

Although … "Poor Yuri," I whispered to Maria. "Stuck between Pavel and Igor."

She compressed her lips in a way that told me she wanted to laugh. "Yes, indeed. Let's hope dreams of Anna will sustain him."

"It would be my pleasure," Pavel said, responding to Niki's invitation with a flourish of his arm and an elegant bow. He hadn't taken his eyes off Anna since he entered the room. Katya resumed her seat before my daughter did, and I noticed that Anna kept her eyes downcast, looking at neither of our self-invited guests. Unfortunately, a conceited young man might value her demure expression, imagining her as more pliable than she had revealed herself to be over the last month.

Lyuba, in contrast, gazed straight at him. From the side, I couldn't be sure, but her stance reminded me of the day Igor first crossed our yard three years ago, strutting like a peacock. She and Anna had imitated our cousin for an entire afternoon, rushing to the window for more inspiration and giggling as they marched back and forth. Lara, too, regarded Prince Pavel with fascination, although I could see her tugging at Lyuba's sleeve, as if she wanted to resume their interrupted conversation. As I watched them, I could imagine Lyuba gathering material for one of her stories.

Which reminded me that I had yet to show her the book Anfim had brought back for me from his long journey south. I must do that soon.

"Thank you," Igor said, responding belatedly to my sister's invitation to join us. Mishka, ever the perfect steward, signaled to two menservants to lay the new places, and before long, our meal continued as before.

My mind whirled with speculation, however, and the food stuck in my throat. To occupy my hands, I took a piece of kulich and tore it into small pieces. I sipped wine from time to time. But despite my jumbled thoughts and feelings, one question would not be denied.

What is Igor up to now?

At last, we finished our meal and moved to the sitting room. Yuri wasted no time in claiming Anna's company, but as soon as the two of them settled themselves on the window seat, Prince Pavel plomped himself down on my daughter's other side. Yuri's glare should have started a fire in the courtyard, so incendiary was it, but Pavel paid no attention. Drifting by on the pretense of tending the candles that glowed in the icon corner nearby, I heard a stream of the most outrageous flattery issuing from the prince's lips. *Shades of his father!*

Anna, I was pleased to note, stared at Pavel with a kind of dazed amusement, as if she couldn't believe what she was hearing, before thanking him austerely and turning her attention back to Yuri. I grabbed the chance to demand the prince's company and invited Lyuba to sit with us. Of those present, she had the least to fear from Pavel's attentions, because her father had stated that he wouldn't consider a husband for her until the grand prince decided which of his young female subjects to honor with a proposal. And if, as I suspected, Lyuba was collecting material for her next set of tales, why not help her? It went without saying that I wouldn't leave her to handle Pavel alone.

I began the conversation by describing the miniatures in my book and asking her whether she could deduce the title from the images. At first she seemed uncertain, but when I got to the last picture—an emaciated, poorly clad man and a rather elaborately dressed figure (male? female? I couldn't tell), both flat on the ground before a pair of large round tents surrounded by wild animals—her face cleared. "*Layla and Majnun*," she said. "It's one of my favorites. The half-clothed one is Majnun, which means 'crazy man.' He and Layla fell in love when they were young, but her father married her to another, so Majnun roamed the desert like a hermit, creating poems about her; that's where his name comes from. That scene with the animals is the last time they meet before death; they've both fainted from joy."

Impressive. "Thank you," I said. "I'll bring the book next time, and you can tell us the details." I turned to Prince Pavel. "Lyuba is quite the scholar. She knows several languages. Do you read?"

"Enough to handle a prayer book or a land claim," he said with a shrug. "I see no reason to read for pleasure."

Lyuba subjected him to a gaze so penetrating any normal man would have squirmed in his seat. I could guess she viewed Pavel's sentiment as the equivalent of heresy. I expected her to protest, but instead she turned the conversation away from herself. "What form of entertainment do you prefer, Prince, if you don't like to read? Chess, perhaps?"

"Not chess." He shook his head, a flash of distaste visible on his face. "I like to ride to hounds, to hunt bear and boar, to carouse with my friends, to practice my military skills— interests a young lady like yourself would not share. I suppose you spend most of your time embroidering?"

Lyuba, a noted horsewoman who exercised her brother-in-law's falcons and had spent years resisting every effort by her older sister to impart skill with a needle, widened her sparkling eyes in a masterful imitation of awe. "You hunt bear? Isn't that *dangerous*?"

Pavel preened, his chest expanding and his finger caressing his upper lip in a way that only increased his resemblance to his father. "Why, yes. A maddened bear can maul a man beyond hope of recovery. We drive them into pits filled with wooden spikes, but the moment of the kill requires great courage. Only the strongest of warriors attempt such a feat."

"But you, I feel certain, have done so." She shuddered in an exaggerated manner. "I can't help feeling sorry for the bears, though. What harm do they cause if left alone?"

"It's a sport, my dear," he said in lofty tones. "I don't expect you to understand. Does your father not hunt?"

"He hunts with the court. Deer, rabbits—the grand prince receives the credit for those. Let us talk of something else, since the lure of a bear hunt escapes my poor female brain." Again she widened her eyes, and again her speech and gestures suggested that she was gathering material by encouraging him to reveal his prejudices and his folly. Yet Pavel seemed oblivious, as if he couldn't imagine a woman capable of seeing through him, as Lyuba obviously did. "Where was your last military assignment?" she asked.

"Smolensk," he said. "It's a fortress in the west. A long way from Moscow. I don't suppose you've heard of it."

Lyuba bit her lip, held it for a long moment, then released it. She had the history and geography of half the world inscribed in her head at this point, and the idea that she might lack the ability to place Smolensk on a map must try her patience sorely. "I remember it well," she told him in bright, cheerful tones more typical of a besotted maidservant than her sophisticated self. "My brother-in-law was military governor there for a year. Maria and I visited him at Christmas. Did you travel into Lithuania during your posting? As far as Poland, perhaps? I've always wanted to see the royal castle in Cracow. My former stepmother lives there when not at her own estate, and at times she visits the grand duke's palace in Vilnius as well. She says they are quite extraordinary, filled with works of art from all over Europe."

Well, *that* should convince Prince Pavel to stop treating her like a ninny. Watching them, I wondered why he wasn't working harder to impress her. Her fiery beauty, so different from Anna's—copper hair instead of blonde, gray-green eyes rather than blue—combined with her lively wit and slender form would appeal to many men. Of course, I didn't wish such a match on Lyuba, whom I loved as a third daughter, but even if her father failed to step in, I trusted her to rebuff Prince Pavel's advances in ways that Anna couldn't hope to do—yet.

"I did not visit Lithuania," Pavel confessed, looking somewhat chagrined—at the reminder that Alexei outranked him, I assumed. "Unlike your brother-in-law, I was a guardsman, and I stayed in the fortress unless ordered out on a sortie—exercises, you understand; we are not at war with Lithuania." He cast a longing glance over his shoulder to where Anna, deep in conversation with Yuri, gave no sign of noticing anyone else.

His focus on my daughter prevented him from observing the effect of his last comment on Lyuba. Her surface calm broke as annoyance flashed across her face, but then she conquered her emotions once more. "Are you sure?" she cooed at Pavel. "We so often *are* at war with Lithuania. When did we stop fighting?" When I sent her a glance of mingled amusement and warning, she straightened in her seat and pursed her lips; her dancing eyes revealed how close she was to giggling outright.

I couldn't say I blamed her. Pavel's absolute inability to imagine a woman with interests outside the household—or, indeed, any intellect to speak of—had earned him every mocking word Lyuba sent his way. It was like watching a cat toy with a mouse; she operated so far outside his narrow world that he failed even to recognize the blows she landed, let alone the gifts she would bring to the right partner someday.

Of course, Cousin Igor shared Pavel's dismissive attitude, as his behavior toward me during the contract signing demonstrated. That would only strengthen Igor's view of the young prince as a prime candidate for Anna's hand, in addition to the political and professional advantages that close ties to the Shuisky clan would bring. Many mothers—and brides—would agree, oblivious to the hints of something darker beneath Pavel's superficial assets.

But six years with Semyon had convinced me that youth, title, fortune, and good looks offered a place to start. They did not, in themselves, determine happiness in marriage. Watching Pavel in action, I felt ever more certain that he was not the kind of man I would have wanted for Anna, even before we solemnized her contract with Yuri—which made it all the more disturbing that Pavel couldn't take his eyes off my daughter. Instead of responding to Lyuba, he continued to stare at the bench where Anna gazed at her contracted husband as if the room contained only the two of them.

Reviewing what I'd seen so far, I frowned. I didn't believe Pavel had fallen for Anna at first sight. He'd strutted into the dining hall as if he belonged there, and that was before Niki introduced him to us women. And here he was acting as if my daughter were somehow uniquely his. His smugness on entry acquired a new, more troubling aspect. *You expected me*, it said, *and here I am.*

But no one had expected him. No one except Igor, who brought him here.

Having promised him Anna? Despite having signed a contract for her hand two weeks ago?

With anyone else, I wouldn't even entertain such questions. Breaking a marriage contract was difficult, if not impossible—and expensive, to boot. Dissolving this one would alienate Gavriil Vorontsov, and although no one would discount the Shuisky clan as a social and political force, Pavel's powerful uncles had died, one after another, over the last decade and a half. What Igor might hope to gain from such a match remained far from clear.

Yet I couldn't ignore the flush of triumph on my cousin's face. His self-satisfaction equaled Pavel's. They were up to something, and I needed to find out what.

I yearned then for the men to leave, so I could ask Katya a few hard questions. She wouldn't admit her own part in any scheme; I knew better than to imagine she might crack under pressure. But if I expressed a genuine interest in her relationship with my cousin and his friendship with Prince Pavel, I might uncover inconsistencies or prompt unforced statements that would help me figure out what Igor had in mind.

That would have to wait, though, until the men left. At last, after another quarter of an hour or so, Anna's friends arrived, one by one with their mothers. Igor and Prince Pavel said their goodbyes then, and Yuri, Alexei, and Niki went off to look at horses or talk about battles or do whatever men did when they were on their own. Tolya came down from the nursery, where he had eaten dinner, but soon ran off with Laika to play in the courtyard (and, no doubt, dirty and rip his new clothes) with any boys of his age he could find. Lara had been curled up in a corner with a book, oblivious to the adults' conversations, but she set it aside when Anna called to her and accompanied the rest of us to the third floor. Taking the seat my daughter pointed out, right in the center of the group, she listened to the bigger girls chat and watched Anna open her gifts.

Once certain that both Anna and Lara were settled, I seized the opportunity to sit beside Katya. Darya had taken over the management of the party, since we were in her house, and she entertained the three visiting mothers. Together, women and girls made enough noise that I could talk with some assurance that no one would overhear me.

"Do you remember when we were that age?" I asked as an opening gambit, rather than dive into my main concern right away. I gestured at the group surrounding Anna. "In some ways it seems like yesterday, and in others centuries ago. To think that the next year I was married!"

"And I not long after," she said with a sigh. "To that old man who couldn't give me a living child. Although my father did better by me than yours did. Grigory Morozov was kind, at least, like my Uncle Gavriil."

I'd been gazing at the girls—Lara's elfin charm, Lyuba's animation and fire, Anna's serene grace, the three of them standing out from the others, who seemed almost interchangeable. Fair hair, eyes ranging from light brown to blue, pale and pretty, neither too fat nor too thin—even their names were predictable: Elena, Vera, Sophia. And to think that once I'd been like them, poised on the brink of womanhood, my future determined by the choices my father made.

"Yes," I said to Katya. "I like your Uncle Gavriil. He seems sweet. He didn't bear a grudge against me for turning him down, although Igor insisted he did."

"Do you wish you'd accepted him?" She sounded mildly curious, no more.

I shook my head. "I was in love with Anfim. I still am." I paused, not wanting to push her too far too fast. But after a moment I added, "And you? Do you ever regret wedding my cousin?"

She shrugged, an elegant gesture that nonetheless revealed a certain discomfort. "He's not a bad husband. Thinks a lot of himself, but I knew that before I accepted him. He orders me around more than I like. I don't understand his obsession with recovering this estate when a dozen others would do as well. Nor do I understand why he constantly pushes for more, even though we have my uncle's patronage, an adequate income, and a nice place to live. But Igor comes home most nights and he doesn't beat me or embarrass me with women, so on the whole I'm satisfied."

Her description of marriage sounded dreary and depressing compared to the bliss I felt with Anfim, but it did suggest she might not have planned Igor's assault on our estate. Did she know about the threats her husband had made against Anfim, Anna, and me?

I toyed with the idea that I'd wronged her, but I still wasn't certain, so I set the possibility aside for future consideration and pursued another trail. "What possessed him to bring Prince Pavel here today? He seemed almost to be pushing the boy at Anna, although her contract with Yuri strengthens Igor's connection with your uncle. Does he not value that?"

"Oh, he does," Katya said. "He feels betrayed, I think, that Uncle Gavriil agreed to the match without consulting him. And he has a Vorontsov connection through his marriage to me, so he believes he doesn't need another. He doesn't take me into his confidence, you understand. These are my impressions based on what I overhear him say to his cronies. But I believe he would rather wed Anna to a Shuisky prince like Pavel and expand his web of connections in that way. Or to one of the Belsky clan, since Prince Dmitry seems to survive every challenge to his influence."

"But the contract's already signed," I said. "He can't break it without paying hefty penalties."

"Which my uncle would not waive," Katya agreed. "Nor should he. Perhaps Igor has a plan to get the money out of the Shuiskys—as part of a new settlement, you know."

Another disturbing possibility. Gavriil Vorontsov and Niki would continue to back the contract, but since Igor was the official head of the clan, their steadfastness might not be enough to offset Igor's withdrawal of support. I could argue my rights as Anna's mother, and Anfim as her stepfather, but that too might not suffice, given that I had signed the document only as a witness and Anfim not at all. My belief that I had secured my daughter's future took a nasty hit.

I didn't want to share such thoughts with Katya, whose loyalties I still questioned. "It seems that Igor learned the wrong things from his association with Fyodor Koshkin if it causes him to undervalue the relationship with your uncle," I said instead. "What went wrong between Igor and Koshkin, anyway? I recall Koshkin taking Igor to stay at his house after that business with my father's will. Yet these days his name never comes up."

"You're halfway right." She paused while Darya raised a cup filled with cider and toasted Anna on her betrothal. The rest of us rose and repeated the toast, but when we resumed our seats, Katya continued. "Koshkin remained Igor's patron until our wedding, but my uncle wields more power and influence. There's been no break with Koshkin that I know of; Igor just doesn't seek him out anymore."

Which might mean anything from an ongoing scheme concealed by a pretense of indifference to a sundered bond. "Has Igor promised Pavel more than he can deliver, do you think?"

"If by 'more than he can deliver,' you mean Anna's hand, I don't know. As I told you, Igor doesn't discuss his plans with me. He believes women can't handle complexity."

My tension exploded in laughter. "He said that of *you*?" I asked. "How do you keep your mouth shut when he spouts such nonsense?"

That wrung a smile out of her. "With great difficulty," she admitted. "But we don't spend much time together, so I've managed to stay quiet so far. I have more important concerns of my own." She touched her stomach. "Like you and Darya, I'm with child."

"How wonderful!" I was genuinely happy for her. "You've waited so long. More than two years. When did you find out?"

"Oh, it's not the first time." A flash of sorrow crossed her face, and I reached for her hand. "But I waited five months before telling anyone about this one, so I hope for the best. The baby quickened a week ago."

The loose robes we women wore hid the evidence of pregnancy, but I should have noticed the signs. I'd spent too much time readjusting to married life. "I too hope for the best—for both of you," I said. "And Igor, of course." The thought of my ambitious cousin as a competent or caring father strained credulity, but if Katya could tolerate him, it was not for me to criticize.

Darya interrupted us then, and I shared the news with her. "Yours will arrive first," I said to Katya, running a quick calculation in my head. "August. Then Darya's in September, and mine not until October or thereabouts."

Darya and I exchanged glances, and for a tense moment I wondered if she would ask Katya to join us in the countryside. I hoped she wouldn't, because where Katya went, Igor might follow, and that would destroy both the pleasure and the point of our retreat—especially if Igor arrived with Prince Pavel in tow.

My sister must have reached the same conclusion, because she said nothing about our plans to leave Moscow. Instead she called us to circle around Anna, whose friends' mothers were indicating a desire to return to their homes and families. The party ended not long afterward, and by late afternoon Lara, Tolya, Masha, Laika, and I were heading back to our own home.

When we set out that morning, I'd had quite limited expectations of the party. I'd imagined a comfortable afternoon with friends, a celebration of my daughter's steps toward adulthood, another opportunity to take the measure of Yuri Vorontsov, and perhaps a few insights wrung out of Katya. And indeed, all those things had happened. But I'd also run into Cousin Igor, scheming once more, and made the acquaintance of Prince Pavel, clearly a rival for the role of Anna's husband—and an unwelcome one, at that. So I had to worry that he and Igor might find a way to upset my neatly engineered arrangement for my daughter's welfare.

Katya, however, had proven far more forthcoming than I'd anticipated. And the exchange with my cousin, however unpleasant, left me with a better idea of the dangers I faced.

I just had to ensure that Igor didn't bring his scheme, whatever it was, to fruition.

Chapter Fourteen

IN PART TO KEEP OUR COUSIN OFF-BALANCE, AND IN PART to move our own plans along, we left Moscow a few days after the party. Even in carriages laden with goods to last us through the summer, we could cover the distance to my rural estate in eight hours or less. Masha and the boys, as well as Andrusha's nurse, occupied one carriage with Laika, when the dog grew tired of loping beside the horses; Darya, the three girls, and I rode in another. We would stop several times during the journey to stretch our legs and relieve the strain of such cramped quarters. Even so, the lengthening days of early May meant that we could reach our destination long before sunset.

Yuri and Nikita rode alongside, with small contingents of armed guards before and behind to protect us from bandits on the road. A good thing, too, as we had barely passed from sight of the city walls before a group of ruffians in peasant dress topped with quilted armor galloped up, took a good look at the warriors with their spears and sabers, and wheeled into hasty retreat. The zing of unleashed arrows sped them on their way as we tumbled out of the stopped carriage to watch.

"Igor?" I bent forward to whisper the question in my sister's ear, not wanting to cause further alarm among the three girls, who were fluttering and murmuring like a cote of disturbed doves.

Darya shrugged. "Who can know? I doubt it. Bandits aren't uncommon on rural roads. They withdrew fast enough when they saw the guards."

"It's rare for them to attack so close to the city," I pointed out. She acknowledged the truth of that statement with a nod. But with no more information to go on, we reentered the carriage and resumed our journey, grateful that the escort's presence had deflected robbery, injury, or even death among our party.

Yet I wondered. Although I'd seen no familiar faces among the attackers, and nothing distinguished their clothes or manner from other ruffians I'd occasionally encountered on this road, it seemed a little *too* coincidental that we should suffer an attempted assault at a time when we were under threat from our cousin, even though we'd done our best to conceal the news of our departure from him. The possibility that either my sister's household or mine contained a spy loomed ever larger. I could only hope that we had left that informant behind in Moscow.

But in case we had not, I decided to ask Niki to assign half the guards to watch the estate. The other half could relieve them for as long as he and Yuri stayed with us and accompany them if duty called them away.

As the carriages rolled along, the attack continued to nag at me. I'd felt so certain we would be safe if we could only reach Malinino, but I had to face the possibility that I'd been wrong.

How deep did Igor's malice run, and how far would I have to go to combat it?

A peaceful hour or so passed, and our fruitless speculation gradually yielded its place to normal conversation. I didn't forget my questions and fears, but I set them aside for later. "I can't wait to see the house again," I told Darya and the girls as we reached the halfway point. "Why did we stay away for so long? Papa, I know, but he's been gone three years already."

"Habit, I suppose," my sister said. "But you're right: we should have done this ages ago. Anna, do you even remember Malinino?"

Anna rubbed her nose, as if by some magical gesture she could summon the spirit of the past. "Not really," she said after a while. "Maybe when I see it. How old was I?"

I had to stop and think before I could find the right words to answer that question, simple as it seemed on the surface. "You were five the last time I brought you." I hesitated before going on, but she was growing up and soon to be married. I wanted her to hear the full story of her father's disgrace before her in-laws dropped what to them would seem like a casual comment that would rock her world and undermine her trust in me. Here, in this secluded carriage, seemed like as good an opportunity as any. "Rumors reached Moscow of your father's escape from the monastery where he'd been confined, and I wanted to get away from the city in case he came looking for us. It wasn't until we returned in the fall that I learned of his death."

Her mouth opened, but no sound came out. "How did he die?" Lyuba asked.

Lara's sharp intake of breath made me hesitate for a moment before answering, but glancing her way reassured me. I'd startled her, but she knew nothing of Semyon except that he had died. She must wonder what happened to him. I decided it was safe to go on.

Even so, another awkward pause ensued while I decided how much I should say right then. "You've met Alexei's half-brother, Ogodai Khan?"

Lyuba nodded. "At Alexei and Maria's wedding. I was only six then, though, so I don't remember him well. Anna, you met him too."

"No, I didn't." My daughter's voice still sounded as if someone were choking her—the result of hearing about her father, I assumed—but at least she managed a response. "You're forgetting. We didn't become friends until after Maria's wedding."

"Is that possible?" I asked, teasing them. "There's a time before you two became closer than twins?" Lara giggled.

Anna giggled, too, and poked Lyuba, who poked her back. Fifteen or not, they hadn't grown up altogether. "I know who Ogodai Khan is, though," my daughter said. "He's the one who rescued Anfim from the Crimeans."

"Indeed he is," I said. "He's also the man who killed your father."

That provoked more shocked exclamations, even from Darya. Only then did I realize that in my eagerness to put my unwanted first marriage behind me, I'd hidden the full details of its aftermath even from my sister. As briefly as possible, I told them how Semyon had become involved in a plot to kidnap the young grand prince and his brother, how the discovery of my husband's crime had almost brought him to the executioner's block but had instead ended with our divorce and his exile to a monastery. Halfway through, I recalled that Fyodor Koshkin, Lyuba's father, had masterminded the plot and manipulated my husband into joining it, then stepped back and let Semyon take the blame.

I decided not to mention that part, since disillusioning Lyuba as to her father's true nature was her older sister's job, not mine.

"Semyon became a bandit chief after his escape," I told them, simplifying the tale to keep it as clear as possible. "He and his men attacked pilgrims visiting the northern monasteries."

"Like the robbers who attacked us today," Anna said. Her fingers twitched, as if in fear.

"Yes." I leaned forward and covered her hand with mine to comfort her. "But just like today, the pilgrims had defenders. Ogodai and his brother-in-law Daniil captured Semyon and imprisoned him. But he had threatened Ogodai's sister—Nasan, who was a good friend of mine when she lived in Moscow. You remember her, Darya."

My sister nodded. "We attended her wedding." To the man Papa had chosen for my sister, no less.

"I remember her, too," Lyuba interjected. "She wields a sword and a bow, and she can ride anything with four hooves and a neigh—even bareback, Maria says. She sounds like the kind of woman I want to become."

"She and Daniil are a good match," Darya said, as if Lyuba hadn't spoken. Looking at the girls, she added, "They lived next door, in Katya and Dmitry's house, before leaving to join Ogodai Khan's horde. I was nursing Papa then, but I saw Nasan from time to time."

I couldn't miss the questions in the girls' eyes, but not wanting to get sidetracked, I returned to my tale. "Let me finish. Semyon had tried to capture Nasan, so when he later attempted to escape, Ogodai shot him through the heart. You don't threaten the sister of a Tatar khan if you want to live."

They besieged me for details then, and I couldn't blame them. I'd done the same thing myself when I first heard the story from Maria, who had witnessed the entire episode. I answered them as best I could until, somewhat to my relief, the carriage stopped. I heard the jingle of horse tack and the thump of boots hitting the ground. A shaft of light pierced the gloom of our conveyance as the door opened. Nikita stuck his head inside long enough to say, "We're here." The girls piled out first, then Darya followed at a more sedate pace.

I went last, and by the time I set foot on the driveway, Tolya was leaping and shouting while Laika ran circles around him and barked like a mad thing. Masha looked distinctly harried, poor woman, after hours in a carriage with a rambunctious boy, a restless toddler, and a dog. Andrusha's nurse, Nadia, didn't seem much better off, perhaps because her charge howled as if possessed by a house spirit. Yuri, though, had already taken Anna's hand and was ushering her and the other girls toward the house. The ruckus of our arrival alerted those inside, and servants poured out to greet us.

Darya took her son from Nadia's arms and rocked him until he quieted. I stopped long enough to secure Niki's agreement to post guards around the estate, then joined her. "Good thing we sent the servants ahead," I said. "Can you imagine having to get everyone settled without any advance preparation? I hope they have supper waiting."

"I see smoke rising from the kitchen." She pointed to a wooden cottage set aside from the sprawling main house, also made of logs but, unlike our Moscow home, on a single level. "That's a good sign."

Her maid—Alya, who would care for all of us women during this summer break—appeared at the door and bowed, first to Yuri and the girls, then to the rest of us. Petka came right behind her; we'd chosen him to act as steward, since

Mishka remained to supervise the Moscow estate and watch over Anfim's house in our absence. Eva, too, had remained in Moscow; after watching her weep buckets at the idea of heading for the country, I'd decided that insisting on her presence would be more trouble than it was worth. Silly girl—she must have a young man in the town. Or maybe, like Lara, Eva had never experienced life outside the massive city walls.

Her loss, because here we were, surrounded by green grass and scented wildflowers, a briskly flowing stream visible in the distance and bird song rippling from unseen throats among the trees. Before I had time to appreciate the full beauty of the May woods, we entered the house, leaving Niki's and Yuri's warriors outside.

Watching them move into position, I shivered. Despite my best efforts, the lingering menace of my cousin's hatred cast a shadow on the bucolic loveliness of our surroundings.

"I wish Anfim would write," I said to Darya a week later. We sat on a cloth spread under an oak so massive that it must date from the period right after the Flood. When I looked up, morning sunshine dappled the leaves with brilliance, yellow freckles against an ocean of green. It was too early in the year for roses, but I could still smell the violets I'd crushed as I passed. The grass where Tolya romped with Laika was studded with dandelions and daisies; the ripples in the stream beyond, where Lara and Lyuba strolled along the bank while birds called to one another among the weeping willows, glittered like topaz. Yet on the far side of the meadow, the gleam of steel helmets provided a constant reminder that the serenity around us hid a darker truth.

"I fear the worst. That attack on the road still plagues me. I can't believe Igor has forgotten us, although I wish he would."

Andrusha, staggering around the linen cloth between us, gurgled and reached for yet another acorn. Darya grabbed it before he could stuff it in his mouth and tickled him as he emitted a full-throated roar of protest. He dropped to his hands and knees and abandoned his stumbling attempts to walk in favor of a rapid crawl. This time she swept up the acorn before he could reach it and hid it under the cloth. He promptly forgot its existence and accepted a rattle instead.

"It must be worrying," she said. "But suppose the groom didn't deliver your letter? He too could have run into trouble along the way."

A sudden pang gripped my insides at the thought. I clutched at my stomach, and the pain faded, but the fear remained. "That's exactly what bothers me," I gasped.

"Are you all right?" She reached for my hand, and I heard anxiety in her voice.

"Just a spasm. It's easing now." I inhaled, rubbing the slight bulge where, if all went well, I would soon sense the child's fluttering. "I think the baby will be fine. I'm the one who's terrified. If our cousin could hire bandits to attack us, why not Anfim as well?"

"We don't know that Igor ordered the attack on us," Darya reminded me. "And Anfim traveled with a government escort. He'll be safe, I'm sure."

"Don't forget that intruder the guards frightened off the day after we arrived," I said. "I bet if they'd caught him, he would have turned out to work for Igor. The whole thing makes me edgy."

"True," Darya said. "We never had trouble like that before. Do you think we should go back to the city?"

I thought about that, but I couldn't see how we were more vulnerable on a guarded rural estate, where any stranger would stand out, than amid crowded city streets. "No. That would just make life easier for Igor. But I do worry about Anfim. And I miss him. It's been five weeks already. You know how that is."

"I do," she admitted. "Niki left this very morning, and I already yearn for him." She pointed to her left, where Yuri was pushing Anna in a swing. "And I'm glad we came. It's been good for the children. Those two as well."

"You're right." From my seat under the tree, I could see my daughter's flushed face and sparkling eyes, hear her joyous laughter. From Yuri's mischievous expression I deduced he was alternately teasing and flirting with her. "He's such a lovely young man, and he seems to bring out the best in her. Every day I see fewer traces of that shy, biddable girl we've known for so many years." I was proud of the self-assured young woman my Anna was becoming.

"Has he said how long he can stay?" Darya asked. "The more time they spend together, the better."

I shook my head. "He's in no hurry to leave, that much I'm sure of. I suppose it depends on when the summer orders to muster go out. It's usually not until July, right?"

"Usually. I hope Niki isn't called this time. He and Alexei have managed to stay in Moscow for two years, but that can't last forever. Even tsareviches get military assignments." She pulled a handful of last year's dried oak leaves out of Andrusha's clenched fist. He'd reached the edge of the cloth while we talked and now rolled happily in the grass, so preoccupied with the new sensations this movement provoked (or so I assumed) that he forgot to howl at the loss of his captured leaves.

Darya must have fears of her own that she wanted to talk through, because so far she hadn't told me anything I didn't know. Six years with Semyon had burned the timing of military assignments into my brain. Indeed, at times I would have sworn that only his frequent absences kept me sane. "Do you have a special reason to worry?" I asked.

"The groom who called Niki back to Moscow told us that the grand prince is collecting forces in Kolomna to attack Kazan. If that's true, he will summon every nobleman able to fight." She pleated the edge of the cloth, then released the folds to capture Andrusha and return him to her lap. He wriggled free and began rolling once more.

I frowned. A campaign against Kazan, and my husband stuck on the wrong side of it? I didn't like that idea one bit.

The first question sparked a second: could this be another part of Igor's scheme—the reason he pushed the assignment in the first place? But I found it hard to imagine my cousin holding *that* kind of power. "I don't understand," I said. "They sent Anfim and the others to see a man who favors Russia installed on the khan's throne. Why would they attack before the envoys even leave the city?"

"I don't know. Perhaps they have inside information." She stared at the stream, as if oblivious to the impact of her words. That was so unlike her that my anxiety rose even higher.

"Anfim did say the situation in Kazan was unstable. I wonder if he and his party alerted the grand prince's council to potential trouble. But in that case, it seems particularly callous to abandon them." I fought to keep my fears under control. One advantage of marrying a state secretary, I'd thought, would be having him out of harm's way most of the time. The thought of him being trapped in a siege made my earlier fears seem petty.

"They may have left the city already." Darya reached for her son, who had fallen asleep sometime after his most recent roll across the grass. Without waking him, she picked him up and resettled him in the shade, where he lay in angelic stillness. From time to time, he smacked his lips as if nursing.

I shook my head. "Then he would have sent word." Unless they too had suffered an attack on the road. I didn't mention that, though. I'd already silenced Darya with my last objection.

Looking around for something that would distract us from a conversation rapidly descending into unverifiable but frightening speculation, I saw Yuri and Anna, standing close together under a beech tree. As I watched, he bent and touched his lips to hers—gently, supporting her chin with his finger. He pulled back almost right away, and she gazed at him. I couldn't read her expression from her profile, but the way she leaned toward him told me she welcomed his embrace, even if she didn't quite know how to respond.

I wondered if he would repeat the kiss. If he did, I might have to intervene for the sake of propriety, despite the contract that bound them.

He didn't, though. Instead he took her hand and said words I couldn't hear. The two of them walked toward the brook, so I guessed he'd managed to rein in his desire. The sunlight sparked copper highlights in his hair and gold ones in Anna's, giving them the appearance of a fairytale couple.

At the edge of the meadow, on this side of the brook path, I saw Lara and Lyuba gesturing in a way that suggested they were acting out one of Lyuba's stories. I could hear them declaiming but not the actual words. When Yuri and Anna joined them, a quick conversation ensued, accompanied by rapid arm movements. Yuri gripped his chest, moaning, and fell backward onto the grass, an arm over his face. Anna sank gracefully to the ground, lying on one side while Lyuba pretended to resuscitate her and Lara ran to guard them from her brother and the dog, neither of whom paid the least attention to the drama being enacted nearby. That was when I recognized the story as *Layla and Majnun*, which Lyuba had read out to us the evening before from my book, translating the tale from Persian into Russian as she went.

When I glanced Darya's way once more, she raised her eyebrows. "Are you sure it's a good idea to make Yuri and Anna wait until the autumn before they wed?"

"Perhaps not. It seemed like the right choice at the time, but it would be better to marry them sooner than have them anticipate their vows. Or for Igor to find a way to separate them. Either would undo everything we were working to prevent." And if Anfim and I could fall under the spell of passion in our thirties, only a dolt would imagine that a fifteen- and an eighteen-year-old could withstand temptation for long. "Anfim expected to return in a few weeks. Whatever my fears, I have to hope that he's well and on his way back. When he gets here—if he does—I'll talk to him about Anna and Yuri. I left him out of the contract because of the urgency. I don't want to ignore him again if I can help it."

"Agreed," my sister said. "I'll write to Niki as well. Then we can start planning for a summer wedding."

Assuming Igor doesn't scotch our plans. But I kept that thought, too, from my sister. Why torment her with phantoms that might never materialize?

I kept a more watchful eye on Anna and Yuri over the week that followed. With each day that passed, my fears for

Anfim's safety increased. At best, I worried that he might not have received my letter and instead have gone to Moscow, where finding an empty house would alarm him. At worst, I imagined an endless stream of potential mishaps, attacks, even murder. At the estate, we suffered no more incursions, from which I concluded that Igor had changed his plans when he learned we had posted guards. But travelers were always vulnerable, even those under royal escort, so the relative safety of Malinino did not allay my concerns for Anfim's well-being.

I lost color in my cheeks, and my appetite waned. Darya chivvied me into tasting the meals the cook prepared with admirable regularity, but the same food I'd found delicious the week before settled in my stomach like the lead weights used at merchants' stalls to measure purchases of flour and groats.

"You must eat," Darya said for the hundredth time. "You'll harm the baby if you don't."

"I know." I picked up a carved wooden spoon and dipped it into the bowl of fragrant cabbage soup, only to put it down again after the first sip. "And I will, as soon as I see Anfim safe and sound. Even a letter would comfort me, because it would mean that he's still alive, that he has some sense of what's going on and where we are."

Instead, a courier arrived the next day, racing in on a lathered horse. A small escort followed at a slower pace. I picked up my skirt and ran toward him, but Petka reached the man first.

"Let me look after your mount, Sir," our steward said as I approached. "He's fair winded, he is. Needs a good rubdown and some water and oats. Here's the mistress to see to you. Solomonida Petrovna's her name."

"Greetings," I said. "Petka, alert the cook. Our guest will need rest and food as well." The courier was bent over, panting, and showed no sign that he could talk. Petka dipped his head in response and left with the horse.

"Grishka!" Yuri said from behind me, and I heard surprise in his voice. "What brings you here, and in such a hurry? You've half-killed poor Champion."

I turned. "You know him, then?"

"He's one of my father's men," Yuri said. "He fights under my command."

Grishka straightened. "We have our orders, Lord. We're to report to Kolomna by the end of the week." He was still struggling for each breath, and I felt sorry for him. He had ridden himself and his horse hard.

"Show him the way to the kitchen, Yuri, if you please," I said. "The cook will give him beer and food. If you leave the horse here to recover and take one of ours, your father can send someone to exchange them at his leisure. I'll find Anna."

"Agreed." He reached for the courier's elbow and walked him toward the kitchen while I went in search of my daughter.

I found her in the main sitting area, stitching, and explained what had happened. "But that's terrible," she cried. "How can the grand prince be so mean?"

I knew better than to take such questions literally. "It's the way of the world, my darling," I told her. "Yuri will be here in a moment to say goodbye. I'll leave you alone with him, since you're contracted, but only for a short time. He has to return to Moscow to collect his army gear and his men. So if he's to reach Kolomna by the end of the week, he must leave soon. You don't want to get him into trouble." I didn't mention that months might pass before they saw each other again.

Even without that reminder, I worried that she might refuse or burst into tears or take her anger out on me, as she had when she learned of my impending marriage. Still worse would be if she inflicted her grief on Yuri. It was her first time enduring these separations, so much a part of noble life—and unlike many women, she cared for the man who would soon ride away. I knew from my own experience how she felt; I'd found it hard enough to accept that Anfim must leave for Kazan despite his promises to stay with me until our child's birth.

But Anna did not disappoint me. Instead she said, "No, Mama," in a shaky voice. "I won't disgrace you. I know a wife must be brave."

"I'm proud of you," I said, and I was.

Yuri came through the door then. "I'll tell Alya to pack your things," I told him. "I trust you to protect Anna's virtue."

"Thank you," he said. "Of course, I will not abuse your faith in me. And I appreciate your help. I'll need whatever will fit in two saddlebags. Essential items only. I'll have my father send for the rest."

"Of course. It's been years since I supervised in circumstances like these, but I haven't forgotten how it's done. Everything will be ready within the hour." I accepted his renewed thanks and left them, as promised.

Not much more than an hour later, Yuri rode off with his men, leaving behind a tearful Anna. Standing on the porch with my hand in Lara's as we waved goodbye, I too felt sad to see him go. Our magical summer had lost part of its charm, my husband had still not returned or sent word, and storm clouds gathered in the distance, presaging a troubled future.

Then, almost like a sign from above, I felt the first, faint fluttering of my unborn babe. Discreetly, I pressed one palm against my stomach, reveling in that unparalleled sensation, that confirmation of the small life growing inside me.

Anna, sobbing outright now that Yuri had passed from sight, didn't notice. I said nothing; it seemed too cruel at that moment to contrast my happiness with her sorrow. Sharing my good news could wait.

As before, the first sign that my fears might be unwarranted was Tolya shrieking, "Papa, Papa, Papa. Look, Laika, Papa is here!"

I'd gone into the house to escape an imminent drizzle after ordering Tolya to follow me and bring the dog, but when I heard the noise I ran back outside. Lara had already retreated to the sitting room, where Lyuba had promised to read to her, but in response to her brother's shouts, she reappeared at the door. I heard her footsteps behind me as I reached the covered porch.

Anfim stopped his horse, a handsome bay, and dismounted a short way from the entrance to the house. I arrived in time to see him pick up Tolya, by now as brown as an acorn and towheaded as only a sun-loving small boy can be. He clung to his father while Laika gambolled around them, uncaring of the rain that slicked her silky fur.

First things first. I whistled to the dog before she could knock them into the mud by accident. The sound caught Anfim's attention, and he raised an arm in greeting before putting Tolya down and grabbing the horse's reins. The four of them strolled toward us, Laika leading the way.

Next to me, Lara jumped up and down. "Give Papa a quick hug," I told her, "then find Petka and have him send a stable boy to look after Papa's horse." She nodded and ran to do my bidding. Anfim swept her up in his arms, kissed her on both cheeks. I heard a brief exchange I couldn't decipher, then he let her go and she dashed past me on her way to fetch the steward.

Tolya leaped onto the porch in a single bound, the dog close behind him. The two of them shook themselves, sending droplets of rain in every direction. "Tolya!" I said, but he was laughing too hard to hear me.

Under normal circumstances, I'd have stopped and made him listen. But right then, his father looped the horse's reins around one of the carved wooden beams that supported the porch roof and joined us. I wrapped my arms around the neck of the man I loved and left boy and dog to fend for themselves while I surrendered to Anfim's kiss.

Chapter Fifteen

Supper was nothing if not lively. Even Anna forgot her woes when Anfim launched into his story of the khan's installation.

"A massive man," he said, describing Shah-Ali, the grand prince's candidate for the throne. "Too fat to ride; he'd break the poor horses' backs, so he travels everywhere either by litter or, in this case, on one of those huge Tatar carts big enough to carry a tent. And what a tent! Gold silk lined with felt, with scarlet brocade for the roof. It takes six oxen to pull it and a dozen men at the back steadying it as it moves. We followed that cart, surrounded by three thousand guards, from Kasimov to Kazan, cursing its slowness the whole way. The first leg of the journey went twice as fast."

He grinned at Lyuba, regarding him with wide, fascinated eyes. "He looks like that elephant from your book," he added. "Solomonida described it to me when she first told me of Gavriil Vorontsov, but Vorontsov is a skeleton compared to Shah-Ali." While the girls exclaimed at that, he bent to murmur in my ear. "And they say he has a wife and dozens of concubines. Can you imagine what their lives must be like?"

I laughed, so delighted to have him back with me that I would have responded the same way to much less humorous thoughts. "And what of the installation itself? Is it anything like our coronations?"

"Not really. Oh, formal speeches and prayers and that sort of thing, of course. But then they seat the khan on a white rug and raise him three times in acclamation. And wasn't that a scene? It took a small army to lift him. The jewels alone must have weighed as much as Laika—rubies the size of pigeons' eggs, diamonds that must gleam in the dark, strings of pearls that reached his waist, feathers formed from jade in his turban, and emeralds stitched into his cloth-of-gold sleeves. Worth a king's ransom, they were."

Lyuba pulled a piece of paper and a stick of charcoal from a hidden section of her robe and scribbled madly as Anfim talked. Lara would soon be hearing tales of a mysterious sultan and his beautiful but doomed bride, I suspected.

"And what then?" Anna asked. "Was that the whole celebration?"

"Not in the least," Anfim told her. "After the acclamation, they held a feast. No pork and no wine—only that smoky, sour koumiss the Tatars love. I don't like it much, but I drank the toasts so as not to offend. The food was delicious, though—more spicy than we're used to, but I got accustomed to that when I traveled with my brothers."

"What did they serve?" Lyuba held her charcoal high, as if awaiting inspiration.

"Lots of things I didn't recognize, but there were lamb pies and dumplings in broth and chunks of goat on long skewers. A whole sheep's head for the new khan. He doled it out piece by piece to those he wished to honor, including us as ambassadors of the grand prince. Most of it went to the princes, though, which was fine with me. I preferred the pies and the dumplings; even the goat had a strong odor, like old game. There were vegetable dishes, which cleansed the palate; those weren't too different from our Russian versions. The best was a very elaborate rice dish cooked in enormous round pans." He held out his arms in a circle, so that only his middle fingertips touched. "That size. Our translator called it *plov*. I don't remember it from my stay at the Tatar camp, but we ate something similar in Bukhara. We presented the grand prince's gifts before the feast began, and they were well received—a very large suit of armor decorated in bronze was Shah-Ali's favorite. There were gifts for the leading beys and princes as well."

Lyuba resumed her scribbling. Other questions poured in from Lara and Tolya, Anna and Darya, but Anfim held up his hand in silent protest. "I want to hear about your summer. Tell me why you decided to come here, and what you've been doing. But first, a moment." He turned to me and said quietly, "You must eat, my love. You're so thin, and you should be rounded by now. Is our baby well?"

I hadn't noticed that I'd stopped eating, so caught up was I in his story. Thus reminded, I reached for a piece of bread and dipped it in the fragrant whitefish stew in front of me. "It has quickened," I murmured. "The day Yuri left, I felt the child move for the first time. So yes, we are both well."

"Then why are you skin and bones?" He clasped my wrist lightly, and I obliged him by chewing the sopped bread before answering.

"When you didn't return, I became anxious," I admitted. "I couldn't eat, although I promise I tried. I will make up for it now. You will stay with us for a while, will you not? Or must you go to Moscow?"

"I came from Moscow," he said. "I know, your letter told me how to find you on the road, but I had to report to Tretiakov first. We ran into bandits on the way home, and I wanted him to get the information as fast as possible."

"You too?" I strove to keep my voice at a level that would not alarm the children. His words gave shape to my worst fears. "Bandits attacked us as well, on the way here, but our escort drove them off. I've been terrified something similar would happen to you."

He didn't answer at first but stared at me with horrified eyes. "You were attacked on the road? Who would do such a thing?"

His obvious concern touched me. I pulled myself together and said, "I think Igor sent them, but I have no proof. There was an intruder, too, but again the guards chased him away. Since then, nothing. But what of you? Was anyone hurt? Were you?"

He peeled back his sleeve, revealing a bandage that covered most of his right forearm while the children gaped at him. "A scratch. They underestimated the size of our escort, so they attacked but did little damage." He rolled the sleeve down again. "But I recognized one of the men. I don't think they were real bandits but military slaves belonging to Igor Grigorevich. That's what I decided Tretiakov must learn, even if it delayed my return to you. So I would guess you're right, and your cousin is behind all three attempts." His mouth compressed into a thin line. "This has to stop."

I gulped for air. I was glad, of course, that he had suffered only a minor injury, but that Igor ... I couldn't even finish the thought.

Anfim touched a finger to my lips, then caressed my cheek. "We'll discuss the implications later. I can stay for a few weeks. And look after you and the baby, as I see is required."

"I'm glad," I said. "Also that the letter reached you. I feared you'd return to Moscow and panic when you found us gone."

"Fortunately, we ran into the courier as we were leaving Kazan, after the installation. I'll tell you more about that later as well." His finger again brushed my lips, a warning not to speak, then he released me and addressed the others. "I want to hear about your time here—what fun you've had, Lara's embroidery, Anna's young man, Lyuba's stories, everything. Let's start with you, Tolya. You've turned seven since I left, and I swear you've grown a head taller. Do you like that wooden saber and shield I brought you from Kazan?"

Tolya nodded with great enthusiasm. "Mama Shura remembered to bring my armor. The dragons had better watch out tomorrow. I'll be a real bogatyr!"

"So you will." Anfim squeezed my hand under the table. "That was nice of Mama Shura. So tell me, what did you and Laika do while I was away?"

Tolya launched into a saga about the dragons he'd slain and the frogs he had caught. Lara broke into the conversation midway to chatter about the wildflowers she'd plucked and walks by the stream and the tales that she and Lyuba and Anna had brought to life with Yuri's help.

I welcomed their chatter, which gave me time to consider what I'd learned from Anfim. Igor grew bolder with each attack. So far, our escorts had saved us all from serious injury or death. Next time, we might not be so lucky.

Anfim was right. We needed to find a way to rein in my cousin—and soon.

So close to the longest day, dusk would not fall for hours. Hand in hand, Anfim and I strolled across the grass. I'd promised to show him the Malinino of my childhood—the raspberry bushes and birches, the clearing where Niki and the rest of us children pelted a grumpy eleven-year-old Igor with acorns, the rippling light on the brook, the stepping stones that led to its far side. But I also planned to find out more about his mission, and especially his close escape on the road.

As we left the meadow for the woods, I heard Tolya behind us. Revitalized by his meal, he called to Laika, who barked in response. Andrusha protested as his nurse, issuing a stream of commands interspersed with condolences that did nothing to stem the toddler's wails, carried him off to bed. Lara let out a shriek of glee at the sound of a whistle, and I turned my head to see Lyuba, hands on her waist, flapping her elbows like a bird, although I couldn't identify the song. Anna sat on the swing, gliding back and forth as if by doing so she could summon Yuri to her side.

"Do you see why I wanted to bring them here?" I asked my husband. "Lara told me she and Tolya had never left the city. I think all children should have a summer without cares, in a place where they can run and climb, where everything they touch is alive or at least part of the natural world. I have such fond memories of this estate."

"I can imagine," he said. "It's so beautiful, so peaceful. And it's been good for them, I can tell. Lara is happier and more robust than when I left. Tolya is in his element, and no wonder. I would have loved these woods and meadows when I was a boy."

"You never spent time in the country either?" That amazed me, although it shouldn't have. Lara's astonishment when I first raised the idea of visiting Malinino had already shown me that her family had no such tradition.

"We're city people, born and bred." He pulled me behind a tree and looked down at me, smiling. "Although a summer here may change that." He kissed me hungrily, and I responded in kind. After weeks apart, being with him again—my husband, my love—felt like a precious gift.

Sometime later, we sat on a rock near the raspberry bushes, our hands and mouths stained crimson as if we too were children. "Tell me what you didn't say at the supper table." I picked up another berry from the kerchief spread between us and held it out to him. "Start with the attack, and what Tretiakov said when you told him." When we left the house after supper, I had given him the details of our run-ins with the bandits and intruder.

He plucked the berry from my fingers and popped it into his mouth. I saw his Adam's apple move as he swallowed. Then he answered my question. "He was concerned, and rightly so. The force was small, no more than a dozen men, but it tells us that Igor Grigorevich is getting bolder. He's an opportunist, not a planner. An idea enters his head, he tries it out, and if it works, he claims credit for it. If it doesn't, he pretends it has nothing to do with him. This time, though, he's gone too far to back off. I identified his man, and if the authorities find him, they can force a confession out of him. I wonder if Igor understands that. If he does, he may become even more dangerous."

He made a good point, although I didn't like what it implied—that we were still at risk. "Can Tretiakov act against Igor?" I asked. "Or report him to someone who can?"

Anfim shrugged. "He'll tell Gorbaty, and they'll keep a watch on your cousin. He's too high-ranking to accuse without more proof than I can provide. I caught only a glimpse of the man; I could be mistaken. They can't take that chance." When I didn't respond, having no idea what to say, he patted my hand. "But we know the truth, so we can prepare ourselves for Igor's next attempt."

"We need to stop him before then." I put my thoughts from earlier into words. "His next stab in the dark could be fatal."

"Yes," Anfim said. "Tretiakov tells me Igor's been sent to Kolomna, though. With luck, that will keep him busy while we make plans." He patted my hand once more. "I need time to think. Let's talk of something else."

"I'd like to see your wound first," I said. He rolled up his sleeve again, and I undid the bandage. It was a clean slash that ran along the inside of his arm, halfway from his elbow to his wrist, and already scabbed over. Finding no sign of infection, I rewrapped it. "I'll put some ointment on it later. Tell me about the site where the courier reached you."

"Ah." He plucked another berry from the cloth and ate it. "Confession time. You've asked me more than once what took me east, but I have to be careful in Moscow. It's too easy to be overheard there. But here I think it's safe, and after three months as my wife, you've earned the right to hear what your husband is doing."

His trust thrilled me even more than his kiss. "I remember what Niki said about Prince Alexander and his campaign. Was he right?"

Anfim raised one shoulder. I read it as an admission, and he soon confirmed that view. "For the most part," he said. "The installation was real, although I doubt it will have any long-term effect—except to provoke the opposition. By the time we left Kazan, I'd already heard muttered complaints from the same leaders who drove out Shah-Ali's predecessor, as well as rumors that Safa-Girei and his father-in-law are gathering an army to overturn Shah-Ali. That was what Tretiakov wanted to know—whether the Kazanians would remain loyal, as they have not before."

"And Prince Alexander?" I rolled a raspberry back and forth with my index finger, then placed it against my tongue, savoring the tangy sweetness.

"He's pleased with us." He grinned at me and tapped the corner of my lips. "It's good to see you relaxed once more. When I got off that horse, I didn't like the strain I saw on your face."

"I missed you. It's good to have you home. And when you smile at me that way, like a mischievous boy, the resemblance between you and Tolya is so strong it makes me laugh." I fed him the last raspberry. "Why is Prince Alexander pleased?"

"Because we found the opening he's been looking for." He folded the empty kerchief, stood, and held out his uninjured arm. "Come, walk with me, and I'll explain."

I accepted his hand, and we strolled along the brook, away from the house. The soft light, filtered green by the leaves above our heads, mingled with the shushing sound of branches shifting in the breeze. We stepped under a weeping willow, and I stood with my back against the trunk and put my arms around his neck. "Explain. Who knows when you will tell me, if not now?"

The willow branches enclosed us like a secret room, disturbed only by the occasional quack of a duck floating past, the splash of a leaping fish. The scent of mossy earth and the wild roses that grew on the other side of the stream created a sense of magic—like that first night we made love, although so very different. Midsummer, not midwinter, yet the scene generated the same illusion of inhabiting a private world, one where even my beastly cousin could not intrude.

Perhaps Anfim felt it too, because instead of answering he wrapped me in his arms for a lingering kiss. I'd almost forgotten my question when he raised his head and said,

"On the way there, Shah-Ali pointed out a hill not far from Kazan—almost uninhabited, with rivers on two sides, making it easy to defend. He suggested it could become a staging area for launching an attack against the city. We were on our way home when your messenger found us, and we'd stopped to examine it. The khan's instincts are sound. It's not clear how we could build a fortress there without attracting the wrong kind of attention from Kazan, but that, fortunately, is not my job. I relayed the information to Moscow, and the military men will work out the details."

I released a slow breath. After waiting so long for him to confide in me, I felt as if our marriage had entered a new stage. "And when you traveled with your brothers? Were you looking for fortress sites then, too?"

"No, that was more general," he said. "I listened in the bazaars, to hear what people thought when they believed no one could understand them. No one would take me for a Tatar, given the way I look, so they assumed I couldn't speak their language. I can't say I enjoyed my stay in Ogodai Khan's horde, but three months there taught me more than twelve years in the chancery. I'm completely fluent now. That's why Tretiakov asked me to spy for him in the first place. I did take mental notes on the terrain as well, and Tretiakov passed them on to Prince Alexander, but I see the rivers and the roads as a merchant would see them. I learned a fair amount about food supplies and weaponry, though. I think they found that useful."

"And Igor?" I hated to bring up my cousin again, but it seemed important to have a sense of how much harm he could do. "Did he guess you were spying?"

"I didn't tell him." Anfim frowned. "He must have had connections of his own, even then, so he may have found out. But why did you ask? Has Igor done more than you've told me so far?"

"He worries me. He's encouraging Prince Pavel Shuisky to court Anna." I told him about the betrothal party. "And from what you say, he now has the grand prince's ear in Kolomna."

Anfim made a disgusted face at the sound of Shuisky's name. "A popinjay. Young Vorontsov's a far better choice. I met him only once, but he impressed me with his kindness and good sense." He tugged me away from the willow tree. "Let's get back to your nasty cousin later. I want to walk with you through these beautiful woods, then retire to our own chamber where we can—with due deference to our developing son or daughter—celebrate my return."

I saw no reason to argue with that plan, so I let him pull me onto the path and showed him where to find the stepping stones that crossed the stream.

Two weeks later, another courier from Moscow arrived to alert Darya that Niki and Alexei, too, must report to Kolomna. My sister complained bitterly. I sympathized with her, and said so, but I knew the only real remedy was Niki's return unscathed. Had I not tortured myself during Anfim's journey to Kazan? And in Kolomna Igor waited, like a spider, for the first opportunity to entrap us that came his way.

My pregnancy, now visible whenever I removed my encompassing robes, had entered the stage where I felt myself capable of moving mountains. With Anfim at my side, I found my appetite restored. He loved to touch my belly when we were alone, waiting for the flutters that reassured us both that our unborn baby thrived. In this phase of blooming motherhood, I let Lara and Tolya place their palms against my robe to sense the movement of the hidden child, an exercise they found quite miraculous. Lara, especially, rushed to my side when I mentioned that the baby was kicking, then stared at Andrusha as if she imagined the newborn would come out as big as a toddler.

"No, no," I told her one day when she voiced this thought. I held out my arms, bent at the elbows, hands angled neither to left nor to right. "More like this size. Remember when Andrusha was first born? He was tiny compared to how big he is now. We'll swaddle this little one at first to keep him—or her—comfortable, and you'll be able to hold the baby in your arms."

"Was I swaddled? And Tolya?" She sounded incredulous that anyone could confine her energetic brother.

"I expect so," I said. "Newborn babies aren't used to living in this big, wide world of ours with its bright light and loud noises. They're in a dark, enclosed space. So they cry less if they're tightly wrapped." I laughed then. "I wouldn't try that with Tolya now. He'd tear the house down."

When she burst out laughing at the thought, I smiled at her. "I'll show you what to do. You're a wonderful big sister, so I'm sure you'll learn fast and be a great help to me."

Alas, not long after that conversation, a new courier—one I didn't recognize—arrived from Moscow, horse and man as lathered and exhausted as the pair who had dragged Yuri away from us a month ago. Anfim greeted the newcomer by name and, as I had done on that earlier occasion, summoned Petka to care for his mount. Unasked, I ordered the cook to prepare refreshments and received a grateful nod from both men in response. My stomach clenched at the thought that I would soon be overseeing the packing of my husband's things. And what would happen to Anfim—to us—then?

Indeed, when Petka returned from the stable to escort the messenger to the kitchen, Anfim came toward me. The frown on his face was not encouraging.

"You're called away." This time I did not protest. "Where?"

"Kolomna," he said. "A shorter journey this time, but I have to reach the city by July 1."

"Kolomna!" I tried without success to conceal my dismay. "Yuri, Niki, Alexei, and now you—all in Igor's backyard, where he can cause as much trouble as he likes."

Anfim looked resigned but not happy. "Yes, alas. There's a big gathering there, training for a future attack on Kazan. Not the whole army, of course. Some have to stay behind to guard against enemies from the west and south. But several divisions have massed around Kolomna, together with the generals most likely to oversee any future campaign. How else can the grand prince get firsthand experience of command?"

"I see," I told him. "But you're not in the army. Why do they need you?"

"Some kind of administrative problem." He stared at the house rather than me, so I deduced that it was the summons that bothered him, not my questions. "Novgorod is under orders to send a contingent of musketeers to join the military exercises, but there's been some sort of mixup. Tretiakov wants me to find out what went wrong, straighten it out, and report back. As soon as I do, I'll rejoin you here. With luck, the whole thing won't take more than two weeks."

"You know I wish you could stay," I said. "But you can't. Watch out for Cousin Igor, and say hello to Niki and Alexei when you see them. With luck, you'll have a chance to renew your acquaintance with Yuri Gavriilovich and …"

"Give him Anna's love," he finished for me. "I will."

I held out my hand. "Fair enough. Let's get you packed. Tretiakov hasn't given you much time, but I'm sure you can reach Kolomna in three days, even if it rains."

He bent and kissed the tip of my nose. "It won't rain. It wouldn't dare. Am I not traveling on the grand prince's orders? But yes, compared to Kazan, this distance is nothing. Goodness, we're already halfway there!"

Chapter Sixteen

Malinino, July 29, 1546

"I need to speak to you." Anfim tugged at my arm. "In private, without delay." He bent forward and murmured in my ear, "Igor's really done it this time."

"Of course." I flinched at the urgency in his tone. He'd just returned from his journey to Kolomna—with Nikita, who swept Darya into his arms, then stopped to kiss and hug their son before taking her off to walk in the meadow so they could talk.

The children clustered round my husband, Tolya clutching his father's arm. Between demands to show off Laika's latest tricks and pleas for Papa to admire a collection of snail shells and stones, he talked nonstop. Next to him stood Anna, composed on the surface, but the way she clutched her cotton overdress with her hands suggested an agony of impatience. Lyuba and Lara hovered nearby.

"Hush, Tolya," I said. "Give your papa time to breathe before you deluge him with dogs and snails. He has something he needs to discuss with me, so we're going to our own room. You'll have the whole evening to show him your collection and Laika's tricks."

Tolya scrunched up his face, but he knew better than to object. Lara took a step back, as if yielding her place, and I smiled at her. But it was Anna's reaction that caught my attention. Her eyes grew moon-shaped with concern, and I saw her composure crack. What had she heard—or thought she'd heard—in my brief exchange with Anfim?

"Igor's really done it this time," my husband had said. But how?

The only way to find out was to go with Anfim. "Try to keep Tolya out of trouble. We'll be back soon," I said in the most reassuring tone I could muster, then tucked my arm in my husband's and walked to our room at the far end of the house.

"What happened?" I barred the door, moved to the settle at the opposite side of the room, and held out my arm. "You look so grim."

He sat beside me and took my outstretched hand in both of his. We hadn't even kissed in greeting yet, another sign that whatever concerned him was serious. "It's Yuri," he said after a long pause. "He's on his way to the monastery at Ferapontovo. Under orders from the grand prince to become a monk. And that's the *good* news. For a while, I thought the story I'd bring you would be much worse."

"What?" I strove to keep my voice low. No wonder he didn't want to blurt this out in front of Anna. She'd have a fit when she learned she couldn't marry the boy she loved despite our promises. "Why? Something to do with Igor?"

He shook his head like a person trying to clear his mind of unwanted memories. "The whole incident was shocking. I wish I could spare you, but I need to talk—and you need to know what we're dealing with. It started out simply enough. You'll recall that I told you before I left how Tretiakov had received confusing information about the number of musketeers demanded from Novgorod. When I got to Kolomna, I discovered that the reports sent to Moscow were correct. Due to conflicting messages about numbers, the generals were in an uproar because they'd expected many more gunners from Novgorod than they received."

"It sounds like an honest misunderstanding," I said, more bewildered than before.

"And easy to fix, one would think, especially during training exercises," Anfim agreed. "All they had to do was send for the missing men. But no one wanted to break the news to the grand prince, who's becoming more irascible as he grows into his power. The generals settled on Prince Kubensky to perform the unwelcome task, and he passed it on to your cousin Igor."

"Igor," I said with a sigh. "So Igor approached the grand prince. But how did that lead to Yuri becoming a monk?"

Anfim's grip on my hand tightened. "That's where it gets complicated. At first the grand prince wanted nothing to do with the matter. He told Igor to stay nearby and sent Yuri's uncle Demid and Kubensky to deal with those in charge of the Novgorod musketeers. Yuri went with them only because his uncle commanded it. But an hour or two later, Demid reported back, and the grand prince didn't like what he heard. First he turned on your cousin, accusing him of having misrepresented the facts and threatening punishment. Igor cowered, then shifted the blame to Demid and the others— including Yuri. And me, but Demid spoke up for me, saying that Tretiakov had sent me to straighten out the mess. Igor grumbled like the wheels of Elijah's thunder chariot, but he must have decided his chances of wriggling out of trouble were better if he stuck with accusing the Vorontsovs—which didn't make me feel great, I assure you, even if it did save my skin."

"How like Igor. Always ready to sacrifice others," I said bitterly. "I'm glad you escaped unscathed."

"I'll be ever grateful to Demid for that," he said with a rueful smile.

I tightened my grip on his hand. "But how did Igor manage to incriminate Yuri? Any fool knows that a boy of eighteen takes orders from forty-year-olds; he doesn't give them."

"Believe me, pointing that out would not have mollified Grand Prince Ivan," Anfim said. Hearing frustration in his voice, I indicated my understanding with a nod, and he continued. "He expects the nobles to follow his orders, even if he's half their age. And he didn't go after Yuri right away. He targeted Demid first, demanding to know why he hadn't already punished those responsible. Igor at least had the sense not to contradict the grand prince, but Demid chose to argue."

"A bad habit of his, Yuri told us," I said, remembering the day we introduced Anna to her betrothed. "His father kept urging Demid to be more respectful."

"Did he? Too bad Demid didn't listen. He might be alive today if he had."

"Alive?" My throat tightened as I glimpsed for the first time the true horror of the events my husband had witnessed.

"Yes, alive." Anfim released my hand, stood, and paced about the room before returning to sit next to me once more. "Ivan lost his temper. He ordered the three nobles executed— not just Demid and Kubensky but Yuri as well. On the spot, without a chance to confess their sins before they died."

I gasped. Condemn three loyal servitors to Hell for a minor offense? What kind of monster was ruling us?

Anfim went on as if I'd made no sound, as if he couldn't stop. "The soldiers lined them up and beheaded the older men with swords while the grand prince looked on. Then Yuri threw himself full-length on the ground and begged for the grand prince's forgiveness. It worked. Ivan changed his mind and sentenced Yuri to the monastery instead."

He hesitated. I had time to consider and reject a dozen possible causes before he added, "I could see your cousin wasn't happy when the grand prince spared Yuri. He muttered something to Pavel Shuisky—the one you told me was interested in marrying Anna—and the two of them smirked and walked off. When I managed to get close enough to overhear them, Igor was telling Pavel that this result was better than nothing."

"Do you mean forcing the tonsure on Yuri was better than nothing? Igor wanted Yuri to *die* to prevent him from wedding Anna?" I'd harbored few illusions about my cousin, but this went beyond my worst imaginings.

"I believe so," Anfim said. "Igor knew Yuri's death or tonsure would break the contract without any penalty. He saw his chance and took it. That's how his mind works."

I knew he spoke the truth. Yet the reality of it shocked me. "So Demid pays the ultimate penalty, Yuri goes to a monastery—and Igor gets off scot-free?"

Anfim's mouth twisted as if he'd bitten into a sour quince. "Better than scot-free. The grand prince appointed your cousin to fill Kubensky's shoes. In the Great Regiment, no less. As a reward for exposing the Vorontsov traitors and their accomplice Kubensky."

The Great Regiment was the most prestigious of the five divisions. A real twist of the knife, that Igor should reap a reward while Yuri—and my daughter—suffered. "That's the worst news I ever heard," I said. "Thanks be to God that Yuri escaped with his life, but Anna will be heartbroken. She's been longing to see him every day since he left."

My husband pulled me closer, and I rested my head on his shoulder. Whether I sought to give comfort or receive it, I couldn't tell. I suspected Anfim couldn't either.

"There were other penalties, but none so severe," he added in an unsteady voice. "Exile, torture—even of people who didn't side with Vorontsov."

"That makes no sense!"

"I know," he said. "None of it makes much sense. It was unwise of Demid to argue, but he spoke with the best of intentions. He wanted to protect the grand prince's reputation for justice. Hardly a crime that merits the death penalty."

He rubbed his hand across his forehead, as if the memory hurt his brain, before continuing. "There's more. Ivan confiscated the victims' property on behalf of the crown. The family will get the bodies for burial but nothing else."

"How can a boy be so harsh?" I could hardly speak.

"That's the problem in a nutshell. He's not a boy anymore," Anfim said. "He turns sixteen next month, but too many members of his council treat him as the helpless child he was for so long. I suspect he wants the nobles to understand they have to stop telling him what to do, or they'll pay a heavy price."

I considered that. Anfim was probably right, although so extreme a punishment imposed on a pair of close advisers with such haste and cruelty, such lack of concern for the victims' families or even their souls, didn't bode well for the future of the monarchy.

"He confiscated the victims' property," I repeated, only then grasping what I'd heard. "That would make it difficult for Yuri to support a bride even if he hadn't received the order to become a monk." I wondered in passing how Gavriil Vorontsov would react to the news of his son's forced tonsure. They'd seemed close, and although Gavriil had other sons, so his lineage would continue, I suspected he would still mourn the banishment of this one.

"True," Anfim said. "Although estates and income can be restored. The tonsure is a bigger problem. How many people succeed in revoking monastic vows?"

"Very few." I closed my eyes for a moment, casting my thoughts back in time. "It was a good day for Igor. Katya told me he felt betrayed when Gavriil Vorontsov signed the contract against Igor's will. His revenge is complete: Gavriil's brother dead and his son exiled, doomed never to wed. And Anna now has no intended husband to protect her from Prince Pavel or whomever else Igor selects for her. The only thing he didn't manage to do was get you killed as well. He couldn't have planned it better if he tried."

"He didn't have time to plan. He grabbed the opportunity when he saw it, as usual. But that doesn't lessen the damage he's done." Anfim clenched and released his fists, kneading the fabric of my summer frock. "Starting with Anna. She's attached to Yuri, you say?"

"Very much so. She's been counting the days until his return. And I want him to marry her. I trust him to defend her against Igor or anyone else who seeks to hurt her, including Prince Pavel." Recalling that afternoon in the garden when Yuri pushed my daughter on the swing and flirted with her, the glow on her face as he took her hand and walked with her toward the brook, his compliance with Lara's directions to act out the story she and Lyuba were discussing, I strained to hold back tears. So much hope, so much happiness, destroyed by a greedy cousin and a capricious prince. "This is like *Layla and Majnun*."

"*Layla and Majnun?*" Only when I saw my husband's bewildered face did I realize that we'd never discussed the book he'd given me. Between my conversation with Lyuba at the betrothal party and the moment when Yuri's summons to muster made the tale a painful reminder for Anna of love lost, Anfim had been away.

"The book you brought back from Bukhara," I said. "Lyuba recognized it and read it to us. It's a Persian epic poem about lovers separated by an outside force." I conveyed the essence of the plot as succinctly as possible.

"As Anna and Yuri have been by the grand prince's command. Yes, I see."

Thinking of Yuri, Anna, and the affection between them, I couldn't go on at first. "He was so sweet to her," I said after a long pause. "By the time he left here, I think he genuinely loved her. And she loved him. How am I going to explain it to her, Anfim? *Gospodi*, she's only fifteen!"

"I know." Anfim held out his hand. "Let's start with Darya and Nikita, shall we? Among the four of us, maybe we can come up with a plan."

I agreed, so we went off in search of my sister and brother-in-law. A short time later, we discovered the two of them walking near the brook, with no one else in sight. From the grim expression on my sister's face, I deduced that Niki had already shared the news with her. I couldn't think of anything else that would have her whacking rushes with a fallen branch.

"What are we going to do about Igor?" she demanded the moment we got close enough to hear her.

"That's why we're here," I told her. "But before we start on our cousin, I have a more urgent question. How do we break the news to Anna?"

She abandoned her assault on the rushes long enough to meet my eyes. "Well, I did have some thoughts about that."

In the end, we decided to approach Anna as a group and give her a short but accurate explanation of why she could no longer wed Yuri. With Anfim at my back, I volunteered to take the lead. I was her mother, after all.

Lyuba sat with Anna in the central room when we found them. "Where are Lara and Tolya?" I asked. The last thing I wanted was to discuss these events within earshot of children.

"Masha took them to the kitchen," Lyuba said. "Tolya was hungry."

Tolya was always hungry. A boy who ran from dawn to dusk naturally had an appetite as large as the imaginary dragons he chased. "And Lara?" I asked.

"Masha said they should both go," Anna replied. "Lara didn't argue. She's very quick to pick up feelings. She knows something's happened. Are you going to tell me what it is?"

I sat on the bench next to her and clasped her hands, as Anfim had done with me earlier. "Yes, sweeting. It affects you more than any of us."

"May I stay?" Lyuba asked. I glanced at her, noting the tension in her shoulders. It would be good if she stayed—one more person to help my daughter in her moment of crisis.

"Please do," I said. "I have bad news, and you should hear it at the same time as Anna." When Lyuba nodded and leaned forward, as if she could demonstrate caring through the slant of her body, I turned my attention to my daughter. I repeated Anfim's account of the dispute between the grand prince and Yuri's uncle that ended with Demid's beheading and Yuri's banishment. I said nothing about the source of the argument, the other punishments, or even the horrible refusal to grant the condemned spiritual absolution. Nor did I share the overheard conversation between Igor and

Pavel. Instead I finished with the most important point in terms of its effect on her life. "The grand prince ordered Yuri to take monastic vows. He can't marry once he does that."

Anna stared at me as if she couldn't believe what she'd heard. Lyuba rallied faster, moving to sit on the bench at my daughter's other side. She patted Anna's shoulder in a consoling way.

"Yuri almost died?" Anna asked after a while. "For no reason?"

"Yes," I told her. "Because of his uncle's poor judgment. But Yuri begged for forgiveness, even though he'd done nothing wrong, and the grand prince spared his life—on the condition that Yuri leave Moscow and join a monastery in the North. But that means he can't wed you—or anyone. If he disobeys the grand prince, he could still be executed."

I waited, letting her absorb the information at her own pace. Her eyes never left my face. The pause seemed to stretch to infinity before she said, in a small voice I hadn't heard since she turned six, "I won't marry Yuri?"

I bit my lip and shook my head. I'd braced myself for shock, but her reaction was worse than I'd expected. Had Yuri betrayed my trust in a way I hadn't anticipated, leaving my daughter, too, harboring a secret sin? "It's not possible, darling," I said in the most soothing tones I could manage. "Monks are sworn to celibacy. I'm sorry. We all like him so much."

"The grand prince sent him away." She spoke slowly, in a wondering tone. "Took his property and forced him to become a monk. So I can't marry him—or rather, he can't marry me, despite the contract you signed. We'll go back to the city in the autumn, but the ceremony we planned will not take place."

So she *had* understood. "That's right." I wished I could turn back time to the days of scraped knees and pricked fingers, when Mama's hug worked wonders.

Lyuba continued to pat Anna's shoulder, and again I wondered whether there was more to my daughter's reaction than I knew. I reached out my arm, intending to offer comfort.

Before I could touch her, Anna spat, "My life is ruined, and it's your fault. If you'd married Gavriil Vorontsov when he asked instead of *fornicating* with that clerk, Yuri would be here today. I hate the grand prince, and I hate you!"

She ran from the room, leaving the rest of us gaping— except for Lyuba, who sent an apologetic glance our way and raced after her.

"Well, that went horribly," I said. "I have to admit, I expected her to do pretty much anything but blame me. And now I'm wondering whether Yuri took advantage of her innocence behind my back." My head ached with tension and the reverberation of the slammed door, and tears blurred my eyes.

Anfim's arm around my waist offered some comfort, as did the kiss he dropped on my brow, but I still felt like someone run over by a stampeding herd. How could my daughter, even in her misery, be so cruel?

"She's a smart girl," my husband said. "She'll figure out when she calms down that her accusation doesn't make sense. Your cousin shifted blame to the Vorontsovs to save his hide, avenge himself on Gavriil Timofeevich for a perceived slight, and pursue his own choice for Anna's husband by getting rid of Yuri. Your marriage to Gavriil wouldn't have changed any of that. And if you *had* married him, there would have been no contract between Anna and Yuri in the first place. A mother and daughter cannot marry a father and son."

I nodded, accepting his reasoning, although it was Anna's rage, not her irrationality, that worried me. "We didn't tell her what you overheard Igor say to Shuisky. Perhaps we should have."

"I doubt it would have made a difference," Anfim said. "Your daughter lashed out, trying to hurt you as much as she hurts inside. In a way, it shows how much you mean to her. You're the one she trusts to love her no matter how badly she behaves."

Oddly, that comforted me. I squeezed his hand to express my thanks, and he gripped mine in return.

Niki frowned at the wall behind me. "Anfim's right," he said. "But Igor's a menace. We definitely have to do something about Igor. I don't intend to stand by while he shoves Pavel Shuisky down Anna's throat. Or convinces the grand prince to confiscate our estate on his behalf, for that matter."

When I murmured agreement, he turned his attention to my husband. "Did they find that pretend bandit you identified as Igor's man? A confession from him would go a long way to hamstringing the bastard."

"Alas, the man escaped," Anfim said. "Unless he's stupid enough to resurface, we'll need another weapon to subdue Igor Grigorevich."

"I think you're overlooking an important point," Darya interjected. The rest of us stared at her. Like Anna and Lara, Darya so often watched without speaking—even these days, when marriage and motherhood had brought her to a new stage of openness and authority—that people tended to forget how observant she was.

"What?" I asked.

"To us Yuri is a wonderful young man," she explained. "The perfect husband for Anna, gentle and loving yet strong in her defense. And no, I don't think he took advantage of her innocence. They were hardly ever alone, and he showed great respect for her. When did he have a chance to seduce her?"

"You have a point," I said. "I hope you're right. Whatever I did, I did as an adult woman." I smiled at Anfim. "And only with the right man."

"Who had waited for the right woman," he said. "But I believe Darya has something else in mind. Please continue. To us Yuri is a wonderful young man, but ..."

She acknowledged his invitation to proceed with a wave of her hand. "Exactly. We like Yuri. We found him, with help from his cousin Dmitry, and did what we could to push the signing of the contract forward to protect Anna—to thwart Igor, in effect. Naturally Igor wanted Yuri out of the way. Do you remember how our cousin once told me I was his greatest asset? But with help from Alexei and Maria, I managed to circumvent him and wed Niki."

She touched her husband's arm and, when he stroked her cheek in response, went on. "He'd already given up on you, Solomonida, because he couldn't marry you off at thirty-three, and his attempts to manipulate you failed. And although he may be gloating now, he'll soon realize that his success carries a high price: by sacrificing Demid and Yuri out of a misplaced desire for revenge, he's offended his wife and lost Gavriil's support."

I nodded, although I doubted Igor had the capacity to learn from his mistakes. "Go on. You've escaped him, and so have I. And Anna?"

"Anna is his best asset yet," Darya said. "A fifteen-year-old virgin, beautiful and of noble birth, with no contracted husband. You think he wants to wed her to Pavel Shuisky. I don't agree. He may encourage Prince Pavel so he can hold that match in reserve, but why stop there? This is Igor we're talking about, and Igor places no limits on his own ambition. There will be a bride show for Grand Prince Ivan before the end of the year. Why wouldn't he use Anna to become the grand prince's in-law? If he pulls that off, he'll have his pick of any estate in Moscow, including ours, and a lot more besides."

"*Chort vozmi*," Niki and Anfim said in unison. Devil take him.

"We'll need a full military-style campaign to head him off if that's his goal," Anfim added.

"We will indeed," Niki agreed.

I frowned. Anna's future was important, without question, but her present unhappiness concerned me more. "We've wandered off-track. Before we worry about what to do next, we have to console Anna today. If she won't talk to me, who can approach her? Lyuba's a darling, but we can't put the whole burden on a girl."

"I will," Darya said. She didn't look as if she enjoyed the prospect, but who would?

That was when Anfim surprised me. "No," he said. "Let me try. I won't reproach her. I know she's heartbroken. But in attacking my wife, Anna impugns my honor as well. Perhaps it's time she hears, if only gently, that her mother has as much right to love and happiness as she does." And without waiting for attempts at dissuasion, he left the room.

Chapter Seventeen

I HAD MY DOUBTS THAT ANFIM WOULD SUCCEED IN overcoming my daughter's resistance, but within the hour, Anna appeared, alone, her hands gripped together and her eyes fixed on the floor. "I'm sorry, Mama," she said in a voice that sounded stiff, but I knew her well enough to guess that she was fighting tears. "I was abominably rude to you. And not just now but before as well, when you told me you planned to remarry. Please forgive me."

With a sigh of relief, I touched her arm and drew her toward the bench near the window, then urged her to sit. "Can you tell me what made you so angry?"

She shook her head quickly and blinked her eyes. I thought she meant she didn't know, but after a while she whispered, "I was jealous."

"Jealous?" I could hardly believe what I was hearing. "You mean more to me than life!" But as the words left my mouth, I recalled Maria at my wedding feast, as we speculated about the source of my daughter's fury. Maria hadn't spoken specifically of jealousy, more of reluctance to accept that I might experience passion with a man my own age. There was not much difference between that and jealousy, though, when I thought about it.

"Because you loved Anfim more than me," Anna said, her voice a little stronger. I protested, and she raised a hand to stop me from responding. Her tears receded as she made her confession. "It sounds foolish when I say it out loud. But when you told me I could stay with Auntie Darya while you went to live with your husband, I didn't know what to do. Then you helped with Yuri and his Aunt Liza, and I realized you cared for me as much as ever. But when I heard that Yuri and I could never be together, I couldn't bear it. I said the worst thing that came into my head, so you would hurt the way I did."

Her control broke then, and she tumbled into my arms, sobbing. I murmured, "It's all right, darling, everything will work out for the best," over and over, but I could guess that none of it was more than meaningless sound to her. She would recover from this blow sometime, but not soon.

"I will never leave you," I told her when the flood abated at last. "Even after I die, I'll watch over you from Heaven. You will start your own household one day; that's what children do. But we have plenty of time for that. Would you like to stay with Anfim and me when we return to Moscow?"

She nodded, as if still incapable of speech. "Then let's start there," I said. "We can wait until you're ready before we think of marrying you to anyone else, and in the meantime, we'll find a way to protect you from Cousin Igor and his schemes."

Again she nodded, but after a brief pause she sighed. "And the bride show? *Must* I take part in it? I don't hate you, but I detest Grand Prince Ivan. How could I even think of wedding him after what he did to Yuri and his uncle?"

There was no point in arguing with her. Who, in her situation, would not feel the same? To point out that she would have no choice or could change her mind or might fail to attract the attention of the boyars and their wives—who would select the final candidates, meaning that she would never have to face the grand prince—was irrelevant at the moment.

"We'll see what we can do," I promised. "It's early days yet."

That seemed to calm her. She hugged me once more, and I hugged her back. "I love you, sweetheart," I told her after a while. "No matter what happens, you can count on that."

"I know, Mama," she whispered. "I love you, too."

"What did you say to her?" I asked my husband when we could speak freely, nestled together in our own bed.

He patted my rounding stomach and laughed softly when he felt the child kick. "That she means the world to you. That you weren't much older than she is when you married a difficult husband—I didn't say what made him difficult; that's not my tale to tell—and you want to ensure a better future for her. That you spent many years caring for her on your own and have never regretted a single moment of that time, but you deserve happiness, too. That wedding you has brought me nothing but joy. And that she's welcome in my house."

"The same things I said, for the most part." I reveled in the touch of his palm against my cheek. "That's good. She will believe it more readily if she hears it from both of us."

He nodded. "She asked if living with us would spare her from the bride show. Lyuba had suggested as much. I said I didn't know, because a broken promise is worse than one not given. But I told her that staying with us may discourage the Pavel Shuiskys of the world. That seemed to reassure her."

"With luck, it will discourage not just the Pavels but their mothers," I agreed. "Snobs that they are about their noble blood. That will buy us the time we need for her to adjust to losing Yuri and to find another man who will truly care for her. I hope it does make her ineligible for the bride show. I can't blame her for wanting nothing to do with Grand Prince Ivan."

"That whole situation troubles me," he said, barely above a whisper. "The senselessness of the punishment, Ivan's unbridled rage. Combined with boyar ruthlessness and ambition, the grand prince's temperament creates a toxic brew."

I could produce no response to that except a murmured agreement.

Around the middle of August, Anfim received news that Safa-Girei Khan had indeed ousted his rival once more. The Russian candidate, Shah-Ali, didn't even put up a fight: instead he hosted a grand dinner party, got his guests blind drunk, and slipped out of Kazan before Safa-Girei arrived.

"So much for my two months on the road," Anfim said, his voice dry as he related this news. "What a waste of time. I might as well have stayed home and looked after my wife." He gazed at me over the edge of the unfurled scroll. "Tretiakov has called me back to the office. I don't want to leave you again."

"I don't want that either." I sighed. "Let's return to the city. I've loved it here, and I hope we can come again next summer, but it will do us good to have a change of scene. The children can resume their lessons, too, before they forget everything they've learned. I'll speak to Darya."

Niki had also received orders to return to Moscow, as it turned out, and Darya agreed without hesitation to any plan that would keep her family together. And so, as suddenly as we had decided to visit Malinino, we packed up and went home.

It *was* good to see our city house again. Over the course of a few days, we moved Anna's possessions from Darya and Niki's estate and installed her in a bedroom on the third floor, next to Lara's. With her came my maid Eva, who would take care of the three of us, leaving Alya to care for Darya at the family compound.

I hadn't had time to question Eva about her summer and the young man whose attentions had, I assumed, kept her in Moscow before I saw her near the kitchen, deep in conversation with a servant I recognized. I'd encountered the man often during the months that Cousin Igor lorded it at our estate. He was Makar, the servant in charge of Igor's vast wardrobe. But I'd also seen him, I realized, in the street that fateful night when Anfim and I declared our love for each other. At the time, I didn't make the connection: the servant wore a costume; he was the man with the elk antlers who passed us on the street. Watching him with Eva, though, I understood that my cousin's accusation that I'd been "consorting" with Anfim drew on more than supposition or hints from his wife. Had Makar been peddling his master information, with Eva's help, from the beginning? It seemed likely, and it explained how Igor had learned of our journey to Malinino.

When I saw Makar leave, I challenged Eva. She denied everything at first, then broke down when I pointed out how much damage our cousin's attacks could have done and reminded her of the trouble she'd already brewed between me and my daughter with her careless words.

"I meant no harm, Lady," she said. "I thought she should know how the world works. I didn't expect her to get angry with you."

"And Igor Grigorevich?" I demanded. "Does *he* need to know how the world works? How dare you share my private business without my permission?"

"No, Lady, no. You misunderstand. I told only Makar. He was the one who shared the information with his master!"

"That makes no difference," I said in my sternest voice. "I should throw you out of the house!"

She sobbed harder then, because I could do exactly that if I chose. She belonged to me, and if I refused to provide her with food and lodging, she would be in dire straits. I doubted Makar could support her, since he depended as much on my cousin's generosity as she did on mine. And however much Igor had profited from her indiscretion, he would not accept an untrustworthy servant into his household. On the contrary, he'd get rid of Makar rather than deal with either of them.

I waited, unrelenting on the surface, until Eva found her voice. "Forgive me, Lady," she said between hiccups. "I won't offend again."

"Hmm." I pretended to weigh her promise against the harm her careless words had caused, but in reality I was thinking about how to make the best of a bad situation. After letting the pause stretch, I said, "I will forgive you if you do three things. First, you tell me everything you passed on to Makar about me and my household. Second, you find out what he knows about my cousin's plans, especially those that concern Lady Anna, then report that information to me.

And third, I'm about to write a letter to my sister. Deliver it this afternoon and bring me her answer without delay."

Eva bowed until her nose touched her knees and withdrew, wiping away tears. I wasted no time in heading to my husband's study, where I penned a request to Darya. I wanted her to host a meeting with Cousin Igor as soon as he returned from Kolomna, since I knew he wouldn't deign to visit me here. I asked her to pick a weekend day, so that Anfim could attend.

It was time to tackle my cousin head on.

From Eva I learned that she had indeed told Makar about my pregnancy and my visits to Anfim's house. That was useful in terms of clarifying where Igor got his information, but our marriage made it no longer relevant. It was the second part of my deal with Eva that proved its worth, and within a short time.

She came to see me in the main room two days after our confrontation, radiating an air of suppressed excitement. I'd never considered her a handsome girl: she was too thin and washed-out for beauty. But for this brief moment, her pleasure in fulfilling the task I'd assigned her gave her a certain glow.

"What did you find out?" I asked. Anna stood up, as if to leave, but I shook my head at her and she resumed her seat. I wanted her to know that as time went on, I would treat her more and more as an adult.

Eva seemed not to notice. She clasped her hands together and fixed her eyes on my face. "Makar says that Igor Grigorevich sent a message from Kolomna. The grand prince conferred on him the property that belonged to the prince who was executed, and Igor Grigorevich wants Makar to join him with his best outfits so he can make a good showing when he goes to take ownership of the new estate."

"*Bozhe moi*," I said. "Prince Kubensky's property, as well as his military position. How my cousin rises in the world!" Would this royal grant sate Igor's greed to the point where he would abandon his quest to control the land that once belonged to my father? I hoped so, although I feared it might not.

"Yes, Lady," Eva said. "But there's more. Makar heard him, before he went to Kolomna in the spring, talking with Prince Pavel Shuisky about Lady Anna." She bowed to my daughter. "It was after her betrothal party, and the prince was most impressed with her. He told Igor Grigorevich how foolish he'd been to sign the wedding contract, because he— the prince—would have liked to marry her. Igor Grigorevich looked thoughtful, Makar said. He didn't object, but he didn't agree either. He told the prince that many things can happen between signing and wedding. He hinted that he might revoke his consent if the prince offered to cover the penalties for breaking the contract."

Beast. I kept that thought to myself. "And did the prince seem inclined to pay?"

Eva shook her head. "He said he was land-rich but cash-poor. Igor Grigorevich didn't argue. Instead he told the prince there were ways to get rid of Yuri Gavriilovich that didn't involve money. But after the prince left, and Igor Grigorevich's wife asked what Prince Pavel wanted with him, the master told her to mind her own business, because women didn't have the sense to manage worldly affairs. She should stick to her embroidery and the child she has on the way."

I swallowed hard at that last and avoided Anna's eyes, lest I burst out laughing before I discovered whether Eva had more to say. The idea that Katya was less capable than her bumptious husband never failed to amuse me, but more important was that Eva's testimony corroborated what Katya herself had told me. "Excellent work, Eva," I said. "Is there more?"

"No, Lady. May I go now?" She twisted her hands together, and I saw how nervous she was.

"Yes, go," I said, in a firm but kindly tone intended to convey that she was on the road to redemption but not yet wholly forgiven. "You did well. Remember not to gossip to Makar about us, and tell us at once if you hear anything else."

She bowed and departed, and I moved to sit beside my daughter, who looked troubled. "I understand," I told her. "You don't want to marry Prince Pavel. I don't want that for you either. I don't like the way he treats women. We won't let that happen."

"She said Igor promised to get rid of Yuri. Is that true?" She inhaled, a sobbing breath that, combined with her words and the bleakness I glimpsed on her face, suggested she'd absorbed only the part of the conversation that concerned the man she loved.

"I'm afraid it may be," I said. "We're still trying to uncover the truth. I plan to talk with Anfim and your aunt and uncle. Together we may be able to force Igor to admit what he did."

"Our cousin is truly hateful," she whispered, so low that I strained to hear her.

"Don't worry," I assured her. "Whatever we discover, we'll keep you safe from him."

Gradually we restored our usual routine. Lara greeted Father Job with enthusiasm, recording and totaling long columns of numbers with aplomb. Tolya welcomed the reintroduction of restrictions with less enthusiasm, but Lyuba's promise to create a book of stories for him reconciled him to the hours spent on lessons. When classes ended, he still had lots of time to run in the courtyard with Laika, again restored to my sister's household. And although I kept a sharp eye on Eva and watched what I said in her hearing, every day that passed strengthened my conviction that her repentance was sincere.

In anticipation of Igor's return to Moscow, Anfim and I invited Darya and Nikita to a light supper at our house. This second week of August saw the Dormition Fast in full swing, but the dietary rules were not as strict as those for Lent. Cabbage turnovers sautéed in nut oil nestled next to patties formed from dried peas; sliced carrots and cucumbers created a pretty oval around a platter of pink salmon; and a tureen of buckwheat groats steamed nearby. With the last of the season's berries, brought from Malinino, these dishes made for an elegant and satisfying meal.

We sent food for Lara and Tolya to the room I'd set aside for sewing and similar projects. With Eva in attendance and Anna to supervise the children, we adults could talk downstairs with some expectation of privacy. I'd give my daughter a summary of what we decided—part of my effort to respect her increasing maturity—but I considered it too soon to include her in a planning session like this.

With the table set, the initial greetings exchanged, and food before each of us, I explained what I'd wrung out of Eva. "As if Igor weren't enough of a menace," I finished, "we have to assume he knows more or less everything that goes on in both our households. I've threatened to cast Eva into the cold if she dares chatter about us again, and I think I've convinced her that I mean what I say. But of course, I have no way to guarantee that her reformation will stick."

"What do you want out of this meeting?" Nikita took a bite from his turnover and groaned in pleasure.

Anfim picked up the conversational thread. "Some certainty about what your—no, I suppose he's *our*—cousin has done and intends to do." He patted my hand as he said the *our*, and his acknowledgment of the bond between us drew a smile from me. "We have much well-informed speculation, but I'd like a better sense of what we're fighting, so we can focus our efforts in the right place."

"Alas, Igor has no reason to answer our questions," I said. "How can we persuade him? Get him boasting about his accomplishments, perhaps?"

"*Has* he any accomplishments?" Niki speared an inoffensive piece of salmon with his eating knife and glared at it.

"He certainly thinks so," my husband said. "And with some grounds. He's still an associate boyar, still on the royal council, and master of a princely estate, whereas his opponents have been killed, stripped of their property, and driven from power. We can compliment him on his military assignment, encourage him to expand on his relationship with the grand prince, and talk about his summer in Kolomna. I can ask around for details that will convince him to open up."

I wrinkled my nose. "That might work. I'd hate to spend hours listening to him gloat, though, and we can't force him to say what we want to hear. He knows us too well to fall for wide eyes and expressions of boundless interest. I doubt he'll agree to a second meeting, so we need a surefire way to get the information out of him during the first."

"I have an idea," Darya said. The rest of us turned to face her.

"Yes?" I wondered what she'd come up with this time.

"Nutmeg."

"What?" The three of us spoke in concert, and she burst out laughing.

"You should see your faces," she said. "Igor loves to drink, and he doesn't moderate his intake. We could ply him with beer, but he might get sodden and fall asleep before we have a chance to question him. Spiced wine, though—"

Light dawned, and I interrupted her. "Nutmeg—that's perfect! But doesn't it take a while to work?"

The two men were now staring at us both. "What are the pair of you talking about?" Anfim asked.

"Nutmeg causes hallucinations if you take too much of it," Darya explained. "Fear, anxiety, palpitations. Other things too, but those are the effects that might help us. Best of all, it sometimes makes people forget what they said and did under the influence." She looked at me. "Combined with alcohol, it won't take long. But I'll have to find a way to add more to his cup; otherwise you and I can't drink the wine, and that will arouse his suspicions."

The men looked, if possible, even more befuddled by her last statement. "Nutmeg can also cause miscarriages," I told them. "Not in tiny amounts, but we have to ensure that he gets eight to ten times as much as usual if we want it to work." I nodded at my sister. "But you should dose Igor separately anyway; otherwise Anfim and Niki will be affected as well."

"I can leave it out of the wine altogether and add it to his cup right before serving. I'll have the cook make gingerbread with it, too. So long as he eats that and drinks several toasts in a row, he'll get enough to lose control without realizing what's happening. And we can easily turn down food; if he asks, we'll say we ate too much at dinner."

"It's not fatal, is it?" Niki asked. "That would be both a crime and a sin."

"Oh no," Darya said with an airy wave of her hand. "If he were older, I wouldn't try it. He might have a heart attack. But at thirty, he'll get nothing worse than a headache or an upset stomach. I don't want to *kill* him."

Her husband shook his head. "I swear, wife, sometimes you terrify me."

Chapter Eighteen

Moscow, Late August 1546

I SPRANG TO MY FEET AS A BLAST OF NOISE ASSAILED MY ears. My needlework fell unnoticed at my feet. The sound of men's voices, raised to carry great distances across the open steppe and interspersed with a steady drumbeat of hooves, sent terror flowing through my veins like an icy river. Scattered thoughts and images flitted through my head: invasion, raid, burning buildings, women and children driven into slavery, bodies hacked and dying. I couldn't form a coherent sentence, couldn't catch my breath. Run, hide, find the children? I had no idea what to do, no ability to calm myself long enough to plan. The sound flung me back to the summer I turned nine, when the Tatar armies broke through the southern defense lines and attacked Moscow itself. The memories were indelible—the city smoking like a giant bonfire, even the churches crumbling into ash, their holy icons blazing.

Tolya skidded into my sewing room, panting too hard to talk. Not that I could have heard him over the din. The sight of him, so young and defenseless, snapped me back to adulthood. My first task was to assess the danger, so I could decide how best to protect him and Lara, myself and my unborn babe.

Breathing too rapidly for comfort, I stepped over the new shirt I'd been embroidering for Tolya and moved as fast as I could at seven and a half months pregnant. When I reached the threshold where he was doubled over grabbing his midriff, I caught his arm. "Upstairs," I said.

He blinked in confusion. I pointed to the ceiling and, when he straightened, still gasping for air, led the way to the light-filled workroom on the top floor, where we might have a chance of seeing over the city wall and catching a glimpse of whatever lay beyond. Bad or good—and a Tatar raid with two children in the house and a third on the way could never be good—I needed to learn the truth as fast as possible.

Our timing couldn't have been better. We reached the window and Tolya scrambled onto the seat just as a group of horses emerged from among the birch trees that lined the Ordynka—the road to the Horde—and raced toward the Moscow River. The first group soon gave way to others, until hundreds—no thousands, if not tens of thousands—of animals poured like an endless torrent along the dusty highway. Only a handful of them had riders. I saw no warriors armored in chain mail and helmets, no puffs of smoke. The noise, deafening as it was, included no zing of arrows, no clash of swords, no screams of pain.

I collapsed onto the window seat and heaved a huge sigh of relief. My hand instinctively sought my belly to comfort the unborn child. "*Slava Bogu*," I said to Tolya. "We're safe."

He gave no sign of hearing me—not surprising, given the racket outside. I staggered to my feet once more as my mind absorbed what I was seeing and hearing: not a raid for plunder or an invading army but the nomads driving their horse herds to Moscow for sale. The cries came from the herders, sheepskin-clad men as wild as their beasts, which by now had almost reached the river that separated the Kremlin from their pasture grounds. I'd heard that sound every late summer or early fall I'd spent in the city, yet fear always triumphed over experience. Only when I saw the riderless horses could I relax and enjoy the spectacle.

And what a spectacle it was! Anfim, Anna, and Lara arrived as I started to breathe normally at last, and the five of us stood spellbound at the sight. White and black, bay and chestnut, roan and dapple gray, manes of contrasting shades flying in the breeze they themselves had created, the onrushing herd formed patterns of color as intricate as a tapestry. As I watched, the lead horses reached the river and swerved left and right, splitting into two massive streams. The Tatars—who had acted as a barrier along the sides, keeping the milling animals moving forward—responded to some unseen signal and, in a performance even more compelling than their control over the racing steeds, rode around and around the herd in ever-tighter circles until the animals slowed, then stopped. Even from where I stood I could see the heaving sides and hanging heads; the poor creatures must be exhausted.

The sudden silence, broken only by the occasional whinny and Tolya jumping up and down hooting, disoriented me almost as badly as the clamor it replaced. "So few men compared to the number of horses," I said when I could speak. "And yet they bring them to their destination unharmed. It amazes me every time. Or more accurately, it terrifies me every time until I realize they aren't coming after us. *Then* it amazes me."

"Me too," Anfim said. "Especially now, when I have a clear sense of how far they travel. Months on the road, over steppe and through forest, driving animals accustomed to living wild on the grasslands, without saddle or bridle. This is one of my favorite moments of the year. What do you say, Tolya, shall we go and see if Uncle Postnik and his sons are following the horses?"

Tolya shrieked his approval, and I laughed. "Have fun. If you find them, bring them here for dinner. I'll tell the cook to prepare extra food. Anna and Lara, come with me, and we'll make sure everything's ready."

And off they went, father and son, returning two hours later with my brother-in-law and a pair of strapping nephews who, after some initial trepidation, soon warmed up enough to entertain us with stories of what they'd experienced while trailing the nomadic riders and their animals.

It made for a memorable evening.

Not long after the arrival of the horse herds, Igor returned to Moscow, and we could put Darya's plan into motion. I arrayed myself in the most elaborate robes I possessed that could expand to cover my advanced state of pregnancy. By then I had about five weeks to wait before Anfim's new son or daughter arrived. In the month since we came back from Malinino, I had overseen the refurbishing of the cradle that once held Lara and Tolya and acquired a nursemaid who would take primary responsibility for the baby, leaving Masha free to concentrate on the older children.

On the day selected for the meeting, we dispatched Anna and Lara to Maria's house, where they would remain safely out of earshot. We gave in to Tolya's desperate pleas for a reunion with his favorite dog, given how unlikely it was that he would pay any attention to what the grownups wanted to discuss. By the time Anfim, Tolya, and I entered the carriage to travel the short distance to Darya and Nikita's estate, I felt as prepared as I would ever be to impose my will on Igor, with a little help from Darya's nutmeg.

I noticed as soon as I entered the main sitting room that our cousin had not dressed up for the occasion. Even Anfim, resplendent in the russet robe he'd worn for our wedding, outshone Igor. I read our cousin's plain clothes as evidence of disinterest or disrespect. Not, perhaps, a promising beginning.

"Welcome home," I began in an attempt to put Igor in a more cooperative frame of mind. "It's fortunate that you arrived so soon after the birth of your son. You've decided to call him Timofei, Katya said. Congratulations to you both." When Anfim murmured similar phrases, Igor preened as if he'd delivered the child with his own hands. One bridge crossed.

Niki took the wine Darya offered and sipped from it. As I watched, she turned her back on Igor, sprinkled brown powder into his cup, then filled it to the brim with liquid. She winked at me before handing it to him. When he took it, she gave cups, less full and unsprinkled, to Anfim and me before passing out plates of gingerbread to one person after another, ending with herself. I set the plate aside after a bite or two, recalling that it too contained nutmeg, most likely more than the usual amount.

"How long?" I mouthed while her body still blocked my face from Igor's gaze. We had agreed Niki would chat with Igor before we arrived, on the grounds that our cousin would be more inclined to suspect some ulterior motive if he found four of us waiting for him. Admittedly, he and Niki didn't get along, but Niki could at least exchange stories of the Kolomna campaign and ask about Igor's colleagues in the Great Regiment, which was more than the rest of us could manage.

Darya held up one finger, indicating one hour. Seeing the plan well advanced, I dove in. "We asked you to join us," I said to Igor, "so you can tell us what you have in mind now that you've returned to Moscow, cousin. Wouldn't you like to share your thoughts with us, so we can appreciate your genius?"

He tossed back the cup of wine before replying, squinted at it, then held it out for more.

Darya repeated her performance, including the sprinkled nutmeg. "Answer the question," she said when she gave Igor the cup this time, "or no more wine for you."

He sniffed the liquid this time before sipping. "What's in this, anyway? It's very spicy."

"Nothing unusual." Darya gazed at him, her eyes wide and guileless. "Cinnamon, nutmeg, honey, a touch of ginger. It's the same mix you've been drinking since you arrived."

No wonder Igor appeared disheveled. I'd better move faster, then. At the rate he was guzzling wine, the nutmeg would overwhelm him before he revealed the information we sought. I fixed what I hoped was a suitably admiring expression on my face and addressed the topic of most interest to me. "Yes, do tell us. Now that poor Yuri Vorontsov has been sent to the monastery, are you considering a new husband for Anna?"

He took another swig of wine and frowned, gazing not at me but over my shoulder. "Who's that lurking in the doorway?"

"Me," Niki said in a harsh voice. I turned my head toward the sound and discovered he had barred the exit. As I watched, Anfim positioned himself next to Niki, underlining the point that Igor would have to get past them to reach the door.

The effect on our cousin was startling. He cringed, and a flash of fear crossed his face. "Papa?" he stammered. "What brings you here? Are you still after Old Sheremetev's estate? They wouldn't give it to me, but I got another from the grand prince, a better one. It used to belong to Prince Kubensky!" I exhaled, a long, relieved breath. The nutmeg was working, lowering his guard and producing hallucinations. His father had died years ago.

"Why did you want this estate?" I kept my tone gentle so as not to alarm him further.

"To make up for Papa's losses, of course." Igor set down his cup, grabbed his head with both hands, and rocked back and forth. "He gambled everything away." He dropped his hands and glared at Niki. "I'm not a ne'er-do-well like you. I take care of my family."

For that brief moment, I felt sorry for him. "Of course, cousin," I said in a soothing tone. "And look at the success you've achieved. You have land, a fine house, a good wife, and a newborn son. You don't need our estate. You've no reason to worry about Anna's marriage, either. What difference does it make to you?"

He turned bleary eyes on me. "What difference? What *difference*? When she could make me cousin to the grand prince? And if he doesn't choose her, Pavel Shuisky will take her. That will expand my ties among the elite. Why waste her on that silly Vorontsov boy, when she could become a princess—even the *grand* princess? Only a fool like you, Solomonida, would endorse such a match!"

My sympathy for him vanished, and I asked in my stoniest voice, "Did you get rid of Yuri, then?"

"Of course I did." Igor leaned back in his seat and waved a languid hand. It was all I could do not to kick the chair out from under him. "It was easy enough to blame him and his uncle for the mixup with the Novgorodians." He glared in the direction of the door. "That bastard Anfim should have gone down at the same time, but he slithered out of trouble like he always does, curse him. He even dodged the men I sent after him during that mission to Kazan."

Anfim growled in his throat, and I sent him a warning glance. "We thought that was you. I bet you set the bandits on us, too, when we went to Malinino. You're so devilishly clever, cousin. We can hardly keep up with you."

"I did. Makar told me where you'd gone, and I wanted to scare you—teach you a lesson, troublemakers that you are." Oblivious to the fury he was sparking among his listeners, he preened, examining his well-buffed fingernails as if they reflected his own glorious image.

"Oh, you taught us a great deal." With an effort, I kept the sarcasm out of my voice. It was time to solicit some hard information, and I wanted him as cooperative as an obnoxious scourge could be. "Which men did you send?"

Igor mumbled some names, and the next time I looked at my husband, I saw him scribbling on a piece of paper. Hoping Igor would further incriminate himself, I went on. "Tell us more about Yuri. Did you plan for him to die?"

Igor shook his head. "Hoped. Didn't plan." His speech was slurring as the nutmeg spread through his body, and his eyes shone with a maniacal gleam. "Saw my chance and took it. Couldn't guess what the grand prince would do. It's too bad Yuri escaped death, but from the monastery he can't cause any more trouble for me. So that turned out all right."

I stared at him, shocked—not so much by what he'd done, most of which I'd already guessed, but by this reminder of his callousness. He'd destroyed two young people's lives and hurt his patron Gavriil Vorontsov as well as his own wife, who had lost an uncle and a cousin due to his maneuvering. Yet none of the harm he'd inflicted shook Igor's belief that his advancement at court justified any means of attaining his goals.

I checked the faces of the others, wondering if any of them wished to intervene, but they seemed content to let me take the lead. And it did seem best not to confuse Igor in his unsteady state. I doubted he would last much longer before keeling over. I gripped my silken skirt with both hands to stop myself from lunging for his neck and said in tones more biting than was perhaps advisable, "It turned out well for you, I suppose. Did you act on your own, or did someone help you?"

His brow furrowed; then he fixed his eyes on me and glared. "You think me some dolt's puppet?" His scorn yielded to pride, and he puffed out his chest. "I did it myself. You didn't expect me to beat you, did you, Shura? Even though I swore I would. But I did. I win, you lose."

I clenched my hands together until my fingers ached. Whatever happened next—and I harbored no illusions that Igor would change his behavior as a result of this day or even, perhaps, remember my exact words—I would lay out the future for him in terms he could not mistake. "Listen to me, Igrushka. You may be the head of the Bezzubtsev and Sheremetev clans, but you no longer control Anna's marriage. She's Anfim's stepdaughter now, and you're only her second cousin once removed. You have a son, and you can arrange *his* marriage to advance your career. Leave Anna to us."

This little speech was a gamble on my part—and possibly untrue. The privileges of noble birth might well outweigh those of a stepfather from a merchant family, however high his rank in government service. But I hoped to sow a seed that might sprout in Igor's mind even if he didn't remember the details of today's conversation, leaving him with a nagging uncertainty of his own rights where my daughter was concerned.

Anfim had taken a step forward as I began my exhortation, and by the time I reached the end, he was standing behind my chair. His hand settled on my shoulder, and I glanced his way long enough to return his smile before focusing on our cousin once more.

Igor flicked his eyes back and forth between us, and I saw his volatile emotions reflected on his face. "Anfim," he muttered, as if to himself. "That ingrate. Took my bread, then stabbed me in the back—got in my way, sided with Nikita and Darya against me, chased that troublesome harlot." He lurched to his feet and pointed at me as he reached the last word. "You."

"*What* did you call my wife?" At the sound of Anfim's furious voice, my cousin's head swiveled, and he stood there, weaving, not unlike the lumbering bear who'd come so close to toppling me as I left the Christmas party a lifetime ago.

"Oh, there you are. Traitor," Igor mumbled. He was becoming harder to follow as the spiced drink strengthened its hold on him. "Don't deny it. I took you in when you needed help, and how did you reward me? By turning on me to pursue this wily slut." Again he twisted his neck, regarding me with his head tipped to one side, as if he saw me atilt. The movement made him stagger, but he managed to spit out his next words. "I've beaten you once, and I'll do it again if I have to."

My stomach lurched at his renewed threat. The wildness in his eyes showed that he'd moved beyond the realm of rational answers. I'd found out what we wanted to know, and I'd told him clearly to leave Anna alone. Time to let him go while he could still walk.

I pushed myself to standing and looked at my sister. "He's out of his mind. We've learned as much as we can."

Igor grabbed my arm. I pulled away and smacked him, hard. "Don't touch me!"

"Harlot," he snarled once more. "You're a sinner, and I'll touch you any way I want."

Shades of Semyon.

I cringed. Then Anfim cursed, snapping me back to the present. I shoved my cousin in the chest with both hands and watched with satisfaction as he stumbled. A roar sounded behind me—Nikita, surging forward. But it was my husband's fist that connected with Igor's chin and brought him down. While Igor groaned, Anfim planted a foot on the chest of his childhood friend and said, "Do *not* insult my wife."

Igor writhed and moaned, but only when he muttered an apology did Anfim remove his boot. Grumbling under his breath, Igor rolled to his feet and staggered toward the door.

Niki stepped to one side long enough to let him pass, then slammed a hand against Igor's back as he exited, sending him crashing against the far wall.

"Thank you for joining us, Igrushka," Niki said, his voice dripping with sarcasm. "You've proven surprisingly informative. Shall I summon a man to see you home?"

Darya, Anfim, and I rushed for the doorway, curious to see how Igor would reply. He looked at us, one by one, then rubbed his lip, bleeding from its contact with the wall.

"Don't come near me, you brutes." He blinked, as if unsure of what he saw. "I'll get my revenge. Just you wait."

Nikita and Anfim let out a joint roar, and Igor scuttled down the hallway like the rat he was.

He had yet to reach the outer door when Tolya—drawn by the noise, I assumed—came in with Laika at his side. Igor raised a hand. "Useless brat," he said. "Get out of my way."

Tolya drew back, startled. Laika stepped in front of him, her fur bristling and a low growl emanating from her throat. Igor stared at the dog, transfixed. "Is that a wolf?"

When no one replied, he shook his head and staggered forward. She lunged, knocking him flat, then stood over him and bared her teeth, as if threatening to bite him if he so much as stirred.

Only then did I grasp what was happening. I'd assumed Igor was the one person she would not touch, even to safeguard Tolya, but I'd misjudged her.

I wrestled with the temptation to let Laika bite my cousin—and won, although the devil perched on my shoulder whispered that Igor deserved far worse. "Tolya," I said, keeping my voice calm. "Back up, slowly. Go to the top of the stairs and call Laika, then take her to the stables until Igor Grigorevich leaves. She thinks he wants to hurt you." When Tolya had taken several steps toward the door, I turned to address my cousin. "If I were you, I wouldn't move a muscle. Silly as it may sound, she's warning you not to attack her pup."

He grumbled objections, but he lay rigid and, after another snarl from the dog, silent. Soon Tolya called Laika's name. Her ears perked, so I knew she was listening. He called again, and she retreated, still bristling and growling in response to Igor's slightest move.

"Now get out," Niki said in disgusted tones when the outer door closed. "Even the dog has more sense than you."

Igor shook his head, his eyes wilder than before. "A wolf and a wolf-boy. What sort of house are you keeping?"

"He needs someone to take him home," I said. "I'll fetch Mishka." When the others nodded, I set off for the servants' stairs, where I found Petka on his way up. "Help Igor Grigorevich," I ordered, then stood aside as he raced to the top two steps at a time. I followed at a slower pace, and by the time I reached the others, Igor had left.

"I guess we overdid the nutmeg," I said as I rejoined my sister. "Did you ever see the like?"

"I don't think we did." Darya, who stood closest to the table holding the wine and gingerbread, raised the container of nutmeg to prove that it was still more than half-full. "Overdo it, that is. Maybe the wine strengthened the effect. But even if we did give him too much, he'll be fine tomorrow. A little headachy and sick, perhaps, which is less than he deserves. It was worth the risk; I learned a lot."

"Me too," I said. "More than I wanted to, in truth. What a dreadful villain he is. Can we bring him to justice?"

Anfim picked up the paper he'd scribbled on. "Not for what he did to Yuri, alas. He lied to Grand Prince Ivan, but to question the ruler's decision would endanger us more than him. But for attacking a royal escort, perhaps. I'll report the names to Tretiakov and see if he can force a confession out of them. Assuming they haven't disappeared, like the one I recognized."

"That's something, I suppose." Although not nearly enough. I had sufficient experience of the court to predict that even if Tretiakov *did* interrogate Igor's servants, they would be more likely to suffer than their master. No carrying rubbish out of the hut, as the saying went—which in this case meant that the privileges of the royal council as a whole must be protected, even if it meant shielding one of its members from well-deserved prosecution. At best, we might see Igor discreetly dispatched to some far-flung post as a disciplinary measure.

The others didn't respond, probably because they had reached the same conclusion. After a few moments of silence, I asked, "Do you think we've stopped him for now?"

Anfim rubbed his knuckles where they'd connected with Igor's chin. A certain glow of satisfaction surrounded him, leading me to suspect that he'd welcomed the opportunity to put Igor in his place at last.

"For a while," he said. "And we did learn a lot. Most important, that we needn't worry about Anna until the grand prince selects a wife."

"Yes, she's safe until the bride show, it seems. Even a stepfather can't keep her out of that." A thought flitted past, and I laughed. "We do have one unexpected ally."

The others regarded me with that wary expression that family members keep for the crazy old aunt in their midst.

"Unexpected ally?" Darya asked.

"Fyodor Koshkin," I told them. "He's kept Lyuba off the marriage market because he hopes to wed her to the grand prince. Do you think he'll stand by and do nothing while Cousin Igor steals the prize of the century out from under his nose?"

"It will be a battle of giants," Darya said in tones of awe. "If it didn't involve Anna and Lyuba, I'd await it with pleasure. There may not be another such contest in our lifetime."

"Giants? A battle of snakes, more like," Niki said dryly. If there was one person on earth he disliked more than Igor, it was Lyuba's cunning, power-hungry father. "Still, I'd back Koshkin against Igor any day."

Knowing them both, I had to agree with him. Our cousin had demonstrated a raw cunning that surprised me, but he couldn't match Koshkin in experience, subtlety, and manipulative ingenuity.

"Here we go then," Anfim said. "First the bride show, then Pavel Shuisky. We'll need all our wits to get Anna through the next year."

"Yes, first comes the bride show," Darya agreed. "And what a show it will be."

"Without a doubt," I said. "What a show it will be."

Chapter Nineteen

A FEW DAYS AFTER THE NUTMEG INCIDENT, DARYA AND I went to our cousin's house to visit Katya and baby Timofei. We kept a sharp eye out for Igor, but he was nowhere to be seen. Katya had a wonderful time telling us how wildly he'd talked after returning from his meeting with us. She didn't ask if we knew what had affected him, and we didn't mention the nutmeg. We couldn't be sure, of course, but from her account it seemed that our cousin might have forgotten many of the day's events. I sent the Virgin Mother a plea that the seed of uncertainty I'd sown would survive, then concentrated on admiring mother and baby in ways that would deflect the attention of jealous wraiths who might otherwise harm the newborn.

"Have you heard from your cousin Yuri since his banishment?" I asked Katya when the tale of wolf-boys and their mothers seemed to have run its course.

"He sent a letter." She rose and rummaged in a basket filled with embroidery threads before drawing out a single sheet of paper, which she held out to me. "It arrived yesterday. I'd hoped one of you would stop by. I can't read it, and I'm reluctant to ask a priest or clerk, in case they share the information with Igor. With him acting so strangely, I don't want to let him know that I have it. He gloated something horrible about Yuri deserving what happened to him and worse, but Yuri's my cousin, and I've always thought him a nice boy. I was glad when I heard he might marry Anna. They're perfect for each other."

Curious, I took the letter from her and perused Yuri's script—neat letters set off by elaborate curlicues at the beginning of paragraphs, an apt mirror of his attentive yet exuberant nature.

"He writes with great circumspection," I said after a while. "As if he hopes we will see the unstated meaning behind his words."

"Poor boy," Darya put in. "He must be in shock. To go within the space of one afternoon from youngest son of the royal favorite, on the brink of marrying a beautiful girl, to a narrow escape from death and a future as a monk would boggle the mind."

"Indeed," Katya said. "But what does he say, Solomonida?"

"That he reached Ferapontovo safely," I told her. "The abbot is a friend of his father's. He doesn't give the man's name. I wonder if it might be Nikolai Kolychev, who lived in this house before you did. He retired to Ferapontovo, as I recall, but he left here almost a decade ago and I have no idea if he's still alive. Either way, life at the monastery is not so dire as Yuri feared it might be. He misses Anna and Moscow, even his military assignments. He sends her his love and says he has fond memories of Malinino." I frowned at the letter, trying to figure out the ending. I had no trouble deciphering the words, but what Yuri meant by them escaped me.

"And?" Katya asked when the silence lengthened.

I didn't want to reveal what I'd seen. It could only cause trouble, most notably for Katya, if she let it slip at the wrong moment, but also for my daughter and the man she loved.

Then an idea occurred to me. Katya might not agree, but the only way to find out was to ask. "May we copy the letter for Anna? Like Yuri, she hasn't recovered from the shock of seeing their contract evaporate overnight, and she would appreciate having this reminder of him to console her as she grieves."

Katya smiled, and touched by the warmth in her eyes, I felt for the first time that she might indeed be wholly our friend. "Keep it," she said. "I don't want Igor to see it. He can't read anymore than I can, but he'll get one of the clerks to tell him what it says, and then it will set him off again. Everyone will be safer if it stays at your house. But before you take it away, read it to me once from beginning to end. And next time I visit you, be ready to write out a reply for me. That's my price for giving the letter to Anna."

"Anfim can send the reply for you, if you like," I said. "He has access to couriers who travel throughout the Russian lands on government business."

"And Yuri can address future letters to Solomonida," Darya added. "Then Igor need never know, unless you choose to tell him."

"Agreed," Katya said. "It will serve my husband right for his malicious attack on my family." She nodded at me. "Please, read me the letter."

I did as she asked—except for the last two sentences, which I felt certain were not intended for her.

Tell Anna to stay strong, Yuri had written. *All is not yet lost.*

Less than a month later, Darya sent word that her labor pains had begun. I had planned to attend the birth, even though I was almost on the brink of confinement, taking

Masha with me as the most experienced of our servants at assisting women in childbirth but leaving Lara and Anna at home. My daughter surprised me, though, by insisting on accompanying Masha in my place.

"You can't go, Mama," she said in the firm tone that I was slowly becoming more accustomed to hearing from her. The letter from Yuri had done her more good than a thousand assurances from the rest of us. "Suppose harm comes to my new brother or sister because you see something a pregnant woman shouldn't see or attract the attention of evil spirits? Masha will tell me what to do, and in case I do marry someday, I need to learn what happens in childbirth. I will be fine."

Tempted to object, I bit my tongue. She was right, and I wanted to encourage her to imagine once more that marriage and motherhood might lie in her future. Fifteen was more than old enough to encounter labor and birth; I'd witnessed my second stepmother, Xenia, bringing forth her son when I was nine. I also had no desire to risk my unborn infant. I wasn't even certain how much help I could offer, being more than eight months along.

"Very well," I said. "Send us word when the child is born, no matter how late at night." I kissed her cheek. "I'm proud of you."

"Of course I will send for you." She hugged me. "Thank you, Mama, for your faith in me."

The next morning, the message came. Darya had given birth to a beautiful, healthy girl they'd named Theodora. Anfim was at the office, but I wrote him a note and dispatched the stable boy to deliver it, then summoned the carriage. I arrived to find Masha caring for my sister and my daughter taking responsibility for her newborn cousin, bathing and wrapping the baby while cooing a long stream of nonsense syllables that soothed the crying child.

"She's a natural mother," Darya told me when I pulled over a stool and sat next to her bedside, and I had to agree.

"You're both well," I said. "You can't imagine how relieved I am."

"Me too." Darya stretched, then turned to face me and touched my protruding stomach. "Your turn next."

Three more weeks passed, by the end of which I felt like the Leviathan of the Scriptures or the elephant to which I had once unkindly compared Gavriil Vorontsov. During that time, Anfim brought news that, as he'd predicted, Igor's servants had been incarcerated for their attack on his government mission, but their master had denied responsibility and, therefore, evaded punishment. It wasn't the outcome we'd hoped for—not even a discreet assignment to a fortress far from Moscow—but it did, or so Anfim argued, put our cousin on notice that future wrongdoing would meet with a harsher response. With the baby so close, I couldn't muster the energy to complain, but I did regret the leniency granted my cousin, especially in contrast to the unfair penalties inflicted on Yuri Vorontsov and his uncle.

At last, the day came when my water broke. I sent for my sister. Anna appeared even before Darya arrived, summoned Masha, and held my hands while we waited. While Anfim paced (according to my sister) outside the door and demanded frequent reports, the three of them escorted me to the bathhouse where, later that evening, a small, red, and wrinkled but healthy boy with strong lungs and the willingness to use them made his appearance. As soon as Masha delivered the afterbirth, Anna set to washing the infant while Masha and Darya looked after me, but my daughter barely had the baby wrapped and in my arms before Anfim came through the door, Lara and Tolya at his heels. Masha dropped a blanket over my lower half, and although I was both exhausted and sore, the sight of my family exclaiming over its newest member sent sparks of joy rippling through my veins.

"What will you call him?" Darya asked Anfim. It was the father's prerogative to name a new baby, but we had discussed it, so I knew what he would say before he spoke.

"Sergei," he said. "After St. Sergius of Radonezh, whom I've always respected. We'll call him Seryozha among ourselves."

I held out our new baby, and my husband took him, cradling his son in his arms and supporting the infant's head with practiced ease. "Sergei Anfimov," I said. "I wish Papa were here. He would be proud of his new grandson." I smiled at my sister. "And granddaughter." She returned the smile, her eyes twinkling.

"He's so little," Lara said. "You told me he would be, but I'd forgotten Andrusha was ever that small. How long will it take him to grow?"

"Not long." Darya touched Seryozha's nose, and he snuggled deeper into Anfim's hold. She drew back and ruffled Tolya's hair, still bleached from his summer in the country. "Just think, seven years, and he'll be as big as Tolya!"

I held out my arms, and Anfim placed the baby in them. I gazed at them one by one: the husband I loved, my darling daughter, the stepchildren who had come to mean so much to me, my sister who had been a companion since her birth, my faithful servant, and now this new life entrusted to my care. Despite everything, I had found the path I'd sought, the one that let me meet my children's needs as well as my own.

The thought sparked a memory of that evening almost three years ago, when I felt alone and unwanted. And although I couldn't identify the source of my certainty, in my heart of hearts I knew that *this* son would not perish before his time, because he had been conceived and born not in sin, as I'd once thought, but as the manifestation of a love that was meant to be. These were gifts that even my wretched cousin Igor could not steal.

"Thank you," I told Anfim.

He leaned forward and kissed me. "No, my dearest wife," he said as he touched our son's head. "Thank *you*. You have brought me more happiness than I can say."

Historical Note

As with its predecessors in this series, *SONG OF THE Sinner* rests on a historical foundation but includes few documented events. Primarily, there are two—at the start and near the finish, like bookends—but they are the most outrageous plot points in the story, so they merit a small amount of explanation.

Throughout Songs of Steppe & Forest and the Legends of the Five Directions series that precedes it, the dominant if often hidden conflict grows from the fact that Grand Prince Vasily III of Moscow died in November 1533, when his eldest son, the future Ivan the Terrible, was three years old. Until April 1538, Grand Princess Elena, the boys' mother (there was a second son, Yuri, but he appears to have been born with physical and/or mental disabilities and was never a serious contender for the throne), managed with the help of her favorite to keep a shaky hand on the reins, but when she died under mysterious circumstances, she left no adult member of the royal family who could stabilize the realm on behalf of her son Ivan, then still only seven. The result was an escalating crisis as various alliances of noble clans fought one another for power.

By the time *Song of the Sinner* opens, Grand Prince Ivan is approaching adulthood (somewhere around fifteen, in

Muscovite terms). The possibility that he would soon rule in fact as well as in name seems to have set off another, more intense round in the struggle, culminating in the attack on Prince Andrei Shuisky on December 29, 1543. According to the historian Mikhail Krom, who wrote a magisterial tome on the events of Ivan's childhood, this attack on Shuisky was the Vorontsovs' revenge for Shuisky's attack on them in September 1543, covered in *Song of the Sisters*. Since the two assaults mirror each other in certain crucial ways, I accept Krom's argument and have used it in my story.

The other bookend—the execution of the Vorontsovs and Prince Kubensky on July 21, 1546—is also part of this ongoing drama. Here, too, historians disagree about the exact sequence of events and the reasons for them, and again I have borrowed Krom's version of the story as the most psychologically and dramatically effective. In reality, the incident was even more brutal than I have portrayed it, resulting in the deaths of not only Fyodor Semyonovich Vorontsov (here called Demid, another name associated with him, to avoid confusion with the fictional character Fyodor Koshkin) but his nephew Vasily Mikhailovich, here renamed Yuri and exiled to a monastery. Although it may sound strange, imprisonment in a monastery was not an uncommon penalty: unlike the wooden houses that prevailed in Russia at this time, the larger monasteries had stone walls, making them effective jails. And forcing a young nobleman to take monastic vows ensured that he would not wed or have legitimate children, thus taking him out of a political game based primarily on marital alliances. Whether Yuri does suffer this fate and what he means by "all is not lost" are questions I address later in the series.

The fluctuations of rule in Kazan from January to July 1546 as khans fled, were installed, then fled once more are also real events and, as suggested here, set up the eventual Russian conquest of the Kazan khanate. One more—and rather bizarre—overlap with history is the explanation for what caused Grand Princess Elena's sudden death. When I wrote *The Shattered Drum*, I believed that her pregnancy and attempted abortion were my own inventions. But six months after that book appeared, I learned that modern-day Kremlin scientists had exhumed Elena's body and concluded that she died of a massive hemorrhage after giving birth to a child and ingesting poisonous mushrooms. They fingered the Shuisky clan as the most likely perpetrators. So my only fictitious contributions may have been the identity of the murderer and the use of yew leaves instead of toadstools.

As I mentioned in *Song of the Sisters*, another element of the story that may puzzle readers is Anfim Fadeyev's position as state secretary within the Treasury, despite his obvious involvement in foreign affairs. When I introduced him in *Song of the Shaman*, for the sake of simplicity I described him as a clerk in the Foreign Office. But although many diplomatic documents have survived from the early sixteenth century, attesting that a group of specialized civil servants like Anfim already existed, in 1543–1546 they still worked within the Treasury, which had formal jurisdiction over foreign affairs. It was with the establishment of the Ambassadorial Chancery in 1549 that this group received recognition and its own chancery head, Ivan Viskovaty. The role of state secretary is close to the top of the administrative hierarchy—similar to the position of undersecretary of state in our system, so Anfim's promotion is a major achievement, even if he can never rank as high as someone with noble birth.

With these few exceptions, the plot and characters are entirely my invention, although as always, I have done my best to remain true to the details of food, clothing, housing, gender relations, marriage politics, government administration, social differentiation, and trade as we can recover them from the sparse sources that remain from the sixteenth century.

And yes, even at doses of one to three teaspoons, nutmeg does have psychoactive properties; it can also cause early labor and miscarriage. Used in small amounts as a spice, however, it is quite safe.

Last but not least, I summarize here my note on naming conventions found in *Song of the Sisters*. In the sixteenth century, names and the forms they took conveyed a lot about a person's social status, but family names were still malleable: even among the elite, surnames changed with every generation. I have therefore imposed a degree of consistency on my characters that did not exist in reality. Solomonida Petrovna is a formal greeting, at the level of Lady Sheremeteva, used by strangers and subordinates. Shura, Dasha, Niki, and Katya express intimacy and affection; Shurenka points to even greater closeness. Igrushka, although an affectionate form of Igor, indicates mockery when used by his cousins.

Because family names were not fixed, Anfim Fadeyev (the two-part name, in contrast with the three-part names used by Solomonida and her family and by everyone in Russia today, indicates that he is not a member of the aristocracy) is the son of Faddei but the father of Larisa Anfimova (Larisa/Lara, daughter of Anfim) and Anatoly Anfimov (Anatoly/Tolya, son of Anfim). References to married women alternated, depending on circumstances, between identifications based on their father's name (Solomonida, daughter of Pyotr Sheremetev) and their husband's (Solomonida, wife of Anfim Fadeyev). Because Solomonida, Darya, Katya, and Maria have appeared in previous novels, I use the same surnames for them here to aid in identification, even when their circumstances have changed. Although this introduction is merely the tip of the iceberg, as they say, I hope it will help you make sense of this story.

Acknowledgments

HERE I EXPRESS MY THANKS FOR THE ONGOING HELP FROM my invaluable writers' group, which continues to enrich and inform my writing, and to the other authors of Five Directions Press for their encouragement and support. It is impossible to imagine publishing a novel without them.

In particular, I thank those who read the entire novel before publication: fellow writers P.K. Adams, Courtney J. Hall, and Gabrielle Mathieu. If you enjoyed this book, do check out their titles as well. Russell E. Martin filled me in on Muscovite wedding customs for couples where both husband and wife were previously married. Ann Kleimola remains a fount of inspiration and suggestions—including, in this case, Anfim's investigation of the causeway near Kazan (the eventual location of the Sviyazhsk Fortress, from which Russia launched its successful conquest in 1552) and the psychedelic effects of nutmeg. She has saved me from more historical errors than I can count, even though she and I both specialize in Muscovite history, and at this point I am deep in her debt.

To my husband and son—and, of course, the cat, who monitored my progress every day in my office and purred encouragingly while draping herself in front of the monitor—words cannot express my gratitude.

The Author

As a child, C. P. Lesley thought everyone made up stories while falling asleep. It never occurred to her that anyone would pay her for them, and for a long time, she was right—no one would. But after years of producing horrible prose, reading books about novel writing, and pestering hapless fellow-writers and friends to read her drafts, some of the advice stuck, and she finished *The Not Exactly Scarlet Pimpernel*, then *The Golden Lynx* and its sequels: *The Winged Horse*, *The Swan Princess*, *The Vermilion Bird*, and *The Shattered Drum*. Five Directions Press published *Song of the Siren* in 2019, *Song of the Shaman* in 2020, and *Song of the Sisters* in 2021. You can find Juliana's, Grusha's, and Darya's stories, respectively, in those last three novels.

She is currently working on the fifth in her Songs of Steppe & Forest series, *Song of the Storyteller*, which explores Lyuba's efforts to find happiness despite her father's plans to use her marriage to support his political intrigues. Lesley has also started a joint project with fellow novelist P.K. Adams, author of the Jagiellon Mysteries and a duology on Hildegard of Bingen. The new series begins in Muscovy in 1553. The first novel, tentatively titled *The Merchants' Tale*, takes place against the backdrop of Tudor sailors' discovery of a northern route to Russia and their encounter with the young Ivan the Terrible and his in-laws, the ancestors of the Romanov dynasty.

When not thinking up new ways to torture her characters, Lesley edits other people's manuscripts, reads voraciously, maintains her website, and practices classical ballet—an interest reflected in *Desert Flower* and *Kingdom of the Shades* (Tarkei Chronicles 1 and 2). She also hosts New Books in Historical Fiction, a podcast channel on the New Books Network. You can find out more about her at www.cplesley.com.

FORTHCOMING FROM FIVE DIRECTIONS PRESS

Song of the Storyteller

SONGS OF STEPPE & FOREST 5

Moscow, December 1546

I HAVE ALWAYS LOVED STORIES. SINCE THE DAY DEAR Father Job introduced me to the art of making meaningful marks with a pen on a piece of paper, the magic of the written word has called to me. From a young age, I yearned to record the legends and tales of my family, renowned in both forest and steppe, but I would have laughed at the idea that I myself might ever have a story worth telling. Foresight being a gift limited to sorceresses and wizards, I did not predict even when the day dawned—on the fourteenth of December, a Tuesday—that I would soon be caught up in a contest for the hand of the ruler of all Russia. Who could imagine Lyuba, lover of books, as one among a hundred girls, most of them eager to join our sovereign in the Dance of Isaiah, the central moment of an Orthodox Christian wedding?

In fact, on that long-ago morning my immediate goal was to resist the demands of my older sister, Maria, that I supervise the maids as they tackled the weekly wash. We were ensconced in the sitting room where Maria loved to sew (and tormented me with exercises in needlework that led only to tangled threads, malformed stitches, and bouts of bad temper), and we sat on one of the heated, padded benches that edged each of the four tiled walls. Brilliant light flooded the room from above, colored insets in the glass casting jewel-like shadows on the richly patterned carpets that lined the floor. Nevertheless, so close to the shortest day the drafts that wafted past the leaded settings of the panes were chilly enough to send shivers down my arms despite the fur wrapped around my silk-clad shoulders. I was glad of the warmth beneath me.

Despite my sister's obsession with laundry—and in general her insistence on supervising tasks that Tanya, our extremely competent housekeeper, could and did oversee with great efficiency—I loved Maria as I loved few other people. Fourteen years my senior, she had been more mother than sibling to me for as long as I could remember. She had overseen my upbringing since I was six. Even so, she didn't share my fascination with books. For her, an embroidery needle marked civilization's highest achievement. And in her hands it did.

"But Lyuba," she protested. "You must learn to order your household. You turned sixteen a few months ago, and whether or not Papa succeeds in having you summoned to the grand prince's bride show, he will certainly arrange a match for you within the year."

I repressed a shudder at that last. I couldn't decide which possibility was worse: marriage to Grand Prince Ivan—who, despite any allure generated by his power and wealth, was at heart suspicious, dictatorial, and given to fits of uncontrolled rage—or an alliance with a stranger selected by Papa to advance his own interests at court. As for the bride show, I couldn't imagine what that might be like, since the last one had taken place four years before my birth, when the present grand prince's father married Ivan's mother. All I knew from hearsay was that a call had gone out across the Russian lands, summoning noble virgins to Moscow. What happened after they arrived remained shrouded in mystery.

Although it would make a wonderful story. At times, alone in my room, I imagined the possibilities: maidens dressed in elaborate silks and velvets bowing one by one to the ruler, strolling past him as he decided which one he would pick, while the haughty boyars whispered encouragement and speculated in corners and their wives prodded each girl forward, pulling her away as she reached the end of her walk without receiving the wedding ring and kerchief that would signal Ivan's acceptance. There would be backbiting and subtle shoving, perhaps some nasty tricks to undermine this potential bride or that. All I needed was the right frame: a powerful sultan, perhaps, like the one Sheherezade lulled with her yarns, saving herself from death. How dreadful to survive a bride show only to find oneself married to a monster. What a dramatic tale that would be!

Meanwhile, my sister was tapping her foot and waiting for an answer. Reflexively, I tucked a stray copper strand back into my braid, as if only concern for my own untidy appearance could have delayed my response. "I know how the washing should be done," I reminded her. "But I promised Tolya another story if he studied well for Father Job, and I have yet to start on it."

This excuse had the virtue of truth. Tolya—the seven-year-old stepbrother of my best friend, Anna—fancied himself an epic knight. I had promised him a book of fairytales if he applied himself to his lessons, although exactly when I delivered each one was up to me. But Maria knew that I enjoyed writing far more than watching maids dunk dirty linen into soapy water, so the chances she would accept my explanation were slim.

She narrowed her brown eyes—so different from my gray-green, one shade darker than a cat's, although our hair was the same rich auburn—and I prepared myself to hear that my ploy had failed. After a brief pause, though, she managed a curt nod. I waited until I'd left the women's sitting room for the study belonging to my brother-in-law Alexei before I released a sigh of relief and put sloshy thoughts of laundry behind me.

As I walked down the stairs, I reveled in the prospect of several hours to wander in the land of story, undistracted by friends or family. Alexei seldom bothered me while I wrote, but in any case I'd heard him storming around the house an hour ago grumbling about some council session at the Kremlin that required the attendance of the high nobility, including himself. Although the son of a Tatar khan whom I hadn't seen since I was six, Alexei had converted to Christianity and entered Russian service just before he married Maria. As a Christian, he could no longer become a khan himself, but he bore the title "tsarevich," meaning "son of a khan," and that put him at the very top of the court hierarchy, just below the royal family. As a rule, he stayed as far away from the messy and cut-throat politics of the court as he could, but even he had to respond to a direct summons. So, still grumbling, he'd mounted his horse and ridden off, with his aide—Nikita Andreevich, Anna's uncle—in attendance a short time ago. Since Niki, a gifted artist, was the only other person allowed to work in Alexei's sanctum, I felt certain I'd have it to myself.

Running my fingers down the banister as I descended from the women's quarters on the third floor to the study on the second, I put myself in writing mood by imagining what I would do first when I reached my destination. I could spend time preparing my quill and cherishing the roughness of fresh paper, the oddly compelling acridity of new-mixed ink. I might stroll the room, inhaling the aromas of leather and parchment, imagining how my tale of knight and dragon should unfold. Or should I sit down and start writing with no preparation other than checking the sharpness of my pen and the presence of a sufficiently large stack of paper? Sometimes my best ideas came to me out of the blue.

In the end, though, none of that happened. When I walked through the door, I stopped short, feet riveted to the floor, and stared. A tall, dark-haired stranger in riding dress, topped with a robe of rich crimson trimmed in sable, stood near the window, paging his way through a stack of paper that I recognized as my unfinished book of tales.

https://www.fivedirectionspress.com/song-of-the-storyteller

WHO IS THE GOLDEN LYNX?

This question drives the first book in Legends of the Five Directions, a series that will sweep you to the distant world of sixteenth-century Russia, amid the descendants of Genghis Khan and courts that could teach the Borgias a thing or two about political ambition, assassination, and chicanery. Follow Nasan and her kinsfolk as they struggle for power, honor, identity, and love in Moscow, across the steppe, and through the vast forests of the Russian North.

"A 'ripping good yarn,' as adventure stories have always been. Enter the exotic, cut-throat world of sixteenth-century Muscovy in the company of a Tatar princess whose skills would have made her equally a heroine on the American frontier. The Kremlin court of the not-yet-Terrible toddler Ivan and his mother-regent Elena Glinskaya, boyar intrigue, arranged political marriages, spirit animals and ancestors pointing the way to restoring balance and order in the universe—what more could a reader want except further adventures, which are heralded by the advent of another animal messenger?"

—Ann M. Kleimola, professor *emerita* of Russian history

Find out more at http://www.fivedirectionspress.com/boxsets.

www.ingramcontent.com/pod-product-compliance
Lightning Source LLC
Chambersburg PA
CBHW020224260626
47156CB00002B/524